# MERCILESS

### AN OPTION ZERO NOVEL

## CHRISTY REECE

Merciless
An Option Zero Novel
Published by Christy Reece
Cover Art by Patricia Schmitt/Pickyme
Copyright 2020 by Christy Reece
ISBN: 978-1-7337257-3-6

To obtain permission to excerpt portions of the text, please contact the author at Christy@christyreece.com.

# MERCILESS

*Somewhere between darkness and the dawn lies a truth that could get them killed.*

Years ago, Asher Drake lost everything he loved. He had followed the rules, done the right thing, and was repaid with betrayal. Now, as leader of Option Zero, he plays by his own rules and handles things a different way. Ash knows he might not live to see another day, but one thing is certain, he will fight till his last breath for what's right.

Out of dark desperation, Jules Stone became someone else. Having experienced the worst of humanity, she battles her demons by fighting for those who can't fight for themselves. But the shadows linger. When an opportunity arises to pay a debt, Jules accepts the offer, hopeful that the shadows will disappear forever.

Secure in the knowledge that power is the ultimate weapon and truth is only a matter of perception, an enemy watches, waiting for the perfect moment to strike.

Putting aside the pain of the past, Ash and Jules must join forces and fight their demons together before the darkness becomes permanent and destroys them both.

*"What lies behind us and what lies before us are but tiny matters compared to what lies within us."* —Ralph Waldo Emerson

# CHAPTER ONE

**Colombia**

Things were quiet. Maybe too quiet. Standing on the front porch of the safe house, Asher Drake shrugged off the unease. Paranoia, nothing more. Typical reaction from a Marine who'd seen more than his share of bloodshed and bullets. But this wasn't war, and he was no longer an active-duty Marine. Time to get his head back into what peace looked like.

As he perused the neighborhood, he couldn't imagine a more serene setting. Maybe not a Norman Rockwell painting, but the backdrop was as close as he'd seen in this part of the country. Nestled in an upper-middle-class neighborhood, with sidewalks, freshly mowed lawns, and the occasional basketball hoop in the driveway, the entire area reeked of safety. The house belonged to a local businessman who was apparently happy to rent his home out for a generous amount of money while he vacationed in another part of the world.

The assignment was boring, but that was okay. He was

more than ready for a low-key, fluff job. He'd been preparing to go back to the States and continue his life with Meg, when Yeager Bates, an old friend from high school, had texted him with the offer. Bates was former Army and ran a private security firm in the States. The firm was looking for a couple extra military types to protect some bigwigs for a business meeting with locals. A couple of days, tops. Good money. Was he interested?

The answer had been an easy "hell yeah." With the extra cash, he'd be able to put more down on the house Meg had found for them.

Making babies with Meg, having a house in a nice neighborhood, and living a fulfilling, peaceful life were his goals. With interviews set up next week for several promising job opportunities, life was looking pretty damn sweet.

He and Meg had been working toward this since they'd graduated from high school. They'd gotten married right before his first deployment, but they'd decided to put everything else on hold till he was home for good. At last, everything was falling into place.

They had agreed to wait until he was finished with his service before trying to get pregnant. Meg was eager to get started. And Ash was more than eager to help her get there.

A scuffing noise had him whirling around to see Yeager coming toward him with the big, easy grin he'd had since Ash had known him. "Still twitchy?" Yeager asked.

"Hell, does it ever go away?"

Yeager gave a dry huff of a laugh. "I'll let you know."

He hadn't seen Yeager in years, but between a late-night card game and an early-morning run, they'd been able to catch up. "I've got no activity on this side," Ash said. "You?"

"Quiet as a church during confession."

"Mayhugh ready to go?" Ash asked.

"Just about. Last time I saw him, he was chowing down on some kind of pastry and reading his email."

The man they were protecting, Frank Mayhugh, was the president of a manufacturing company in the Midwest. Why he'd come to this small town in Colombia for a business meeting was anyone's guess. He and Yeager were to make sure he stayed safe while he was here. So far, it'd been a piece-of-cake assignment.

"You know what this meeting is about?"

"Not really. I was told the basics. A meeting with locals about some kind of business venture. My business has been slow lately. The money was way too good to pass up."

"I hear that."

A voice came through his earbud. "Mr. Mayhugh is ready to leave."

"Copy that," Yeager said. He met Ash's eyes. "Let's move."

With one more glance around the quiet, peaceful surroundings, Ash followed his friend.

THE MEETING WAS in full swing. Ash had watched from his post as a dozen well-dressed men and women walked into a large conference room. Their expressions ranged from excitement to harried to frowns of worry. What they were discussing behind closed doors was still a mystery.

Again, he couldn't help but wonder about this location. They were about twenty miles from Bogota in an area that no one in their right mind would call an appropriate setting for a business meeting. He'd asked around, and so far no one seemed to know exactly what the meeting was about or why they'd chosen this place to have it. And why were the buildings here in the first place? They were surrounded by wilderness on all sides. Who puts a large office complex in the middle of a freaking jungle?

His gut told him he needed to find out what was going on. When details were this sketchy, there was usually a reason. And it was rarely good.

"Drake, you copy?"

At the urgency in Yeager's voice, Ash went stiff. "Yeah. What's up?"

"You close to the entrance?"

"Yes."

"There's a convoy coming this way. Not sure they're headed for us, but stay alert just in case."

Yeager was on the roof as a lookout. They were taking turns between each other and two of Yeager's security men, Jeff Mason and Cort Dunley, who were guarding a couple of other people at the meeting.

Already on his way, Ash responded quietly, "Will do."

Arriving at the entrance within seconds, he noted both Dunley and Mason were standing across from each other outside on the small portico. Ash pushed the door open and stuck his head out. "You hear that?"

"Did he say convoy?" Mason asked.

"Yeah. And since we're the only building, no way it's not coming here."

Dunley turned toward the door. "We need to—"

"They stopped," Bates said in Ash's ear.

"Okay. Let's alert everyone just in case we—" Ash broke off at his friend's soft curse. "What's wrong?"

"Ah, hell, Ash."

"What?" Ash barked.

"They've got a rocket launcher."

"Get down here, Bates. Now!" He looked at the other two men. "Let's get them out."

They ran back inside. Their number one priority was

protecting the people in the room. That meant getting them out of the building before the walls exploded around them.

Two men stood at the outside of the double-door entrance. Ash ran toward them, shouting, "We've got trouble. Get everyone out!"

Looking more irritated than alarmed, one of the guys said, "What the hell are you talking about?"

Ignoring the idiot, Ash jerked the door open. A hand pulled at his arm. "Hey, you can't go in there. This is a private—"

He shoved the guy away and ran inside. "Everybody out! We've got heavy fire coming our way!"

Either these people had been expecting trouble, or they were hyperconscious of the dangerous location. Men and women jumped up, grabbed laptops, papers, and briefcases, and hurried toward Ash.

Noting that Mayhugh was in the middle of the pack, Ash turned to lead them to safety. He had studied the blueprints of the building this morning. The side door was not only closer but also led to the parking lot where several SUVs and a passenger van were parked.

"This way," he yelled.

He heard a curse from the direction of the door. Mason ran toward him, fury on his face. "The door's locked. They'll have to go out the front."

Turning, he yelled at the small crowd, "Change of plans. We're going out the front."

"Over here!" Dunley shouted from the front door.

Ash barked, "Move!" and shoved them forward.

As if in slow motion, he watched the people scramble to get out. A couple of them were pushing others out of the way to try to save themselves. One woman went down, and Ash reached for her. Picking her up, he ran toward the door, set her on her feet, and shoved her out.

Yeager's voice sounded in his ear, "Incoming!"

A half second later, hell exploded.

Glass shattered, bricks hurled through the air, and the world went black. Ash threw himself out the door and landed hard several feet away from the building. If he lost consciousness, it was for only a second or two. When he raised his head, he saw that a thick cloud of dust and debris surrounded what was once a large office complex.

Stumbling to his feet, his ears ringing, a haze of confusion covered his thoughts. Eyes stinging from blast debris, he squinted through the thick fog of smoke. Had they gotten everyone out? The last thing he remembered was practically throwing a woman through the door. Had she survived?

Shaking his head to clear it, he stumbled toward the demolished building. Whatever had hit them had done more damage than one rocket shell. There had to have been two or three. The entire building lay on the ground, smoldering.

He touched his ear, noting that he'd lost his earbud. What about Yeager and the other men? Had they survived?

"Over here!" The shout came from within the rubble.

The dust was settling some, leaving a hazy, blurry image of the destruction that surrounded him. Ash spotted a man lying beneath a steel beam. His torso and head were clear, but his legs were pinned. The man was Yeager Bates.

Ash ran forward, stepping over debris, pieces of clothing, and other items. When he reached Yeager, he was relieved to see a grin on the man's face. "Told everybody to get out and forgot to take that advice myself."

Stooping down, Ash tried to lift the beam with no luck. "I need to find a rod or something to bolster this thing." His eyes searched for something sturdy. Everything looked too twisted or damaged. "Hang on." He glanced back at Yeager's face. "How bad is it?"

He grimaced, tried to move. "Can't tell. Nothing hurts."

Standing, Ash surveyed the area. It was amazingly empty of people. Had everyone else died in the blast? How was that possible? He remembered several people exiting the building. Where were they?

"You need help?"

He glanced behind him. Mason and Dunley were headed his way. Mason had blood running down the side of his face, and Dunley was limping and holding his left arm at his side. They were banged up but very much alive.

"Yeah. Bates is pinned."

They went to work, shoving and lifting, trying to get the beam to move even an inch. In the midst of grunting and cursing at their slow progress, the rumble of a helicopter caught their attention.

Ash straightened and peered toward the area where the noise was coming from. Was this help, or had the bastards found another way to get to them?

A heavy breeze swept the area, clearing the air. About two hundred yards away, a Chinook helicopter was touching down. Ash watched as a horde of people appeared from behind some big bushes and ran toward the chopper. A man dressed in black jumped to the ground and herded the people onto the chopper.

Relief flooded him. At least they had help.

He shouted and waved his arms, making sure that the pilot saw him. It was a long distance away, but Ash knew he'd been spotted. The pilot looked directly at him, but there was no nod or the slightest acknowledgment.

The realization hit him seconds before the giant bird lifted from the ground and took off. "They're leaving us."

"No way in hell," Mason snarled. "They can't—"

But they had. Standing in the midst of destruction and death, next to a man pinned beneath a gargantuan beam, Ash watched the helicopter grow smaller and smaller until it was a dot in the sky.

The sound of a vehicle caught his attention. Hopeful that this was a sign that they hadn't been abandoned, Ash turned. The truck that had fired the rockets was coming toward them. This was no rescue. This was an army headed to finish the job.

They needed to get the hell out of here. They had arrived in several vehicles. If they could hold the bastards off for a few minutes, maybe they could tie a rope to one of the larger SUVs and dislodge the beam. Then they'd hightail it out of here.

His eyes darted to the parking lot that had been on the other side of the building and his heart sank.

Reading him correctly, Dunley said, "They're demolished. Mason and I checked before we headed this way."

Ash exchanged a look with each man, silently acknowledging what had happened. They had been left behind. And they had no way out.

They were military, trained to fight till their last breath. And that's what they would do.

But if he survived, Ash swore that he would spend the rest of his life hunting down the people who left them to die.

CHAPTER TWO

**Spokane, Washington**

Lucy Carson pulled into her driveway, put the car in park, and pressed her forehead against the steering wheel. She still had no answers. For the past two hours, she had been driving around the city, trying to come up with the right words. How had life suddenly become so complicated? She and her dad had always had a special bond. He was her hero. But the last couple of months, they'd argued more than they'd talked. She had disappointed him—she knew that. Her parents' approval meant everything to her. They had stood by her, believed in her, and had been her cheerleaders all her life.

This was different, though. She was twenty-one years old, had just graduated from college, and would soon use her degree in art history to work at one of the top museums in the state. No, it wasn't a high paying job, but as she had tried to explain, starting at the bottom was one of the best ways to learn. Art, in its many forms and fashions, was a field that both fascinated and inspired her. Her dad thought it was impractical and frivolous.

This was the first problem they had not been able to talk through. He was an attorney, and his fondest wish was for her to go to law school and join him in his practice. It was his dream, but it had never been hers.

She had tried, she really had. She'd even taken several pre-law courses and had done well in them, but neither her heart nor her imagination had been engaged. Being a lawyer was not what she wanted.

The dinner tonight was to have been a celebration of her graduation, but it had turned into a shouting match by the end of the meal. Oh, how she wanted to snatch back those words she'd spouted off to him. The restaurant had been full of diners, and she had embarrassed her parents by not only shouting at them, but also by storming out of the restaurant. They had raised her better, expected more from her. She expected more from herself. It didn't matter that her dad had started the argument, she should have controlled her temper.

Now she needed to figure out how to apologize but still make him understand that she could not do what he wanted. She had to live her own life.

She wished Rob had been there with her. Even though he also disagreed with her decision, he would have smoothed things over with her dad. They'd been dating for almost a year, and both her parents approved. Which was no surprise. Rob was in law school and in his own words, loving every moment. That was Rob's dream and she was happy for him. But again, it wasn't hers.

Resolved, Lucy opened the car door and stepped out onto the driveway. Either way, she had to talk to her dad tonight, to at least apologize. She wouldn't be able to sleep until she did, even if it was just a quick *I'm sorry*. She could wait to have a more open discussion tomorrow, after they'd both had a good night's sleep. But she had to apologize tonight.

She turned the key in the lock and pushed the front door open. For the first time, she noticed that though the porch light was on, all the lights inside the house were off. That was unusual. Her parents were night owls and often went to bed long after she'd turned in for the night. It was only a little after eleven. Maybe they were in their bedroom. The master bedroom faced the back of the house and couldn't be seen from the front.

She set the security alarm and headed upstairs. As she trudged up the stairway, she continued to work on the words that would help her dad understand without causing more hard feelings. Hurting him was the last thing she wanted.

She stopped at her parents' bedroom and knocked on the door. When she didn't hear an answer, she frowned, noting that no light shone under the door. Surely they were home. The garage door had been closed, and she hadn't thought to check to see if her dad's SUV was parked inside.

She turned the doorknob and opened the door. The stench of something raw and wild hit her like a violent wave. Breath catching in her lungs, she took a step back. *What the—?*

Reaching for the wall light switch, she flipped it on and faced a nightmare of horrors. Blood everywhere. Everywhere! The walls, the ceiling.

Barely able to comprehend the scene, she took in the morass in the center of the room. The people on the bed were unrecognizable. Her mind refused to accept that they were her parents. They couldn't be. This. Could. Not. Be. Happening! She felt a scream inside her, boiling to get out, but she couldn't make a sound. She was frozen, not breathing. Unable to think.

How long she stood there she would never know. She didn't hear him behind her. It hadn't registered that anyone else was in the house. Something hard started to wrap around her waist. Lucy looked down to see a long arm, hairy and saturated in blood, slowly snaking around her body. She was pulled back into a hard chest, and a man with fetid breath whispered hotly into her ear, "Hello, Lucy. I've been waiting for you."

Run!

Her body screamed at her to move, her sluggish mind urged her to get up. This was her chance…maybe her last chance. He was asleep. She could hear him snoring in the next room. And he was drunk. If she was lucky, he'd be unconscious for several more hours.

Lucky? She swallowed a bitter laugh. There was no such thing. For her, there was only survival.

She gazed down at her hands, barely comprehending that they were her own. They were bloody, nails ripped to the quick, wrists bruised and scratched. She had fought him—at least she'd had that. She had fought and she had lost.

Hopelessness overwhelmed her. Closing her eyes, she sank deeper into her corner. Maybe it was better this way. She had no one—she was nothing. He had taken everything from her. What was the point in going on? Maybe he would just kill her. Maybe she would let him. She wouldn't keep fighting him. When his big hands wrapped around her neck again, she would let him do what he wanted. She almost hadn't come back the last time. Maybe she wouldn't next time.

She didn't know how long she'd been here. Weeks. Maybe months. Time had become an endless nightmare of pain and degradation. Everything she had loved, everyone she had loved, was gone. If she closed her eyes and concentrated hard, she could still see her mom's sweet smile, see her dad's face light up with laughter. Those memories were fading though. Lately those images were superimposed with the brutal, vile memories of her parents' lying in rivers of blood.

Her heart cried out at the injustice, at the cruelty. They had never hurt anyone, had been the best, most loving parents in the world. Why had this happened to them? It wasn't fair!

How she missed them…oh sweet Lord, how she missed them. She would never get the chance again to tell them how much she loved them. How grateful she was for them. Or how very sorry she was for behaving so selfishly at the restaurant. If only she had one more chance. But she didn't. All her chances had disintegrated.

Oblivion beckoned. Death held out its arms, offering a comforting embrace. A sweet release from the pain. From the heartache. She closed her eyes…sinking, sinking…

Lucy jerked awake with a gasp. Her eyes darted around the room. What was that? Was he awake? Was he coming for her? How long had she been unconscious? Why hadn't she run when she'd had the chance? She didn't want to die. She wanted to live. She wanted to make this bastard pay. The only way to do that was to run, get help. They would find him, and they would punish him for what he'd done. To her parents. To her.

The small, dark room gave her no answers. Stinking of mildew and rotted food, the room had been her only scenery since he'd brought her here. The lone window across from her was a small one that had been boarded up years ago. The wood was old and rotting but had held firm against her pitiful efforts to remove it. She had spent hours trying to pry even one board loose, with no results other than splinters and bloody fingers.

She hadn't heard any outside sounds, but the room was solidly built. Maybe even soundproof. She had no idea if she was in the middle of a city or in a forest, miles from civilization. She'd heard no noises. Even if she got out, would anyone be around to help her?

One thing was for sure: If she didn't get out, she wouldn't survive. And she wanted to live. She would live and make this monster pay for everything he'd taken from her, everything he'd done.

Going to her knees, she summoned the strength she would need. Every part of her body cried out for her to stop. It hurt too much! Cuts, barely healed, popped open, warm blood oozed down her torso, her legs. When she grimaced with pain, the cuts on her cheek tore open. Would she bleed to death before she found help? Was there any point in even trying to escape?

She shut down the doubts. She couldn't…she wouldn't stop. She had to get out of here. If it was the last thing she did, she had to at least try.

Dragging herself to her feet, she leaned against the wall to catch her breath. Minimal food and water had left her depleted, incredibly weak. The blood loss hadn't helped. None of those things mattered…she couldn't let any of that stop her.

Her hands unsteady, she carefully slid her wrists from the cuffs. Not only had he grown lax, sure that she could never escape him, she had discovered that she'd lost so much weight, the cuffs were much looser. With an enormous amount of tugging and pulling, plus the slickness of blood from her raw skin, she had been able to slide out of them. When he'd come in to check on her earlier, she'd hurriedly put them on again.

Now, she laid them on the floor, taking care to not let them clank together. She straightened to stand, and a wave of dizziness swept through her. Clutching at the wall, she held on until the room righted itself. Breath gasped out of her lungs, and she realized that part of her dizziness had been from holding her breath.

Shivering, she looked down at the thin, white T-shirt she was wearing. He'd thrown it at her a few days ago when she'd told him she was cold. It hadn't been clean then and was now even worse. Stained with blood, sweat, and other bodily fluids she didn't want to think about, it stank, as did she. That couldn't be helped. She couldn't take the time to look for anything warmer or fresher. She had to get out of here.

Speed and stealth were of equal importance. He could wake at any moment. Just because he was drunk didn't mean he couldn't hurt her. Some of her most vicious beatings had come during his drunken episodes.

How had she never known people like him existed? Her parents had been both amazing and lovingly protective. She had read about monsters like this bastard in news stories, but they had been about other people. She had lived a charmed life, never really acknowledging that true evil existed or that it could touch her.

Feeling as awkward as an infant learning to walk, Lucy wobbled her way to the door. He had come in to check on her earlier and had forgotten to turn the lock when he left. When she hadn't heard that familiar click, she had known this was her chance. Her first one in weeks. She couldn't mess this up. She might never get another one.

Holding her breath again, she put her ear to the door. Yes, he was still sleeping. Deeply this time. The snoring had softened, and his breathing was shallow. That didn't mean he wouldn't wake at the slightest noise. She'd learned, to her detriment, that he was a light sleeper even when he drank himself into a stupor.

She eased the door open. He was on the sofa. Though it was all the way across the room and she could see only the sofa's back from this angle, a limp, booted foot hung over the armrest.

The door to the outside was the sweetest sight ever, and it was only a few feet away. The small window at the top indicated it was night. She told herself that was good. She would be harder to find in the dark. Freedom could be hers.

She took three steps toward the door and then stopped. The knife he'd used to cut her clothes off that first day lay on the counter. He had used it several times since then to terrorize her, and on several occasions he had cut her. She could turn the tables. She could grab the knife, and before he knew it, she could stab him through his cold, rotten heart. He would never hurt her or anyone again. His death would never make up for what he'd done, but it would be a good start.

Her hand shaking with both excitement and fear, she grabbed the knife and turned to the couch. She stood above him. How could someone so evil look so ordinary? He was only in his mid-twenties, with pale, thinning hair and a small scar on the bridge of his nose. He looked like someone you'd pass on the street and not consider the least bit dangerous. That couldn't be further from the truth. If he opened his eyes, the illusion of normality, of sanity, would disappear, and the darkness in his soul would gleam bright.

The knife gripped in her hand, hatred and revulsion boiled through her veins. She raised the knife high. Getting the blade through his chest wall might take more strength than she had, but she remembered enough from her biology classes to know where to stab for maximum damage.

The knife arced down. It was a quarter inch from his

thick neck when she stopped. Could she do this? Could she actually kill? Take a life, rotten though it was?

She wanted this monster to suffer. Wanted to see him behind bars, writhing in agony. For what he had done, he would be on death row, and one day full justice would come to him. Killing him now would be too easy for him.

Still hanging on to the knife, Lucy backed away. Doing an about-face, she headed to the door.

Run, run, run. That's all she needed to concentrate on. She got to the door and heard a groan. He was waking up!

Giving up on stealth, she yanked the door open and ran.

About a hundred yards away, she ventured a look back. She saw no movement, no activity. Maybe he hadn't heard her leave after all.

For the first time, she got a look at her torture house. Though dawn had yet to break, it was light enough to see the derelict old cabin. The porch was sagging, and broken shutters hung drunkenly from dirty windows. Tall weeds and sparse grass surrounded the structure. It reeked of evil and was the perfect residence for the devil who lived within its walls.

The creaking of the front door jerked her out of her trance. She'd just been standing here, staring at the house as if she wasn't running from a demon. She kicked her brain back into gear and started running again.

Seconds later, an ungodly squeal of rage echoed through the woods. He'd discovered she had escaped! If he found her, she knew without a doubt he would kill her this time.

Telling her weak legs and malnourished body to move, she picked up her pace and ran like the devil himself was chasing her. Because he was.

For what felt like an hour, she ran as fast and as hard as she could. Her bare feet were bleeding and numb from the cold, her limbs felt like rubber, and her side ached as if it would rip open if she took one more step. She had no choice but to stop. Leaning against a tree, she bent forward. Ragged breath whistled out of her aching lungs like a sick locomotive. If a herd of stampeding horses had been following her, she wouldn't have heard them.

As she fought to breathe, she raised her head to judge her surroundings. She was deep in the woods. It was now early morning, and the rising sun mesmerized her with its piercing light, its welcoming heat. It was the most beautiful sight she'd ever witnessed. How long had it been since she'd been outdoors? The fresh air was intoxicating, the sun a warming solace to her battered soul.

Something that felt like optimism soared through her. Yes, she could do this. She had escaped the bastard. He had no idea which direction she'd headed. There was no way he could find her now. All she had to do was get to a phone or find someone who could call for help.

Energy flowed through her body. She straightened, drew in another shaky breath. She had no idea where she was going or even if there was help ahead. All she knew was the sun was so beautiful and so bright, and it called to her unlike anything ever had before. Something told her if she followed the sun, it would take her exactly where she needed to go.

Lucy took a step and then another, her eyes never leaving the bright beacon of hope. How far she walked she would never know. What seemed like hours later, sounds of civilization caught her attention. Noise, like large machinery, drew her toward one area. One foot in front of the other became her only focus. When she saw a construction site and a group of men standing around looking at something in the ground, she opened her mouth to say something, and nothing emerged. She tried again. Still nothing.

Doing the only thing she knew to do, she continued to

put one foot in front of the other and shuffled forward. She heard someone shout. A few more shouts joined in.

Lucy felt herself falling, and then strong arms caught her. She closed her eyes on a sobbing sigh. She was safe. She had escaped her nightmare. The monster could never hurt her again.

If only she had known how wrong she was.

# CHAPTER THREE

**Twelve years later**
**Memphis, Tennessee**

I t was a good night to catch a killer.

Flipping her long blond hair over her shoulder, Jules Stone took a practiced, casual glance around the stylish bar. The dark, shiny tables and high ceilings gave off the ambience of wealth and class. George's Place was just one of a new crop of meeting places for the young and single in the city. Trendy food, medium-to high-priced liquor, and a good sound system made George's Place one of the most popular.

The bar was filling up and soon would be too crowded to give her the view she needed. It made sense that Thursday night would bring in more people than earlier in the week. The weekend was coming, and people wanted to get their celebration on early. That didn't bode well for her, though. Too many people meant she could get lost in the crowd. She didn't want to get lost. She wanted to be noticed, to be seen.

Perhaps she should have dressed more provocatively. She'd opted for casual but feminine, but maybe she should have stepped it up a notch and gone for sexy and seductive. The lightweight turquoise sweater was snug and molded to her shape nicely but didn't show even a hint of cleavage. Her jeans hugged her long legs but would probably have looked sexier paired with something besides running shoes. She had decided on them for two reasons. First, heels made her taller, and while five foot eight wasn't all that tall, she wanted to appear as petite as possible. Second, she needed to be able to move fast. Wearing heels would slow her down and could get her killed.

Deciding there was nothing she could do about her clothing choice, she took a long swallow of her drink and then gasped, trying not to choke. She'd ordered a virgin screwdriver—okay yes, basically orange juice—but she had wanted it to look like the actual cocktail. Apparently the bartender had missed the *virgin* part of her order. She wasn't a teetotaler, but a glass of wine once or twice a month was her limit. Anything that obscured or deadened her senses was something she avoided at all costs.

She couldn't order another drink…not yet. That would look odd, and the last thing she wanted was to look like an anomaly. She needed to seem like any other eager young woman hoping to make a connection but not quite sure how to go about the process. That was the killer's preferred target.

This was her second bar tonight and her eleventh this week. She'd started her search earlier than usual, hoping to hit at least five before she called it quits for the night. A week of trolling bars and drinking virgin screwdrivers was about as boring as it sounded. She had turned down nice young men hoping for a connection and not-so-nice young men looking for a hookup and had consumed so much orange juice she had amusedly wondered if her blood might actually have a tinge of orange. Not a bad thing to have if you're from

Tennessee. Jules wasn't. Her home base was in Flagstaff, Arizona, and as much as she longed to go back there, she couldn't. Not until the job was finished.

Patrick Lyle Meeks had cut a deadly swath throughout the Southeast and apparently didn't intend to quit anytime soon. Jules was going to do her best to make him change his mind. Meeks's preferred victims were young blond women who were either alone, or he'd been able to cull them away from the crowd.

Meeks wasn't shy about leaving his DNA. The authorities had identified him after his second kill. An arrest for assault years ago—resulting only in probation and community service—had given them the results quickly. His identity wasn't the problem—finding him had been much harder.

The FBI believed Meeks had left his DNA through carelessness. Jules disagreed. Meeks had money, enough so that he was able to have multiple identities and vehicles, along with several hideouts. He was from New Jersey and for some reason had decided to make a name for himself by heading south and killing whoever caught his fancy. Though his bank accounts were frozen, Jules believed he had planned this carefully and had hidden funds. And it was her opinion that the low-life bastard was thoroughly enjoying himself.

Photographs of him had been splashed all over the news. You couldn't turn on the television or read an online news service without seeing his face. Meeks likely loved the publicity, the notoriety. He was an egomaniac who got off on killing women and then flaunting that he wasn't getting caught. Having his photo everywhere was icing on the cake.

Jules knew this type of killer all too well.

She took another sip of her drink and barely held back a grimace. Even though the ice had melted, weakening the taste of the alcohol, it was still awful. Waving down a server, she asked for another one, making sure this time that the woman understood she wanted orange juice only.

Admittedly, the reason for the screwdrivers seemed lame, as the FBI had pointed out, but in her estimation, it was worth pursuing. Four of the five women Meeks had killed had consumed screwdrivers the night they were targeted. The fact that he had killed them *with* screwdrivers couldn't be a coincidence.

Zeke Sheridan, the FBI agent in charge of the investigation, thought she was on a wild-goose chase that could get her killed. They had sparred verbally over the phone and once in person. Each time, Sheridan had dismissed her screwdriver theory as conjecture and warned her repeatedly to stay out of the case. And just like all the other times, Jules had no intention of following his advice.

No, this wasn't her job. No one was paying her to hunt down a killer. She did this for herself. And yes, she easily acknowledged that she could be killed, but she could not stop herself from going after the fiend. He was so arrogant, so damn sure he wouldn't be caught. She would show him he was wrong.

Her eyes roamed the room, searching. The bar was getting almost too crowded, and Jules wondered if staying here any longer made sense. She was likely just one in a hundred young women. There was no proof that Meeks was still in Memphis. The last woman he'd abducted and killed was found four days ago. He could have gone on to greener, less risky pastures. Jules didn't think so. He had an established pattern, and she didn't think he'd break it. Meeks usually killed twice before he moved on to a new city. Two murders in Little Rock and two in Atlanta. As far as anyone knew, he had killed only one woman in Memphis. He had one more to go before he was finished here.

"Here you go, hon."

Smiling her thanks to the server who delivered her fresh drink, Jules took a sip of her faux cocktail, and that's when she spotted him. He was looking right at her, and when they made eye contact, he smiled.

He had altered his appearance. A wider nose, fuller lips, and round, dark-rimmed glasses. His hair was lighter than in his photos, and he was sporting a gold hoop in his right earlobe. He looked different, but not so much that she didn't recognize him.

Now to get him to take the bait.

She lifted her drink in an awkward kind of toast, gave him a soft, shy smile, and took a sip. That was all it took.

In seconds, he was standing at her table. A quiver of apprehension shivered up her spine. She was a foot away from a cold-blooded, sadistic serial killer. It wasn't the first time she'd been in the presence of true evil. And just like those other times, nausea rose up and tried to strangle her. Fight-or-flight instinct told her to get the hell out of here before it was too late. Jules stiffened her spine, the fear and revulsion shoved into the corner where they belonged. She knew how to handle monsters.

"Mind if I sit down?"

She offered him another shy smile and a quick nod. "Sure."

Meeks sat down and immediately held out his hand. "I'm Charlie."

She shook his hand, not surprised by the strength of his grasp. It took some muscle to skewer someone with a screwdriver.

"Hi, Charlie. Nice to meet you. I'm Sandy."

"You're drinking a screwdriver, right?"

"Yes." She giggled nervously. "I figure with all the vitamin C, it's got to be good for me."

"That's my favorite drink, too. Can I buy you another one?"

She held up her thankfully full glass. "I'm good for right now." Breaking eye contact, she gazed around and then returned her eyes to his. "Do you come here often?"

"No. My first time. You?"

"My first time, too. I was supposed to meet a friend, but she bailed at the last minute." She shrugged. "I decided I didn't want to stay in tonight, so I thought I'd give it a go."

"I'm glad you did. Do you live in Memphis?"

"Yes. In Midtown. I work at the bank at Highland and Poplar Avenue."

"Hey, that's where I bank."

Either he had an account under another name, or he was lying to make it seem as if they had something in common. Didn't really matter, but it was interesting to see him work his sick game.

"It's a small world."

He grinned. "We're practically best friends already."

She giggled and took another small swallow of her drink. She didn't want it to get so low that he would order another one. Asking for a virgin screwdriver might push him away.

The sound of the music increased as a DJ came onto the small stage above the dance floor.

"Would you like to dance?"

Since having his hands on her was something she didn't want to contend with, she shook her head. "Thanks, but I don't really like to dance."

"Me either, but it's getting loud in here, and I'd really like to have a conversation with you without shouting. Would you want to go to a coffee shop or something?"

Biting her lip in indecision, she said, "Well…I—"

He held up his hands, all innocence. "I promise I'm a nice guy."

"Okay. That sounds like fun."

Acting the gentleman, which would impress any girl, Meeks stood and held out his hand to help her move around the table and step down. Still holding her hand, he led her through the crowd and out the door.

As no woman had survived to tell, it wasn't clear what happened between the pickup and the abduction. Jules was about to find out.

Once outside, they stopped on the sidewalk. "There's a place over on 4th Street that makes the best lattes in town. Sound good to you?"

"Sure. My car's just around the corner. I can follow you."

"No need. I'm parked right over there." He pointed toward a darkened alleyway, where a few cars were parked. "We can ride over together, and I'll bring you back." She was sure his kind smile was meant to support his claim that he was a nice guy. "It'll give us more time to talk."

Getting into a car with a stranger was not a good idea for anyone. Getting into a car with a known serial killer was a very bad idea. Jules knew what she was doing. No one had trained harder, was better equipped, or more determined.

Her hand still in his, she let him lead her to a silver Mercedes SUV. They had speculated that Meeks had a garage filled with expensive cars. He was a multimillionaire, having inherited much of his wealth from his deceased parents and almost doubling it since. Now, for some reason, he preferred killing. There was all sorts of speculation about when and why he'd begun killing. All sorts of theories that something must have triggered his psycho tendencies. Jules didn't care about his reasons. She just wanted to stop him.

He opened the passenger door for her, and the instant her foot touched the floorboard, a screwdriver was pressed to her throat. "Get in," Meeks snarled.

She had assumed he would wait until he got her into the

car before he pulled his weapon on her. Why hadn't he? She could still scream and attract attention. Even though they were hidden in an alleyway, if she made a noise of distress, people would come running. Was this part of the thrill for him? Or had something spooked him?

"What are you doing?" The tremor in her voice had more to do with fury than fear.

The screwdriver dug deeper into her skin. "I said get in the car."

Screaming was out. The last thing she wanted to do was get someone else hurt. She had her gun in her bra holster, but that would mean making a sudden movement, which might get her stabbed.

He was standing behind her, the screwdriver pressed on her carotid. One hard jab, and she could bleed out before help reached her. Since they were about the same height, she chose to shock him with a hard and startling head-butt to his nose. He let loose a pained grunt, and she felt the give of cartilage. She'd definitely cracked something.

The screwdriver clanked to the sidewalk—he'd dropped his weapon. Jules turned swiftly and swung her forearm against his head, slamming it into the back passenger window. She followed with a knee to the groin, but he recovered quickly, slugging the side of her head with his fist. She felt the impact through her whole body and fell backward, landing on the pavement.

Blood covering his face, Meeks jumped into the passenger side of his vehicle. She got to her feet in time to see him climb over the console to the driver's side. She reached for the door handle, but it was too late. The vehicle started up, and he tore out of the parking lot.

## CHAPTER FOUR

Jules ran to her vehicle, hitting the remote starter before she was halfway there. The instant she was inside, she shifted into drive and followed. No way was he getting away from her. No way in hell.

Swooping in and out of traffic, she rounded a curve. Meeks was five cars ahead of her. She could see the unique taillights of his SUV. He had opted to stay off the interstate, which made things a littler trickier for them both. He was a good driver and had no issues with speeding and changing lanes, but the heavy traffic wasn't conducive for a quick getaway. Jules, on the other hand, was caught behind two cars whose drivers seemed determined to go the same speed and hold up both lanes.

Keeping her eyes on Meeks's vehicle, she pressed the screen on her dashboard and brought up her most recent calls. While Zeke Sheridan might not be happy about her continued involvement in the case, he needed to know about this.

The instant Sheridan answered, Jules said, "I'm following Meeks."

She had to give the FBI agent credit. Instead of asking how she'd found him or blasting her for her interference, he said, "Where are you?"

"He just turned onto Poplar Avenue. He's about four cars ahead of me. Driving a silver Mercedes SUV." She rattled off the license plate.

Before he could ask another question, Jules said urgently, "Listen, I think he's getting on the interstate, headed toward the Hernando de Soto Bridge."

"He's going into Arkansas."

"Yeah, looks like. I'll stay with him."

"What are you driving?"

"Dark blue Ford Mustang."

"Okay. I'll alert the highway patrol. Stay with him, but do not approach. Understand?"

She ended the call without making a promise she couldn't keep. No way was this maniac getting away from her. She would do what she had to do.

Zooming down the interstate made it easier for her to keep up with him. She didn't think he'd spotted her yet. She was hanging back several car lengths. The night was dark, with clouds covering the sliver of moon. With her dark car, she was just one of a dozen cars behind him.

He crossed the bridge, and still no patrol cars were in sight. Jules continued to stay several cars behind him. Ten miles into Arkansas, the silver SUV took an exit. Jules took the exit, along with another car. Would Meeks head back to Memphis, or did he have a place to hole up nearby in Arkansas?

The SUV turned onto a four-lane highway. Traffic was lighter now, and Jules stayed back even farther. They continued for several more miles, and Jules was starting to get more concerned. Was he driving aimlessly, or did he have a destination? When he finally turned into the parking lot of a small motel, she breathed her first easy breath.

She slowed her vehicle but didn't pull into the parking lot. If he was turning around, she wanted to be ready. When he parked in a spot on one side of the building, Jules drove to the second entrance and parked on the other side. Hiding her vehicle between a large SUV and a cargo van gave her the cover she needed to slip out of her car undetected.

Hugging the brick wall, Jules inched her way toward the front of the motel. Would Meeks go to the lobby and check in, or did he already have a room here? She peered around the corner. The light inside his vehicle was on, and the look on his face would be comical if this weren't so deadly serious. Dried blood covered half his face, his nose was swollen to twice its size, and she was happy to see that he had lost a front tooth, too. Obviously infuriated that his plans to kill tonight had been thwarted, he was shouting at the mirror on his sun visor as he tried to wipe the blood from his face.

Since he would spot her if she came around the front, Jules had no choice but to try to come at him from behind. That would mean going around the motel. She didn't like the idea of letting him out of her sight, but she had no choice if she wanted to surprise him.

The need to do so vanished when she saw his eyes widen. She spared a glance around and saw that the sign next to the door where she stood had a glass-like appearance. He had seen her reflection.

The engine of his SUV started up again. Jules had a decision to make. If she went back to her car, she could lose him. As he began to back out of his parking space, she made the choice. Pulling her SIG Sauer from the bra holster beneath her arm, she headed straight for him.

Meeks was driving toward the exit. Adrenaline pumping, Jules ran full force toward the SUV. He was a killer and wouldn't hesitate to run her over. She refused to let that stop her. The instant Meeks spotted her, he turned the steering wheel, stomped on the gas, and zoomed toward her.

Jules jerked to a halt. Holding her gun with both hands, she aimed at his head and fired. The windshield cracked, but the bullet didn't penetrate. Bulletproof glass? The SUV didn't slow. Jules kept firing. Half a second before he ran her down, she threw herself out of the way. The front fender caught her left hip, taking her off her feet. She landed, rolled over, and came up on one knee. He might have bulletproof glass, but no way did he have bulletproof tires. She fired, taking out the left front and rear tires. The SUV traveled a few more feet and then slammed into a light pole. Steam rose from the front end. Meeks would not be driving away in that vehicle.

Seconds later, sirens blaring, five police cars roared into the parking lot.

Breathless, Jules put her gun on the pavement several inches from her body and stayed on her knees. If the police saw her with a weapon, they'd have every right to assume she was a threat.

She didn't mind waiting. Besides needing to catch her breath, the adrenaline rush was gone, making her aware of aches and pains throughout her body. None of that mattered, though, as extreme satisfaction flowed through her. She had done what she'd come here to do.

FIFTEEN MINUTES after he'd arrived on the scene, FBI agent Zeke Sheridan sauntered over. Jules was sitting on the curb, icing her hip and getting her scrapes treated by a paramedic.

His expression was solemn, but there was a twinkle in his light green gaze. "I thought I told you to stay out of it."

"Following orders is not my strong point." She glanced over at Meeks, who was lying on a gurney, handcuffed to the railing, and babbling about a crazy female stalker who had attacked him without provocation. "He going to be okay?"

"Healthy enough to stand trial for five murders." He nodded toward the ice bag on her hip. "You hurt?"

"Just bruises and scrapes." She gave a smile of thanks to the paramedic and stood. "So, are we okay?"

Sheridan held out his hand. "We're good. We'll be in touch."

After shaking his hand, Jules headed slowly to her car. A hot bath and the carton of ice cream in her hotel mini fridge were calling her name.

She was almost to her car when Sheridan called out from behind her. "You ever think about working for us? We have some cool toys."

She threw him a grin over her shoulder. "Thanks for the offer, but I told you I don't follow orders very well."

With one last wave, she opened her door and climbed into the driver's seat. She was already stiffening up and would likely have to crawl out of her car to get to her hotel room. It would be worth it, though. Meeks would never be free again. He'd left too much DNA at his crime scenes to get out of this. She'd done the job she'd set out to do and felt damn good about that.

Tugging off the blond wig, Jules pulled pins from her hair, sighing in relief as a cascade of strawberry-blond strands settled around her shoulders. Moving her neck and shoulders to get the kinks out, she steered her car back toward Memphis. Bright lights outlining the bridge twinkled in the distance, and Jules had to fight the unusual temptation to stay just one more day to explore the fascinating city. She pushed aside the unusual longing. She didn't do tours or take vacations.

Most people would call her crazy for getting involved in something so risky. It wasn't like she didn't have a full-time job already. Because of her reputation and the skills she'd acquired, she had more than enough work to keep her busy without seeking out more. Others might consider her arrogant. Risk was the least of her worries, and arrogance had nothing to do with it. She had survived the unimaginable. So many others hadn't. And while she had long passed the point where guilt and grief made her wish she had died, too, she couldn't live without doing all she could.

Keeping herself out of the limelight was getting harder. Barely a handful of people knew about her. The more she involved herself, the greater her chances of being found out. Serial-killer cases tended to get more publicity, which meant the people who caught them got noticed, too. Publicity was the last thing Jules wanted. She didn't hunt serial killers for fame and most certainly not for money. Some might call this her destiny. Jules didn't know about that. All she knew was she had survived for a reason. If she had the skills to save a life or bring a monster to justice, how could she not do all she could?

Her phone buzzed, and she glanced at the caller ID on the dash screen. There were only one or two people she could bear talking with tonight. When she saw the area code, her heart skipped several beats. Not a friend, but most definitely someone she wanted to talk to.

Giving herself no time to hesitate or second-guess her decision, she slid into another persona, answering with a brisk, "Yes?"

"Is this Ms. Diamond? Ms. Jessie Diamond?"

"Yes. This is Jess. Who's this?"

"Ms. Diamond, my name is Lisa Steiner. I'm Senator Nora Turner's personal aide. The senator wondered if you'd have time to meet with her about a possible job opportunity."

"I'm not into politics."

"Politics aren't involved."

Jules rolled her eyes at that extremely false statement. "What kind of job, then?"

She asked the question more to see what kind of reason Steiner would give. She had been speculating about how Turner would approach her.

"This is a personal matter. Not one we can discuss on the phone."

"The payout?"

"Let's just say you won't be disappointed by our offer."

"When and where?"

"The senator is on the road in Ohio, conducting town hall meetings. Can you be in Cincinnati on Thursday afternoon?"

"That should work. Where and what time?"

"I'll text you the details."

Ending the call, Jules took a moment to savor this victory. She had a lot of work ahead of her and would likely experience more emotions than she'd allowed herself to feel for years, but she could not turn her back on this. For a short time, she would put aside her need to hunt killers and do what she had dreamed of doing for years. It was time, way past time, to pay a debt.

# CHAPTER FIVE

**Budapest, Hungary**

Asher Drake stepped out of the limousine and onto the sidewalk in front of the massive hotel. Head cocked at an arrogant angle, he asked, "We ready?"

Serena Donavan, Option Zero's head communications specialist, answered in his ear. "Good to go on our end."

"Okay. Let's do this."

Nodding at the dour doorman standing at the entrance to one of Budapest's oldest and most exclusive hotels, Ash, known only as Humphrey here, strode inside. Impeccably dressed in an eight-thousand-dollar suit made from the finest of wools, he wore a.testoni shoes and a Christian Lacroix tie. A dark brown wig with a receding hairline gave the impression that he was trying and not succeeding to hold on to as much hair as possible. He had a bit of putty at his nose and chin, bushy dark brows, contact lenses the color of dry mud covering distinctive blue eyes, and a set of veneers over his teeth that gave him a pointed, piranha-looking smile. Even Ash's own mother, rest her soul, wouldn't recognize him.

Anyone who looked at the man named Humphrey would see what he wanted them to see—wealth, supreme arrogance, and a disdain for most of mankind. Ash had played the role more times than he could count. It was actually a comfortable one, as not giving a damn came easily to him.

As he sauntered through the lobby, he was aware of the whispers, the stares. A few recognized him, most didn't, but he ensured he made an impact that everyone would remember. Humphrey was a man who made things happen. He might not give a damn about people, but he definitely wanted them to give a damn about him. Egomaniacal Behavior 101.

Humphrey did not have an entourage. That was part of his mystique. It was rumored that he had killed ten men in less than a minute because they betrayed him. That was an exaggeration. It had been only six, and his reasons had nothing to do with betrayal.

He didn't slow down when he neared the elevators. The doors magically opened for him the instant he arrived. Anyone watching might believe he had the power to call forth an elevator by sheer magnetism alone. They didn't know that he had people controlling the hotel elevators. It was an amusing parlor trick that went well with the mystique he had cultivated.

The doors closed and the elevator rose slowly toward the penthouse suite. As he was alone and the cameras had been disarmed, he repositioned his earwig and asked, "Any interference with the communication?"

"Clear as a bell. Pure as the driven snow. Perfect as a spring morning on the moors of my beloved homeland."

Ash winced at Sean Donavan's ridiculously cheerful tone. Donavan had just returned from his honeymoon and had yet to come down from the clouds. His wife, Serena, gave a soft chuckle and said, "Shh."

Sean and Serena's romantic relationship had caused no problems. As usual, they were on the mark professionally and did their jobs well. When they'd announced their engagement last year, Ash had wondered if things would change. They hadn't. In fact, other than the annoying cheerful attitude from Sean and the happy glow on Serena's face, nothing was different. He was glad of that, as he'd hate to lose either of them.

The elevator jarred a bit when it stopped at the top floor. The doors slid open, and Humphrey emerged. In a glance, he noted the guard count was exceptionally high. Not that unusual for a meeting such as this. The reputation he'd developed for Humphrey almost required additional protection. Perhaps it was small-minded of him, but Ash enjoyed knowing that he had created that kind of fear in these people.

In an odd way, Humphrey's deadly reputation made Ash's job harder. Taking out the infamous Humphrey would be a gold star on someone's assassination list. It would likely happen someday. For right now, Humphrey offered a valuable commodity that gave him a certain amount of protection. Didn't mean some hothead looking to make a name for himself wouldn't take the risk, but that was the game he played.

A barely perceptible nod at the behemoth guarding the door gave the man permission to commence a search. Jerking his head at the two bodyguards standing behind Humphrey, the behemoth gave the order.

Holding his arms up and out, he allowed the pat-down. Not carrying a weapon into a meeting with a well-known weapons broker might have seemed insane. A gun wasn't necessary. If he wanted anyone dead, Humphrey could find ten household items to do the job just as well.

Search complete, the grim-faced guard muttered something, and whoever was on the other side opened the door. Another guard, slightly smaller than the others, stood there. "Mr. Humphrey, please come inside. Omar is waiting."

Omar Schrader was a slight man with spindly legs, thinning hair, and an unfortunate overbite. He looked as dangerous as a sickly kitten. Behind that unassuming appearance was an intelligent, lethal man whose appetite for money was matched only by his voracious need for beautiful women. Omar relied on his wealth and influence to get him the latter.

Beady eyes twinkling, Omar held out his hand. "Humphrey, my dear friend. How delightful to see you again."

Shaking the other man's hand was like holding an eel, both cold and slimy. Humphrey resisted the urge to wipe his hand the instant the shake was over. Insulting Omar was not a good idea.

"You're looking well, Omar."

Omar gave a gap-toothed grin. "Clean living. You should try it."

"And then where would people go when they need what I supply?"

"Excellent point. I understand you have something new to offer?"

"Experimental and tested on a limited basis only. However, the first one to make the right offer will be the first one to get the weapon."

"I am intrigued. Tell me more."

Humphrey nodded toward one of the men who had searched him. The flash drive had been taken from him when he arrived. Omar waved his hand, giving the guard permission to return it.

Humphrey went to a laptop sitting on a desk and inserted the drive. A few clicks later, a legitimate-looking formula appeared. Omar was no chemist, but he was educated in a variety of deadly things. The compounds in the formula could indeed kill thousands when mixed together, perhaps millions. It was authentic-looking enough to fool even the most experienced weapons dealer and would get Humphrey where he wanted to go. Omar was a go-between. He would review the information, and if he approved, he would then sell it to a client, taking a substantial fee for himself.

Glasses propped on the edge of his nose, all humor replaced with a serious, studious look, Omar sat at the desk and reviewed the deadly information.

Humphrey stood several feet away. Not by any change in his demeanor did he give away his tenseness. He had been assured that the formula looked so authentic that ninety-nine percent of the world's chemists would not immediately detect the flaw. The other one percent was worrisome, but Omar was no chemist, which provided a certain amount of assurance that the formula would pass muster.

Omar glanced over his shoulder. "You have a recording of the tests?"

"Just one. As you know"—Humphrey offered a small, feral smile—"finding a large group of people to agree to die for the sake of science is difficult." He nodded toward the screen. "Click on the second file."

Turning back, Omar did just that and watched, mesmerized, as five people seemingly unaware of their fate were spritzed with a clear, odorless substance. Seconds later, chaos erupted on the screen.

Even though it was fake, watching people act out horrendous deaths was not pleasant. Having been told the performance would be for an obscure horror movie, the actors had been paid well for an hour of their time. They had walked out of the studio unaware that they'd played a part in setting a trap for a mass murderer.

Still not sure they'd pulled it off, Humphrey raised an arrogant brow and brazened it out. "Well?"

"You have outdone yourself, my friend. This will attract many."

The "many" didn't hold Ash's interest. There was no shortage of people looking to kill for various reasons. Many would be interested in owning this type of bioweapon. Only a few could afford to pay the exorbitant price Humphrey would demand. There was only one man in particular they were targeting. Carl Lang had already proven his willingness to murder large numbers of people for both fun and profit. They were counting on this weapon being right up his alley.

"Your asking price?"

"Two hundred fifty million."

"That's quite a lot of money."

"Considering the product, I believe the amount is more than justified."

"Hmm." Behind Omar's thick glasses, his eyes glistened with greed. "Considering the buyers we will be dealing with, the risks are higher than normal. I'll want more than my usual cut."

Before Humphrey could protest, Omar was quick to add, "Be assured, I don't think you'll have any problem getting your asking price." He pulled out the flash drive, closed the laptop, and stood. "I'll set up the auction and get back to you on the final bid."

"No."

Omar froze, cocked his head. "No?"

"I want to attend the auction. I have too much on the line this time."

"Do you dare imply that I would cheat you?"

Omar would cheat his own mother if the price was right. Humphrey walked a fragile line here, but he had no choice. The only way to get to his target was to be invited to the auction. He was counting on Lang being the highest bidder. Others would try, but Lang had the money, which made him the most dangerous for right now.

"Cheat me? No, of course not, Omar. However, we've known each other long enough that you should trust me. This is the most valuable product I've ever offered. I deserve to be involved with the whole process."

Beady eyes narrowed, gleaming with malice. "Or I could just keep the formula and leave you out altogether."

"You can't do that."

"Oh, really?" Omar sent a look to one of his men, and weapons were drawn. A smug smile lifted Omar's thin lips. "What, may I ask, is keeping me from doing that very thing?"

Without blinking an eye, Humphrey nodded at the laptop. "Plug in the drive again, and you'll see."

Omar inserted the drive. When neither of the files appeared on the screen, the amoral weapons broker whirled around, his eyes spitting furious indignation. "What have you done?"

"Just a little insurance policy. The instant you clicked off the flash drive, all information was destroyed. I have the original in a safe place."

Omar turned back to the laptop and continued to try to pull up the information. After several minutes, he closed the laptop and stood. Facing Humphrey, Omar gave a tight smile. "Well played, my friend. Careful you don't play too hard, though. You might get burned."

"Ah, Omar." Humphrey sighed, shaking his head. "We've known each other too long to play games. Do we have a deal or not?"

"I will have to confer with my associates before I can make such a promise."

Omar was still trying to play games, but instead of calling him on it, Humphrey chose to appeal to his ego. "You set up the auctions. You invite who you want. You're the man in charge."

Omar's smile indicated he'd scored with that last comment. "That is true. Very well, my friend. I will arrange the auction and contact you with the location. Just be sure that when you come, you bring a drive that does not do a disappearing act. Yes?"

Humphrey grinned. Omar was a slimy weasel, but he could be likable as long as you didn't turn your back to him.

"Excellent. I'll be sure to bring you a bottle of Balvenie Scotch to celebrate."

Omar clapped his hands together with glee. "You know my weakness. Very well. We will drink it together after we make the sale."

With a small salute, Humphrey walked out the door. He looked neither left nor right, knowing eyes would be on him until he entered the elevator. As before, the elevator doors opened like magic, and Humphrey stepped inside.

The instant the elevator doors closed, Ash spoke into the mic doing double duty as a cuff link. "We're in."

## CHAPTER SIX

Jules had been watching him for a while. For someone trained in covert ops, Asher Drake was surprisingly easy to track. Of course she had studied him. Knowing everything about her targets was her number one rule. And she had learned everything she could about this man long before she'd accepted this job.

Orders from her new employer were simple, straightforward. Watch Drake. See where he goes, what he does, who he meets, what he says. Proceed with caution. Don't approach, don't engage. Not yet. Report your findings.

Couldn't get much easier than that.

Of course, she had no intention of following orders, most especially the last one. Jules had engineered this job for her own purpose. If her employer found out her reasons, she would lose the job, possibly her life. The risk was nothing new to her, but there was the added benefit of doing the exact opposite of what she'd been told to do. Considering who her employer was, disobeying orders had never felt so good.

She was playing a dangerous game, one she wasn't certain

she would win. But she had no choice but to try. Some things were worth fighting for, and a few things were worth dying for. This was one of those things.

Besides, it could be worse. How many people would love to be sitting at a sidewalk café in the middle of one of the most beautiful cities in the world, sipping coffee and enjoying a delicious Dobos torte? Not to mention the sheer enjoyment of watching an unarguably gorgeous man.

Asher Drake's physical bio said he was thirty-eight years old, six-three, weighed around two hundred ten, and had blond hair and blue eyes. The bio didn't do justice to the man. It said nothing about shoulders broad enough to carry a grown man through a desert or a hard, athletic body built for strength and endurance. And blond hair? Not exactly. From this angle, the color was more of a summer wheat, but in the direct sunlight, she had counted at least four shades of blond, a little bit of brown, and maybe a hint of auburn. It was somewhat shaggy, as if he hadn't had a cut in a while. The longish, unkempt style suited him. His skin was a light golden bronze. He had high, sculpted cheekbones, a sharp nose, and a chin squaring toward stubborn. She suspected that centuries ago, his Viking ancestors had conquered foreign lands and created new worlds. Asher Drake looked like he had inherited every bit of that power and arrogance.

The man was a demon in some people's eyes, but in others' he was a hero. She often wondered how he thought of himself. When he looked in the mirror, who and what did he see?

She and Asher Drake would meet soon. There was no other option if she was to achieve her goals. He could never find out her real purpose. She told herself her reasoning was sound. It wasn't pertinent to her quest. She told herself that this job, while quite different than any others, was still just a job.

At some point, she hoped to believe it was true.

Either way, until it was done, until she was satisfied she had done all that she could, she would be sticking to Asher Drake like glue.

ASH DRAINED the last of his coffee as he debated how to handle the situation. The lovely young woman following him obviously wanted something. He was used to being followed —he'd been under surveillance much of his adult life for one thing or another. He'd gotten accustomed to it, learned to accept it as a part of doing the kind of business he did. This was the first time he had wanted to introduce himself to his tail.

He couldn't say what made him want to detour from the norm, other than this woman was different. Attractive, yes. Bordering on stunning. Hair several shades away from true auburn fell past her shoulders in thick, soft waves. She wore a long-sleeved, boat-necked dress of deep blue, and before she'd sat down, he'd caught a glimpse of truly spectacular legs. Her skin was fair, and even from here he could tell she had freckles on her face, shoulders—probably all over her body.

She looked altogether too wholesome to be doing this job. He supposed that's why she'd been chosen—she looked like a fresh-faced innocent who might run at the first sign of trouble. He was quite sure that wasn't the case. Innocents weren't assigned to tail him. Didn't matter what country or government was footing the bill, only a seasoned, well-trained operative would get this assignment. Which made her all the more attractive.

That was an anomaly in itself. He didn't date, not really. He had a few female acquaintances he would see from time to time. Other than companionship and a few steamy moments to take the edge off, he liked that they expected nothing from him.

Since she had been assigned to follow him, this woman, wholesome or not, should know the score.

Standing, he threw down a handful of forints and headed her way. He saw the widening of her eyes as they met his. Yeah, he definitely wanted to get to know this woman.

*CRAP. Crap. Crap.* He was coming toward her. Had spotted her. She had intended for them to meet, but not like this. And not this soon. She wasn't prepared, wasn't ready for their first meeting. How would she…

Jules shut down the panic. Just because it wasn't happening the way she'd planned didn't mean she couldn't use it to her advantage. She was no neophyte, and this wasn't her first rodeo. She was a professional and knew how to play the game.

Seconds before he arrived at her table, she stood and gave him a smile that could melt the coldest of hearts. "You caught me."

Appreciation gleamed in his eyes. "I certainly did."

"What am I to do now?"

"I'd say that's up to you."

Holding out her hand, she kept her eyes locked with his as she felt his large hand engulf hers. The description from his bio had been wrong again. Blue eyes? Not exactly. The color was the blue found in the deepest, darkest depths of the ocean. Unfathomable and endless.

Jules felt her world tilt on its axis.

Gathering her wits took longer than she had anticipated, as did retrieving her hand from his. He'd held on to it longer than was socially acceptable, and she found herself almost breathless from the small but obvious gesture of attraction.

"Are you on holiday?" Cheesy opening line, but she was flummoxed for something more meaningful and intelligent right now.

"You tell me."

"Excuse me?"

"You've been following me for two days. I thought you might've already figured that out."

If she'd had any chance of getting back on even ground, he had just destroyed that hope. When had she gotten so complacent that she couldn't tail a mark without getting caught? She refused to accept the whispering accusation in her head that told her she'd wanted the meeting to happen and therefore hadn't been as invisible as she could have been.

*Regroup, Jules, before you ruin everything.*

Giving a self-conscious tilt of her head, she confessed, "A friend of mine told me about you. I wanted to observe you before we met."

"Is that right?" He waved his hand toward the chair she'd been sitting in, and with much less grace than she wanted, Jules plopped down.

Pulling out a chair on the other side of the small table, he sat and then crossed his legs in a supremely confident manner. "Tell me who your friend is, what your friend told you, and then tell me why you wanted this meeting."

This part should be easy. With expert help, she had created this cover story. As much of it was true, the words should flow effortlessly from her lips. She hadn't, however, expected to have these other feelings get in the way. The success of her mission required her to maintain as much emotional distance as possible. Being attracted to her mark was a very bad idea.

The reminder was a good one, settling her nerves. Instead of answering his question, she glanced around and said softly, "It's a delicate issue. Can we go somewhere more private and talk?"

"Here's fine."

She couldn't blame him for his mistrust—it was well earned. But it did make things a bit trickier for her. Eyes and ears could be anywhere, everywhere.

"Very well. My name is Juliet Stone. Jules to my friends." The words, at last, came easily to her lips. "And the friend who told me about you is Kate Walker. She said you could help me."

His nod was almost imperceptible, as was the lessening of tension in that granite jaw. Someone else might not have noticed the change, but she had studied this man back and forth. She knew him.

"How is Kate? Still fighting the good fight in Washington?"

Her smile was genuine, as was her admiration. "Good try, but you know full well that Kate wouldn't be caught within a hundred miles of DC again."

"And how do you know Kate?"

"I interviewed with her when she was at the FBI." Not technically true, but close enough. "I didn't get the job, but we stayed in contact."

And because it was one hundred percent true, she added, "Friends like Kate don't come along very often."

WELL, hell. He liked her. And he couldn't say that about many people. But there was something about Juliet Stone that made him want to smile. Since smiling had become as rare as unicorns in the last few years, that in itself was an anomaly he wanted to explore.

Using Kate's name was a powerful move. Kate Walker had been his mentor when he'd first started with the FBI. Though she had left the agency before his life fell apart, their friendship had remained solid. He owed her for many things, but mostly for saving his sanity. Outside of OZ, she was the only person he completely trusted.

"And what is it you need help with, Ms. Stone?"

She hesitated, looking around at their surroundings again, showing that she really was worried about someone overhearing.

"If you're concerned about eavesdroppers, don't be. The couple sitting to our left works for me. The older gentleman on the right is a regular at the café and comes here daily. He has four cats, is an avid reader of historical fiction, and lost his wife of forty-five years two years ago last summer.

"The people at the other tables aren't close enough to hear you. Also, I've noticed you move your head and tilt your face often to avoid anyone being able to read your lips."

The tension in her shoulders lessened somewhat. "Okay. Good. I'm a freelance security specialist, specializing in corporate and government espionage. I've been hired by a small think tank out of California. Their job is to analyze and anticipate terrorist threats against the US before they can happen. They believe they have a mole within their organization. One who could take the information they've discovered and sell it to one of our enemies for the sole purpose of creating a terrorist attack they're trying to prevent. I've been asked to identify the traitor."

"Why you? Seems like this would be something the government might want to handle themselves."

"They want an independent, nonpartisan person to evaluate the threat. I've developed a reputation for such things."

"I see." He inclined his head. "Go on."

"I've thoroughly investigated each member of the team. They're a small group of thirty-four, so it should be easy to narrow it down to find him or her. So far, I've had no luck."

"How is Kate involved?"

"She's not…except to suggest that I contact you. She told me about you…about your organization, Option Zero."

"What did she tell you?"

"That you are a straight shooter. You won't stop until a job is finished. And through your organization, you have contacts and ties most intelligence agencies only dream of having. She said you see things in intel that others can't. And you're one of the few people she trusts."

"How is it you think that I or my organization can help?"

"I know that OZ doesn't always abide by the rules. It's going to take some rule-breaking to find the culprit."

"And you don't break rules?"

For the first time since they'd met, a genuine, full-blown smile curved her lips, and Ash caught his breath. He had suspected that this woman could be stunning, and she had just proven him right.

"On the contrary. I'm an avid rule-breaker. However, this particular job will require specific rule-breaking skills."

"And you think I'm your man."

Her eyes widened slightly, and he was gratified to realize he wasn't the only one feeling the tug of attraction.

Oh yeah, he definitely wanted to break some rules with Jules Stone.

CHAPTER SEVEN

Jules eyed the man sitting on the sofa beside her. They'd met just over an hour ago, and now here he was in her hotel room, helping her. She hadn't expected him to agree so quickly and certainly hadn't expected him to be available immediately. She had thought she'd have to do a lot more convincing. Thought that he would do a more thorough check on her before he made a commitment. He'd texted with someone on the walk to the hotel, but that couldn't have given him much information.

Even though she had studied everything about him, there were certain things she couldn't know. Not only did the man make quick decisions, he wasn't one to do so unless he was sure of the outcome. To know that he trusted her meant more to her than she wanted to accept.

Meeting Asher Drake was one of the most surreal moments of her life. Working with him was even more so.

The elevator ride had been another thing she hadn't expected. Being in an enclosed space with him—only him. There were things she wanted to say, questions she longed to ask. But she couldn't. They were personal and not germane to her set tasks. To maintain the professionalism she'd worked so hard for, she had to keep her distance.

"What's wrong?" he asked.

She had already decided she would be as honest as possible. That didn't negate the lies she would have to tell, but every time she could give him the truth, she would. "I didn't expect you to help me so quickly. We've already cleared three employees, and you've been here less than an hour."

"It helps to have a variety of contacts who have connections."

"You mean a variety of people who owe you something."

"Doesn't hurt."

"Do you enjoy what you do?"

"What is it you think I do?"

She knew exactly what he did—or as much as anyone knew outside of his organization. Most of his work was classified. She knew that OZ took jobs no one else would take on or were often deemed too dangerous. Kate had once told her that Asher Drake had a lot in common with Saint Jude, the patron saint of lost causes.

So yes, she knew what he did, but she wanted to hear it in his words.

"Kate told me that you right wrongs."

His shout of laughter was both startling and massively appealing. This man could charm a snake with his wit and calm the devil with his cunning, but his laughter was a game changer. Not only was the sound deep and rich in timbre, his sensuous mouth tilted invitingly, and his amazing eyes glinted, turning them an even more mesmerizing shade of blue.

Jules's breath hitched in her throat. She had honestly never been this attracted to anyone. The inconvenience alone was mind-boggling.

"Kate has blinders on when it comes to OZ."

"So you don't right wrongs?"

"Sometimes. Other times, we destroy."

"How so?"

"That's classified."

"Do you break laws?"

His mouth twitched with a wry grin. "Occasionally, yeah. You got a problem with that, maybe you don't need to be working with me."

"Do you hurt people?"

"Sometimes."

"Good people?"

"You think the lines are that distinct? Good people, bad people?"

"You don't?"

"I think there's good and bad in almost everyone."

"Almost? So you think there are some who are irredeemable?"

"Without a doubt. Don't you?"

Oh, most definitely, but they were getting into territory she needed to avoid at all costs. "Yeah, I do."

"What else do you know about OZ?"

"Kate said you take broken people and give them purpose."

He shrugged. "We're all broken in some way. Some are just better at hiding it than others."

She refused to get pulled into this particular discussion. No one knew better than she did just how broken she was, but like Asher Drake and the people at OZ, she had reinvented herself and found a purpose.

"You're right." She made her answer short, hoping he'd leave the subject behind. Handing him another file, she hurried on, "This is Angelo Rodrigo. He was my first suspect."

Even though she knew he was looking at her very closely,

she didn't meet his eyes. If she did, he would see things she wasn't prepared to address.

Thankfully, after several taut seconds, he took the file from her. "Why was Rodrigo your first suspect?"

"He's the newest member of the team. After reviewing his file, I felt his background wasn't as thoroughly investigated as it would have been if he weren't so talented. He has three doctorate degrees and is only thirty years old. We have plenty of enemies that would pay top dollar to someone with Rodrigo's talents. He has a young family and lives in a modest two-bedroom apartment."

"No indiscretions?"

"Only one that I could find. When he was thirteen, he hacked into his school's network and changed some grades. He was suspended and had to do some community service."

"So you think that's where he started on his life of crime."

Even though she detected no humor in his expression, she got the idea that she had amused him somehow.

"Possibly."

"Tell me more."


As Ash listened to Jules give her opinion on Rodrigo, another part of his mind concentrated on her. She had secrets, that was a given. Everyone had them. But he sensed hers were more complicated than most.

Agreeing to help find a criminal for this type of crime was a no-brainer. He had people who could dig out intel that only God himself knew. Finding out if a man or woman in a group of thirty-four was a double agent, or worse, should be a couple days' work at the most. That wasn't the reason he'd agreed—at least not the only one. He wanted to know more about Jules Stone. What made her tick? What secrets lay behind those crystal-clear gray-green eyes? Was her creamy skin as satiny-soft as it appeared? And would her lips taste as sweet as they looked?

Ash moved uncomfortably as desire stirred. Not the time or the place.

Already knowing Rodrigo was not the culprit, he wanted to know why Jules had changed her mind. "You no longer think he's the one. Why's that?"

"How'd you know I changed my mind?"

"You implied it when you said he was your first suspect. Also, your tone of voice. It grew warmer as you described him."

Her eyes flickered down, and he knew his words had disturbed her. Why? Because he could read her? In his line of work, reading people was as natural as breathing. She would be glad to know that she was tougher to read than most.

He could tell her that. Maybe it would make her lower her guard. With anyone else, he probably would have done so, but not with this woman. Not yet. For right now, Ash found himself wanting to get to know her on her own terms.

Not that he wouldn't check her out thoroughly before they became any more involved. There were way too many people who wanted him dead. While his death would happen someday, he'd prefer that it not happen because of his stupidity or carelessness.

Even though he'd vetted her with a quick text to Kate on the way over here, his thoughts still surprised him. That was definitely not his usual style, but then again, neither was Jules Stone. Kate had given a glowing recommendation. That endorsement went a long way in easing his initial concerns, but caution, as always, was his number one ally.

"You're right about Rodrigo." She gave a small shrug. "While none of them give off vibes of being anything other than dedicated to the job they were hired for, he's one of the few who completely blew me away."

"How so?"

"He's so authentically humble, almost as if he's embarrassed by his brilliance. I can no more see him betraying his country than I can see myself doing so."

"And the hacking charge?"

"He changed only one person's grades, a girl he had a crush on. He did it to impress her."

"Ah, young love. So do you have a new suspect?"

Her sigh held frustration. "No. While not all of them have the most pleasant of personalities, none of them strike me as being capable of doing something like this."

"Then let's find the culprit."

NOT EVEN BOTHERING to hide her astonishment, Jules watched as Asher Drake set to work. A flurry of texts were followed by various phone calls in which he would mutter one or two words and then listen. She counted three different languages and at least a half-dozen dialects. She had known about his talents, his skills, and that he had a tremendous warren of connections throughout the world. But this was even more than she'd anticipated. He used his abilities with amazing efficiency and his contacts with forceful arrogance. She doubted people said no to him very often.

Two hours and fourteen minutes later, he looked up with an odd gleam in his eyes. "Got her."

"Her?"

"Libby Billings."

"But she's the one who hired me. Why would she ask me to find the traitor when she's the one?"

"To throw everyone off." He glanced down at his phone. "She knew there was going to be an inquiry. Their contract is up for renewal, and some questions were being asked. She agreed to hire an outside investigator."

"I don't know if I should be insulted that she thought I wouldn't be good enough to find the truth, or impressed that she had the gall to try to pull this off."

"I'd say this, like many things, was a desperate attempt to delay the inevitable."

At those words, Jules's antenna went on high alert. She studied the man beside her with care. Had that been a veiled reference to her own deception, or was she being more paranoid than usual? Seeing nothing concerning in his expression, she dismissed her fears. Everything was going exactly as planned.

His next words, lethal in their quietness, jarred her out of her self-congratulatory haze.

"So, Jules, are you ready to tell me what this is really all about, or do you want to continue to play games?"

## CHAPTER EIGHT

W atching her reaction closely, Ash took in her shock but saw no real guilt. A light flush of pink rose on her face, and her pupils dilated slightly.

"What do you mean?"

"You disappoint me, Ms. Stone. I thought you would come up with a better response than that."

She blew out a shaky sigh, and he realized she was more upset than she let on. That knowledge both surprised and concerned him. He was usually better at reading people, but just in the brief few hours he had known her, she had fooled him several times.

She gave a nervous, self-conscious little laugh. "What gave me away?"

"The case, for one. My people found your traitor faster than yours simply because of the network we've created. You would have found her within a week."

She grimaced. "It took ten days. Most of the people I use are freelancers themselves. I had to get in line."

"So I just spent an afternoon discovering a criminal you've already identified?"

"It was the only way I knew to get your attention. I knew you'd see past the ruse eventually...I didn't expect you to catch on so soon, though."

"Then let's stop playing games. Tell me the real reason I'm here."

"Very well. I want to work for OZ."

"And you thought lying to me was a good way to get a job? Tell me you're not that naïve."

"Not naïve at all. I also wanted to see if you were as good as Kate described."

"So this was a test, a job interview of sorts?"

"You're angry."

"Really? What gave me away?"

"You're too calm."

He couldn't deny the anger, but it had less to do with being used and more to do with who had used him. He had thought they had a connection, and now he wondered if he'd seen what he wanted to see.

He stood, gave an abrupt nod. "It's been a while since I've been duped, so I'll give you credit for that. I don't play games and don't associate with people who do. Goodbye, Ms. Stone."

"Mr. Drake...Ash...wait, please."

He was halfway to the door, but he stopped and turned. "One chance to change my mind. Use it wisely."

Jules waited a second to gather her thoughts. Asher Drake wasn't the kind of man who gave second chances. He definitely wouldn't give her a third. She had made a complete mess of things. If she had told him the full truth, she wasn't sure she could have screwed things up more than this. Believing she could play it her way without getting burned had been foolish.

"I don't trust easily." She said the words haltingly, but no truer words had ever come from her mouth. "I wanted to…I needed to…" When had lying been so difficult? For the past ten years, that's all she'd known. But this? This was different, so very different.

"You needed to know if I'm as good as you were told."

He said it without an ounce of ego. He knew his worth—what he had and could accomplish. And miraculously, he had given her an out. She grabbed on to it gratefully. "Yes."

He headed back to her, his intent unclear until he stopped in front of her. Grabbing her shoulders, he pulled her to her feet and brought her face within an inch of his. "Lie to me again, and you won't like the consequences. Understand?"

She tried to swallow, but her mouth was so dry she made only a strange sound in her throat that could have been a moan.

He shook her lightly. "I'm waiting for an answer, Jules."

"Yes…okay. Again, I'm sorry. I won't…"

He let her go and stepped back. "I have some things I need to do. I'll be back tonight at seven. We'll have dinner, and you'll answer all my questions. Correct?"

"Yes."

He walked out the door before she could come up with anything else to say. On one level, his high-handedness and arrogance were both insulting and off-putting. But she had reason to know that his arrogance was well earned, and she found she couldn't hold on to an ounce of resentment about that. She had deceived him and deserved his wrath.

She had created the ruse for two reasons. One, she wanted to see if what she'd been told was true. Was Asher Drake really that good? If not, she might have considered backing away and going about this a different way. What she had discovered in those hours of watching him work was that the intel she'd received was somewhat inaccurate. Asher

Drake wasn't just good at digging out secrets, he was a master.

The second reason for the ruse was much more self-serving. She had wanted to watch him work. See him on a different level. Over the years, she had built him up in her mind. Would the reality live up to her imaginings? He had. So much more than she'd ever expected.

Why hadn't she been able to fool him as she could so many others? Was it because a part of her wanted him to know the truth? To go ahead and face the pain…get it out of the way? She'd never considered herself a masochist, but she was no stranger to self-flagellation. Was that the reason, or was there something more?

If he found out the truth, everything could be ruined. She had worked too hard for this opportunity to screw things up now. Too much was riding on achieving her goals. She owed him this. She owed him much more, but this would have to do.

ASH STOPPED on the other side of the door and cursed softly. What was it about Jules Stone? With anyone else, he would've issued a carefully worded threat and been out the door without looking back. Instead, he'd given her another chance.

And she was still lying. Even as he'd told her he'd give her one more chance, he already knew that she wouldn't tell him the full truth. She didn't trust him. He understood that to a point. After what happened in Colombia, he'd trusted only a few. After Meg's death, that number had shrunk to barely a handful.

Whoever had hurt Jules had damaged her. He could identify with that, but that didn't mean he'd give her a free pass.

He should've called her out on her continued lies immediately, but the terror he'd glimpsed in her eyes had pierced something inside of him, so he'd relented. He detected no evil in her intent, only an extreme caution. And something else…dammit, what was she hiding?

Ash headed to the elevator. He'd wait till he got to a secure phone before he called Kate and demanded to know more about the woman she'd sent to him. However, he had his own avenue he would pursue. And it was the best there was.

He pounded out a brief, tersely worded text to the op center at OZ headquarters: *Juliet Stone. Get me everything.*

# CHAPTER NINE

Ten minutes after Ash left her hotel room, a cellphone chimed. Every part of Jules's body went stiff with tension. She'd placed the burner phone in the bottom drawer of the dresser, under a pile of clothing. Yes, to keep it hidden, but mostly because she didn't want to hear from the only person who had the number.

The call had come quicker than she had anticipated, and the timing sucked. Having Ash call her out on her lies had rattled her more than she wanted to admit. She desperately needed to regroup before her meeting tonight, settle her thoughts and repurpose her mission. She didn't have time to play politics.

Snatching the phone from its hiding place, Jules snapped out, "Diamond," hoping the caller would get the message that this was not a good time to talk.

"Hello, my dear. I understand you've made contact already. Good going." The woman might have meant it as a compliment, but she made it sound like Jules had arranged a sleazy hookup.

"How do you know I made contact?"

"I have eyes and ears everywhere."

That was no surprise. Even though this woman had hired her, Jules knew she trusted few people, which was likely how she maintained her position.

"Yes, we've met."

"And?"

"And what? We've met. That's it."

"He was in your hotel room for over two hours."

Jules closed her eyes. She had known she would be under surveillance, at least until Turner decided she could be trusted. But this? Even if she were legitimately working for the woman, this kind of scrutiny went way beyond acceptable.

"Listen, you hired me to do a job. If I have to have a tail, and you continue to keep checking up on me, then I'm not the right person for this job. You need to find someone else."

Turner gave a huff of exasperation. "No one is impeding your job, Ms. Diamond. However, I have a lot on the line, and I—"

"And you need to either trust me to do the job or find someone else. What's it going to be?"

Yes, she was sounding like a hard-ass, but that's exactly the kind of person this woman respected. Jules had carefully cultivated her undercover persona. Hard-as-nails Jessie Diamond took no prisoners. Allowing the senator to bully and push her around without protest would be out of character.

"Very well," Turner conceded. "I'll have my people return home. But you need to give me something. You were with him for several hours. You must have learned something."

Oh, she had learned a lot, but nothing Turner could know.

"We're just getting to know each other. He's not going to share anything of value until he knows he can trust me."

"How are you going to get him to trust you? He trusts almost no one."

With good reason.

"Let me worry about that."

"All right, but I'm paying you a lot of money to get what I need. Don't disappoint me, Ms. Diamond. I'm not a person you want to cross."

"My reputation speaks for itself."

"Of course. So what's next?"

If the woman expected a daily briefing, she was going to be sorely disappointed. However, Jules gave her the next step, hoping to appease her.

"I'm having dinner with him tonight."

"Then I won't keep you. You'll want to look your best for what comes next."

Even though the words had never actually been said, Jules knew her employer had no issues if she chose to sleep with Asher Drake to get the intel she needed. This woman's opinion meant less than nothing to her, but she couldn't let on that her agenda was in direct opposition to the reason she'd been hired. Her only option was to keep up the pretense until it was no longer necessary.

"I'll get back with you as soon as I have something to report."

She ended the call before the woman could respond. There was nothing more to say.

Returning the phone to the drawer, Jules grabbed her running clothes. Her muscles were tense, almost bunched. She had known this would be a difficult assignment but hadn't counted on how much it would cost her physically. The hotel had a decent gym, and she'd spent an hour there this morning. Bashing the boxing bag had helped release a lot of pent-up energy, but there was nothing like a run to work out her worries.

She dressed quickly in thin sweats and her favorite running shoes and was out the door within five minutes. As she headed down the stairway, she gathered her hair into a thick ponytail. By the time she was outside, she was limber enough to start out at a quick pace.

Turning left out of the hotel, she went toward the running path she'd discovered yesterday. Though there were several, she would have to take the shortest route today. Preparing for her dinner with Asher Drake would take more than her usual five-minute beauty regimen.

Two minutes after leaving the hotel, she spotted her tail. Drake's or her employer's? Didn't really matter at this point. She needed this run and refused to let anyone destroy her enjoyment. Stretching her long legs, Jules put on the speed.

Running alongside the beautiful Danube was something she'd always wanted to do, and with each step, her worries lessened. It didn't matter that her first meeting with Asher Drake hadn't gone as planned. She had achieved what she'd wanted even earlier than expected. The fact that there was an attraction between them was an anomaly. It would pass.

Asking him for a job had been in the back of her mind all along. She wasn't impulsive, but she hadn't known for sure she would ask until the words had come from her mouth. It just made sense. Working for OZ would give her the access to Drake that she needed, impressing Turner in the process. And the work would be fascinating.

Once she'd accomplished her goals, she'd return home, to the life she'd built for herself. This was just a slight detour but would be so very worthwhile.

Even though her mind zoomed with various issues and plans, she never lost her situational awareness. Those days were gone for good. She'd worked her ass off to become someone else. In both body and mind, she was a completely different person. Even the nightmares had retreated to only occasionally, when she was tired or emotionally over-wrought. Just like everything else she didn't want in her life, Jules battled them ruthlessly until they were almost nonexistent.

Because of one horrific event, all her hopes and dreams had changed focus. While she could deeply regret the cause for that change, she could not regret the direction her life had taken. The choices she'd made weren't the only ones she could have made. She could have gone in a thousand different directions, but her life and work suited who she was now.

Did Asher Drake feel the same way? His work wasn't completely different than before his life was torn apart, but how he went about it had definitely changed.

Jules made her way back to the hotel, noting that her tail had given up on her. That told her that it had been Turner's man and not one of OZ's people.

If the woman had lied and still planned to have her watched, she would have to get even more blunt than she'd been earlier. Asher Drake would spot a tail even quicker than Jules. The last thing she needed was for the OZ leader to wonder why his potential new employee was being followed. If he caught the man, he'd extract information from him—of that she had no doubt. Drake was known to be a master of inquisition.

Finding out Jules was working for one of Asher Drake's biggest enemies would be a disaster of epic proportions.

## CHAPTER TEN

Ash stood at the entrance to the restaurant, spotting Jules instantly. A half hour before their meeting time, he had texted her, asking that she meet him at the restaurant. Going up to her hotel room again was out. Until he knew her better, what she wanted from him, their meetings needed to be in public places. He still didn't have a good grasp on Juliet Stone. He anticipated more lies at their dinner meeting.

What he had learned in the last few hours intrigued him immensely. In fact, he could not remember ever being this fascinated. The question that simmered in his head the most, though, was why did she continue to lie? Her résumé was not only easily proven, it was quite impressive. So why the deceit?

The instant she saw him, she gave him a quick, simple smile and stood to greet him.

"I'm glad you suggested this restaurant," she said. "The concierge at my hotel recommended it when I first arrived."

He waited until she'd settled back into her chair before sitting across from her. "I never miss the opportunity to come here when I'm in Budapest. They have the best goulash in the city."

"Do you come to Budapest often?"

"On occasion. How about you?"

"This is my first visit. I already know I want to return so I can explore."

"It's a great city with an incredible history. Let me tell you about it."

Throughout their meal, Ash concentrated on entertaining his dining companion with interesting tidbits about the city. To anyone looking on, they appeared to be having a delightful and friendly dinner. Only he and Jules were aware of the undercurrents that were as taut as a piano wire.

Her appearance was once again breathtaking. Wearing an off-the-shoulder white dress that made her skin glow, Jules Stone had the kind of beauty that was both timeless and seemingly effortless. Several people had given her second and third glances. Ash had come prepared to get answers but found himself delaying the inevitable. It had been a long time since he'd enjoyed an evening this much.

They both declined dessert but asked for coffee. When their cups were filled with steaming liquid and Jules had taken her first careful sip, Ash knew he could no longer put it off. The pretense needed to end.

"So tell me the story of Juliet Stone."

The smile she gave him would have fooled almost anyone. Ash wasn't just anyone. He sat back and waited for the lies to begin.

THOUGH SHE HAD ENJOYED the easygoing camaraderie, Jules couldn't deny the relief of finally getting to the reason for their dinner meeting. She had been tense during their meal, anticipating when the questions would begin. Now that they had arrived, she settled herself down. She had lived this lie for over a decade; she knew it by heart.

"I was born and raised in Franklin, Tennessee. I'm an only child. My parents owned a chain of dry cleaners. I graduated from the University of Tennessee with a degree in art design."

"You didn't want to join your father's business?"

She didn't outwardly flinch but felt a tightening in her stomach muscles all the same. "No. That kind of business never interested me."

"So how does a woman with a degree in art design become a freelance security specialist?"

He had already done his homework, and that was what she wanted and expected. Her profession was legitimate, and she had many clients he could talk with if he wanted references. Not everything was a lie, but the next few were necessary.

"After graduation, a friend and I took a month to travel through Europe. We were at a nightclub and met some guys. I'd never considered myself naïve—I knew the signs to look for, but they fooled us both. Our drinks were spiked with something. I woke up in the trunk of a car. I had no idea where April was or where I was being taken.

"I won't go into detail about what happened, but I did manage to escape. April wasn't so lucky. She was found in a ditch along the roadway just outside of Rome. She had severe allergies and always carried an EpiPen wherever she went. Whatever we were given, she was apparently allergic to it and died."

"I'm sorry."

"It was a hideous, tragic event that never should have happened. It changed my world, my entire way of thinking about things. I think, more than anything, I was angry. I had no training, no protection against the evils of the world."

"So you learned how to kick ass."

"In a manner of speaking."

"You didn't consider law enforcement? Military?"

"As I mentioned, following rules is not my strong point. My mom and dad knew that whcn I made up my mind, there was no changing it. They encouraged me to try the FBI. They had a couple of friends who'd worked for them at one time."

"Is that how you met Kate?"

She grimaced and then gave a slight grin. "Yes and no. I went in for an interview, but halfway through, I got frustrated and ended it. The interviewer and I both agreed it just wasn't going to work.

"I was agitated…upset. Nothing was working out the way I'd hoped. I was distracted, not looking where I was going, and slammed full force into Kate as she was coming in the door I was exiting. I knocked her to the ground, and her coffee splattered all over both of us."

"Knowing Kate, you got an earful."

"And then some. But when she calmed down, she said something extraordinary that changed my whole life."

"What did she say?"

"If you put that kind of energy into doing something worthwhile, you could change the world."

"That sounds like Kate."

"I told her once that if she ever got tired of chasing bad guys, she would do great as a fortune cookie writer."

"Bet that went over well."

"You know Kate. She gave me a witty, profane answer and a couple of insults, and we were good."

"So how did Kate help you?"

The correct answer was she had saved her life and so much more, but Jules gave him what she could, which was still very much the truth. "She helped me refocus. To see purpose when there didn't seem to be any."

"Your credentials are both surprising and impressive. How did you get so good, so fast?"

She opened her mouth to answer, but the waiter appeared at their table with their check. Explaining all the training she had gone through, the ups and downs she had endured was best shared in private.

"Can we go somewhere less crowded and finish?"

"Of course."

She watched as Ash took care of their bill, his expression unreadable. He likely already knew every single thing she had told him. Her story was as airtight as if she'd actually lived the life she had just described. Every ounce of it could be verified. If asked, she could produce a variety of people who would swear she was exactly who she said she was. Childhood friends, her second-grade teacher, even the first boy she'd ever kissed. There wasn't a hole or even a slight wrinkle that could be questioned.

No one ever need know that it was all a huge, elaborate lie.

THEY ENDED up in a small nightclub a block from her hotel. Ash let Jules lead the way. She apparently had an agenda and her story mapped out well in advance. He would play it her way for now. Would she dig a hole with her lies that she couldn't get out of, or did she have an exit strategy?

It had crossed his mind that seduction was part of her agenda. Sex was often a prerequisite to getting information from a target. That would be no hardship. He wouldn't give up any intel, but if she wanted to give it a try, he wouldn't object.

The instant they entered the popular nightclub, he reversed his opinion. This was not a place for the distraction of seduction. It was a place of avoidance. Did she think she was finished sharing for the night? If so, she was wrong.

Without telling her why, Ash walked away from her and had a few words with the manager. Less than a minute later, they were ushered to a small private room in the back.

Though she looked a little discombobulated, she rallied quickly and gave him a quick smile. The room was set up for a small private party, with just a few chairs and tables. The music was less loud here, too. At least he could hear himself think.

They ordered drinks he suspected neither of them wanted. Their dinner conversation had been a prequel. Now he wanted it all. She would either lay it on the table for him, or he'd walk away. Yeah, he'd have some regrets. She was the most intriguing woman he'd met in years. Didn't mean he was a fool.

"It's time to be straight with me, Jules. You've told me what you want me to know. Now, I'm ready to hear what I want to know."

The flare of confusion in her eyes was real. "I'm not sure what you mean. I've answered all of your questions, and I—"

"Yes, you've given me answers to my questions. So we'll start there. Tell me how a small-town girl from Tennessee became a hunter of serial killers."

Ah, there it was. For the first time, he knew he had truly stumped her. Oddly enough, he felt no triumph. What she did was damn dangerous and incredibly brave.

"How did you come by that information?"

At least she hadn't tried to deny it…he had to give her that. "I think you underestimate OZ's network of intel."

"I didn't think so, but apparently I have. Only a handful of people, if that, know about my involvement. Mind telling me who gave you this information?"

"Like I said, Jules, I have a good network."

She opened her mouth, most likely to ask another question, but Ash held up his hand. "Let's cut to the chase. If you really want to work for OZ, answer the question."

She looked away for a mere second, and he prepared himself for another lie. When she turned back to him, he saw something different in her eyes. He knew that this time at least he was actually going to get the truth.

"The first one was by sheer accident. I happened to be in Baton Rouge on a job." She shrugged. "Attempted-bribery case. They wanted an independent investigator to sit in on an interrogation. I was headed to the airport and stopped at a service station to fill up my car before returning it to the rental agency. I saw this guy inside the store eyeing two young women who had also stopped for gas. I didn't like the way he was looking at them and thought I'd just walk over and have a talk with him. Just to see what he might say."

Saying her actions were stupid was probably not the best way to get her to keep talking, so he held back his words and gave a nod of encouragement.

"The closer I got, the more skittish he seemed. There was no mistaking that he was hiding something. He turned away quickly, like he didn't want me to see his face. That definitely caught my attention.

"I read all sorts of newspapers and online reports. It's a hobby of mine. So I knew about the murders. Four teenage girls in the area had disappeared over the past couple of years. Three of them had been found dead. One of them survived but could give very few details. Her description of the killer was vague, but she did remember one distinctive characteristic."

"What was that?"

"He had a scar across his neck, as if he'd at one time been strangled with a garrote. When he turned away to avoid me, the collar of his shirt shifted, and I saw the scar."

"What did you do?"

"I knew if I pulled out my phone and called someone, he'd see me and run. I had a choice to make. So I did take out my phone, but I walked around to the back of the building as if trying to get away from him. I took the chance that he would follow me to shut me up."

"And that's what he did?"

"Yes. He was middle-aged, not terribly fit. I was able to take him down with little effort."

He doubted it had been as easy as her explanation implied. Murderers didn't give up easily, and serial killers knew how to kill. That was what they specialized in, after all. Still, he didn't ask for details. He'd already determined that she was well trained and quite likely lethal.

"Since I didn't want the publicity that would come with catching him, I knocked him out and handcuffed him to a light pole. I used his phone to call the police and told them where he was."

"Why didn't you want credit? It would have given your security business a boost."

"I don't want that kind of boost."

"But you were found out anyway?"

"Yes, but not for a while, and thanks to Kate's connections, the ones who know agreed to keep it quiet. Or at least I thought they had."

"Don't worry, your secret is safe. I'm surprised you didn't ask if it was Kate who told me."

"Kate doesn't divulge secrets."

"Very true. So based upon that experience, you decided you were good at finding serial killers?"

"Not really…that was a lucky break. But I did decide to test the territory. I've only been involved in five cases."

"And apprehended three on your own."

She stared at him for a long moment and then nodded slowly. "You really do have connections."

"That shouldn't surprise you."

"It doesn't. I knew you did, but I've worked hard at keeping myself out of the limelight."

"That's not going to change. If you don't know already, I'm not big on getting attention either."

"Thank you. So what now?"

"Not so fast. How'd it happen? Why this kind of career?"

She seemed to sink into her chair as she sighed. "It's simple, really. After I recovered from my ordeal in Europe, I knew I couldn't go back to who I was before. I wasn't the same person. And I swore I'd never be that helpless again. I'd had no training. No way to fight these people. Neither did April.

"My parents indulged me—how could they not? They were so grateful to have me back safely. I told them I wanted to make sure it never happened to me again. So instead of pursuing a career in design, I devoted all of my time to becoming the type of fighter that would never be taken again."

"And you became some kind of avenging angel?"

She gave a dry laugh. "Not exactly. I wanted to save lives, stop bad guys."

"But not through any kind of law enforcement agency. Those pesky rules again."

She just shrugged, smiled.

"Kate was the one who gave you the idea to go out on your own?"

"Yes."

"So why does someone with such a stellar reputation want to work for a secretive, off-the-books organization like OZ?"

"I think you might be overstating my reputation."

"I don't think so. According to my sources, besides helping apprehend serial killers, you have single-handedly saved the lives of schoolchildren, government officials, and average citizens."

"'Single-handedly' is definitcly a stretch. I have a few trusted associates who have helped."

"So again, why do you want to work for OZ?"

"Because I want to do more."

"And that's the best answer you have?"

"It's the truth."

"You're telling me you've been doing this for more than a half-dozen years. Answering to no one. Making your own decisions. Taking the jobs you want to take and being very successful at it. And now you suddenly want to work for someone else?"

She looked down at her feet, and he knew the next thing that came out of her mouth would be a lie.

When she raised her head, tears glistened in her eyes. "Did your research dig up any intel on Fran Johnson?"

"No."

"That's not a surprise. They want to keep it a secret. Pretend it never happened."

"And what is 'it'?"

"Fran was a key witness in a murder investigation involving a crime family in Pittsburgh. They knew there was a mole, possibly several moles, within the Justice Department. I was tasked with finding the mole.

"I found him, but he turned out to be the mayor's nephew. Fran was killed. I got the boot, and the department covered it up. Case dismissed for lack of evidence."

"And you think that wouldn't have happened if OZ had been involved?"

"I know it wouldn't have happened. OZ is too powerful."

"I think you overestimate what we can do. We have a lot more enemies than allies."

"Maybe so, but you wouldn't let them get away with it. You would have found a way to expose who they are and what they did."

Ash considered her story. It was easily verifiable, which meant there was some truth to her words. She was still holding back, though. He needed to make a decision. He didn't have to know everything about the people he employed, but he damn well needed to trust them.

Was Jules's reticence a natural part of her private self, or was it something more? Kate's endorsement went a long way in helping him decide. She was responsible for sending Jasmine McAlister to him. Jazz, as she liked to be called, was one of his most valuable operatives.

Ash looked at Jules long and hard, and she withstood his scrutiny unflinchingly.

"OZ has rules. Not a lot, but a few. We might be more lenient in some areas, but the rules we have are written in stone. Anyone who violates one is out on his or her ass."

"I'm not opposed to rules when they make sense."

That wasn't a resounding agreement that she would follow the rules blindly, but he was okay with that. If she had indicated otherwise, they might have had a problem. He relied on his people to make good decisions and do what made sense. Micromanaging was not his way.

"Most of my operatives live close to our home base. You got a problem moving?"

"No. I live outside Flagstaff in an older two-story house I renovated. I live on the second floor, and my office is on the first. I should have no problem renting it out."

"OZ employees are expected to be on call 24/7. You could be gone for weeks or months at a time. No spouse or significant other that's going to resent your absence?"

"No."

She didn't elaborate, and he didn't probe further. The intel he'd received had already confirmed that she had no current romantic relationships. In fact, from what he could tell, she didn't date. Period.

"You'll have to go through a rigorous physical and psychological exam. Plus, a six-month probation period. One screw-up and you're out. I don't give second chances."

"Not a problem."

Before he committed, he had one more question he needed her to answer. If she denied the truth or brushed it off as nonsensical, he'd have his answer.

"How are we going to handle this heat between us?"

# CHAPTER ELEVEN

The question took Jules's breath away. She had been doing so well, answering every question without any real hesitancy. Yes, the fact that he knew about her "extracurricular" work had been startling, but she'd rallied and thought she'd done quite well. But this? This was not something she'd anticipated.

She couldn't deny the attraction. That would be an obvious lie. Nor did she want to pretend it meant nothing, because in all honesty, it was one of the sweetest emotions she'd felt in years. Jules did the only thing she knew to do. She asked her own straightforward question.

"Are you opposed to being involved with one of your operatives, or have you just never been attracted to one of them?"

"I have many attractive employees, but not one of them has made me want to kiss every part of her."

Her heartbeat tripled, and heat flooded her body. This man and his blunt honesty were both unexpected and incredibly appealing.

Before she could come up with a response, he added,

"And before you tell me this kind of talk is out of line in an interview, I'll tell you I know that. But not being forthright about things is not my way. Whatever your answer is, you need to know that up front."

"Your honesty is much appreciated. So what should we do?"

"You have two choices. Work for me, and anything between us is off the table. Or don't take the job, and we can have a short-term relationship."

"Short term?"

"I don't do permanent."

Okay, there was honesty, and then there was brutal honesty.

"So it's either one or the other?"

It was an obviously rhetorical question, and he didn't bother to respond.

Even though there was only one answer she could give, for just a second she allowed herself the fantasy of giving a different one. What would it feel like to be with a man like Asher Drake? She'd already known he was a man of integrity and strength. And now, having met him and gotten to know him on a personal basis, the things he made her feel were unlike anything she'd ever experienced. What would it be like to have him touch her, kiss her? Give herself over to the kind of pleasure she'd never before felt?

"Jules?"

Jerked out of the hopeless fantasy, she gave him the only answer she could. "I want to work for OZ."

For just a second, she thought she saw disappointment flicker in his eyes, but if it had been there, he quickly covered it with the arrogant blandness she was coming to recognize as his standard expression.

Without another word, he stood and held out his hand. She allowed him to pull her to her feet, wondering exactly what she had gotten herself into. By working with him, she was putting herself in a precarious position. She had her own agenda. If she didn't get her head straight and remember exactly why she was here, she would mess all of this up. There was too much at stake to jeopardize her goals.

They didn't talk as they walked back to her hotel. For someone who rarely felt nervous, she was suddenly incredibly so. Just because they were attracted to each other didn't mean anything, really. She had met dozens…okay, not dozens, but a few men she had felt attracted to. Not one of them had made her the slightest bit nervous. But this wasn't just anyone. This was Asher Drake, a man she had studied like no one else.

She wasn't sure what she expected when they arrived at her room. She had admitted an attraction to this man, and they had both agreed it wasn't something they could explore. He didn't get involved with his employees, and she had an agenda that was in direct conflict with any kind of intimacy with her target.

None of that mattered when they were standing at her hotel door. Her heart was racing like she was a teenager in the throes of her first crush. She held her breath, unsure of the next move.

Asher Drake had no such problem. With a curt nod, he said, "I'll be in touch." The words were terse, his face expressionless as he walked away.

She gave a laughing sigh. The man was nothing if not unpredictable, and despite all the whispered warnings in her mind, she knew she was going to have a difficult time controlling her response to him. She had never been so utterly fascinated by anyone as she was by Asher Drake.

Her timing, as usual, sucked.

The instant she entered her room, the musings of her mercurial heart abruptly ended. She was not alone.

The intruder sat in the darkness of a corner. Jules could just make out an indistinguishable shadowy image. She couldn't even tell if the person was male or female. She cursed softly. She had been distracted, unprepared. Two things she'd sworn would never happen to her again.

"You failed the first test, Ms. Stone," a female voice said, its owner sounding amused.

"Who are you?"

"Your trainer."

"For?"

"Your new employment."

"I only agreed to work for OZ a few moments ago. How did you know?"

"I imagine Drake anticipated your answer. He's smart like that. You, on the other hand, I'm not so sure about. Drake told me you're quick on the uptake. I may have to disavow him of his opinion."

Jules couldn't argue with that. She was being slow in comprehending. "Ash didn't tell me the training would begin so soon."

"Ash, is it?"

The amused speculation in the woman's voice was irritating, but again Jules couldn't argue with her reasons. She was being uncharacteristically stupid.

Regrouping, she took a breath and said, "That's his name, isn't it?"

This time, a soft laugh came from the corner. "Yes, I do believe it is."

Okay, she had not only sounded defensive but just a little immature, too. Tired of the games, Jules reached back and hit the light switch. In an instant, light flooded the room, and she saw the woman was little more than a sprite.

"Don't let my size deceive you. I can kick your ass."

"I believe you."

"Why?"

"Because you wouldn't work for OZ if you couldn't."

"Good answer. And you're right. But let's talk about you. Think you can do the same thing?"

"Do I think I can kick your ass? Am I going to have to?"

"Mine and a few others."

"When does this training begin?"

"It already has. We'll travel back to the States in an hour. Get your things, and let's go."

No. That couldn't happen. For her plan to work, she had to be at least in the same city with Drake. Not being in the same country would severely limit her ability to do her job.

Jules eyed the woman, assessing her words. "You're bluffing."

"Oh, really? Why do you say that?"

"For one thing, you're obviously here in Budapest for a job."

"So? Drake has reassigned me."

"Then your job must not be very important for him to be able to do without you so easily."

A gleam of admiration flared in the woman's dark eyes. "Not too many people have the guts to insult me to my face."

"You'll soon learn that I'm quite gutsy."

"You'll need to be." She abruptly stood, and Jules noted that the woman wasn't as small as she'd first thought. Maybe five-two, five-three, but she was thin, almost fragile-looking. She also had an unhealthy pallor. This OZ operative was apparently so valuable that Drake needed her even in her sickly state.

"I'll be here at seven a.m."

"Why?"

"To brief you on the op."

"I'll be on an OZ op already?"

"OZ employees are on call from day one. We don't bring people on unless they're already fully trained."

"If that's the case, what are you planning to train me to do?"

"You need to learn the OZ way."

Before Jules could question what exactly that meant, the woman added, "If *trainer* doesn't suit you, you can call me your watcher." She tilted her head. "You come highly recommended—Kate doesn't suffer fools gladly, but you damn well better be worth the trouble."

She paused as if waiting for a response. When Jules didn't respond, she continued, "Drake gave you your conditions for employment, but I'll give you one more. Screw this op up, and you'll regret ever hearing about OZ."

Not waiting for Jules's reply, the woman silently passed by Jules and opened the door.

"Just one question."

The woman turned, arching a questioning brow.

"You got a name?"

"Yes." Without another word, the woman walked out.

WITH MORE DETERMINATION THAN GRACE, Jazz McAlister made her way to the elevator. She had booked a room three floors below Juliet Stone's. She figured she had just enough strength left to make it there before she collapsed. Drake would bench her if he knew how weak she really was. She didn't intend for him find out. If she didn't work, she didn't function. Work kept her sane...well, as sane as people like her ever got.

When the elevator doors opened, she waltzed in as if she hadn't a care in the world. Even though the elevator was empty, she kept up the appearance. Bravado had been her mainstay for years, and right now it was the only thing keeping her on her feet. When she got to her room, she'd let her guard down.

The instant she entered her room, her legs threatened to give out on her, and she managed to make it to the bed before she collapsed. Never one to shirk her duties, she quickly texted her boss and gave him her opinion. Drake was right. As impressive as Juliet Stone appeared to be on paper, she was hiding something.

She would definitely be keeping her eye on OZ's newest operative.

As soon as the door closed behind her intruder, Jules dropped onto the sofa. She felt like she'd lived a lifetime in just one day. Not only had she met the man who had fascinated her for years, she had agreed to work for him. If that were all, it would be more than enough, but there was something else…something monumental. They were more than mildly attracted to each other. The complications were endless and mind-blowing.

In her heart of hearts, she wasn't surprised at the attraction. How many times had she stared at his photo and wondered about him? She had built up Asher Drake in her mind, but she had assumed that once she met the real man, he wouldn't live up to her expectations. She'd been wrong. He was more, so much more, than she had ever dreamed. Complicated, amazingly sexy, and bone-chillingly perceptive.

She was playing with fire, and even though she knew she would get burned, she couldn't stay away from the heat. For the first time in years, she felt truly alive.

The ring of her phone drew her from her exhausted

musings. Pulling it from her purse, she grimaced as she saw the name of the caller. Taking a deep breath, she slid her finger over the answer icon. She had some fast-talking to do.

"What the hell, Jules?"

Despite her friend's tone, Jules couldn't help but smile. Having known Kate for well over a decade, she knew the anger would come from concern. Kate Walker was at the top of an exceedingly short list of people she trusted.

"And hello to you, too."

"You're going to work for OZ? Are you insane?"

"Oh, I think that ship sailed a long time ago, don't you?"

"Don't be glib. How on earth do you think this is going to work?"

"It'll give me access I wouldn't have from the outside, which should impress Turner. I need to be as convincing as possible. Plus, I'll be a good operative."

"No question about that, but it's going to put you in more danger, too."

"I'll play it out for as long as I can. You said you thought you were close to finding what you need."

"I am, but 'close' is a relative term. It could still be months away."

"Then I'll stick it out until then or until I no longer have a choice, whichever comes first."

"You know he'll find out the truth eventually."

"Not necessarily. I've covered my tracks."

"He's the best in the business of uncovering tracks."

Asher Drake had definitely proven that tonight. Not once had she anticipated that he would find out about her penchant for hunting serial killers. Still, she believed this cover was as solid as possible.

"I'm worried for you, Jules. You might get more than you bargained for."

"I thought you trusted me to handle this."

"I do. Or at least I did until Ash texted me that you told him you want to work for him."

When Jules didn't reply, Kate sighed and added, "You planned to ask him for a job all along, didn't you?"

"Yes and no. I didn't start out with that intention, but the more I thought about it, the more sense it made."

"I thought you were just going to observe for a while before you introduced yourself."

"He made me. I had no choice but to play it out."

"That's because he's the best there is, Jules. You know that. You're playing a dangerous game with a very dangerous man. I know you don't necessarily see him that way, but you don't know Asher Drake like I do."

"I thought you liked and admired him."

"I do, but that doesn't mean I don't see him for what he is."

"I know what I'm doing."

"Guess it wouldn't do any good to ask you to reconsider telling him who you really are."

"Absolutely not."

"I think you'd be surprised at his reaction."

"Let's not do this again, Kate. If I tell him, you know what he'll do. He'll want to know everything, and we'll be right back where we started."

"All right. I'll drop it for now. Now tell me what happened."

"I figure you know most of it. Ash said he checked in with you."

"Ha. That just shows you how little you know about the man. His text was five words. Your name and then 'Tell me everything.'"

"Whatever you told him must have worked."

"I just told him that I think a lot of you and he can trust you. I imagine I'll hear from him again."

"Considering he caught me in a lie, he might question your judgment from now on."

"Uh-oh. I told you he's got some kind of sixth sense when it comes to lies. How angry was he?"

"Enough to threaten that if I do it again, I won't like the consequences. Not angry enough to walk away."

"I just hope you don't regret this decision."

So did she. "I didn't expect him to know about the serial-killer cases."

"I warned you. The man is good. Do not, at any point, underestimate him."

No, she wouldn't. She'd learned her lesson about that. The other issue, she wasn't quite sure how to handle. "There's another complication."

"What?"

"There's an attraction I didn't anticipate."

"For you or for him?"

"Both."

"Oh, Jules."

Those two softly spoken words held a wealth of meaning.

"I know. It's stupid. Nothing will come of it. We both agreed if I went to work for OZ, we couldn't pursue anything. It'll pass."

"For your sake, I hope so, but let me ask you this. What's your endgame here? Once this is over and you've done what you need to do, what happens?"

"I'll leave. You know the reason I'm doing this."

"Yes, but I also know that your emotions are tied up with this case. And when emotions are involved, things don't always turn out the way we planned."

"You're right, but right now I just need to get this done. What happens after that we'll just have to wait and see."

"You know I'm only a phone call away."

"Thanks, and I love you for it."

"Love you, too. Get some rest. You've got to be exhausted."

"Yeah. And my day might be longer tomorrow. One of OZ's employees was waiting for me in my room. She says she's my trainer."

"What's her name?"

"She didn't say. She's petite, has short, ink-black hair, dark brown eyes, and looks like she might have been sick recently."

"Jasmine McAlister, or Jazz. She was injured on an op a few months back. Don't let her size or weak appearance fool you. She's a tough one."

"So she told me."

"Believe her."

"I will. I'll do fine. Remember, I'm a tough cookie, too."

"Yes, you are."

"Night, Kate."

"Night, Jules."

After ending the call, Jules sat for a while and just appreciated the silence. The day had brought more challenges than she'd expected. When she'd set out on this quest, she'd had one goal. That hadn't changed. And what she'd told Kate was the truth. Working with Asher Drake would assist her in achieving that goal even better than she had hoped, but it also complicated things. She had no real exit strategy. And if her new boss found out who'd sent her here, she had a feeling complications would be the least of her worries.

## CHAPTER TWELVE

The flight to Timisoara, Romania, would be a short one. Ten minutes after takeoff, Ash stood at the front of the plane's cabin to brief his people. Five OZ operatives had traveled to Budapest with him. The sixth, his newest hire, sat in the second row of seats. Judging by the slight stiffness of her shoulders, he discerned that Jules Stone was feeling a little out of her element.

This op in Romania had been planned long before Humphrey's meeting with Omar Schrader had been scheduled. He hadn't mentioned it to Jules last night. One of the requirements of an OZ operative was to be ready for anything at a moment's notice. There were still things she needed to do to prove herself, but this would be a good starter test.

Despite her seeming uncertainty, Ash had every confidence that Jules was a good fit for OZ. Not only did she have the required skills and drive, she had the leadership qualities needed to head up a mission. That she didn't like rules, as she'd confessed, wasn't an issue. He could work around any problems on that front. His biggest concern, admittedly a large one, was that she still wasn't being entirely truthful. Even though the stories she'd told him yesterday had checked out, his gut told him she was hiding things. Until he was completely certain of her, he and Jazz would be keeping a close eye on her.

"Okay, listen up. This is a brief flight, so we'll need to be ready to hit the ground running when we land. We'll do a quick run-through now to make sure we're still on the same page and one last review once we're on the ground. Before we get started, though, let me introduce you to OZ's newest team member, Jules Stone. She can get you up to date on her background later. Till then, be assured she is well trained and ready for action." He glanced around at the other operatives. "Any questions?"

When there was no response, Ash went on. "Jazz, I need you running point on communications. Stone will be with you."

He didn't expect any argument. Jazz didn't think he was aware of how weak she still was. He had been there when she was injured, and he knew full well she wasn't physically healthy enough to be on the job. He also knew that she needed to work. Downtime for Jazz was a dangerous thing. If she didn't work, she went places in her mind that she needed to avoid. Her assignment on this op, while important, could have been done by one of the others, but this would keep her busy and involved without any undue stress on her body. Besides, he knew how it felt to need something to concentrate on other than your own tortured thoughts.

"Stone, I'll skim the basics of the op. Jazz can fill in the blanks." Ash didn't wait for her response but continued on, "Andrei Dalca has been on our radar for years. He's involved in a multitude of crimes, including human trafficking, illegal arms, drug running, and money laundering. The Romanian government has spent millions of dollars and thousands of man-hours trying to catch him in the act. So far, he's been untouchable. But we've found a way into his inner circle."

Ash clicked the remote in his hand, and the photo of a beautiful, dark-haired woman with unfathomable light blue eyes appeared. "Eve Wells, OZ operative. She infiltrated the man's inner circle through Dalca's wife's brother, Darius Vasile.

"Darius thinks himself a lady's man and has fallen for Kimberly Lowe, Eve's undercover name, quite hard. She's been his exclusive girlfriend for over five months. Not only has she been inside Dalca's primary residence multiple times, last week she infiltrated his private office. She found the evidence we've been searching for. We now have enough to make something stick."

Ash didn't allow himself to speculate on how Eve was holding up. He knew this op had been a difficult one for her, and he hoped it wasn't destroying the sometimes tenuous lid she kept on her fury. Even as much as he knew she was the one person who would do whatever it took to get what was needed on Dalca, he knew the price she might have to pay. He worried that it might take all she had to give, but that would be a problem for another day.

Ash clicked the remote again, revealing their destination. "Dalca is at his main residence this weekend. He's having a small gathering to celebrate a new venture. We're not sure what that new venture entails. Doesn't really matter, because thanks to Eve, we now have a way inside his compound and the intel to destroy him.

"Each of you has the blueprints of the residence, as well as the layout of the grounds, on your tablets. Once we've secured Dalca, we'll transport him a mile from the compound, where Romanian authorities will receive him.

"Let's review our roles." He nodded at Xavier Quinn, his second-in-command for this op, to take over the briefing.

Xavier knew the mission as well as Ash did. Allowing him to go over the rest of the op with the team would give Ash a chance to observe them. They worked flawlessly together, but throwing a new part into a finely tuned machine could disrupt the performance. He not only wanted to assess how they responded to their new team member, but he needed to watch Jules's demeanor as well. He'd told her she was on probation, and he meant every word. Her experience and Kate's recommendation could go only so far. How she behaved on her first mission would be the key to moving forward or letting her go before trouble could start.

JULES HAD an unfettered view of everyone. She and Jazz, who had finally shared her name, had arrived at the small airstrip ahead of the other OZ team members. Being the first ones here had given her an advantage as Jazz had murmured each person's name when they stepped onto the plane.

Since no one seemed surprised to see her, she figured they'd been forewarned, most likely by the OZ leader.

Jules noted that each operative appeared to be serious, focused, and in excellent physical condition. Collectively, they were tough-looking professionals and as intimidating as hell.

What Jazz hadn't said about Xavier Quinn had been telling. She'd said his name like she had the others', but the tenseness of her body and the longing Jules had glimpsed in the other woman's eyes, albeit briefly, told her more than words ever could.

Asher Drake might discourage romantic relationships within OZ, but that didn't mean they didn't occur.

When Serena and Sean Donavan arrived, that proved her point. Jazz told her they'd just returned from their honeymoon a few days ago and were so much in love that everyone else wanted to gag. Her soft, affectionate tone belied the words. Jules suspected that beneath Jasmine McAlister's tough exterior lay a tender, romantic heart.

She had watched in rapt attention as Asher Drake had joined them. Though nothing was said, the demeanor of the group shifted from semi-relaxed to alert attention. Just in those few seconds, it was easy to surmise that these people respected their leader.

The case involving the head of a crime family was no big surprise, other than the knowledge that OZ was working for the Romanian government.

Kate had told her that OZ's connections and influence reached all corners of the earth. What wasn't clear was how Asher Drake had created such a network in a relatively short period of time.

She was drawn from her musings when Xavier Quinn unfolded his large frame and stood. Facing the group, he pinpointed Jazz with his gaze before sweeping it over the rest of the group. She felt the woman beside her stiffen. Xavier's harsh features were both alarming and mesmerizing. The fierceness of his expression was set off by startling silver eyes the color of old pewter. With thick, short hair the color of deepest night, broad shoulders, and a mouth that looked like it hadn't moved from flat-line grim in years, he was easily the most intimidating of the group.

Xavier stood to the left of his boss. The screen revealed an aerial view of a multibuilding compound surrounded by a high brick wall. Sidewalks, pathways, verdant green lawns, and colorful flowerbeds separated the buildings. The estate reminded Jules of a large, luxurious apartment complex.

"As you can see, the place is huge and a fortress. There are five buildings, and the one in the back is the main house. The two on the left are guesthouses. The smaller one in the back on the right is the pool house, and the one beside it is where Dalca keeps his cars and other toys.

"The party will be in the main house. We anticipate a dozen or so guests. Three of them are known associates of Dalca. The others are family and close friends. We're not after anyone but Dalca, and we'll do our best to maintain Eve's cover."

"Our best? Exactly what does that mean?"

Jules glanced to her right, where a tall blond man sat. He'd been introduced to her as Gideon Wright, and though he'd seemed pleasant at the time, the expression on his face indicated he was a wolf in sheep's clothing. What had set him off?

"Just like what I said, Gideon. If this doesn't fly, Eve may need to stay inside."

"She's been there five damn months," Gideon snarled.

Ash sent Gideon a questioning look. "She knew going in that it could take several months. Has she said it's been too much for her?"

"Of course not. You know Eve. She's going to do the job no matter what."

"Isn't that what we all do?" Ash asked quietly.

As if aware he'd started an argument he had no hope of winning, Gideon shrugged. "It is."

Going forward as if there'd been no disruption, Xavier brought up another photo. This one of a middle-aged man with cold, hard eyes and an arrogant smirk. "Our target, Andrei Dalca. Eve's job will be to contain the partygoers in one room. It'll be easier to ensure everyone's safety if they're all together when we go in."

"Any idea how many guards are on the premises?"

So involved in the op's details, Jules asked the question without thinking of the protocol. Thankfully, no one seemed surprised by or resentful of her interruption.

"That's our biggest issue," Xavier answered. "On any given day, Dalca has about a half dozen. When he has guests, it usually increases. We do know that they'll be heavily armed and have posts around the entire perimeter. Ash and I will neutralize the ones surrounding the far west side. That'll give you and Jazz the opportunity to get inside the communications center. Jazz will block all communications going in and out except for ours. You'll need to stay there in case someone escapes us and tries to repair their comms. The rest of us have our assignments."

Sending his boss a look, Xavier handed Ash the remote and then settled into his chair again.

His gaze taking in everyone, the OZ leader said calmly, "This is how it's going to go down."

## CHAPTER THIRTEEN

A quarter mile from Dalca's compound, the team drove their vehicles onto a narrow road. Obscured by overgrown bushes and trees, it was the perfect place to hide their transportation. They'd take it on foot from here.

No one spoke. Each person had their job and knew it well. Most important was the first assignment, which was to disable the cameras and cut off all communication within the compound and to the outside. The last thing they wanted was for someone to call in reinforcements. Once comms were down, the team would systematically disarm and neutralize the guards and then converge on the party.

Ash spared Jules a glance. The team had accepted that she was on the op, but that didn't mean they accepted her as one of their own. She'd have to prove herself, and he didn't plan on making any special accommodations. She wouldn't want any concessions, and he wasn't one to make them for anyone.

She was checking out the weapons she'd been given, a Glock 19 and KA-BAR knife. She needed to be comfortable with both, and he approved of the ease and care in which she handled each weapon. She likely had favorites of her own—most professionals did—but she'd do fine with the loaners. He wasn't surprised to see the glitter of excitement in her eyes. Just in the few hours he'd spent with her yesterday, he had recognized a kindred spirit. She enjoyed this kind of work. In his opinion, that was a must. If you didn't get a little pumped with adrenaline going into an op, you didn't have the edge you needed. On top of that, life was too short to do something you didn't enjoy.

She looked ready and able to perform the job assigned. What did concern him, though, was how she separated herself from the others. While the rest of the team stood grouped together, she stood several feet away. Yeah, she was the new kid on the block and likely didn't feel she belonged yet, but he relied on his people to work as a team. That needed to happen immediately.

He'd have to keep an eye on that.

His gaze went to Jazz and then to Jules. "Ready?"

When they both nodded, he jerked his head, and the team moved forward as one. They were at the compound within minutes. Thanks to Eve, they knew the best place to breach the wall. The blind spot, about ten feet wide, gave them just enough room to throw a rope over and climb up. Once they were all over the wall, things became trickier.

In silence, they surrounded the communications building. Xavier crept up on the lone guard. Choking him into unconsciousness, he quickly zip-tied his hands and feet, while Jazz slapped tape over his mouth. Xavier and Gideon carried him around a corner, propping him up against a far wall behind some shrubbery.

With that taken care of, Ash carefully eased the door open. As expected, three Dalca employees sat at their stations, surrounded by thirty monitors. He was glad to note that not only were their backs to him, but not one of them appeared to be alarmed, confirming that the team's arrival hadn't been detected.

Ash, Gideon, and Xavier each grabbed a man and, using the same tactic Xavier had used on the guard, easily took them out.

Leaving Gideon and Xavier to secure the unconscious men, Ash jerked his head toward the monitors. "Get started, Jazz. We'll want a complete outage of the phones as well as camera access."

"Got it." She sat down at one of the computer stations and went to work.

His eyes went to their newest operative. "Keep a watch out. Let us know if there's any trouble."

Jules gave an abrupt nod of acknowledgment and her eyes spoke of understanding. She knew her role. Ash had no idea if she was tech savvy enough to help Jazz, but that wasn't necessary for this op. Before Jazz had become a field operative, she had worked the technical side. She could do this alone with no issues. If they were discovered, Jazz would likely be too weak to defend herself. Jules would be her eyes and her protector.

Comfortable with the setup, Ash turned to the others. "Let's get to work."

With that, he and the rest of the team walked out the door.


JULES WATCHED Ash and the others leave. Part of her wanted to be in on the action, but another part was satisfied to stay behind. Ash trusted her to watch Jazz's back. That meant something.

"You need me to help with anything?" Jules asked. She wasn't the most tech-savvy person, but she figured she could press whatever keys Jazz told her to press.

"I'm good. Just keep watch."

Doing just that, Jules went to the small window over-looking the grounds. While a part of her focused on looking for threats, her mind reviewed the last half hour. The ease with which the op had gone so far was hard to comprehend. She had been on enough missions of her own to recognize the extreme professionalism and skill of the operatives. Each knew his or her job. There was no questioning, no pulling rank. There was mutual respect, mutual trust.

"Okay," Jazz announced behind her. "All comms are down. Other than our team, no one can call in or out."

Glancing over her shoulder, she noted the gleam in Jazz's eyes. The look of a person who knew she'd done good.

"Is it always like this?"

"Like what?"

"I don't know." She shrugged. "Quiet. Smooth. The way the team took out the comms people was as silent and effi-cient as any I've ever seen."

Jazz gave an abrupt laugh, then grabbed her right side and winced. "I wish. But sometimes, yeah. It's smooth and quick. Other times, not so much. Predicting what people will do when they're in a panic isn't always easy."

"You were hurt on your last op?"

Another wince crossed the other woman's face, but Jules didn't think it was from pain.

"Yeah," she said. "You could say that."

"Mind talking about it?"

"I can't give you any details. You don't have the clearance for that yet. But I can say we were in Africa dealing with a group of extremists. I happened to get in the way of one who thought jumping off a cliff would be a good way to go out. Unfortunately, he took me with him."

"How on earth did you survive?"

"About halfway down, I managed to shake loose of the

guy. A tree branch was sticking out of the side of the cliff. I grabbed on to it. He kept going, and I slammed down onto a rock that was jutting out."

"When did that happen?"

"About four months ago."

"How badly were you hurt?"

"A few broken ribs, punctured lung. You know the drill."

Just in the short conversation, Jules had learned quite a bit about Jazz McAlister. First, the woman was incredibly brave. To have survived what had likely been life-threatening injuries took strength and courage. And no way was she healthy or fully recovered from her injuries, but she was obviously determined to keep working. That took focus and a deep commitment.

To ease the defensive look lingering on Jazz's expressive face, Jules inclined her head toward one of the blank monitors. "Are all OZ operatives as technically savvy as you are?"

Jazz eyes twinkled with amusement. It struck Jules then that Jasmine McAlister was actually quite lovely. She wore almost no makeup and could easily pass as a teenager if she wanted. Jules got the feeling that Jazz purposely hid her beauty.

"Serena is our tech and communications leader. She has a group of five that work directly under her."

"But she's an operative, too?"

"Yes. She and Sean work well together, so when the entire team is on an op, she usually joins us. The rest of us have adequate tech skills. Well, except for Xavier." Her smile grew wider as her eyes softened. "He can barely work a toaster."

Just like that, Jules saw something else. Something Jazz would most definitely deny. She was in love with Xavier Quinn.

~

ASH MOVED through the bushes that lined the paths separating the buildings. He and his team had disabled and disarmed ten guards so far. He hadn't heard from Eve since they'd arrived, but that wasn't a concern. She likely had her comms off. She knew her job, and he trusted her to do it.

"Just took out another guard." The edginess in Gideon's voice put Ash on alert. "He was headed to the communications building. There was a man in front of him. I couldn't get to him without raising an alarm."

"Understood." Ash clicked a button on his earwig. "Stone, can you hear me?"

"Yes."

"You have a guard coming your way. You up to taking care of him?"

"Of course."

He didn't think they knew each other well enough for her to understand his underlying meaning. Jazz was in no shape to take on a rabbit, much less an armed soldier. Would Jules read between the lines?

Apparently so, as she added softly, "I've got this, Ash. No worries."

Satisfied that it would be taken care of, Ash turned his earwig back on for the rest of the team. Even though things were going smoothly, he was getting that twitchy feeling between his shoulder blades. It was rarely wrong.

"Let's get Dalca and get the hell out of here."

JULES PULLED the Glock from the holster on her thigh. Even though she was comfortable with the model, she preferred her own SIG Sauer. She checked the chamber once more, noting Jazz was doing the same with her weapon.

The other woman hadn't heard Ash's side of the conversation, but she'd heard Jules's response and no doubt knew what was about to go down. Hopefully, she didn't think she needed to prove herself.

To dispel that concern, Jules went to the door, saying, "Time to earn my keep."

"Wait," Jazz said.

Holding back a sigh, Jules turned. They didn't have time for an argument.

Jazz eyed her calmly for a second and then surprised Jules by saying, "Kick his butt."

Giving her a quick smile, Jules opened the door and peered out, left and right. She saw no one. Closing the door behind her, she dashed to a large bush a few feet away. She didn't know which direction he'd be coming from, but she should be able to grab him before he made it to the door. She didn't have to wait long.

Running footsteps moved toward her. When he rounded the corner, Jules knew a moment of regret. He looked like he was barely out of his teens and likely had something to prove, too. It couldn't be helped. Pushing emotions to the back where they belonged, she concentrated on the matter at hand. What the young man lacked in years, he more than made up for in bulk. A surprise attack would be her best bet.

She waited until he passed her and then was on him in an instant. Going in low, she took him down from the back, at his knees, hitting hard. He fell forward, and they both grunted. The kid was at least two hundred fifty pounds, most of it solid muscle. Giving him no time to react, Jules wrapped her arms around the soldier's thick neck. She squeezed with just the right amount of pressure. Doing what was normal, the kid grabbed her arm to try to dislodge her. When that didn't work, he went to his feet with her still hanging on to his back. Even though her feet were about a foot above the ground, Jules held tight. He tried to swing her around, and still she held, still squeezing. With one last attempt to get her off his back, the kid threw himself backward and slammed her against the brick wall.

She grunted at the explosion of pain but managed to keep the pressure on his windpipe. The young man dropped to his knees and at last lost consciousness.

Rolling off him, Jules looked up into Jazz's grinning face. "You looked like a flea crawling all over a rhino, but damn if you didn't get the job done."

Breathless, Jules made the effort to give her a thumbs-up. Jazz produced a zip tie and took care of the man's hands and feet, along with putting tape over his mouth. Between the two of them, they managed to hide him behind a bush. The deed was done in a matter of minutes, and they finished up just in time to hear Ash say, "Okay, let's get this done."

# CHAPTER FOURTEEN

Eve Wells took another surreptitious glance at her watch, a gift from Darius Vasile. She missed her OZ-issued watch, which performed multiple functions. This flashy bauble only told the time, but the glittery, overdone style fit her gold-digger persona to a T.

Only a few more moments, and her team would strike. This assignment should end today and, in her estimation, couldn't be over soon enough. Five months as Kimberly Lowe—Kimmie to her friends—had been more than enough. Acting as if she hadn't a thought in her head other than looking pretty was more than even a seasoned spy like herself should have to endure.

Crossing one long, silky leg over the other, she added a soft, exaggerated sigh with the movement, drawing both male and female attention. While the women glared daggers, the men eyed her with the type of hunger that would have made Eve Wells go after them with a biting comment or the closest weapon. As Kimmie, the beautiful, useless bimbo, she gave the languid smile of a hungry cat on the prowl.

After all, a girl had to have her fun.

The drawing room, though enormous, was one of the loveliest rooms in the house. Its six sofas, five chairs, numerous occasional tables, and baby grand piano in the corner spoke of taste, decadence, and extreme wealth. She had been a guest in this house many times and had visited every room in the compound at least once. Darius loved showing off the home he intended to own someday. He had explained that his brother-in-law, Andrei Dalca, was twenty years older and smoked like a chimney in winter. Since Andrei had no children or siblings, Darius firmly believed he would inherit everything. Because of Andrei's unhealthy life-style, Darius anticipated gaining that wealth sooner rather than later.

She knew the OZ team was already here, and since no alarms had been raised, everything was going according to plan. The dinner had been lavish and decadent. The wine had been flowing, and the laughter had gotten louder. Ash had said he wanted everyone relaxed and mellow, assured of their invincibility. These people looked about as relaxed as they were going to get.

To counteract the boredom of the aimless discussion going on around her, Eve mentally reviewed the details of the op. The last communication she'd received from her boss was a coded message this morning via text. Anyone who happened to see it would have assumed it was a spam message, but she'd learned OZ codes and way of messaging the first month she'd been on the job. And since the messages were often disguised as advertisements for a gross or unpleasant product or procedure, she'd also learned her boss, Asher Drake, had a screwy sense of humor. One of the many reasons she liked the man.

This morning's message had been short, to the point, and descriptively unpleasant. Eve was glad she'd been alone when she'd read it, as she had broken out into a fit of giggles.

*Kool-Eaze is a Breeze! Are you in hemorrhoid hell? Are they grouped together? Painful and sore? Itching? Help is on the way! Try our soothing balm today and feel amazing, glorious relief by evening. In eight to nine hours, they'll be completely gone! Our soothing ointment will make the burn disappear and the swelling vanish! Order within the next eight hours and get another tube for free! Loved ones will thank you for it!*

Translation: Group everyone into one room. The op would go down between eight and nine o'clock this evening. And her OZ team members were looking forward to seeing her again.

The plan was a simple one, which was the norm for OZ, as simplicity usually had the best chance for success. Putting too many complications into a mission was a good way to ensure the operation went sour.

Her one assignment tonight was ensuring everyone stayed in this room. Once Dalca's guards were neutralized, unable to communicate the threat, the OZ team would appear. Having everyone together would ensure the safety of her team, as well as Dalca and his people.

She glanced around the room, taking in the evening's guest. Dalca, of course, held center stage. A tall man with a slender build and dark eyes, his expression was one of arrogant authority. There was, though, a small gleam in his eyes that was worrisome. Dalca didn't get excited about much, but for some reason he seemed uncharacteristically pleased tonight. What was that about?

Her gaze moved to the other occupants. Dalca's wife sat beside him, but Eve noticed she wasn't touching him. Even without knowing their background, it was obvious the woman disliked her husband immensely. Portia Dalca was a year older than her husband and looked ten times that. Being married to a controlling bastard couldn't be easy. Eve might have felt sorry for her if not for the pesky fact that the woman ran part of her husband's business. In Eve's opinion, Portia and Andrei were made for each other.

The guests included Daniel Balan, Dalca's attorney, and Maria, his wife. The others were an odd assortment of Dalca's relatives and the guest of honor, Henri Burman and his wife, Greta. Eve suspected Henri was the reason Dalca looked so pleased with himself. As Burman was a wealthy financier from Germany, it stood to reason that he and Dalca had likely made a lucrative deal of some sort.

The plan was for Eve to be taken away along with the other guests. Until they knew the charges would stick, she wouldn't break her cover. Though it wasn't ideal, she had worked too hard to risk walking away too soon. It had been her suggestion to stay undercover until everyone was satisfied that Dalca would be convicted. Ash had agreed with her assessment.

Gideon would no doubt have a different opinion.

The thought of Gideon Wright made her want to smile. It had been five months since she'd seen her friend. Even though they often communicated via text using OZ code, it wasn't the same as talking with him or seeing him. Gideon Wright had been her best friend for years, long before she'd joined the OZ team. Eve missed his sharp wit and dry sense of humor. Once he learned she might have to maintain her cover for a while longer, she figured she'd get an earful. That was okay. She knew how to give it right back to him. That's what made their friendship work.

"Darling." The heavily accented voice sounded behind her.

Putting on a sultry smile, she turned to the handsome man leaning over her. Darius Vasile was probably the easiest mark she'd ever targeted. She had met him, interestingly enough, through an online dating site. Though Darius cultivated a reputation that he was a player, she had done a thorough investigation and learned that despite his looks and money, he had difficulty keeping a girlfriend for more than a couple of months. He'd turned to online dating for assistance, and she had been there to swoop him up. It hadn't taken her long to figure out why he couldn't maintain a romantic relationship. The man was the neediest, most annoying human being she'd ever met.

"I'm bored."

Sounding like a whiny adolescent was one of Darius's least-admirable qualities.

She giggled softly, as he would expect. "Then come sit by me so I can entertain you."

Needing no further encouragement, Darius settled onto the arm of her chair and nuzzled her neck. Covering her shudder of revulsion with another giggle, she reminded herself this was the job. She closed the door on Eve Wells and turned into his arms, becoming Kimmie once more.

"That's odd," Burman said. "My phone has no signal."

Trying not to stiffen, Eve looked over Darius's shoulder. Burman had a frown on his face as he held up his phone. A small triumphant zing went through her. The action was about to begin.

"Perhaps I can get a signal in another part of the house," Burman said. "I need to make a call."

Eve pulled herself from Darius's clinging arms. To ensure everyone's safety, no one could leave this room. She opened her mouth to grab everyone's attention, but before she could say anything, Greta Burman gave an exasperated snort of disgust. "The only reason you want to use the phone is to call your mistress."

Everyone, including Eve, fell into a stunned silence. Though Greta had been drinking steadily all night, she had spoken barely two words. Apparently, the alcohol, along with anger at her husband, had given her extra courage.

Eve kept her mouth closed and let the scene play out. The reason for staying in this room didn't matter…it just needed to happen.

Greta stood and began to pace around the sofa, where her shocked husband continued to sit. "I have given you twenty years of my life, two beautiful children, and put up with your obnoxious family, and you repay me by sleeping with your harlot!"

"Greta!" Henri whispered harshly. "This is neither the time nor the place. Stop it right this minute. I'll—"

"You'll what?" She reached for her small evening bag on the sofa and pulled out a Ruger .38 Special. "Teach me a lesson?"

Eve swallowed a groan. Of all the times for Greta to assert herself. While she could applaud the woman's show of independence and fortitude, doing so with a gun in her hand and too much alcohol in her blood was not the best way.

Ash and Gideon would be here any moment. The last thing they needed when they barged through the doors was to find a drunken, unstable woman brandishing a gun.

Disarming Greta while still acting as if she didn't have a brain in her head would be tricky, but Eve had no choice. She had to get that gun out of the way.

Jumping to her feet, Eve cried out in a shrill voice, "What is she doing? Oh, Darius, she has a gun! Get it before she shoots me."

Darius whirled around to gape at her. "What?"

Eve's voice went even shriller. "She's going to shoot me!"

Everyone, including Greta, was looking at her as if she'd dropped in from outer space. With all eyes on the witless Kimmie, Eve took advantage. Running for the door as if in a panic, she stumbled and fell on top of Greta, knocking into the woman so hard the gun flew out of her hand, sliding across the hardwood floor and under one of the sofas.

Barely a second later, the door busted open. Asher Drake and Gideon Wright stood there, holding guns.

Eve cursed under her breath. Perfect timing, as always.

ASH HAD BEEN surprised many times in his life. To see the elegant and capable Eve Wells sprawled on top of another woman, while others stood around them gaping, was surprising indeed. He'd told her to create a distraction if necessary. Apparently, she had.

"Hands up, everyone."

Dalca abruptly came out of his shocked trance and sprang to his feet. "What is the meaning of this? Who are you people? What are you doing in my home?"

"We're here for you, Dalca. No one needs to get hurt."

"This is outrageous. Get out of my house immediately before I call the authorities."

"The authorities are not your friends today, Dalca. Make it easy on yourself and everyone else and give up."

Dalca glanced over at the man to his left and then returned his gaze to Ash. "May I confer with my attorney?"

"You can confer all you want when we get you to a secure facility. For now, keep your hands where we can see them." He nodded at the women still on the floor. "You two, get up and go stand over there."

"There's a—"

Eve's words were cut off when Dalca dived for something on the floor and came up with a gun. Grabbing the woman standing beside him, he pulled her in front of him and held the gun to her head.

Ah, hell. Tapping his earwig once, Ash spoke softly, "Plan B."

Holding his gun steady, Ash advanced toward Dalca. "You don't want to do this, Dalca. It won't have a good ending."

"If I put the gun down and surrender, it won't have a good ending either."

Ash took another step closer. "Perhaps, but at least you'd be alive."

"Don't come any closer, or I'll shoot her."

"Shooting your attorney's wife might put a crimp in your relationship."

Finally coming out of his shock, Balan snapped, "Andrei, unhand my wife immediately."

In response, Dalca pulled the woman even closer to him, blocking Ash's chance for a clean shot. "Attorneys are easy to find."

"Adding murder to the list of your charges will not help your cause."

"You won't let me kill her."

Ash cocked his head. "I won't?"

"No. You're going to get me safely out of here. I'll release her when I'm safe."

"I think you've been watching too much television. That's not how I operate."

"I know your kind. You will do whatever you have to do to prevent bloodshed."

"I don't think you've ever come across my kind before."

"Maybe not." Swinging the gun away from the woman he was holding, he fired, hitting Gideon.

Eve screamed and ran toward the fallen operative. A second later, five more operatives burst into the room, all their weapons aimed at Dalca.

Well, this had gone to hell in a hurry. Without taking his eyes off the idiot in front of him, he growled at Xavier, "Take care of Gideon."

"Kimmie," Darius snapped, "come away from that man."

Holding her hands over Gideon's injury, her eyes wild with grief, Eve snapped, "Shut up, Darius."

"It's bad, Ash," Xavier said. "We need to get him out of here."

Without being told, Jules eased past Ash and circled behind Dalca. So focused on Ash, Dalca never noticed her until she had her gun pressed against the back of his head.

Her eyes on Ash, Jules spoke with soft menace into Dalca's ear, "I'm the newest member of this team and have a lot to prove. Killing you would only help me."

"That would be murder," Dalca snarled. "You can't do that."

Ash gave a mean grin. "You just shot one of my best men. You think getting rid of a weasel like you would bother us?"

"You can't just—"

"We can and we will."

Jules pressed the gun harder against Dalca's head. "Want me to shoot him here, boss?"

"Yeah. That oughta do it."

"Wait! Wait!" Dalca screamed. "I give up."

"Take his gun, Stone. If he even twitches, shoot him."

Jules took the gun from the man's hand and within seconds had him lying on the floor and zip-tied.

Ash glanced around. The rest of Dalca's guests were huddled in a corner.

"Sean, you and Serena gather everyone in the van. Xavier, you and Eve take care of Gideon."

Eve looked up at Ash. "But I—"

"I think your cover is blown."

She shook her head, misery in her eyes. "I'm so sorry, Ash."

"We'll sort it all out. Just take care of him."

And they would have to sort it all out. What had been going as smooth as ice had turned into a shitstorm. And if they lost Gideon? Hell, he wasn't sure the team could survive another loss. The last one had almost destroyed them.

# CHAPTER FIFTEEN

They were headed back to the States hours later before Jules got the chance to talk with Ash. He had removed himself from the group, spending much of his time on his phone. For anyone else, it might look as though he were coldly removed from the drama around them, but Jules knew that wasn't the case. He was focused on what needed to be done, but his eyes told another story. He was concerned for his injured operative and quietly furious at how the op had gone down.

Gideon had been in surgery when they'd left the hospital in Timisoara. Eve had promised to call the moment he was out. If there was anyone who felt worse than Ash about how the op had gone down, it was Eve Wells. Jules didn't know the woman at all, but she easily recognized the signs of grief and massive guilt. She was well versed in both those emotions.

Sitting in one of the seats in the back of the plane, Jules got an uninterrupted view of Ash talking in a low tone with Xavier Quinn, who was on one of the sofas at the front. She couldn't hear what the two men were saying, but judging by their grim expressions, it wasn't pleasant.

Several moments later, Ash walked down the aisle toward her. With a heavy sigh, he dropped down into the seat across from her. "Eve called. Gideon's out of surgery. He lost a lot of blood, but thankfully the bullet missed his femoral artery. They repaired the damage, but it's going to be a few months before he's fully operational again."

"Thank God for that. It could have been so much worse." When he didn't answer, Jules couldn't keep from saying, "You know what happened wasn't your fault."

Those amazing eyes cut over to her, and for the first time in hours, she saw something besides sorrow in them. Fury flared, pure and bright. Her comment had definitely pissed him off.

"And just whose fault is it?"

"How about Dalca's for being such a slug and trying to use a human being as a shield? Or the woman who thought pulling a gun on her husband in a room full of people was a good idea?"

"Doesn't negate my responsibility. I should have anticipated and—"

"Anticipated is one thing. Being able to predict the future is something else."

"Predicting human behavior is my job. Desperate people act in irrational ways. It was my op, my responsibility. Period."

Arguing would do no good. He was set on taking this on his own shoulders.

"What's going to happen to Dalca?"

"That's up to the Romanian authorities. The intel Eve obtained should give them what they need to put him away. If not…" He shrugged. "Eve's cover is blown, so we're probably out of it either way."

"She could have saved her cover…explained away her concern for Gideon as compassion for a stranger."

"Possibly. Yeah, probably. She's my best deep-cover operative. She could've pulled it off."

"Then why—"

"She and Gideon go back several years. The speed of his recovery might hinge on having her close by."

"You care about your people."

"Hell yeah, I care. Bullets and death have the ability to either bring people together or separate them forever. There's not an OZ employee I wouldn't die for, and every one of them would do the same. It's how we survive." He sent her a searing look. "You good with that?"

Was she good with possibly giving up her life for a virtual stranger? Yes, she was. That question had been asked and answered a long time ago.

"I am."

His nod of approval meant something to her. They had both started out with different lives, but fate, or whoever was in charge of hellish situations, had put them at odds with a normal life. Both of them had survived the only way they knew how.

"So what's next on OZ's agenda?"

"We'll regroup, then start on our next assignment."

"I need to go home for a few days. Take care of some personal business."

"Understood. You'll need to report to the company doctor a week from Monday. I'll text you the details."

"Doctor?"

"For a complete physical. You look to be in good health, but I don't take on operatives without knowing that for sure."

That made sense. Being an OZ operative would likely be physically grueling.

"All right. And then—"

"Then you'll be taken to a secure training facility. Put through the standard tests. Shooting, physicality, hand-to-hand. It's a rough two days, but it'll tell us what we need to know. Better yet, it'll show you what we expect."

Jules swallowed. She hadn't assumed she could just walk onto the team without proving herself, but this seemed extreme.

"You look surprised."

"I am. A little."

"Today's op was a low-key one. We don't get many like that. When you've got a submachine gun going at you or an RPG headed your way, you'll appreciate being in top physical condition."

"Makes sense. What else?"

"After you've completed your tests and I've seen the results, I'll contact you with where to go for your implant."

"My what?"

"Tracker. OZ operatives work deep cover. My people don't check in with me unless they have intel or require assistance, but I need to know where they are at all times." He waited a half second and then added, "You got a problem with that, OZ might not be the best fit for you after all."

Even though what he said made sense, it was difficult to agree to such an invasion of privacy. Everyone, even OZ operatives, had a right to a private life, didn't they?

"You won't be the first person to balk at the requirement. No hard feelings if you want to back out."

Backing out was not an option. She had to have this job.

"I will agree to the tracker, but I don't have to like it."

A small smile twitched at his mouth. "I'm sure there will be several things you won't like."

"And you don't care, do you?"

"As we discussed, I don't have a lot of rules, but the ones I do have are set in granite."

"Your way or the highway."

"You get dead or go missing, it's on me. I don't like it when that happens, so yeah, my way or nothing."

A saner part of her told her to protest more. He might be the leader of OZ and her new boss, but the autocratic attitude could get old fast. But she could also understand his reasons. OZ operatives operated in the most dangerous parts of the world. If an operative disappeared, being able to find them quickly could be the difference between life and death.

"What happens to the people who leave OZ? I'm assuming the tracker can be easily removed?"

"It can and it is. But if you have it removed while you're an OZ operative, you're out permanently."

"Understood. What else do I need to do?"

"The physical, skill tests, and the tracker are the biggest issues. The rest we can discuss when you come back."

"I'll need to find a place to live close to headquarters."

"Closest town is about five miles away. You can stay at the op center as long as you need. We have apartments there."

That would help with the transition, but she definitely would need her own place and space.

"Hmm. Awkward question, but where is OZ headquarters?"

Humor briefly eased his harsh expression. "Montana. I'll send you a map."

She nodded. She'd been to Montana on a case once, but that was pretty much all she knew of the state. She'd do some research once she got the location.

"With Gideon out and Jazz on modified assignments, you'll need to hit the ground running when you get back."

Jules nodded, but something was bothering her. "You and

your team have accepted me awfully easily. I didn't think it would be this smooth."

"It's not, so don't take it for granted. I trust Kate more than anyone else in the world. If she says you're legit, you are. And your reputation for getting the job done is impressive. You're a good fit for OZ."

Before she could bask in his approval, he added, "We still have a problem, though."

"What's that?"

"You're keeping something from me. You've got secrets… everybody does. I've got no problem with that as long as they don't affect the team."

He went to his feet and then looked down at her, his expression icy once again. "If those secrets ever put my people or a mission in jeopardy, you'll regret it with your last breath. Understand?"

"The last thing I would do is hurt you or this team, Ash," Jules said quietly.

With a curt nod, he turned and headed back to the front of the plane.

When he was several feet away, Jules blew out a long, ragged breath. It wasn't every day that one received a death threat from an employer, but she knew that was exactly what he'd meant.

# CHAPTER SIXTEEN

**Montana**
**OZ Headquarters**

Ash sat at his desk and reviewed the job requests. Since OZ operated under the radar, all of the requests had been vetted and validated. The team had been back from Romania for over a week, but he held back on choosing the next op. Not only did his people need some downtime, they were a couple of operatives short.

When he'd started Option Zero, he'd had two major goals. First, he would choose only the jobs that interested him. And second, he would choose the ones that appeared hopeless. A lot of different agencies and organizations assisted people throughout the world, but few focused on the situations that looked hopeless or impossible. He understood that. People helped where they could do the most good. But what about the others? The ones that seemed doomed to failure? The jobs that no one else wanted were the ones he wanted. Why? Because he and his people knew all about helplessness and hopelessness. They'd been there, done that, and had the scars to prove it. This was where they could make a difference.

Creating OZ had saved him. After he'd lost Meg, he'd lost himself. Hadn't cared about anyone or anything. He might've stayed that way if it hadn't been for Kate. He was already out of the FBI by then, spending most of his time so filled with hatred, he was surprised it hadn't smothered him.

Kate had been dealing with her own issues. She had chased a serial killer for years and ended up leaving the Agency before he had been caught. On her way out, she had recommended Ash to take the lead on the case. In a round-about way, that had led to Meg's death.

Not that he didn't feel the full weight of Meg's death on his own shoulders. John Leland Clark had been the most evil and vile kind of human being, killing without remorse across the western United States and enjoying every moment of his far-reaching fame. But in the end, Clark had been used as a weapon for someone else's evil agenda.

Ash had gotten his man. That was one thing that Asher Drake could say about himself. He damn well had gotten his man. But at what cost?

There was no denying that he and Meg had been struggling. After Colombia and then Syria, he hadn't been the same man. Even though he'd fought many battles while in the Marines, he'd always known what he was fighting for and that he'd had a whole country backing him. In the jungles of Colombia and then the desert of Syria, it had been all about survival.

Returning home hadn't brought the peace he sought. He was justifiably angry, and not being able to get any answers only made things worse. Meg had expected the man she married to return to her, and instead she'd gotten a damaged and bitter one. She'd done her best. He gave her all the credit for trying. And for a while, in his first few years with the FBI, things had seemed to be back on track. Even though he hadn't gotten the answers he sought, he had been doing his best to look toward the future. All of that had changed when he'd turned on the television one day to see a woman running for political office. That woman was Nora Turner. After searching for years, trying to solve the mystery of what had gone down in Colombia, he discovered that one of the people who'd been there was an up and coming politician.

Seeing Turner had reopened wounds that had never completely healed. Confronting her had been a mistake. She had denied everything, of course, and Ash had ended up looking like a crazed maniac. The FBI had taken a dim view of one of their agents accusing a popular politician of treasonous acts and murder.

Everything had begun a downward spiral. Meg's death at the hands of a serial killer had been the final and most brutal blow to his dream of a happy, peaceful existence.

Convicted of the murder of twenty-seven people, Clark was now rotting in a prison cell in Colorado. In Ash's mind, he had killed twenty-eight. The one victim who had managed to escape him had committed suicide several months after her rescue. Without a doubt, Clark was directly responsible for her suicide.

The bastard was on death row, but Ash hoped his execution never happened. Death was too good for the monster. Better that the scum live to a ripe old age, withering away. Maybe it wasn't a just sentence, but as there was no fitting punishment for what Clark had done, it would have to do.

Losing Meg had been like losing himself all over again. They'd been childhood sweethearts and had planned to grow old together. Life and other shit had happened to derail that happiness, but it was all on Ash that Meg died. He had to live with that guilt, and for a very long time, he hadn't wanted to live at all.

Kate refused to give up on him. She was the one who came to him about Laurie, a four-year-old girl who was kidnapped from her home by her Afghani father and taken back to Afghanistan. The father was rumored to have ties to the Taliban. While both governments sympathized with the mother's plight, little was being done about bringing her back home. Kate asked Ash to give it a try.

After talking with the mother, seeing the love and fear she had for her child, Ash felt a determination he hadn't felt in years. This, he could do. This, he could handle. In this, he could make a difference.

The next day, he called the five people he trusted most—Xavier Quinn, Gideon Wright, Liam Stryker, Sean Donavan, and Nick Hawthorne—and told them what he planned. There was no hesitation. He had been through hell with these men. Ash knew them as well as he knew himself. He knew what their answers would be. All were in.

Under the cover of night, they broke into the father's house, rescued the girl, and returned her to her mother.

Kate took care of arranging new names and a new life for the child and her mother. And Asher Drake had found a new purpose. Seeing the reunion between mother and daughter gave Ash the biggest sense of peace he'd felt since losing Meg. He had skills and he could use them—but only on his terms.

Six years later, he was the leader of one of the most hated and respected organizations in the world. OZ didn't exist, at least on paper. They worked under the cover of anonymity and free rein—as long as they didn't get caught. If that ever happened, they would be tried and convicted, without support from any government.

Receiving intel from multiple sources throughout the world enabled OZ to do things ordinary citizens could never accomplish. Ash didn't take these things for granted. He knew they were living on borrowed time. Many had tried to take them down, and at some point someone would succeed. It was a price he was willing to pay.

No OZ employee came on board without knowing that they could be killed or imprisoned on any op. And that was why he had created a team that would watch each other's backs. No one else would.

Hiring Jules Stone was a risk, but not only had Kate vouched for her, Ash instinctively trusted her. Yes, she had secrets, and he'd get to them eventually. Trust didn't come easy for any of his people. They'd been hurt and broken just about as badly as anyone could be, but they had been able to reinvent themselves and turn their brokenness into a purpose.

Jules had been hurt, too. He could see it in her eyes. At some point, she might share her pain with him. That would be her choice.

The attraction between them was something he had no choice but to ignore. He couldn't afford the distraction. Staying focused was how he made it through each day. Giving in to temptation was not only self-destructive, but also pointless. He would never fall in love again.

Jules would be an asset to the team. Over the past week, she had passed her physical evaluation and operational skill tests without the slightest glitch. The reports he'd received were impressive. Plus, she had handled herself well in Romania. The op had turned sour in the blink of an eye, and she had rolled with the situation, reading Dalca correctly. The man had been in a panic, and while he'd shown himself to be dangerous by shooting Gideon, his number one priority was self-preservation. Dalca had really believed that Jules would shoot him. Hell, she'd been so convincing that Ash had almost believed it himself. But he'd seen the expression in her eyes, had read her intent. Everything had worked out in the best way possible.

Except for Gideon.

Ash shoved away from his desk and went to the window. The sky was the kind of blue that no man could re-create. The sun blazed down on majestic snowcapped mountains, offering peace and solace. He and Gideon had hiked those mountains, camped beneath the stars, and shared stories.

If not for Gideon, Ash wasn't sure he'd be alive today. He'd been there for him during his darkest moments after he'd lost Meg. He owed the man a lot. And even though Gideon would heal, it infuriated Ash that he'd been hurt in the first place. He placed his people above the op—always. He had to. If he didn't, no one else would. Yeah, they put their lives on the line for others, but first and foremost, he took care of his people.

And he had failed not once, but twice. They'd lost Nick Hawthorne, Hawke to his friends, several years ago. Not in the same way, but Ash still held himself responsible for that one, too. That op had gone south from the get-go, and by the end of the night, he'd had to say goodbye to one of his best operatives.

Even though he lived with the knowledge that he or any of his people could be taken out on any op, it didn't make the bitter pill of grief easier to swallow when it happened.

Returning to his desk, Ash went back to the list of requests and dug in. Lost in the specifics of a particularly intriguing case, he didn't come up for air until his phone buzzed. He glanced at the readout, and a slight smile played at his mouth.

Pressing the answer icon, he put the call on speaker and leaned back in his chair. "Calling to check on your charge, Kate?"

His friend laughed softly. "You know me too well, Ash. How's she doing?"

"I'm surprised you haven't asked her yourself."

"I did, but she's gone all closemouthed on me. Guess she took the 'what happens at OZ stays at OZ' seriously."

That was good to know. "She handled herself well on the first op."

"She'll be a positive addition to the team."

"That's the hope." Since he knew Kate always had a double, sometimes triple, agenda, he asked, "You got something for OZ?"

"Maybe. I'm handling it myself for right now. I might send you some notes soon. Get your take."

"Always happy to give my opinion."

Kate snorted. "Don't I know it."

Ash grinned at the jibe. "What else?"

"Anything on our mutual enemy on your end?"

"Not much more than since we last talked. You?"

"Actually, yes. I have a couple of meetings set up. I think they might give us what we need."

"Take care, Kate. You know what she's capable of."

"Yes, unfortunately, we both know. Her days are numbered, Ash. I promise you that."

"I hope you're right, but once you have the intel, let me take it from there. I'll take the heat. She's already got me in her crosshairs. No need to add you to her list of targets."

"It won't come to that. We can't let her go that far. She's gone way too far already."

Kate was right about that. But Ash didn't discount anything when it came to the senator. He and Turner became enemies long before Ash created OZ. Though *enemy* was a mild word for what he felt for the woman. It was more, much more, than that. Not being able to prove anything didn't make the facts any less true.

Twice now, Nora Turner had tried to destroy him. The first time hadn't been personal, but the second attempt had been target-specific. She had wanted Asher Drake out of the way. She had succeeded, but not in the way she planned. Turner might think that the third time would be the charm, but Ash was going to do everything within his power to see that the senator went down instead. It was way past time for her to pay.

The woman was an extremely influential politician with connections that reached far and wide. Ash was a man who knew how to root out intel that Turner would kill to keep buried. It was a race to see who would get to the finish line first.

"I'm getting closer on my end, too," Ash continued. "There's no need for you to be involved, but whatever intel you can send will only help."

"You'll know as soon as I have anything. In the meantime, I'm only a phone call or text away. Just say the word. I've got your back."

"You're the best of the best, Kate."

"Keep in touch, my friend."

"Will do."

Ash ended the call, and like many times when his mind was on something else, he'd made an unconscious decision. OZ would take the job he'd been reviewing when Kate called. Now he just needed to talk with the operatives who would be working the case with him.

And when Jules Stone arrived, she'd be thrown into the deep end of the pool very quickly. He had no doubt that she was an excellent swimmer.

# CHAPTER SEVENTEEN

**Brooklyn, Ohio**

E ntering the small, nondescript hotel lobby, Jules made her way to the single elevator. She hadn't planned on seeing Turner before she headed to Montana. She'd spent two days in a flurry of packing and making arrangements for her indefinite absence. Then she had flown to an obscure little town in rural Virginia, where for three days she endured the requirements to become a full-fledged OZ operative.

She had flown back to Arizona yesterday, looking forward to one last day of peace and quiet before leaving for her new job. The tests she had endured had been exhausting. A grueling five-hour physical and endurance test had left her aching in every muscle, but it had been the psych evaluations that left her drained. Her answers had not been challenged, and though she hadn't been uncomfortable with the questions asked, by the time she was finished, all those aching muscles had been knotted with tension.

She topped off her time there by getting a small implant

under her left arm. As much as she needed and wanted to do this job, she was close to her limit on the invasion of her personal space. Having been on her own for so long, making her own choices and relying only on herself, this new job with OZ was going to be a challenge.

After all of that, a girl wanted to have at least one day to herself. She had walked into her house with only two things on her mind—a long, hot shower and a small glass of wine. Those plans were destroyed when the last person she wanted to hear from called and demanded a meeting the next day.

As tough as the OZ tests had been, she'd repeat them ten times over to avoid seeing the woman she despised with every fiber of her being. But that was the job. One she had worked and manipulated herself. She would do what she had to do no matter how distasteful.

She dressed for the meeting in a red power suit. Clothes did not make the woman, but they could be used as armor to hide the truth. And since almost every word that was to come out of her mouth during this meeting would be a lie, Jules needed all the help she could get.

The door to the hotel room opened before she could knock, telling her that once again Senator Turner had informants everywhere. Another reminder of the thin tightrope Jules walked.

"Ms. Diamond, please come this way."

Lisa Steiner, Turner's personal aide, was a young, ambitious-looking woman who walked with a bounce in her step and wore a perpetual wrinkle between her brows. Her light brown hair was pulled away from her face in a no-nonsense bun. She wore a sedate navy skirt paired with a blue-and-white-pinstriped blouse and sensible two-inch heels. Thick black-rimmed glasses finished off the serious look.

"The senator can give you seven minutes."

Reminding the aide that it was Turner, not Jules, who

requested the meeting was pointless. If it were up to Jules, she'd be in her vehicle headed to Montana.

"That shouldn't be a problem," Jules answered. "I don't have anything to report." Those were the exact words she'd used when Turner had called her. Since she had been on the job exactly one day, she wasn't quite sure what intel Turner thought she could have gathered. However, alienating the woman so soon after being hired was not the best way to ensure long-term employment. So Jules would play the game until it was no longer necessary.

The aide didn't bother to respond. She knocked on a door and then opened it to reveal Senator Nora Turner sitting at a desk, peering at her laptop. She raised her head when Steiner announced, "Ms. Diamond has arrived."

"Excellent. Please make sure we're not disturbed, Lisa."

"Of course."

The instant the door closed, the senator stood. In her late forties, Turner wore minimal makeup and was attractive without being pretty. She was medium height and a little on the thin side. Her dark brown hair was straight and glossy and fell to her shoulders with a slight curl. Her business suit of baby blue was both feminine and professional.

Jules had studied the woman almost as much as she had studied Asher Drake. Once the president and CEO of a large tech company she had started, Turner held years of experience in the private sector before she threw her hat in the ring to run for her first political office. She'd served as a state representative for two terms and had been a senator for one so far. Her chances looked good for reelection in another landslide.

She was single, had no children, and apparently no real family. When asked once how she could identify with people with children when she had none of her own, she'd said she had given all of that up so others could have what she didn't.

Those words became an unofficial campaign slogan and had ended up making her a household name. The dedicated public servant who lived only to serve others had somehow played well and was believed by the masses.

Ridiculously ironic words for a woman who was directly responsible for destroying Asher Drake's family.

"Well?" Turner snapped.

"Well, what?"

"What have you learned?"

Jules and Kate had worked hard to create just the right kind of amoral mercenary in Jessie Diamond. Kate had used her expertise in creating a new identity and a rock-solid backstory. A dishonorable discharge from the military, gun for hire on occasion, and a slight gambling problem made for the perfect cover. With almost no ethics and a need for a constant flow of cash, Jessie Diamond was the type of woman who would do just about anything for the right price.

While Jules had prepped herself on the backstory, making sure she knew Jessie's life as if she'd lived every moment of it, Kate had used her contacts to spread the word, oh-so-subtly, that Jessie Diamond was good at squirreling out information others couldn't and that she had few limits on just how low she would go.

Even though they'd cultivated Diamond's reputation as a woman who worked fast and efficiently to get the job done, the senator expecting results this soon was beyond ridiculous. Turner knew that. So was this more of her power games or something else?

"Nothing yet."

"But you've been with him for several days. Even went away with him somewhere. Surely my name came up."

Seriously? The woman's ego knew no bounds.

"No, your name didn't come up. I just started working

there. Mentioning you would definitely make Drake suspicious. It's going to take some time."

"How much time? I'm paying you for results, not a good time."

Grinding her teeth to stop the words stuck in her throat, Jules reminded herself what she was working toward and why. Losing her cool now would ruin everything. She could not, however, let this woman believe she was at her beck and call. Hard-hitting Jessie Diamond was no pushover.

"If I'm going to do my job, I need full autonomy."

"What does that mean?"

"It means that I won't be contacting you until I have intel to report. And do not contact me again. Ever."

"I am paying your salary, young woman. I do not appreciate your attitude."

"Then find someone else to do the job."

Jules didn't dare show an ounce of weakness. Her ground wasn't as shaky as it could be. The senator would find it difficult to get someone else to infiltrate OZ. Even if Turner fired her, Jules would continue at OZ. Still, for this part of her plan to work, she needed to have Turner's ear. And she needed to make damn sure no one else tried to infiltrate OZ.

For several silent moments, it was a staring contest between two very stubborn women. Finally, a sparkle of appreciation gleamed in Turner's eyes. "I respect a person who can stand up to me. Not many can. Don't disappoint me."

Jules gave a brief nod. "I'll let you know as soon as I have something."

Before Turner could respond, Jules was out the door. If she had to stay one more moment in the woman's insufferable presence, she would not be responsible for the consequences.

Now she needed to fly back home, get her car, and head

to Montana. She had a job to do. One way or the other, Turner would pay for what she had done to Asher Drake. No matter what it took, Jules would make sure of that.

FROWNING, Nora stared at the door through which Jessie Diamond had just exited. There was something about the young woman she didn't quite trust. The girl had certainly stood her ground, which Nora admired, but there was something…

Ms. Diamond had the kind of reputation that Nora admired. She was known as one who got the job done, kept her mouth shut and her wits about her, and didn't let pesky ethics or a conscience get in her way. Those kinds of people were Nora's favorite kind.

She reassured herself that Diamond could do the job for which she'd been hired. Once she was through with him, Asher Drake wouldn't know what hit him.

Drake blamed her for what happened in Colombia. She had honestly thought all those men died. It had been a messy, ill-thought-out plan, and she wanted nothing more than to put that day behind her.

Nora and her associates had been lucky to get out alive. Chaos had surrounded them as glass and debris zoomed through the air. It had taken every bit of her courage and willpower to escape. She still bore a horrible scar from a cut on her arm.

Drake wasn't the only one who blamed Nora for the debacle. In her opinion, that was grossly unfair. Okay, yes, she coordinated the meeting, but she also brought in extra security to keep everyone safe. Was it her fault they failed? Instead of placing the blame where it belonged, she was held responsible for the entire disaster.

In hindsight, she should have ensured there were no survivors. When the helicopter had lifted from the ground, she had looked down at the destruction and believed that no one would survive. The cartel that had attacked them had been closing in. Even though she'd seen a couple of men running around, she had assumed they'd be dead in moments. How was she to know that Asher Drake would live to tell the tale?

Putting that horrendous day behind her had been her only option. And if Drake had been killed that day, she would have been able to do so. Instead, he was the sole survivor and refused to let that day die a natural death. He continued to chisel away at what happened, trying to uncover the truth.

Despite all the frustration and aggravation, Drake and his people wouldn't succeed. The truth was buried so deep that no one, not even the OZ organization, could dig that far. All the people who'd been there were either dead or had as much to lose as Nora. No one was going to talk. But that didn't mean Drake couldn't cause problems.

While Drake had some influential friends, they weren't even close to being as powerful as Nora's. Plus, Drake had his organization to be concerned with. He had people to protect and a lot to lose.

She needed to rid herself of Asher Drake for good. The first time she'd tried had been an abysmal failure. At the time, it had looked like the perfect solution, and she hadn't gotten her hands dirty at all. A serial killer bent on revenge escapes and goes after the man who put him away? It should have worked. But it didn't. Instead of Drake dying, his wife died instead. What a mess that had been. All that remained was a man even more bent on revenge than before and another black mark on Nora's record.

This time, she was going with a professional. Jessie Diamond was going to fix her problem. Once Drake was ruined, she could put all that nasty business behind her, once and for all.

If that didn't work out, Nora had one last option. She had been assured that Diamond could handle that as well. No matter what, Asher Drake had to be stopped. If that meant he had to stop breathing, then so be it.

# CHAPTER EIGHTEEN

**Montana**
**OZ Headquarters**

The instant the SUV entered OZ territory, Ash had the vehicle on his radar and a visual on the security monitor. The newest member of OZ had arrived. He had wondered if she would make it in time. The plane was fueled up and ready to go. With regret, he'd had to put a hold on the job he had originally chosen. Liam Stryker was on an op and needed backup now.

Ash met Jules at the door and had to ignore the gut-punch of attraction. Dressed in an above-the-knee multicolored dress, she looked like she'd be much more comfortable at an afternoon social than on an OZ op. For just an instant, he had the unusual wish that they could be two people with nothing more on their minds than going out for an enjoyable evening while they explored this sizzle of heat between them. Instead, they were headed into darkness.

Which was, he reminded himself, exactly where he was the most comfortable.

"You have any trouble finding the place?"

She gave a light laugh. "Since this place doesn't even have an address, finding it without the coordinates you sent would have been impossible."

"That's the point. Keeps us off the radar." He glanced over to the small parking area where she'd left her SUV. "You got stuff to unload?"

"Not a lot. Just a couple of boxes and suitcases. I put most of my personal stuff in storage."

"Got your go bag with you?"

She shifted a bag hanging from her left shoulder. "Always."

"Good. We're going. Leave your vehicle unlocked, and someone will unload your stuff and store it till you get back."

"Where are we going?"

"Washington."

"DC?"

"No. State."

She stood on her toes to peer over his shoulder. "Just us?"

"Jazz and Xavier are already on the plane. I'll brief you on the way." He shifted the duffel bag on his shoulder. "Let's go. Our pilot's waiting."

She followed him to his vehicle and, on the way, clicked her key fob to unlock her car. "Tell whomever unloads my car that the candy wrappers in the floorboard are from the previous owner."

He sent her a grin as they got into his vehicle. "You a chocoholic, Stone?"

"Recovering. I've now gone half chocolate, half caramel."

"There's a difference?"

"If you have to ask, then there's no hope for you to understand."

"I'll take your word for it. Other than your sugar overload, did you have a successful trip?"

"Yes. I got everything done that I needed to."

"I got your reports in. You'll be pleased to know that despite your chocolate addiction, you passed your physical with flying colors. You scored in the top twenty percent on your skill and endurance tests."

She grimaced. "Just the top twenty?"

"If it helps, you're competing against a couple of SEALs and an Army Ranger. I'd say that's damn good."

Looking more than a little pleased with herself, she nodded. "That definitely helps."

He veered out onto the main highway. The small airport they used was only a few miles away. "Any difficulty with the tracker implant?"

She grimaced, revealing her distaste. "Yes and no."

"Explain."

"It was basically painless, but—"

"But you feel it's an invasion of your privacy."

"That's an understatement."

"Understandable, but it saves lives. Talk to Jazz about it sometime."

"Did it come in handy when she was injured?"

"No. We were all there then."

"Bad time?"

"Yeah. A real bad time."

That had been one of OZ's darkest days. Xavier had told him that sometimes at night, when demons pounded, he could still see Jazz flying off the cliff with that maniac holding on to her. That was no surprise. It had taken all of Ash's strength to keep Xavier from following her over the edge.

That Jazz had survived was a miracle only God could grant. But she still hadn't recovered. Not fully.

"It's amazing what the human spirit can endure."

He cut his eyes over to the woman beside him. What had

she endured? She had told him a few things, but those were facts, not feelings. How had she handled the pain and the grief? Did she still struggle?

As if aware of his thoughts, she said in a rush, "Tell me about this op. A new one or ongoing?"

"Ongoing. One of our people, Liam Stryker, has been undercover at a sanctuary in Haleyville called the Brotherhood of Solace. It's located about twenty miles from Wenatchee. Ever heard of it?"

"No."

"Not much there, mostly wilderness. I spent a lot of time in Washington a few years back. Lots of desolate places like that. People get lost. Some never get found."

Out of the corner of his eye, Ash watched Jules stiffen at his words. Something was bothering her about this conversation. The tension in her body was palpable.

Shooting her a frown, he asked, "You okay?"

Her expression carefully bland, she shrugged. "I'm fine. Just thinking about how awful it would be to be lost in the wilderness. So this sanctuary, is it a cult?"

"Doesn't claim to be one, but yeah, that's exactly what it is."

"And what's OZ's mission?"

"To infiltrate and monitor. There have been rumors that the Brotherhood has been keeping people against their will. Nothing substantial as of yet. The local authorities can't do anything until there's proof of a crime."

"So how did OZ get involved? Did someone come to you with their suspicions?"

"In a way, yes. Stryker's sister, Elena, is a freelance crime reporter. She was writing an article on the cult. She texted Liam and told him about it, said she was considering trying to join to get more intel for her article. That's the last time he heard from her."

"So she's disappeared, and Liam has infiltrated, trying to find her?"

"He managed to infiltrate, but there's a hiccup."

"What's that?"

"He's disappeared, too."

JULES WAITED for Ash to continue, but he'd stopped with those stark words. "And?"

"And we're going to find him."

"I feel like I'm missing something here. You don't seem that concerned."

"Curious more than concerned."

"Why?"

The SUV pulled into a small hangar where OZ's Gulfstream G550 waited to take off.

Putting the vehicle in park, Ash glanced over at Jules. "We'll go over the op details on the plane. To give you a quick review of why I'm not that concerned, I'll just say that Liam Stryker is one of the most self-sufficient and crafty people I've ever known. I've seen him make escapes even Houdini would've admired."

"So you don't think he's in danger?"

"Yeah, he's in danger, but not for a minute do I think he's in trouble."

And Jules understood exactly what he meant. Ash knew his operative could handle any danger that came his way.

"So if he's not in trouble, what are we going to do?"

"Make sure he stays that way." He opened the driver's door. "Let's go."

Jules grabbed her go bag and headed to the jet. She heard Ash behind her, talking to someone about moving his vehicle. Despite his words, she had the feeling that he was more than a little concerned for his operative.

She stepped onto the plane and saw that while Ash wouldn't admit concern, Jazz had no problem showing hers. She was sitting at a table, her laptop in front of her. A frown of concentration on her face, she glanced up at Jules. "Welcome to a new nightmare."

～

## The Brotherhood of Solace
## Haleyville, Washington

LIAM STRYKER ROLLED over and puked up his guts on the cold, damp earth. He hadn't felt this sick since his junior year of college when Miranda What's-Her-Name dumped him for the quarterback, and he'd drowned his sorrows in the cheapest whiskey he could find. It'd taken him a helluva lot longer to get over the hangover than it had his broken heart.

But this was a lot worse than a hangover. Stupid to have drank that bottle of water. They'd laced it with something, of course. By the time he'd realized it, he'd been throwing his guts up. And then it'd been too late. They'd jumped him from behind. He was a decent one-on-one or one-on-two fighter, but four-on-one with agony boiling in his belly was just damn unfair. It'd almost been a relief when they'd finally knocked him unconscious.

He'd woken on the floor of this musty-smelling basement with his hands tied behind him, a giant booted foot kicking the hell out of him, and an ugly visage hovering over him.

Things had gone from bad to real bad. If he wasn't mistaken, the first kick had cracked a rib.

"You ready to talk?"

Liam blinked up at the snarling face of Malcolm Murray, or as he was known around the compound, Malcolm the Great. He seemed to enjoy the moniker, but Liam figured the

"Great" part had more to do with his gargantuan nose than any greatness Malcolm might possess.

"I'll be glad to talk to you." Liam answered in what he thought was a reasonable tone, especially since the bastard had been beating the crap out of him for the last half hour. "Just ask me a question that I know the answer to."

"Your mouth will get you killed, young man."

"And here I thought it would be my wild ways with women that would finally do me in."

Once again, Malcolm slammed a giant fist into Liam's gut. Since he had nothing left to throw up this time, Liam rolled over and could only gag through the pain. Ragged breaths wheezed out of him as he glared over his shoulder at Malcolm. "I'm beginning to question that slogan you have at the front of the compound. You know, the one that says 'we love you no matter what'? Not feeling the love here, Mal. Not at all."

"Love is for those who follow the rules. You broke them when you allowed our sister to escape."

"Your sister? Listen, you giant-nosed prick, she's not *your* sister."

"Of course she is. The moment she entered our gates, she became ours."

Fury washed through him, easing the pain. This filthy creep and his so-called brothers were going to pay for every ounce of fear they'd put Elena through. If there was one comfort in all of this, it was that she had escaped. He hadn't been sure they could pull it off, but by sheer determination and a little ass-kicking, she had gotten out.

Now he just needed to do the same.

The cavalry would be coming at some point. The plan was for Elena to find the car he'd hidden two miles up the road, drive into town, and alert the authorities. And while he knew that would happen, he also knew the OZ team was on their way. Of this, he had no doubt. Knowing Ash, Liam figured OZ would make it here long before anyone else. He was supposed to have checked in a couple of hours ago. Five minutes after his missed check-in, Ash would've sent out the alert, and they'd be on their way.

Liam didn't have faith in a lot of things anymore, but Asher Drake and his OZ brothers had never let him down. They'd met in the midst of blood and bullets. No one should have come out of that hellhole alive.

A bond of brotherhood had been created that no one could break. When Ash had formed Option Zero and told Liam its purpose, a herd of rhinos couldn't have kept him from joining.

Not a second had passed that he didn't thank the good Lord above that he'd accepted the offer. They'd done some good things…honorable things. He'd almost lost his way, but OZ brought him back home.

He wasn't finished yet…not by a long shot. He had a lot more to accomplish and one very specific goal to achieve. The Brotherhood of Solace and most especially the big-nosed buffoon Malcolm the Great was not going to stop him.

So yeah, Ash and the team were probably only an hour or two away, but that wouldn't keep him from trying to get out on his own. They hadn't nicknamed him Magic Man for nothing.

## CHAPTER NINETEEN

The hidden opening to the Brotherhood of Solace compound was about as well hidden as the entrance to OZ. They could track Liam's signal to inside the compound, but they might've passed by the entrance if Liam hadn't described the location early on. Ash spotted at least five cameras in various areas around the entrance. Those had been taken care of by Jazz, who had jammed them. If anyone on the compound looked at the monitors, they'd see the image of what the cameras were filming the instant they were frozen. Unless someone kept an extremely close eye on them, no one should be able to detect a difference.

He had expected to hear from Liam by now. The man knew ways of escape few people thought of, or would consider, and a talent for getting out of impossible situations. Xavier had nicknamed him Magic Man. But now, Ash would admit concern for his friend. Because of his tracker, they could pinpoint Liam's location. What they couldn't detect was whether he was still breathing.

Ash prayed he was alive. Either way, they were going in to rescue their man.

Running along the perimeter, Ash headed toward the area where his team waited. Jazz would remain outside to monitor the comms. If Liam called in, she'd be the first to know.

"Okay. We ready?"

"Ready," Xavier answered.

"Ready," Jules echoed.

"Let's go." Glancing down at his phone display, Ash noted Liam's tracker hadn't moved. And thanks to the camera drone they'd launched when they first arrived, they knew the building where Liam was being held. Problem was, it happened to be in the middle of the compound, surrounded by buildings on every side. They'd spotted three guards roaming the grounds. It was going to be a challenge to get in without alerting someone.

Fortunately, they had a plan for that, too.

WITH ASH and Xavier following some distance behind her, Jules waltzed into the compound as if she belonged there. Still wearing the dress and shoes she'd arrived at OZ in, she had added a little lip gloss and mascara and pulled her hair back with a barrette. Even she had to admit the look took about five years off her age and gave her the appearance of innocence—something she'd lost over a decade ago.

There were eight squat and unimaginative buildings in the compound, with narrow roads between them that were graveled and uneven. Whatever the Brotherhood did with the money they stole from their members, they certainly didn't use it to pretty up the place.

"Hold back, Stone," Ash said from behind her. "We've got company."

Jules stopped at the corner of one of the buildings and looked back to see Ash deliver an uppercut to a man's thick jaw, knocking him off his feet. The man slammed back into a wall and slid to the ground.

Within seconds, Xavier had secured his hands and feet, slapped tape over his mouth, and dragged him around a dark corner of the building.

"Okay," Ash said. "Let's keep moving."

Jules took off again. Even though the cameras were down, the lights from the giant streetlamps blazed like beacons. They had opted not to cut the power, so walking through the compound without being spotted was a challenge. Still, she was almost to the middle of the compound before anyone noticed her.

"Who are you?"

The man was fortyish, medium height, and slender. Jules saw no weapons and surmised he wasn't a guard, but one of the residents. That didn't mean he couldn't cause trouble. Knowing Ash and Xavier were right behind her, hidden, was a comfort. They still didn't know exactly what these people were about. However, the way this guy was leering at her, she was getting a good idea.

Offering her most winsome smile, Jules said shyly, "I'm new here."

"Is that right? Anybody claim you yet?"

Oh, that didn't sound good at all. Even though her first instinct was to kick this bozo into the next county, she only shook her head. "I just arrived today."

"What's your name?"

"Susie Hopper."

"Well, hello there, Susie. I'm Brother Joe. Welcome to your new home."

Jules took a step back and whispered, "Brother Joe, you're in big trouble."

Reacting as she'd hoped, Brother Joe leaned down to try to hear what she was saying. "What's that now?"

Jules grabbed his right arm, jerked him forward, twisted his arm behind his back, and turned him around, shoving him into Ash's waiting fist. Brother Joe went down hard. Xavier was on him in a second, securing his hands behind his back and then slapping tape over his mouth.

Brother Joe's eyes were a bit glazed, but that didn't stop him from letting loose muffled curses from beneath the tape.

"Better put him out for a while," Ash said softly.

Xavier tapped him on the head with his gun, and Brother Joe's eyes slid closed.

"Let's move quickly," Ash said. "Maybe we can avoid any others."

They ran toward the building where Liam's tracker led them. No matter how much she resented the tracker requirement for OZ operatives, she had to admit that it came in handy this time.

"Ash." The urgency in Jazz's voice caught everyone's attention.

"What's wrong?" Ash said.

"You got police and the county sheriff headed your way."

"How'd that happen?"

"Elena apparently got away and called 911."

"Let's move faster," Ash growled.

Jules knew the reason. OZ tried to stay out of law officials' business unless specifically asked. They did their best work under the guise of anonymity and secrecy.

At the building where Liam was, Ash tried the door, noting it was locked. Taking a small pouch from his pocket, he pulled out tools and had the door unlocked in seconds.

Gun at the ready, Jules went in low. Xavier went in high. Checking the feed on his phone, Ash whispered, "Basement."

She knew they'd normally clear the building before going to the basement, but time was short. They needed to grab Liam and get out before anyone else showed up.

They walked into a kitchen area and headed toward a closed door. "Jules," Ash said over his shoulder, "stay up top and keep watch. Xavier and I will—"

"Looking for someone?"

They whirled, guns pointed at the door. A battered and bleeding man leaned against the doorjamb. Both Ash and Xavier rushed forward and caught him before he could fall.

"Where are you hurt?" Xavier asked.

"Mostly bruises, but I might have a couple of broken ribs." He grimaced and shifted, showing he was favoring his left leg. "Might have a broken foot, too. Bastard dropped a cement block on me."

"Where's that asshole now?"

Liam grinned, his white teeth stark against his bloodied face. "On the ground with a goose egg the size of Texas on the back on his head."

"We've got company coming, so we need to get out of here."

"That means Elena got away, called the cops."

"Yeah."

Liam nodded. "Let's go."

"Can you walk?"

"With a little help."

With Xavier on one side and Ash on the other, they carried Liam toward the door. Jules went ahead of them to clear the way. The night was still quiet, and no one seemed to be about, but that was going to change soon. When the authorities arrived, this place and its residents were going to get an unpleasant surprise.

As she passed each building, she couldn't help but wonder how many people were being held here against their will. Were they waiting, hoping that someone would show up to rescue them? Even though she knew help was on the way, she had an urge to find those victims and help them.

She knew how it felt to be helpless and lost, to feel as though there was no hope. Being back in Washington for the first time in years brought back memories she had furiously worked to destroy. What if someone behind those walls was enduring something similar? How could she not act?

She glanced back at Ash, and it was as if he read her mind. "They'll get help soon. We need to focus on the mission."

Okay, okay. The reminder was a good one. Help was coming.

They made it to their vehicle without incident. Jazz was in the driver's seat of the SUV, engine running. In thirty seconds or less, they'd loaded Liam into the back and were racing down the highway.

Hearing sirens in the distance, Ash said, "Pull over into that area over there, Jazz, and kill the lights. They see traffic on this road, they'll assume it's related to the Brotherhood."

"I'll need to call Elena and let her know I'm okay," Liam said.

As Jazz pulled into a clearing, she looked in the rearview mirror. "I talked with her, Liam. She's aware we went in to get you."

"That's good. Thanks, Jazz."

They waited, holding their breath as several patrol cars raced by, lights flashing but sirens silent.

Five minutes after the last patrol car passed, Jazz drove the car out of the woods and headed out again, away from the Brotherhood of Solace.

CHAPTER TWENTY

Ash stretched his long legs out in front of him. Half an hour after they left the Brotherhood, they were on the plane and speeding down the runway. Being able to land so close to the compound had been a plus.

Liam had insisted on calling Elena to ensure she was all right. It was no surprise to Ash that she was already back at the compound, assisting law enforcement in helping the victims and gathering more intel for her story. If there was one thing he had discovered about the Strykers, it was that they did not quit.

Fortunately, Liam's injuries weren't as bad as they'd feared. He had multiple contusions all over his body, a couple of bruised ribs, and a deep bruise on his foot. Could've been a whole lot worse.

Both Xavier and Jazz were tending to him. All OZ operatives had medical training up to a point. That was something Jules would need training on, but that would have to wait. For the first time in a long while, they were short-staffed. With Jazz not fully recovered, they had been running lean, though efficiently enough. But now Gideon was on medical leave for at least three months, and Liam would be out of commission for a couple of weeks.

And while Eve was not injured, she was on a much-deserved holiday.

Being down four operatives would curtail OZ's activities significantly. With the bioweapon auction coming up soon, they would need everyone on board and as healthy as possible. Apprehending Carl Lang was one of the most important operations OZ had ever endeavored. Countless lives would be saved, and one less soulless bastard would be able to wreak havoc on the innocent.

Grabbing his burner phone, Ash checked for any new communication and cursed softly at the text from Omar. Instead of setting a date for the auction, Omar had thrown a small kink into the plan. He wanted to have another meeting. This time, a long weekend at his estate, and Humphrey was to bring a companion.

Ash considered his options. He had to go, there was no choice in that. Omar would see his refusal as an insult. The man was too important to the mission to create hard feelings at this stage.

Showing up alone might work okay. Humphrey was cold, arrogant, and didn't give a damn what people thought of him. However, Ash had also developed Humphrey as a ladies' man. Going stag would go against that reputation. Ash needed a female operative to accompany Humphrey.

Eve was by far OZ's best undercover operative. She could accept a role in one minute and become that person the next. But for the first time ever, he'd noticed a brittleness in Eve's demeanor. He figured it was from her worry over Gideon and the stress of maintaining her undercover persona for so long. Asking her to come off her leave wasn't something he felt comfortable doing. She needed the downtime.

He had three other options, but they were questionable at

best. Jazz was not good at undercover. She wore her emotions on her sleeve and couldn't act worth a damn. Her instincts and incredible courage made up for any deficiencies in that area, but for this op, she was out, especially with her current physical limitations.

Serena would do fine. She had a varied background, including undercover work, but he didn't want to draw her away from her present assignment. They were getting close to getting the intel they needed on Turner. The last thing he wanted was to put a halt to that investigation.

That left Jules. She had proven herself proficient in several areas already. Had come in with almost no prep and helped facilitate two successful missions. Her aptitude for undercover remained to be seen.

Ash knew he was hesitating for another reason. For the first time in years, he was having trouble holding back his attraction to her. There was something special about Jules Stone. A chemistry he hadn't experienced with any other woman. He liked her easygoing attitude, her adaptability. She had a self-deprecating manner, but stood up for herself, showing she was a strong, self-assured person. He also liked her laughter, her quick wit. The way she—

He went to his feet. Truth was, there were altogether too many things he liked about her. None of that could matter. He had a job to do, and so did she. As long as he made certain things clear to her, they should be fine. He was no teenager in the throes of first love or lust. He knew how to play the game. Now he needed to make sure she did, too.

Glancing toward the back of the plane, where she was seated, he noted she was staring at her laptop with a frown of concentration.

"Stone."

She jerked her head up. "Yes?"

"Need to see you."

She clicked a few keys, closed the laptop, and stood. As she made her way to him, he tried to dispassionately see her as a woman Humphrey would be interested in having in his bed. Without a doubt, she was an attractive woman, but the wholesome, girl-next-door look would not fly. They'd need to work on that.

As she drew closer, he nodded toward a small curtained-off enclosure. Looking curious, she followed him.

"Need to talk with you about an ongoing op."

"Okay."

Ash gave her a condensed version, seeing no reason to go into a great deal of detail as this point. Once they were back at the operations center, he'd bring her up to speed. For now, he needed to explain the job requirements.

"I received an invitation from Omar Schrader to join him for the weekend. He's also invited my romantic partner."

"Okay."

"I've already thrown you into the deep end of the pool, so we haven't discussed this part of your job requirements. Going undercover as a romantic couple doesn't happen that frequently, but it does happen on occasion."

"That shouldn't be a problem. I've done undercover work. Acting as your girlfriend shouldn't be an issue."

"We'll have to be affectionate with each other."

She frowned then, and he could see she was beginning to see the issue of concern. "How affectionate?"

"In public, nothing more than an occasional touch. Maybe a short kiss."

"And in private?"

"I'm going to do my best to convince Omar, without offending him, that we'll stay in a hotel. If I can do that, we might have to contend with a passionate kiss or two in the lobby to make it convincing."

"And if you can't convince him?"

"Then there will be more than a few passionate kisses." He eyed her closely. "How do you feel about that?"

"I'll be fine."

Would she? Ash moved close. Crowding her, he put his hand on her shoulder, caressed down her arm, and tried to ignore the silky creaminess of her skin. He was giving her a test, but his body apparently didn't get that message as thick heat flooded through his veins.

Her eyes wide, she stuttered, "Wh-what are you doing?"

"Gauging how you react to my touch. It's not very flattering."

"What?"

"You're as stiff as a board, and you have an expression on your face as if I'm trying to sell you a used vacuum cleaner."

"That'll change when we're on the job."

Ash shook his head. "Not gonna fly. You're an OZ operative. You're always on the job."

She lowered her gaze for an instant and then raised her head to look up at him. Her expression…her entire demeanor had changed. A smile lifted her mouth into an expression of sensuous hunger. Her eyes glittered with heat and life. And somehow, she'd managed a slight, pink blush in her cheeks. Without moving, she seemed to draw closer as her fingertips lightly touched his face in the hottest, most sensual caress he'd ever felt. Every part of his body zinged to life.

"Umm…that's…" He cleared his throat. "Better."

Her eyes gleaming with triumph, she whispered softly, "Just doing my job."

"Oh, excuse me."

Jules whirled around. She'd been so immersed in the moment with Ash that she hadn't heard Jazz move the curtain aside. From the look on the other woman's face, she certainly hadn't expected to find her boss and the newest member of their team in each other's arms.

A different kind of heat flushed Jules's face.

Apparently not the least bit embarrassed, Ash explained, "Omar Schrader has invited Humphrey and a companion to his estate this weekend. Stone and I will be attending."

Comprehension replaced Jazz's startled look. "Gotcha." She turned her attention to Jules. "I'll get Rose to send you a stats questionnaire."

"So I'm going to finally get a chance to interact with the elusive Rose Wilson."

Over the past few days, Jules had heard Rose Wilson mentioned several times.

Jazz's mouth tilted in an affectionate smile. "Like I said before. Rose is the person who actually runs OZ."

Jules noticed Ash didn't dispute the claim.

"What's a stats questionnaire?"

"You'll need to provide your sizes and list things you'll need to be convincing in your cover. Rose can provide you with whatever you need for the op. Clothes, shoes, other accessories."

"As soon as I hear back from Omar, we'll have a briefing." Ash's gaze swept over Jules, and she felt her body heat up again. "You good with everything?"

"Of course."

With a nod, he headed back to the main area of the plane, leaving Jules and Jazz with an awkward silence.

"You're attracted to him."

Jules heard no disapproval in Jazz's tone, only a mild curiosity. Still, admitting an attraction to Ash was not a good idea.

"I'm a professional. I can make people see what I want them to see."

Obviously not believing her, Jazz raised her eyebrows. "Oh yeah? Might want to work on your performance a little bit."

Before Jules could argue, Jazz added, "You'd be good for him. He needs someone in his life."

Pretending to have no interest in the conversation would be pointless. "Ash doesn't have relationships?"

"Not really. I think he sees someone from time to time, but it's nothing serious. He's not had anything even remotely permanent since he lost Meg."

"His wife?"

"Yeah."

"You knew her?"

"No. I know only what Xavier has told me. She was apparently an amazing woman. But then, she'd have to be for Ash to have loved her."

"You think a lot of him."

"Hands down, one of the best men I've ever known."

"How long have you worked together?"

Jazz's face went blank. "Long enough." She pulled her phone from her pocket. "I'll send a text to Rose to get that questionnaire to you."

"I didn't mean to pry, Jazz."

"It's no big."

Blowing out a ragged breath, Jules took a moment to center herself. Ash had thrown her into a maelstrom of both mental and physical confusion. And truthfully, she was completely and utterly terrified. Fighting her attraction to Ash had been no problem so far. They'd been so busy she hadn't had time to even think about the effect he had on her. But pretending to be his girlfriend, accepting his kisses and caresses as if she belonged to him, would be another matter.

What she had told him was true. She was very good at undercover and could usually adapt a persona as her own without an ounce of hesitation. Having become someone else years ago had trained her to adjust to her circumstances. And while she was more comfortable working alone, she had on occasion worked with a partner. A mutual goal of bringing down evil had always been incentive enough to overlook any awkwardness.

But she had to admit this would be a challenge of a different kind. She knew going in that the job would be hard. Knowing all she did about Asher Drake, all that he had done, she figured she'd built him up in her head. But meeting the man, working with him, was doing nothing but confirming her opinion. Ash was a man of honor, intelligence, and amazing courage. He had fascinated her for years, and Jules knew the image she'd had of him was only going to get stronger.

The moment he'd touched her tonight added a new wrinkle. She had never in her life felt desire like that. One simple touch—nothing more—had ignited a heat and need within her. There was attraction, and then there was *this*.

Admittedly, she wasn't the most experienced when it came to romantic relationships. She dated, not a lot, but some. She had even gone out with one guy five times. Unfortunately, on the fifth date, he had surprised her with a romantic weekend at a small cabin in the woods. She had managed to make an excuse to leave before full-blown hysteria had set in, but she'd still ended up making a complete fool of herself. That had been the last she'd seen of him.

Pain in her hand pulled her from her thoughts. She had been gripping the marble countertop. She took a deep breath and stiffened her spine. She was here to do a job and to pay a debt. Staying focused on her goals was the way she survived. That couldn't change now. Her personal feelings and hang-ups couldn't matter.

"Ladies and gentlemen." The pilot's calm, baritone voice came over the intercom. "Looks like we're in for some stormy weather up ahead. Might want to buckle up for the rest of the flight. Things could get bumpy."

As she headed back to her seat, Jules couldn't help but wonder if the pilot's words were an omen for what was coming.

CHAPTER TWENTY-ONE

**Omar Schrader's Estate**
**Slovakia**

O ne thing Ash had learned about his newest operative.
Never, ever underestimate her. He knew Eve was
good at undercover, but Jules would give her a run for her
money.

While waiting for his undercover partner to arrive at the
airport, he had expected the wholesome-looking, girl-next-
door Jules Stone. The woman who appeared before him,
though, was a pampered, snobbish, ethereal beauty. An ice
princess who looked down on the rest of humanity was
exactly the kind of woman Humphrey would find most
appealing.

Ash had chartered a private jet. Not only would Omar
expect Humphrey to have the most luxurious and expensive
one on the market, he would know the minute the plane
landed. No way did Ash want OZ's plane anywhere close to
Omar and his goons.

A limousine had been waiting for them when they landed

and had whisked them away in minutes with barely a glance from the Customs agents. Half an hour later, they were driving down a long, narrow drive, and Omar's estate came into view. Ash's first thought was that being a weapons broker was an enormously lucrative occupation. His second thought was they were likely on their own once they entered the mansion. Omar was paranoid for a reason. No way would he allow outside transmissions within his residence.

Ash glanced over at his partner and was once again struck by the incredible change, not only in her looks but also in her demeanor. Juliet Stone was a lovely woman with animated features and a smile like sunshine. Elsa Olsen looked as though a smile would fracture her beautiful face.

He had briefed Jules on Schrader's background, as well as the bioweapon Humphrey was selling. Elsa Olsen was the perfect complement to Humphrey's cold arrogance and Jules Stone would be able to pick up nuances he could miss.

Though Omar's past dealings with Humphrey had always been mutually beneficial, this was a different kind of business deal. Was this invitation merely a ploy to get Humphrey alone and force him to give up the formula? Omar was a sleaze, but for the most part, he'd always been up front. Even in the harsh, cold world of weapons dealing, a man's word held consequences.

No matter the reason, Ash and Jules would be ready. Xavier and Jazz were parked in an RV three miles from the estate. They could offer assistance in a matter of minutes.

A slender hand caressed his thigh, reminding him that the woman beside him knew her role. He had been distracted, lost in thought. She was doing the right thing to bring him back to the here and now.

Humphrey sent Elsa a predatory, hungry look. "Have I told you how beautiful you are?"

Her expression one of supreme confidence, Elsa drawled,

"Yes, but a woman never gets tired of hearing such things, darling."

The chauffeur's eyes shifted to give them a glance in the rearview mirror. Knowing he would be reporting to Omar everything he observed, Ash pulled Jules to him, touched his mouth to hers. It was for show, but that didn't keep his body from responding. Her lips were as luscious and sweet as he had imagined. There was only the slightest amount of tension in her body at the beginning, and then she seemed to sink into him. The embrace lasted less than a minute, but Ash knew, audience or not, he could have continued for much longer.

When he pulled away, her lips were plump and moist, and her breathing was slightly elevated. It was gratifying to see he wasn't the only one who was affected.

"Really, Humphrey darling, must you in front of the help?"

An icy bucket of water dumped over his head couldn't have had more of an impact. Even as his body rejected her icy tone, Ash was grateful for her words. Jules's response was exactly how they'd decided she should play Elsa. A sexy ice queen with an arrogant, entitled demeanor.

"I must."

Her smile frigid, she replied, "Then I shall insist upon my own rewards."

"And what would those be?"

She leaned forward to whisper in his ear. To the chauffeur, it would look as though she were whispering something wicked and sexy. Nothing could have been further from the truth.

"I counted three people at the airport watching us. I'm assuming they were Omar's."

Nuzzling her neck, Ash responded, "Yeah, I saw them, too. He's going to keep a careful eye on us this weekend."

"Think something spooked him?"

"Not sure. We'll see."

"Excuse me, Mr. Humphrey. We have arrived."

Of course they had, but staying in the limo and pretending to make out while Omar was likely waiting was a game of one-upmanship. Besides the fact that Ash was truly enjoying himself. Which was as insane a thought as he'd had in years.

Ash pulled away from her and murmured, "More of that later."

She responded with a cool smile, but Ash saw something in her eyes that had nothing to do with the cold and calculating Elsa Olsen and everything to do with the warm-blooded, vibrant Jules Stone.

Despite the serious circumstances of this undercover mission, Ash was going to thoroughly enjoy his time with this beautiful woman.

ELSA OLSEN STEPPED out of the limo, a wealthy, entitled, and self-described fashion icon. She was quite bored with the world and found little amusement in anything. The much older and exceedingly dangerous Humphrey was the most exciting man she'd met in years. A part of her was enamored of the danger, and another part was scared, which made it all the more exciting.

Playing a rich society girl was a different role for Jules, but she anticipated no real issue. Becoming someone else was always easy for her. Being herself was where she usually had trouble.

Which was exactly why her heart was pounding much faster than it should be. Ash's kiss had sent her entire body into a heated frenzy. She was professional enough to maintain the icy expression of Elsa, but the woman inside was all

Jules, and she was feeling decidedly unprofessional. How had one kiss made such a difference?

She dared a look over at Ash, still amazed at the transformation. When she'd first arrived at the airport and saw who was waiting for her, she'd done a double-take. Even though Rose had shown her a photo of Humphrey, it had still been hard for her mind to grasp that behind the receding hairline, ugly brown eyes, and pointy-tooth smile was the very handsome Asher Drake. When he'd said in a very quiet, growling voice, "You look lovely, Elsa," shivers had spiraled throughout her body. The voice had been all Asher Drake.

"Humphrey, my friend. So glad you could join me."

Jules looked up at the man descending the steps toward them. Omar Schrader was exactly how Ash had described him. He had a slender build, thinning hair, and intelligence in his evil eyes. Taking his welcoming smile at face value would be a deadly mistake. This man could be lethal.

"It's good to see you." Humphrey held out his hand to shake Schrader's and then turned to Elsa. "Let me introduce you to Elsa Olsen."

"What a delight, my dear." Using old-world charm by taking her hand and kissing it made no difference in Jules's assessment of the man.

"Very good to meet you, Mr. Schrader, and thank you for the invitation to your lovely home."

"My pleasure, I assure you." He made a sweeping gesture. "Come, let me show you around. Boris will take your luggage to your room."

Despite the fact that Omar Schrader was a weapons broker and quite likely many other evil things, his home was lovely. And Omar was a gracious host, taking them through several rooms, sharing amusing anecdotes of the mansion's history. He ended the tour with refreshments on the west portico that faced a small pond. The sun was setting, and with ducks and geese floating on the water, the entire scene was almost poetic.

A stern-looking middle-aged man wearing a butler's uniform served them drinks and light snacks. Omar munched on caviar and chilled lobster with single-minded focus for several minutes and then sat back in his chair with a beatific smile.

"You have an extraordinary home, Omar," Humphrey said.

"Thank you, my friend. I'm so pleased you and Elsa accepted my invitation. And I'm very happy that I was able to persuade you to stay here instead of at a hotel. I think you'll be happy about that, too."

Humphrey's smile stayed in place, but his eyes narrowed. "Oh? Why is that?"

"Because someone wants to meet you."

"And who would that someone be?" Humphrey's tone was quiet but carried the sharp blade of lethalness.

Omar let loose a loud giggle, startling the ducks and geese, who quacked and honked in protest. Several flew away. No one at the table gave them obvious notice. The atmosphere had just zoomed from low-key to almost deadly.

Neither she nor Ash was armed. They had been patted down before they'd been allowed to get into the limo. However, she had learned that one used what one had available. Utensils on the table could be wielded with lethal precision in an instant.

"Now, now. No one for you to be worried about. I don't want to spoil the surprise. You'll meet him at dinner."

"I don't like surprises, Omar. People in our line of work rarely do."

"I guarantee that you'll like this one."

Jules knew that while Humphrey maintained his semi-friendly demeanor, Ash was calculating exactly what Omar had up his sleeve and if they should take evasive action.

Several tense seconds passed. Jules stayed quiet. Elsa would have no opinion and little interest in such things. Nor would her opinion be welcomed. She had a role to play, but Jules most definitely had an opinion. She believed they should stay and play this out. Omar wasn't stupid enough to double-cross Humphrey. The reputation Ash had built for him precluded even the most arrogant from taking such a chance. Omar had called them to his home for a reason, but she didn't believe it was about betrayal.

Though she couldn't say anything without appearing to try to influence Humphrey, Jules shifted subtly, allowing her hand to drop to her side and then onto Ash's thigh. She squeezed it firmly. Would he understand her meaning?

The tension in him lessened almost immediately. "Then I will look forward to meeting him."

"Excellent. He'll be here at seven for dinner."

"Then we'll want to make ourselves presentable." Standing, Humphrey held out his hand to Elsa. As soon as she was at his side, he nodded stiffly at Omar. "We'll see you in a couple of hours."

Omar stayed seated, looking altogether too pleased with himself. The jovial atmosphere had vanished completely, replaced with a formal stiffness in Humphrey and an odd gleam in Omar's eyes.

As she followed Ash to their room, Jules maintained her icy demeanor, but her mind was whirling with the implications. Who was this mysterious person Omar wanted Humphrey to meet? And why had the man looked so supremely pleased with himself?

CHAPTER TWENTY-TWO

His jaw clamped with tension, Ash strode into the suite that had been assigned to them. He paid no attention to the décor other than to give a cursory glance around to determine where the bugs and cameras might be hidden. Problem was, there was no time for an in-depth search. Decisions needed to be made.

His bag was beside the bed, and while he was sure Omar's people had searched it, unless they'd gone through an entire box of condoms, no one would have spotted his jammer. Covered in a foil packet the size of a condom, the jammer was a prototype and not yet on the market. He was confident the device had not been detected.

The instant the door was closed, still in his Humphrey persona, he said, "Let's take a shower."

Stalking over to his luggage, he unzipped a side pocket and pulled the condom box from his travel bag.

Though her eyes might have dilated slightly, Jules thankfully didn't ask questions or protest. They had talked about touching and kissing, but taking a shower together had not been mentioned. He actually hadn't planned on communicating this way, but one sure way they could talk without Omar overhearing was beneath a flood of water. Later, when and if they returned to the room, he'd take more time and hunt down the bugs and cameras. In a pinch, this would have to do.

Grabbing her by the arm, he pulled her along with him toward the bathroom. And Jules, being the professional she was, gave him a sultry, inviting smile and slid her arm around his waist.

When they entered the bathroom, things became a little more complicated. Ash had little modesty. He'd played sports, been in the military. Plus, the life he lived didn't exactly fit with being insecure about his body. Jules might view things from a different perspective. That couldn't be helped. He'd do his damnedest to keep his gaze at eye level. That was the best he could offer.

When he began to strip, her eyes got noticeably wider. She turned her back to him, and Ash knew a moment of regret. She wasn't ready for this. Instead, she surprised him and said, "Can you help me with my zipper?"

Grateful for her professionalism, Ash moved closer. While he unzipped her dress, he whispered in her ear, "You're doing great."

She threw him a sexy smile over her shoulder and allowed the dress to pool at her feet. Left only in a lacy bra and almost sheer panties, she turned to face him.

Ash had to force himself to turn away. This was the least appropriate moment to give in to his attraction. Not only were they in the home of a deadly weapons broker, there was a surprise coming their way. As happy as Omar had seemed to be, Ash knew whoever was coming tonight would not be a pleasant encounter.

He quickly finished stripping and then headed to the shower. With the jammer on the counter, the cameras and listening devices should be inoperable, but for this particular conversation, he could take no chances. Keeping his back to her, Ash pressed buttons for temperature and steam, then another to turn on the water. Large enough to comfortably fit a half-dozen people, the shower stall featured every luxurious amenity possible.

Turning back to Jules, he held out his hand. His eyes carefully on her face, he did his best to give her a reassuring look without going out of character. Surprising him, she winked slightly and said, "Make sure it's warm enough, Humphrey. You know how I love steam."

"I think this will be to your liking."

The steam was already filling the stall and should give them the privacy they'd need. Taking her hand, he led her into the middle of the shower and wrapped his arms around her. His mind told him to ignore the fact that a beautiful, naked woman was pressed up against him. His body told his mind to shut the hell up.

Hoping she'd ignore the obvious signs of his arousal, Ash held Jules close. The pounding shower and rising steam gave them the cover they needed. His mouth at her ear, Ash whispered, "Sorry about this. The jammer is likely working, but I couldn't take the chance."

"Not a problem. We're good."

"I wanted to talk to you about Omar's surprise."

"Do you know what it is?"

"I have a good idea. I think he's invited Lang here to meet Humphrey."

Jules's body stiffened. "You think he's going to try to take the formula from you?"

"Doubtful. I think Lang's planning on offering a lot of money at the auction and wants to meet the seller before he makes that decision."

"How do you want to handle this?"

"We'll go ahead as planned. If we can't talk to each other, we'll have to improvise. If we can, we'll use sign language."

She pulled her head back slightly to look at him. "You can sign?"

"Yeah. You do, too. Right?"

"Yes…my mother, she…" She trailed off and then said again, "Yes."

"Good. Follow my lead. If I don't check in with Xavier, he can have the team here in a matter of hours. Or, if we have to, we'll fight our way out."

Ash hoped it wouldn't come to that. Not only would he and Jules be in great danger, the chances of getting to Carl Lang were phenomenally smaller. There was still no substantial proof that would tie him to any of the terrorist events. The auction was going to be their chance to catch him in the act.

"Ash?"

"Yeah?"

"Think it might be getting a little too steamy in here?"

While he'd been standing here, ruminating and, okay, yeah, enjoying having Jules in his arms, the entire bathroom had filled with thick steam.

"I'll get out and let you shower. I can shower after you."

"Won't it look strange for you to come back in here?" Before he could answer, she rushed on, "The shower is big enough for the two of us. Let's finish and get out. Okay?"

Tenderness flooded through him. He knew she was uncomfortable like this, but she was thinking of the mission. Instead of doing the wise thing—keeping his focus solely on the mission—Ash did something totally out of character.

His mouth still pressed up against her ear, he said, "Jules, mind if I kiss you for real?"

"I'd be disappointed if you didn't."

From the moment he'd met her, Jules Stone had been

surprising him. This was no exception. With a groan, Ash took a step back and, cupping her face in his hands, put his mouth to her wet, steamy, and delicious lips. Careful to resist moving his hands, he put all of his energy and focus into making love to her mouth.

For the first time ever, his mind was not on the job. Just once…just this once, Ash put the mission on hold and took this moment for himself.

ASH'S LIPS were like fire, devouring hers with an all-consuming heat. She wanted to sink into him, let him devour all of her. Though his hands stayed put, Jules couldn't help but wish they wouldn't. The thought of those large, callused hands roaming over her sent a floodgate of need through her body.

The entire time he'd been whispering to her about Schrader and the new complication, she had been hyper-aware that she was standing naked in the arms of an equally naked Asher Drake. Concentrating on his words had been more challenging than she'd ever thought possible. For years, the job, whatever it was at the time, always came first. It was how she kept focused on the here and now and not on the past. But never had she been more tempted to forget the job.

Having him ask if he could kiss her for real was one of the sweetest moments of her life. But this? This wasn't sweet. This was raw, savage, beautiful—an experience beyond her imaginings. Ash's mouth ate at hers as if he was starving for her taste.

Recognizing his restraint in not touching her, Jules grabbed hold of his upper arms to balance herself. The tension in them told her how much he held himself back.

When he drew away from her, they were both breathing heavily. Ash leaned his forehead against hers, and they stood in the middle of the over-steamed shower, gasping like two long-distance runners who'd just finished a harrowing race.

"Guess we'd better shower before the steam runs out."

Jules nodded. Words were beyond her at the moment. She'd just had one of the most sensual and profound moments of her life, but when she walked out of the shower, she would be Elsa again…coolly composed. She needed to get her game face on and fast.

Pulling away from him, she turned and hurriedly soaped her body and rinsed. She'd worry about her hair later. She could hear Ash behind her, doing the same thing. When they walked out of the shower, all the thoughts and feelings that kiss had invoked would have to be put on the back burner. They were here to do a job, and if Carl Lang was indeed Schrader's special guest, outmaneuvering both men would require all of their wits.

## CHAPTER TWENTY-THREE

M asks securely in place, Ash and Jules headed downstairs. Things might have gotten a little out of control in the shower, but they'd put that behind them for now. They had a job to do.

Her hair pulled away from her face, Jules carried herself like an ice princess, walking with an air of superiority, confident in her beauty and place in the world. The off-the-shoulder black cocktail dress, which landed a couple of inches above the knee, perfectly displayed her lovely arms and legs. Ash had done a double take when he'd seen her. He wasn't worried about Omar crossing the line with her. She wasn't Schrader's type. On the other hand, Carl Lang's appetite for beautiful women who challenged him was well documented. Elsa Olsen was just his type.

When he'd helped her with the clasp of her necklace, he'd whispered that fact in her ear. She had given him a subtle nod, and that was all Ash had needed. Jules could handle herself with anyone. Of that, he had no doubt.

The instant they arrived in the foyer, Omar was there to

greet them. He was dressed in formal attire and looked as nervous as a teenager at his first prom. Either this deal meant more to him than Ash had anticipated, or there was an even bigger surprise coming. He gave Jules's elbow a little warning squeeze. Something was off here, and he needed both of them to be prepared for anything.

"Elsa, don't you look lovely."

With a queenly nod, Elsa acknowledged the compliment and allowed Omar to take her hand and lead her into one of the large living rooms they'd been shown earlier.

Ash was only a few steps behind them, his eyes and ears open for whatever came next. At the entrance, Omar stopped and looked over his shoulder toward Humphrey. "I told you I had a surprise."

Omar stepped aside, allowing Ash to see the three other occupants of the room. A man and a woman stood beside a chair. The man was heavily muscled and had the empty expression of a ruthless killer.

The woman on the other side of the chair was an attractive brunette in her mid-forties. She wore a slight smile, as if she were enjoying a private joke. Ash thought she looked vaguely familiar.

When his eyes lit on the third person, the man sitting in the chair, he knew why the woman looked familiar and why she was smiling. The seated man was one of the most notorious mass murderers of this century. He was believed to have been in on at least eight terrorist attacks in the last decade. He had little to no allegiance to any country, nor did he have any kind of religious leanings. He killed for money, for fame, and for the sheer enjoyment of taking lives.

There was one other unique fact about Günter Rhinehart: The man was supposed to be dead.

Ash cursed himself for his lack of foresight. He'd been so

focused on Carl Lang being here and dealing with him, he hadn't for an instant considered that Omar had found a much more deadly buyer for the bioweapon.

Jules glanced over at him, and though her expression never changed, he saw the knowledge in her eyes. She, too, recognized the man.

Omar whirled around and clapped his hands as if he were a child at his own birthday party. "This is my biggest delight of the year. I can see you're just as surprised as I'd hoped you'd be, Humphrey."

Yeah, he was surprised, and he'd like nothing better than to grab hold of Omar's skinny neck and squeeze until his eyes bugged out. The bastard knew exactly what kind of destruction Rhinehart would inflict if he got hold of a deadly bioweapon such as the one Humphrey was selling. And he did not care.

"This is indeed a surprise." Humphrey's voice held both surprise and delight at the turn of events. "I'm assuming you have an additional buyer for my product?"

"Not additional. Exclusive. Günter is willing to pay an exorbitant amount to ensure he's the only bidder."

Well, this op had taken a downward turn in a hurry. Ash had a choice to make. He could take down Rhinehart and his goons, capturing an evil man whom the world believed to be dead. His cover would be blown, and he'd have Omar and his guards to contend with, too. Between him and Jules, it'd be a rough go, but they had the element of surprise going for them.

Another option might be harder to pull off and was iffier. Could he manipulate the situation so that Rhinehart and Lang bid against each other, giving him access to both of them? Turning Rhinehart down and insisting on going to auction as planned could have deadly consequences.

Offending the bastard might be the last thing he did. Plus, he'd be putting Jules at greater risk. That wasn't something he took lightly. She had agreed to work with OZ, knowing the danger, but this was different. She didn't sign up for certain death. That's exactly what she'd get if this plan went awry.

"Darling," Elsa said calmly, "introduce me to our new friends."

With those words, Ash knew she was all in on whatever decision he made. If it wouldn't have been completely out of character for Humphrey and Elsa, he would've grabbed her and kissed her in front of everyone.

In a split second, he decided on a third option. Günter Rhinehart could not leave here alive.

Taking Jules's hand, he moved toward the trio. Rhinehart had an unhealthy pallor, so even though he wasn't dead, the explosion thought to have killed him had done some kind of damage. He was, unfortunately, breathing, and that meant he was still a threat.

Standing before the murderer of thousands, Ash held out his hand. When Rhinehart merely shook his head, Ash looked down curiously and noted that one of the man's hands was mangled, and the other was missing three fingers. Rhinehart was notorious for making his own bombs and had apparently had an accident with one of them. Or had the explosion that was supposed to have killed him destroyed his hands? Either way, Ash was glad to see that there was some justice in the world.

"Please excuse me for not rising, Mr. Humphrey. As you can see, I am a bit under the weather."

"Many believe you dead."

"And that is exactly what I want them to think. With enough money and influence, you can make people believe anything."

Yes, but only for a short while. The truth always came out. Maybe not as quickly as some would like, but usually someone or something revealed the secrets.

"I'm sure you're right. May I present my companion, Elsa Olsen. Elsa, this is Günter Rhinehart, one of the most hated and revered men of this century."

"Lovely to meet you, Mr. Rhinehart."

"And you as well, Ms. Olsen. May I introduce my companion, Renee Kirkson."

As the two women nodded greetings to each other, Ash studied Rhinehart's female companion. Their relationship had been well known, and since Renee hadn't been seen since the blast, it was believed she had been killed alongside him. There wasn't much known about Rhinehart's private life, but Ash had seen many reports in which a wife and several young children were mentioned. Were they holed away somewhere, or did they, too, believe he was dead?

"And this is?" Ash raised a questioning brow at the large man standing beside Rhinehart's chair.

As if the man was of no consequence, Rhinehart flicked a mangled hand with a careless gesture. "Fredric, my bodyguard."

There was a small awkward silence and then Omar, practically glowing with pride, said, "Now that we've all met each other, let's get refreshments all around. Dinner will be ready in a half hour or so. After that, we'll get down to business."

Humphrey and Elsa settled onto a sofa together. And while he made small talk and pretended to enjoy the hors d'oeuvres, he gauged the atmosphere and the man across from him. One wrong move, one way or the other, and everything could implode. He and Jules would be lucky to get out of the resulting mess alive.

By the time the dinner bell rang, Ash had devised a plan.

It was risky and could blow up in their faces, but it was the only one he believed might work for what they needed.

Now if he could just get the message to the woman beside him.

# CHAPTER TWENTY-FOUR

Jules often faced danger without blinking an eye. She hadn't chosen what had happened to her, but she had made the choice on how to live in the aftermath. There had been circumstances when she felt that if she even twitched, she could be dead. This was one of those times.

The monster before them, enjoying his steak, which Renee cut up and fed to him, was the vilest kind of evil. Every news outlet in the world had covered him, and there had been numerous celebrations at the news of his death. And he should be dead. Three other countries had joined with the US to hunt down this man. They had found him in a warehouse outside of London. Troops had surrounded the building, and they'd been set to go in and capture him when the entire building exploded. Days of searching the debris had finally uncovered Rhinehart's mangled body. The entire world had breathed a sigh of relief.

So how was it he was sitting across from her now?

She didn't yet know what Ash planned. If necessary, the two of them could take on Rhinehart and his two companions. The woman's mild manner didn't fool her. If she was loyal to this creature, then she was deadly. Three against two weren't bad odds, but what about Schrader? Omar talked a good game, but she couldn't see him fighting hand-to-hand. She could, however, imagine he had no problem with shooting anyone. And strolling through the house earlier today, she had spotted at least a dozen guards roaming the grounds.

She would follow Ash's lead, whatever he chose to do. From the beginning, she had known that working for OZ could cost her everything, including her life. She hadn't expected it to happen so soon, but she was prepared for whatever came next. Twelve years ago, she had survived against impossible odds. Maybe tonight, for this one event, was the reason.

The meal in front of her was lovely, but sitting across from a mass murderer greatly diminished her appetite. She forced herself to eat anyway. Until she knew Ash's plan, she couldn't draw attention to herself.

Fortunately, Ash was seated beside her. When she felt his hand on her thigh, she lowered her gaze in the pretense of concentrating on her meal. When he signed the words, her heart caught in her throat, but she knew she hadn't misunderstood him. This was as serious as it got. Rhinehart was going to die tonight.

Jules dropped her hand to her lap and signed, "When?"

Ash's reply came swiftly. "After dinner." His fingers moved rapidly as he spelled out what he needed her to do.

She had trusted Asher Drake long before she'd met him. Even though he didn't know it, would never know it, she would follow him anywhere.

Preparing herself, Jules took a silent, deep breath and then threw a polite smile to Omar. "The meal is delicious, Mr. Schrader."

"Thank you, my dear. I'm glad you're enjoying it, but

please, you must call me Omar. Humphrey and I have been friends for years. It's only right that his lady love is my friend, too."

"Thank you, Omar. And please call me Elsa."

"Delighted to do so."

They went on to have a trite, frivolous conversation about the weather and wine preferences. Humphrey provided a couple of amusing anecdotes that made Omar laugh. The couple across from them kept out of the conversation. Rhinehart chewed, swallowed, and waited for his next bite from Renee. Though her expression didn't change from the blank one that seemed frozen on her face, Jules had to wonder how she felt about being a nursemaid. The woman's own food was getting cold.

By the time the meal was over, a headache pounded and every particle in Jules's body felt explosive with tension. How the next few minutes played out was anyone's guess, but one thing was certain: Günter Rhinehart would not leave this house alive.

For the first time since they'd sat down to eat, Rhinehart spoke. "Now that our meal has finished, I would like to begin our talks. We will be leaving within the hour."

No one mentioned that Renee had not taken more than a couple of bites from her plate. The man was finished with his meal, so apparently that meant Renee was, too.

Omar's expression was one of both excitement and confusion. "But we have rooms ready for you to stay the night. We—"

"I don't sleep in anyone else's home. How do you think I've stayed alive all these years?"

"Of course, of course." Standing, Omar pointed to a door. "Elsa, if you and Ms. Kirkson would head to the front parlor, you'll find coffee and desserts have been provided. It will—"

"No. Renee does not leave my side."

"But we'll be talking business. I'm sure the ladies would prefer to—"

"Renee knows almost as much about my business as I do. She stays with me."

Humphrey added, "I prefer that Elsa remain with me as well. She's quite adept at business herself."

Looking a bit deflated that his plans had been rearranged, Omar shrugged. "Of course. That is not a problem. Let's proceed to the library."

With Omar leading the way, the eclectic group headed to the library. It had been obvious from Rhinehart's demeanor that he was paranoid and trusted no one but Renee and Fredric. This became more apparent when he insisted that Humphrey and Elsa go ahead of he and Renee. The man likely wanted no one behind him other than his bodyguard, who walked several steps behind him.

Playing on Rhinehart's paranoia would be Jules's gateway.

When they were all seated and one of Schrader's servants had served coffee and then left, Omar nodded toward Rhinehart. "Do you have questions before we begin our talks?"

"A few." A gleam in his eyes, Rhinehart gave Humphrey an assessing gaze. "Tell me about your product."

"It was created to cure a blood disease, but an enterprising young scientist realized that with a few elemental changes, it could be made into an odorless, almost invisible substance. One drop can kill a grown man within a matter of seconds."

"How is it distributed?"

"In any way you like. We used a spray bottle for our experiment, but a canister introduced into an air vent could reach hundreds."

"This scientist who created the weapon, where is he now?"

"*She* is no longer alive. The product is mine exclusively."

"I see. While a canister sounds quite intriguing, I am looking for—how should I say it?—more bang for my buck."

There was no mistaking Rhinehart's meaning. He wanted to kill more than just a few hundred people. If she and Ash didn't end the man here and now, he would find some way, somehow, to accomplish his goal.

"With the formula, you should be able to create as much as you like. But you also must understand that if you're going to offer an amount that would keep me from auctioning it off, it's going to need to be substantial."

"How does three hundred million sound?"

There was complete silence after everyone took a startled breath. That was double what Ash had told Jules he'd proposed to Omar.

Before anyone could question the stunning amount, Rhinehart went on to explain, "As you might guess, I am not in good health. I fear I will soon be unable to make the impact I've always longed to make. This would be my swan song, you might say."

Humphrey gave a cold smile. "It would be a song for the ages."

"Excellent. So do we have a deal?"

"Omar"—Humphrey turned to Schrader—"what do you think?"

"I don't believe you would get near that amount at auction."

"I concur. Very well. I will—"

Jules felt the slightest nudge from Ash and knew this was her cue. She leaned over to him and, in a loud, urgent whisper, said, "Did you just hear a helicopter?"

All eyes zeroed in on Elsa, but it was Rhinehart who said, "What did you say?"

She gave him a polite smile but directed her question to Schrader. "Do you have a helicopter, Omar?"

Not yet catching on, Omar sent her a polite, distracted smile and shook his head. "No. I am not a fan of flying. Anywhere I need to go, I prefer to drive. So, gentlemen, do we have a deal? I'd like to—"

Out of the corner of her eye, she saw Rhinehart stiffen. "Why did you ask the question, Ms. Olsen?" His voice held more than a shade of suspicion.

All innocence, Elsa shrugged. "I thought I heard a helicopter."

Building on that theme, Humphrey sent Omar a concerned look. "You know, I thought I heard something, too. Perhaps there's an airfield close by?"

Rhinehart's entire body went stiff with fury. "Have you betrayed me, Omar?"

His eyes round and startled behind his glasses, Schrader shook his head. "Of course not. I would never—"

"Then why did we all hear a helicopter?" Rhinehart asked.

"You heard it, too?" Omar started to rise. "Perhaps I should—"

"Stay seated," Rhinehart snapped at Omar and then bellowed, "Fredric!"

Fredric was at his boss's side in an instant. "Yes?"

"We must leave."

"No," Omar said. "This is ridiculous." Disregarding Rhinehart's orders to stay seated, Omar stood, gesturing wildly. "I assure you there is no helicopter. No one else is coming. You're completely safe here. I would never—"

Hoping to add to the growing paranoia, Elsa said, "Oh, Humphrey, perhaps we should go, too."

"No!" Omar shouted. "This is—"

A gun appeared in Fredric's hand, pointed at Omar.

Looking more insulted than frightened, Omar snapped, "I told you there were to be no weapons at this meeting."

"Understand this, Omar. I have no need of you," Rhinehart snarled. "Fredric could shoot you, and the deal with Mr. Humphrey would still go through."

"How dare you?" Omar barked.

The drama center stage held everyone's attention, giving Ash the opportunity to skirt behind both Fredric and Rhinehart, snagging the poker from the fireplace on the way.

"Do it," Rhinehart barked. "Shoot him!"

Before Fredric could get a shot off, Ash swung the poker, crashing it hard across the back of Fredric's skull. The big man teetered. Ash grabbed the gun from Fredric's hand before he keeled over.

Squealing like an enraged hyena, Renee lunged toward Ash, a knife glinting in her hand. Jules flew through the air, tackling the other woman before she could make contact with Ash. They fell to the floor together.

ASH WHIRLED to see Jules and Renee grappling for a knife. He rushed forward and then jerked to a stop when he heard a gunshot. Looking back, he saw Omar slump to the floor.

Holding a gun awkwardly in his damaged hand, Rhinehart turned to Humphrey. "Now you don't have to share your profit."

Ash raised Fredric's pistol and fired rapidly, hitting Rhinehart in the head and then the chest. He turned just in time to see Jules plunge the knife into Renee's chest. The woman grasped hold of Jules's hair, pulling her forward.

Ash leaped over a coffee table and kicked at Renee's arm, forcing her to let Jules go.

"You hurt?"

Gasping, her head still slumped over Renee's body, she said, "No, I'm okay."

Turning, he rushed toward Omar, glad to see that the bullet was a through-and-through to the man's shoulder.

Having Omar dead would seriously impede his ability to go through with the auction and get to Lang.

"Omar, can you hear me?"

Schrader opened his eyes and said weakly, "The man's insane."

Since the idiot was stating the obvious, Ash saw no reason to point out that Omar should have been smart enough to figure that out. When dealing with psychopathic people, crazy things tended to happen.

Grabbing a handful of napkins from the coffee table, he pressed them to Omar's shoulder. "I'm surprised none of your guards showed up."

"At Rhinehart's insistence, I told them to stay back unless I called for them."

As that was one of the dumbest things he'd ever heard, Ash couldn't help but ask, "How the hell have you stayed alive all these years?"

Giving him a weak smile, Omar said, "My charm and good looks?"

Shaking his head, Ash stood and strode over to Jules, who was still on her knees beside Renee's body. "You sure you're okay?"

"She's dead."

"If you hadn't tackled her when you did, she would have killed me."

She looked up at him then, and he realized she was in shock. Regret mingled with tenderness. This was most likely her first kill. Killing someone was never easy, but Ash knew from experience that the first one lingered forever.

When he held out his hand to pull her up, he saw another reason for her shock. She was bleeding.

"Where are you cut?"

"My arm. Maybe my shoulder. Not sure."

Ash lifted her in his arms and laid her on the sofa. "Omar, this might be a good time to get your people in here."

Omar had propped himself up against the back of a chair. "Just sent a text. Should be here in a few minutes. A doctor, too."

Ash nodded absently, his concern for Jules overriding anything else. Her face was sheet-white, and she was beginning to shiver. Shrugging out of his jacket, he covered her and then examined her arm. She had two cuts. The one on the top of her shoulder wasn't deep. The other, on her forearm, would require a few stitches. He quickly checked the rest of her body but saw no other obvious injuries. Her pulse was strong and steady.

"You did good," Ash said quietly.

"Thanks. It got messy."

"Yeah."

"How's Omar?"

"He'll live. He—"

What sounded like a herd of thundering boots rushing toward them had Ash surging to his feet. Six men, all armed to the teeth, exploded into the room.

Omar shouted, "Stop. Everything's under control." He nodded toward the three bloody bodies in the middle of the room. "Take them out of here. I'll decide later what to do with them."

While the men carried out his orders, an older, heavyset man carrying a medical bag squatted down in front of Omar. As he tended to Omar's wound, the weapons broker grinned over at Ash. "You saved my life."

Ash nodded his agreement and let that stand. As Jules had said, it had been messy but necessary. Günter Rhinehart should have died long ago. Right now, Ash's priority was Jules. He might have saved Omar's life, but she had saved Ash's.

# CHAPTER TWENTY-FIVE

The knife in her hand dripped with blood as she stood over the dead man. Making another downward swipe, the knife plunged deep into his black, rotted heart. She lifted the knife and struck again. The man opened his eyes and grinned up at her, his teeth stained with blood. "You'll never kill me. I'll always be with you. You'll always belong to me. No matter what."

With a shrill scream, she plunged the knife again and again. He had to die. This time, she would kill him. This time, he wouldn't escape. Maniacal laughter pierced her eardrums. He wouldn't die… Why wouldn't he die?

Jules dropped the knife and covered her ears. The man popped up from the sofa and reached for her. Her heart pounding with horror, she screamed and turned to run. A long, bloody hand reached out and grabbed her. Sharp, jagged nails dug into her skin, each cut scorching like streaks of fire.

Using the only defense she had left, she screamed again.

"Jules. Wake up. You're having a nightmare."

She opened her mouth to scream again. Why wouldn't he

die? How many times had she tried and failed? Why couldn't she kill him?

"Jules." Hands shook her firmly. "Wake up. Now!"

She jerked awake, her eyes opening to see Ash's concerned face above her. "What happened?"

"You were having a nightmare."

She glanced around the bedroom, alarmed that she didn't recognize her surroundings. "Where are we?"

"A hotel. I convinced Omar we needed to leave. The doctor gave you something that knocked you out."

Jules pushed to sit up, wincing at the pain. Her shoulder and arm hurt, and her entire body felt as though she'd been beaten.

"Here, let me help you." Picking her up as if she were a child, Ash propped her against the headboard. "How are you feeling?"

The correct answer was "weak and vulnerable." They were two of her most hated emotions and ones she had fought too hard to let take over. Taking a breath, she said, "A little tired but okay."

"There's no shame in being overwhelmed or scared."

There was for her. She had spent almost two years being terrified of everything and everyone. Returning to that mentality, even for a few moments, was something she refused to allow.

So why were tears coming from her eyes?

Ash's arms encircled her, and Jules gave in. Burying her face against his chest, she let go of the horror and the fear from the night before. That moment, when she'd plunged the knife into Renee and felt her body go limp, would remain in her memory forever. That she'd had no choice made little difference. Maybe in time she'd be able to see things from a clearer perspective, but for right now, she needed this time to come to grips with taking a life.

Ash held her close, not asking questions or even giving empty platitudes. He just held her, which was exactly what she needed.

Several minutes later, Jules took a deep breath and pulled away. "I'm sorry. That's probably not what you expect from an OZ operative."

"You lose your humanity, you lose everything. You saved my life, but that doesn't mean you can't regret the way things happened."

She shuddered out another breath. "I'm glad you're okay." She couldn't tell him that she'd often had nightmares about his death. Asher Drake had come close to dying many times, but she felt that only one of those times was her fault.

"And keep in mind that as messy as it was, we saved lives last night. Rhinehart was set on killing as many people as he possibly could. If we'd let him leave, he would have found a way to succeed."

"How was it possible that the man was even alive?"

"That's something I'm sure people are asking each other today."

"People know about it?"

"Only the ones who need to know. As far as the rest of the world is concerned, Rhinehart died in that blast two years ago."

"Does it ever get to be too much for you? Seeing evil every day and knowing that for every monster you take down, there are a hundred more out there?"

"On occasion. But when I focus on what I can do in that moment, it helps."

Feeling a thousand times better for having talked about it, Jules drew completely away from Ash. "How's Omar doing?"

"Better than he deserves, that's for damn sure."

"Maybe he learned a lesson."

"Won't make him less evil, but he does owe Humphrey a favor, so there's that."

"So what now?"

"Omar was a little loopy when we left, but I imagine I'll be hearing from him soon. He'll want to make sure the auction goes well since his brilliant idea was such a debacle."

"How did you know it would work—the helicopter thing?"

"I know what paranoid looks like. All he needed was a little help to tip him over."

"Were you hurt? I kind of lost focus after…everything."

"No. Not even a bruise, thanks to you." He stood and glanced over his shoulder. "I ordered breakfast. You feel up to eating?"

"Maybe after a shower."

He touched her shoulder. "Mind if I check your cuts?"

She glanced down, noticing the bandages on her shoulder and arm. "Did I get stitches?"

"Two on your shoulder and eight on your arm. Also, you had cuts on your right hip and left leg that I missed at first."

She barely remembered those wounds. The images in her head were of Renee's cherry-red face, filled with an intense hatred and determination, followed by shock when Jules slid the knife into her.

"She would have killed me if I hadn't killed her."

"Yes, she would have. And if she had lived, she might have tried to carry out Rhinehart's plan in order to honor him."

Jules let that settle in her mind. While she could regret the necessity of taking a life, she also understood that she'd had only two choices. She refused to regret being the one who lived.

Apparently realizing she needed to process the information, Ash proceeded to check her wounds. Though they would cause her some pain for a few days, she knew she was fortunate they weren't worse.

"They look good. Omar's doctor didn't even think they'll leave scars." He stood and headed to the other room. "I'll let you shower. Leave the door open in case you feel faint."

Jules waited until he was out of the room before she placed her feet on the floor. Other than a little weak-kneed and sore, she felt fine. Taking a shower and then getting some food inside her would go a long way to making her feel normal again.

ASH POURED himself another cup of coffee while he kept an ear out for any sign that Jules was in trouble. She might told him she felt fine and tried to convince herself as well, but the haunted look in her eyes said something else. She was still suffering. Crying in his arms had been a good start, but she was a long way from being fine.

He didn't bother wishing that things had turned out differently. Ash had learned long ago that "wishing" got you nowhere. When he had accepted Omar's invitation, he had done so to continue to help Humphrey establish trust in a somewhat tenuous relationship with a weapons dealer. Killing a known terrorist and two of his associates certainly hadn't been on his radar. Even though he'd done what was necessary, and had most certainly saved lives by taking Rhinehart out, that didn't mean he had enjoyed the deed. He'd done his share, but killing was and always would be the last resort. There had been no other choice. Jules had known that, but that didn't mean it hadn't cost her.

That was why they were going to take a few days here. Staying holed up in the hotel would give Jules time to heal. He could work from here and be available when she was ready to talk.

And since lying to himself was not his way, he could admit to a purely selfish reason: He wanted to get to know her better. She had told him some things, and Kate had filled in some blanks for him, but there was so much more to Jules Stone. They both knew she had secrets. It was his policy that as long as an operative's secrets didn't interfere with his or her job, they were welcome to keep them. This was different. For the first time since Meg, he realized he wanted to get to know a woman on a personal basis.

There would be complications. In the years since he'd started OZ, he had never once considered breaking his self-imposed rule of not getting involved with a co-worker. That wasn't a rule he imposed on any of his employees. As long as the liaisons didn't compromise the job, their private lives were their own business. And since OZ was an off-the-books secret organization, relationship choices could be severely limited. Only made sense that they gravitated toward one another.

When the shower cut off, Ash took the domes off the food he'd ordered and fixed a plate for himself and one for Jules. He didn't know what type of food she liked, but there was a variety to choose from.

"Um, Ash, where are we?"

He grinned at her. She was wearing a hotel robe that practically swallowed her and a definite frown of irritation.

"Missoula, Montana."

"How? I don't even remember getting on the plane."

"That's because you slept the entire flight. I figured you'd wake up when we got off the plane, but you were sleeping deep."

The doctor had told him that would likely happen. Not only had she been exhausted and in shock, the blood loss had left her body depleted.

"I'm surprised we didn't just go on to OZ headquarters."

"The amenities are better here." He nodded toward the plate he'd fixed for her. "Come eat."

Still looking a little uneasy, Jules sat across from him at the small table. He waited until she'd taken a few sips of coffee before saying quietly, "We both need a few days to recover."

"I'm—"

He held up a hand to cut her off. "Don't say you're fine. You're not. You need some downtime."

The emotions on her face were a testament to just how unfine she really was. From the moment he'd met her, he was impressed with her composure and ability to hide her thoughts. Not so today. He saw anger, frustration, sadness, and, if he wasn't mistaken, trepidation.

The last one concerned him the most. "This suite has two bedrooms."

Pink washed over her face, giving her a healthier glow. "I wasn't worried about that."

"We did kiss."

"Yes, well, that was under extraordinary circumstances."

"So you're saying that if it had been anyone else standing in the shower with you, your naked body pressed against his, you would have responded the same way?"

"Yes. No." She shook her head quickly. "I don't know. I just…"

He was pushing her, and that wasn't fair. Changing the subject, he said, "Do you see Kate often?"

Jules's mind whirled at the change of subject. She was just coming to terms with having been unconscious, unaware of where she was or what was happening to her. Waking up in a strange bed, wearing only her bra and panties had been startling to say the least. Learning she was in Montana had been even more of a shock. But now she learned that Ash wanted them to stay at the hotel for a few days. Together. If that wasn't enough, he had confronted her about their kiss. For someone who tried to be in control at all times, she found all of this to be just a bit much.

Grateful he'd thrown her a lifeline by asking about Kate, she said, "Not as much as I would like. We talk almost weekly, though. What about you?"

"Haven't seen her in over a year. We check in with each other often."

Jules knew that Kate was an important intel resource for OZ, and though she knew quite a bit about how they'd met, she wanted Ash's perspective.

She wanted to talk to him about so many things. Things she hadn't thought they'd ever get a chance to discuss. Even if she couldn't tell him everything, she wanted him to know, someway, that she was so very sorry about what happened.

"You look like you're about to fall out of your chair."

Exhaustion wrapped around her like a heavy, smothering coat. She hadn't felt this exhausted and weak in years.

"Why do I feel so tired? I can barely keep my eyes open."

"Aftereffects of shock. I'm glad to see you did eat a little."

She blinked at her plate, surprised that she had indeed eaten half of the rather large serving of scrambled eggs and toast. She'd even drank an entire glass of milk.

"Why don't you go lie down again? After a few more hours of sleep, you should feel a lot better."

"You seem to know a lot about that."

"That's because I've been there."

She wanted to ask him how and when, but her mouth refused to form the words as her brain fogged once more. Before she realized it, Ash was standing beside her and lifting her in his arms.

"I can walk."

"Carrying a beautiful woman to bed, even if it is just to sleep, will never be a hardship."

She was vaguely aware of how good it felt to be in his arms and thought she might have mumbled something about that. By the time he placed her on the bed, she was on the verge of sleep. Her eyes felt as though stones had been placed on the lids, weighing them down. She did manage to blink them open slightly, and her sluggish brain vaguely registered the tenderness in his eyes. Her heart performed a tiny somersault, and she mumbled something a second before unconsciousness claimed her.

I'M SO SORRY.

What was she sorry about? Jules's words before she'd dropped off to sleep hounded Ash. He told himself she could have simply meant that she was sorry she was so sleepy, or something equally innocuous. His gut told him it was something else. What that something was he had no idea. But he intended to find out.

Grabbing the secure satellite phone, he punched in a number he rarely called. He and Kate communicated in various ways, but using a phone was usually his last choice.

Kate answered on the first ring, which meant she was expecting his call.

"You guys okay?"

"News travels fast."

"It does when it's this big. But you and Jules…you're both okay?"

"We're fine. Jules got a little banged up, but nothing serious."

"Can I talk to her?"

"She's asleep. I'll get her to call you when she wakes."

"I can't believe the bastard was still alive. We found his body…supposedly had verifiable proof."

"He faked it somehow. I think he might've been injured then…just not killed. His hands were messed up, and he was in poor health."

"And he was looking for one last boom."

"Something like that. We had no choice but to stop him permanently."

"I agree. Jules do okay?"

"She did great. Acted like a pro, but it cost her."

Neither of them needed to go beyond those words. They both knew the cost of taking a life.

"Everything still in place for the auction?"

"Yes." Just because he'd saved Omar's life, Ash didn't expect any special favors from the weapons broker. The man might've been an idiot for inviting a psychopath to dinner and expecting him to play nice, but that didn't mean he would cut any corners in the upcoming auction. It might, in fact, make him more wary.

"That's good. I have no news on this end, if that's why you're calling."

"It's not. I wanted to talk about Jules. She's hiding something."

"Aren't we all?"

"Don't give me that, Kate. We've known each other too long to play games."

"I'm not playing, Ash. You know as well as I do that we all have things we don't want to share with others. And Jules is one of the most private people I've ever known."

"But you know what she's hiding."

"Yes, but it's not my story to tell. Have you asked her?"

"Haven't had a chance. The day after we met, she was on an op. Things haven't really slowed down to have any kind of real conversation."

"Sounds like you're both taking some downtime now. Maybe you can talk to her. Be aware that reticence doesn't necessarily mean a person is hiding something incriminating."

There was no need for that reminder. He lived in the shadows. Closemouthed reticence was SOP.

"My gut says it's something more than that."

"You're a good interrogator. I have no doubt that you'll uncover the truth. Just remember: Not everyone sees things the way we do."

Ash ended the call, not satisfied, but at least he knew he was on the right track. Jules was indeed hiding something from him. Question was, why had she apologized to him?

## CHAPTER TWENTY-SIX

J ules took one last bite of her pizza slice and then put it
aside, pleasantly full. For the last day and a half, she'd
done nothing but eat and sleep. Her wounds were still
sore, and nightmares still woke her, but all in all she felt a
thousand times stronger than she had when she woke
yesterday morning.

In a surprising turn of events, Ash had been both kind
and gentle. Not that she'd thought he was deliberately mean,
but he was a tough, straightforward man. Seeing his gentler
side stirred emotions within her that had no place in their
relationship. Not only was he her boss, but she was keeping a
mountain of secrets from him. If he discovered even one of
them, his attitude toward her would quickly change.

"Finished?"

"Yes, thanks."

Speculatively, she watched Ash clean up the coffee table.
Every time she'd asked if she could help, he had declined.
Was it his way to do everything himself, or was he being
polite? Either way, it needed to stop. She was almost one
hundred percent again and needed him to see that.

When he came back and sat on the other end of the sofa from her, she said, "So when are we going back to work?"

"In a few days. Don't worry. The rest of the team is keeping busy. OZ never sleeps."

"I feel fine. There's no need to stay away on my account."

For several long seconds, he eyed her as if he were a scientist and she were an interesting specimen he'd never encountered. Jules held his gaze, refusing to give him an inch. She knew her strengths, knew what she could handle.

"Did you know that you scream in your sleep?"

He said the statement so mildly, one would think he was discussing the weather. Still, her heart gave an extra thud of dread. Her nightmares were not a topic for discussion.

Refusing to allow him to put her on the defensive, Jules matched his mild tone when she answered. "I've never taken anyone's life. Even though it was self-defense, I would think nightmares would be normal. Doesn't mean they'll have any impact on my job."

For the most part, until this latest event, she had been able to relegate the nightmares and night terrors to only a couple every month or so. Even then, they usually came after she'd hunted down a killer. She had known they were back, she just hadn't known that she'd screamed out loud.

"Can't argue that. I have them on occasion, too."

Barely breathing, she waited for more questions. Asher Drake was known for not backing down. Talking about her nightmares without discussing their content would be impossible. She wasn't ready to go that far. When he found out the truth, everything would end. It was too soon. She had accomplished nothing. She had to have more time.

"What made you decide to create OZ?"

The lame attempt to change the subject brought a slightly raised brow, but no other reaction. And he did her a favor by actually answering the question.

"A lot of different reasons. After I left the FBI, I didn't do anything for a while. Kate called and asked for a favor. It felt good to be doing something productive again…to help someone. After that, another job cropped up, then another. We were a group of friends with specific skills that could be utilized to do good things. We worked well together, trusted each other. We just needed a name and a place to work from."

"And Option Zero? How'd that name come about?"

He lifted a shoulder in a casual shrug, but his words were some of the most profound she'd ever heard. "At our core, that's who we are. We help people who have nowhere else to turn, who have zero options. We've been there ourselves. The name made sense to us."

And that was one of the biggest reasons Asher Drake fascinated her so much. She knew his past…knew the things he'd been through. Instead of allowing bitterness and grief to overtake him, he had let his circumstances motivate him to help others.

In part, he was the reason she hunted down killers. Yes, she did so because of her past, but Ash was the person she'd had in the back of her mind when she'd first started hunting. Like Ash, she had a unique perspective and specific abilities. She, too, had been stuck in limbo for a long time, unable to get past her pain. Hunting monsters became her way of coping.

"I know I've only been involved in a couple of ops, but neither of them was to help just one individual."

"Some are, some aren't. A few are ongoing. Even though I make the final decision, we have a meeting once a week to discuss possible cases. Everyone gives input."

"Kate said that you have a tremendous network to pull from. How did you gain so much trust in such a short amount of time? OZ has only been in existence…what? Five years?"

"I think you're confusing trust with need. We're given intel to handle a situation. What we aren't given we get through any means necessary to accomplish our objectives."

"Like what?"

"Barter, bribe, coerce, intimidate. It's not always pretty, but to get the results we need, we sometimes have to get creative with our intel gathering."

"What are some of the ongoing cases?"

"The one with Schrader is our biggest."

"How did it come about?"

Jules listened as Ash described the care he'd taken in creating Humphrey, fascinated by the intricate details. She had a lot of experience with creating a false identity, but OZ had taken this to a completely different level. Breathing life into a nonexistent person was one thing. Faking identifications and past history were done all the time for various reasons. Creating a man with Humphrey's reputation was an undertaking few could carry off.

"Through Humphrey, we've been able to apprehend some low-level arms dealers and one terrorist wannabe. Taking Carl Lang down will be our most ambitious project so far."

"Will you retire Humphrey after this?"

"Hard to say. Hate to lose what we've built. We've put so much work into him. But if by sacrificing Humphrey, we successfully take Lang, it'll be worth it."

"When do you think the auction will take place?"

"Within the next couple of weeks. Even though he's injured, Omar won't put it off. He takes pride in his negotiations, and since his latest one was an abysmal failure, he'll want to put it behind him as soon as possible."

"Will this op involve the whole team?"

"Yeah. All hands on deck."

"You're Navy?"

"Marine."

"For how long?"

"Eight years active."

"Once a Marine, always a Marine?"

"Yeah."

"You didn't want to make it a career?"

"Thought long and hard about it, but—" A shadow crossed his face, and he shrugged. "I was married then. Meg and I wanted kids, but we both wanted to be there for them. We decided to wait until I got out to start a family."

"That didn't work out."

"No. We had trouble conceiving...then trouble elsewhere. It wasn't in the cards."

"I'm sorry."

"I guess you know what happened."

"Some of it."

"Never saw it coming."

"How could you? You'd caught the monster. How could you know he would escape?"

"It was my job to know. I failed at both."

"Both?"

"My job as a husband was to protect my wife. My job as an agent was to expect shit like that to happen and be prepared to handle it."

Insisting that Meg's death wasn't his fault would do no good. She knew more than her share about that kind of guilt. No matter what you did, no matter how hard you tried, it clung to you like a leech. Eventually, that guilt became embedded inside you, became a part of who you were, what decisions you made.

"You managed to catch him again."

"Yeah." His disgust evident. "I did do that."

Unable to stop herself, Jules reached for his hand and

squeezed it gently. It wasn't much…it wasn't anything, really. Right now, this was all she had.

"You quit the agency after that?"

His smile was bitter. "'Quit' might not be the right word. More like I was encouraged to leave."

"You apprehended a sadistic serial killer twice. What would make them…"

"Let's just say that the Bureau doesn't take kindly to one of their agents accusing a sitting senator of arranging a murder."

She told herself to stop right there. She knew the story. There was no reason for him to tell it. She knew every intricate detail of how Clark had been apprehended. Cockiness or carelessness, maybe both, had finally led the FBI to a hole in the wall motel in Oregon where he'd been staying while terrorizing another city.

The first takedown had been quick, without even a hint of bloodshed. But then the bastard had inexplicably escaped. The second capture had been neither quick nor bloodless. Clark had been lying in wait, ready to kill Ash. The tables had turned dramatically. FBI Agent Asher Drake had singlehandedly almost beaten the monster to death.

She also knew all about the senator. There was nothing new that Ash could tell her. But she had to ask more questions for two reasons. First, she needed to hear the facts from Ash, no matter how painful they would be to hear. And second, not asking questions would look suspicious. What person wouldn't want answers after his statement?

"You think someone…a senator…arranged for Clark's release?"

"Escape, not release. And I don't think it, I know it. Proving it is another issue altogether."

"But why—"

"It's a long story. Condensed version is I was in Colombia

on what I thought was a simple protection detail. We got attacked by a local cartel. The people we were protecting heloed out of there, leaving us to fight our way out. Senator Nora Turner was one of those people."

"Why would…"

"That's what I've been trying to find out since I recognized her. I confronted her, and she denied it, of course.

"Then we caught a break and finally captured Clark. He was tried and convicted, headed to prison for the rest of his life. His transportation had some problems. Next thing I knew, he'd escaped."

"And he found you and your wife."

"Yeah…he found us."

"And you think…sorry, you believe Turner arranged all of it. But why? If she wanted you dead, wouldn't it be a lot easier to just hire someone to kill you?"

"Maybe. I don't know what her thinking was. My instincts tell me she did it to make it look as though Clark had a vendetta against me."

"But you don't think that's the case?"

"Oh, I'm sure he has a vendetta against me, but how many people would have the ability to find a lake house five hours away from my home? Clark had to have connections and intel to find me. The only person who was remotely interested in seeing me dead back then was Turner. She got the intel to Clark and made arrangements for his escape. He took care of the rest."

"Have you asked her?"

"Not exactly. I confronted her on the steps of the Capitol. Got arrested. Somehow, the press never reported anything about it. I was given the opportunity to resign from the FBI and ordered to stay away from Turner."

"Have you?"

"No, I have not."

She almost smiled at that adamant reply. Giving up was not in Asher Drake's DNA.

"And OZ is working to find proof for you?"

"Yes. And we will. One day, maybe when she least expects it, Nora Turner will finally get exactly what she deserves."

Jules's heart squeezed. She so wanted to tell him the truth. But she kept her mouth closed. If he knew what Turner was up to, what would he do?

Ash had given a succinct, condensed version of what had happened. The pain and guilt she knew he must feel were deeply buried. Determination to bring Turner down had taken the forefront, which was how Asher Drake coped. She understood that kind of coping mechanism all too well.

Jules had watched all the drama from the sidelines, unable to do anything other than swear that someday, somehow, she would find a way to help Asher Drake get the justice he sought.

She would not stop until she had fulfilled that promise.

## CHAPTER TWENTY-SEVEN

H is right fist slammed into the leather boxing bag, followed by his left. He repeated the process again and again, looking for relief from a multitude of frustrations. Ash had to give himself credit. He definitely knew how to spoil a mood. He'd initiated the conversation, hoping to get Jules to talk about herself and her issues. Instead, he'd ended up talking about how his monumental screw-up had gotten his wife killed.

The conversation had halted after that. Even though he might've gotten Jules to talk, his mood had taken a downturn. His only choice had been to get away from her for a while. The hotel gym offered him just what he needed. A half hour at the boxing bag had given him a much-needed release.

The bag in front of him alternated between two faces. One was the chubby-cheeked, innocuous-looking visage that hid a sadistic, cold-blooded killer. The other was a strong, female face belonging to the woman who had manipulated a broken system for no other reason than to cover her own ass.

Only a few people knew the true events of that night. One of the biggest reasons was because Ash had no proof. On the surface, it had looked like a series of unfortunate, completely unrelated events. Events that had enabled a serial killer to escape and find the FBI agent who months before had apprehended him. The van transporting the criminal to the maximum-security prison had broken down. New transportation had been called, but had somehow been delayed. During that time, John Leland Clark had taken down two guards and escaped. How Clark had been able to find the lake house remained a mystery, but powerful people had ways of obtaining information. He knew to the depths of his soul that Nora Turner was responsible. She had used her power with single-minded ruthlessness to get her way.

Regret was a helluva thing. If he hadn't pushed Turner about her involvement in the incident in Colombia, Meg would still be alive. In demanding justice for the men who'd died, he had become a target. And Meg had lost her life.

With no proof of Turner's involvement, Ash had come off looking like a grieving, paranoid fool with an ax to grind. But he knew who was responsible, and he would have proof someday. He would not stop until he got justice for Meg. And for the men Turner was responsible for leaving behind.

They were getting closer. Even though the cover-up appeared impenetrable, Ash was finally seeing cracks in the surface. He just needed a little more time.

"Are you okay?"

He'd been pounding so hard, so deep in thought, he hadn't been aware of his surroundings. A great way to get himself killed.

The compassion in Jules's eyes was almost his undoing. She had strength, kindness, intelligence, and wit. Plus, she possessed a strong desire to right wrongs and see that justice was served. From her beauty, to her strength of character, to her skill as an operative—all of her attracted him like no one had since Meg.

The temptation of losing himself in Jules's soft body and comforting arms was almost undeniable. Forgetting his tortured thoughts, even for a few minutes, would be a reprieve he longed for with an aching intensity. Damned if he would do that to her. He had never used a woman in his life, and he would not start now.

"I'm fine. Sorry. Sometimes, the only thing that helps is to pound the hell out of something."

"Totally understand. It's my favorite way, too." She touched her shoulder and grimaced. "I think my arm is a little too sore for that, but a half hour on the treadmill would be good."

They were back to being polite strangers. While he regretted that, it was for the best. His thoughts about Jules had been altogether too tender. There was little room in his life for those kinds of feelings, especially for an OZ operative.

Giving her a nod, he headed to the exit. "I'll leave you to it."

"Wait…Ash. I wanted to ask…I mean, I wanted to say that if you ever need someone to talk to about…things, I'm a good listener."

There was that wash of tenderness again. Before he could give in to temptation, he gave her a quick nod of thanks and walked out the door.

THE INSTANT the door slammed closed, Jules let out a shaky breath. Seeing Ash's pain was a difficult thing to bear. Would it get better once he got the justice he deserved? She could only hope.

Knowing she had no choice but to proceed, Jules pulled the burner phone from her pocket. She'd hidden the phone in a secret sleeve of her suitcase, but today was the first time she'd checked for messages. There were five missed calls and five voice mails. All from the same person, each one demanding information.

Telling Turner not to call her had been like telling the wind not to blow. The woman's persistence would have been admirable if she'd been doing this for any other reason than to protect herself.

Jules pressed the callback key and rolled her eyes when Turner answered on the first ring with a grating, "It's about damn time. Where have you been? I've been calling you for days."

Giving the excuse that she'd been busy wasn't going to work this time. The senator was expecting results. If Jules didn't give her something, Turner might fire her on the spot. That couldn't happen. At least not yet.

"I overheard a conversation this morning that could be exactly what you're looking for." Jules sold the lie, embellishing certain elements to make it seem as if, with the right spin, Asher Drake were skirting the edges of treason.

"This is perfect!"

"It's not much right now. I'll be able to gather more soon. I—"

"It's a great start. We can build on it…make it seem a whole lot worse. One tiny seed of doubt can grow into a forest of suspicion. By the time we're through with him, Asher Drake won't be able to get a job as a gravedigger. Once he's gone, it's just a matter of time before that ridiculous organization of his is history, too."

Jules ground her teeth so hard, her jaws ached. Asher Drake and Option Zero saved countless lives and brought evil people to justice. Calling them a "ridiculous organization" was like calling Turner an honorable human being.

This might be the toughest job she'd ever had. Pretending excitement to ruin a good man, all the while acting as if she were in cahoots with a woman she despised. But if this worked, it would be one of the most worthwhile things she'd ever done.

"When can you get me names and locations?"

"I don't know yet. I'm still trying to gain his trust. He's still careful around me."

"Don't worry about getting everything. If you can get me just one name, I'll have my people start working up a story."

"I'll see what I can do."

"Excellent." There were voices in the background, and Turner hurriedly said, "I've got to go. Good work, Ms. Diamond. I look forward to hearing from you again very soon."

The call went dead. Resisting the urge to throw the phone across the room and watch it shatter, Jules slid it back into her pocket. She had bought herself some more time. How much she didn't know.

Striding over to the treadmill, Jules set a brutal pace. Every time she talked with the woman, she felt the need for a bath afterward. Even though she was doing this for all the right reasons, she still felt disloyal, as if she were betraying Ash instead of helping him.

Going undercover was nothing new for her. She was used to taking on jobs that required gaining intel covertly. Assuming an undercover persona was a routine part of her job. Sometimes, she enjoyed the pretense. Other times, it was monotonous. But it was still just a job. What she was doing here with Ash wasn't just a job. It was personal, very personal. If she failed…

No, there was no room for failure. Ash deserved justice, and she was going to do whatever it took to get it for him.

Ash heard Jules enter the hotel room. After a hot shower,

he felt calmer, ready to focus on the here and now. He wanted to talk about her nightmares. To find out if she'd had counseling for them, or if she needed counseling now. She'd experienced a traumatic event. If she needed help, he intended to get it for her.

The majority of OZ operatives were military-trained. They had seen war and its aftermath. Just because Jules was skilled in weapons and hand-to-hand fighting didn't mean she was prepared to deal with the emotions that came with taking a life. That was something each of them had to come to terms with in their own way. If her nightmares were related to what had happened to Renee and Rhinehart, then they needed to be addressed.

She was downing some water when he walked into the living area. When she spotted him, she smiled. "You look like you feel better."

"Nothing like beating the hell out of something to give you perspective."

"Agreed." She headed toward her bedroom. "I'm going to take a shower."

"Come out when you're finished. I want to talk to you about something."

"Anything wrong?"

"No. Not really." Thinking he'd get a more honest answer from her if he took a direct approach, he added, "We never did talk about your nightmares."

The smile slid from her face. "There's nothing to talk about. They happen. I deal with them."

"So you have them a lot?"

"From time to time. I told you they're not a big deal and won't affect my job performance."

"Your job isn't in jeopardy, Stone. But if you're having the nightmares because of what happened at Omar's, we need to address them. Ignoring a problem doesn't make it go away."

She came toward him, her eyes gleaming with anger. "Is that right?" Stopping inches from his face, she challenged, "Isn't that what you did?"

"What are you talking about?"

"The kiss in the shower? You're just ignoring what happened there."

"First, I didn't know that was a problem. Second, if you want to talk about it, then let's talk about it."

"There's nothing to talk about."

"Exactly." Ash shook his head. "Gotta tell you, Stone, that wasn't your best deflection."

Heat sizzling in her eyes, she took a step forward. "How's this for deflection?"

She was playing games, and while he could appreciate the tactic for what it was, he was also having all sorts of fantasies of letting her get away with it. Her face was flushed with color, and her lips looked tempting and delicious. His mouth watered as he remembered her taste.

"Where you going with this, Jules?"

"Where do you want me to go, Ash?"

He had to give her credit. As other needs made themselves known, his concern for her nightmares was shoved to the back of his mind. Only by concentrating on his responsibilities was he able to keep from grabbing her and showing her exactly where he wanted to go.

"Never figured you for a coward."

Her head jerked back as if she'd been slapped. "I am not a coward."

"Oh yeah?" He took the last step and pressed his forehead to hers. "You're using this thing between us to deflect my questions. That's beneath you."

JULES CLOSED HER EYES. She wasn't sure she'd ever been this

ashamed. Ash was right on the money. She was trying to use their attraction to distract him. The passion she felt for Ash was the sweetest, most honest emotion she'd had in years. To manipulate him like this was a huge betrayal to these new, incredible feelings.

She backed-up a step and said, "The nightmares started a few days after I was rescued." She couldn't tell him everything, but she could give him this much of the truth. "At first, they were indistinct…blurry. The more I tried to repress them, the stronger and more vivid they became."

"Did you talk to anyone about them?"

"Yes. More than one. Some suggested hypnosis. Others thought meditation would work. A few wanted to give me sleeping pills or anti-anxiety medication. I didn't want a pill or an easy answer. I finally found someone who told me what I needed to hear. She said I wasn't going to get any better until I dealt with my guilt."

"Guilt?"

"For surviving when so…when April didn't. Her parents blamed me for what happened. It was hard to deal with."

"You understand, though, that placing blame is a human reaction that comes from grief. It doesn't mean you were to blame. People lash out because they're hurting."

Yes, she understood that, but when a person was hounded by those grief-stricken people 24/7, the grief that one felt was multiplied greatly. It had been incessant, unending, soul-leaching.

"Jules?"

She brought herself back to the here and now. She needed to end this conversation.

"Yes, I know that, but knowing in your head and feeling it in your heart are often two separate entities."

"So did you…get over the guilt?"

"Not really, but I learned to work through it."

"By hunting serial killers?"

"Something like that."

"Why serial killers?"

Again, she couldn't tell him the full truth, but she gave him what she could. "I guess because of their arrogance… their selfishness. To take a life simply for enjoyment or out of compulsion is the most evil reason I can imagine. It infuriates me."

"Can't argue with you there. So your most recent nightmares…you think they're related to Renee?"

"Maybe…probably some. They usually come when I'm exhausted. Also, I…" She took a breath and gave him another partial truth. "The man…men who took me, one of them had a knife. I guess using a knife to kill Renee brought back some repressed memories."

"I'm sorry about that."

"Don't be. You were right. She would have killed me if I hadn't killed her."

"Thank you for talking with me about it. I know it wasn't easy."

"Thank you for listening."

"Hey, if we don't help each other out, what's the point in existing?" He took a step closer and said, "Now, about that kiss."

Laughing softly, Jules dropped her head onto Ash's chest. In a matter of seconds, she had gone from sorrow and shame to joy and laughter. Ash had done that for her.

"Sorry, buddy, you had your chance."

"You're right." She felt his mouth touch the crown of her head in a soft, quick kiss. "Go take your shower."

With reluctance, she pulled away from him. She was at her bedroom door when he called out to her. "Jules?"

"Yes?"

"Give me another chance on that kiss sometime?"

Another surge of happiness flooded through her. "I'd like that."

As soon as she closed the door behind her, she leaned against it for support. Her legs were suddenly so weak she wasn't sure she could even make it to the bed before she collapsed. Asher Drake had fascinated her for years, but this man with his strength, courage, and incredible charisma was eons beyond the fantasies she had built up in her mind.

As much as she wanted to deny it, she couldn't. She was falling in love with him. And though she had little to no experience in gauging a man's true affection, she couldn't help but believe he felt something for her. Ash was the most authentic and honorable man she'd ever known. The tenderness in his eyes and the gentle way he treated her were real. The passion between them was both explosive and amazingly exciting. He was the kind of man she'd always dreamed of falling in love with, but she had given up on those dreams as fantasies. This wasn't a fantasy…this was as real as possible.

But how would his feelings for her change when he learned that she was the reason his wife had died?

# CHAPTER TWENTY-EIGHT

**OZ Headquarters**

No one would believe this place. Every time Jules rounded another corner, she was amazed at not only how large the facility was, but also the sophistication of the setup. Someone had put an enormous amount of thought into its design.

This was her first official day at OZ, and she was sure her tour guide likely thought her vocabulary was limited to exclamations of "Wow" and "My stars."

"So what do you think?"

She glanced back at Rose Wilson. She'd heard Rose's name mentioned numerous times since she'd become an operative and Jules had been looking forward to meeting the woman. She hadn't been disappointed. Ash had introduced Rose as the person who really ran OZ, and though Rose had smiled, she hadn't disagreed. With hair as white as snow and kind, discerning eyes, Rose Wilson had the kind of beauty that was both endless and ageless. Jules estimated her age as between forty and sixty, but she wasn't even sure of that.

As the woman led her through the maze, pointing out what each area was and how it was incorporated into the overall purpose of OZ, Jules began to see what Ash had meant. This woman knew everything about the organization, from everyday minutiae to the big missions.

"This place is amazing. Was all of this built at one time?"

"The original house was built in the fifties and belonged to a rancher. When he died, his only heir didn't want a ranch, so he sold the house and land to one of those doomsday prepper groups. They're the ones who added the underground. They grew too large and decided to move to a bigger area. The place stood empty for a long while. Ash bought it and renovated it."

Jules was surprised that the rancher had left only one heir, as the enormous house included Ash's office, a large conference room, and five bedroom suites. There was also a large kitchen with every amenity imaginable, as well as a combination living room and den.

She had thought that the house was all there was to see until Rose had shown up at her bedroom door and offered her a tour of the facility.

Standing in the giant communications room, Jules made a slow 360-degree turn. Monitors and computers were everywhere, as were screens of varying sizes. One giant screen covered an entire wall. Five people sat at individual workstations, either typing on their computers or talking on the phone. One of them was Serena, who gave her a quick grin and wave before returning to whatever she was working on at her laptop.

"Kate told me that OZ is bigger than people may think."

"Takes more than a few people to dig out the intel we rely on for our ops."

Jules noted that though the entire area was underground and therefore didn't have windows, the lighting gave off a glow like natural light. Paintings and thriving plants were placed strategically to enhance the area. What should have been dark and depressing was actually a nice, sunny-looking work area.

"How long have you been with OZ?"

"From the beginning. I was working for a tech company in New York. Ash offered me a job, and I've never looked back."

Jules wanted to ask more, but didn't want to sound like an inquisitor. So far, Rose had been amazingly open, but Jules knew that the majority of people working for OZ did so in anonymity.

Leaving the op center, they headed down a long hallway, back to where the tour had begun.

"Your room okay?"

"It's lovely. Whoever decorated the place is very talented."

A smile curved Rose's mouth. "Thank you. I never got to explore those talents in my previous career. Ash gave me carte blanche to decorate as I wanted."

They stopped at the door they'd entered through, and Rose tilted her head toward a set of double doors. "Through there is a gym, swimming pool, rec room, and an indoor shooting range. Feel free to use them anytime."

Though tempted to explore more, Jules resisted and walked out into the sunlight with Rose. The facility's double doors blended into the forest so well, only a person who knew what they were looking for would be able to find the place.

"What happens when there's a heavy snow?"

"We do what we can. Many of us can work from home if necessary. But if they get snowed in here, there are barracks where they can stay."

"I probably need to take some time this afternoon and look for an apartment in town."

"Ash told me you wanted to do that, but there's no real hurry, unless you're adamant about it. You're the only one living in the house right now."

"Ash doesn't live there?"

"No. He's got a house a couple of miles away."

Having a little additional time to look for an apartment would be good, but she had an ingrained need for privacy and her own things.

"If there's nothing going on this afternoon, maybe I'll go—"

Rose glanced down at her watch and shook her head. "Looks like that's out. Ash has called an ops meeting for two o'clock."

Jules looked at her own watch. She had yet to get used to the way Ash and the team communicated with each other. Sure enough, the text indicator light was on. She touched the screen, and Ash's words appeared. The text was short and terse, giving an impression of urgency.

***Ops meeting. 14:00. Mandatory.***

Since that was a half hour from now, she thought to go back inside and take a look at the gym. That idea disappeared when another text message appeared on her screen, this one from Ash but only to her.

***Jules, need to see you ASAP. My office.***

Despite all the stern warnings she'd given her heart over the last couple of days, she couldn't keep it from leaping with joy. Excusing herself from Rose, Jules took the path back to the main house. The closer she got, the less excited she became. What if he had found out something? She knew she was living on borrowed time, but had hoped to have more. After seeing the inner workings of OZ intel, she knew that time might be even shorter. OZ had ways of finding information people didn't want discovered.

She and Ash had stayed in the hotel two more days after

their discussion of her nightmares. Apparently wanting to make sure things weren't awkward between them after that, he hadn't asked any questions more personal than what she wanted from room service and what kinds of movies she liked.

She was aware that Ash had worked most of the time they were there, either on his phone or laptop, but in the evenings, they would watch television or a movie. It had been a relaxing, stress-free time and just what she had needed to recover. Her injuries were almost completely healed, and her nightmares had even gone away.

Spending that extra time with Ash had only increased her awareness of him and how silly and hopeless those feelings were. That didn't keep them from occurring, though, and she had treasured those days of peaceful bliss.

As she knocked on the door, she couldn't help but wonder if the peace was at an end.

ASH WATCHED Jules as she entered his office. The downtime had made a big difference in her appearance. The recovery time at the hotel had been the right thing to do. The news he was about to impart might change that healthy glow, which was exactly the reason he wanted to see her before the ops meeting.

"Heard you got a tour of OZ. What do you think?"

"It's phenomenal, as is Rose."

"Yeah, she is. Don't know what we'd do without her."

"This might be a totally inappropriate question, but where did you get the funding for all of this? The communications center alone has to be worth millions."

"Several. We've built it up over the years. We started with our savings, some personal loans. Some life insurance policies. Whatever we could get together. Some of our jobs have included a nice paycheck. We put as much as we can back into the organization."

"We?"

"The six of us who started OZ. Xavier, Sean, Gideon, Liam, and Hawke."

"Hawke?"

"We lost him a few years back."

"I'm sorry."

Ash accepted her condolences with a nod. Only a handful of people knew the full story of what really happened to Hawke. He didn't like keeping secrets from his team, but in this he'd had no choice.

"So you've been friends with them a long time?"

"Yeah. When you almost die with someone, you form a bond."

"A band of brothers?"

"Something like that."

"You've managed to do a lot with OZ in a relatively short period of time."

"We've been lucky." He nodded to the chairs in front of his desk. "Have a seat. We have a situation I want to discuss with you."

She came toward him, and though she was smiling, he saw something in her eyes that told him she wasn't as relaxed as she was trying to appear.

As soon as she was seated, he walked around the desk and sat in the chair beside her. "I need your honest answer about something."

"Okay…yes…of course."

"Omar called. He's set the auction up for two weeks from today. The timing is good. It'll give us a chance to create some background stories, work different scenarios, and get prepared."

"I'm getting the feeling there's a 'but' attached to that statement."

"Omar insists that you accompany me."

"Why would that be a problem?"

"I need to know how you feel about going back there."

"I'm fine. I—"

Ash held up his hand. "Stop it, Jules. I was there. I saw what happened…how you reacted. I need to know if you can handle it. If you can't, I'll tell Omar we split up, and Eve can attend with me. You can still be part of the op, working in the background with Jazz and Serena. But there's no need for you to go as Elsa."

JULES TOLD herself that she should be touched that Ash had so much concern for his employee. And while intellectually she could accept that, she couldn't help but feel she had disappointed him.

"No, do not even get that in your head," he said.

"What?"

"You handled yourself like the professional you are. I couldn't have asked for more, but a lot has been thrown at you in a short amount of time."

Ash continued to terrify her in how very well he read her. "Then why—"

"Because I need to know you can do this. Not only might this be our only chance to take Lang down, we're dealing with some extremely dangerous people. I need everyone at the top of their game. If things turn sour…"

He didn't need to finish the sentence. These people, including Omar, would kill without a second thought. This wasn't about her ego. This was about bringing down a man who wanted to kill hundreds of innocents. Her employer was asking if she was up to the task.

"I can do the job, Ash."

He nodded and stood, apparently satisfied with her answer. "All right. Then let's head to the conference room and brief the rest of the team."

They walked together out the door. "So Omar has recovered from his wound?"

"He said he has. My sources have told me that the injury is healing much faster than Omar's mental state."

"How so?"

"Apparently, he was more than a little shocked and upset than what he let on."

"Is he blaming us?"

"No. From his perspective, we saved his life. Believe it or not, that was the first time he's ever been injured on the job."

"That doesn't seem quite fair."

"Yeah." Ash threw her a wry grin. "A weapons broker should experience firsthand pain from all the products he's responsible for putting on the market."

Trying to ignore the way his smile affected her was almost impossible. For years, she had wondered if she was too screwed up to actually ever have strong feelings for a man. Her unimpressive dating life certainly bore that out. So why was it that the one man she couldn't have was the one she found herself wanting more than anything in the world?

This was just another example that confirmed her opinion that fairness was nothing more than a fairy tale.

The conference room was already full when they arrived. Jazz and Xavier were engaged in a private conversation in a corner. Sean was talking to Liam Stryker, who still had a nasty bruise on his jaw. Rose and Serena were sitting beside each other, reading something on a laptop.

When Ash closed the door, every one of them stopped what they were doing and went on alert. It wasn't the first time she'd seen the OZ team react to their leader this way, but it again reinforced her opinion that Asher Drake not only had their respect, but also their loyalty.

"Sorry for the short notice. Everyone take a seat, and we'll get started. Schrader called. He's got the auction scheduled for two weeks from today. That'll give us time to put all our covers into place and run through several scenarios."

"Did he name names…say who will be at the auction?" Liam asked.

"He didn't mention any specific players, but I anticipate talking with him again to see if I can wheedle out a name or two. He's throwing a slight wrench into the plan, but it may end up working to our advantage. He's holding some kind of gala the same night. So while everyone is enjoying the party in one part of the house, there will be a party of another kind in another section."

"You think the invited guests will have any idea what he's up to?" Jazz asked.

"Some probably will. A few will likely attend both. I doubt that will include Carl Lang, but who the hell knows with Omar?"

"I'll get our people to start digging," Serena said. "Check the usual suspects. Somebody has got to have access to a guest list."

"Do that. I doubt Omar is going to be so forthcoming as to share every name with me, but I'll do my best to get some of the main players." His eyes continued to focus on Serena. "Also, be on the lookout for chatter. Any kind of talk about either the auction or the party would give us a leg up.

"Dig deep on the dark web. Look out for anything about possible big events. All these people, both famous and infamous, in one place will make it a prime target for their rivals. An uninvited guest, or even one who plans to attend, might take this as an opportunity to take down their competition."

Serena nodded. "Will do."

"So not only are we going to nab Lang, there's a possibility of getting caught in the crossfire of rivals?" Jules said.

"Exactly. That's why this will involve everyone. Whatever special projects any of you have pending need to be put on hold until this is over. If you've got one that's coming to a head, see me after the meeting, and let's talk."

"Will Eve and Gideon be back in time?" Serena asked.

"I talked to Eve yesterday," Jazz said. "She said Gideon's doing well in rehab, and he's as grouchy as an old bear."

A slight grin tugged at Ash's face. "Which means he's getting back to normal. I talked to him a couple of days ago. He's ready to get back to work. He's still on crutches, but knowing Gideon, that's just another weapon he can use. We'll put him with Serena on comms."

"What about Eve?" Jazz asked. "Will she be coming home, too?"

"Yeah. She said she's ready to get back to work. She and Liam will team up and attend as a couple." Ash turned to Rose. "Omar indicated there will be some famous Hollywood faces at the event. Create a cover for Stryker and Eve. Nothing too bold. Up-and-coming power couple—film producers should work. Make their films somewhat obscure so people won't be surprised they've never heard of them. Maybe give them a new project. They can attend the event as if they're looking for financing.

"Xavier and Jazz will be on overwatch. Stone will attend with me as Elsa. Seems Omar has taken a liking to the woman who helped save his life."

Ash was giving her more credit than she deserved, but Jules only gave a small nod of acknowledgment. The nightmares of killing Renee had disappeared. Though she wouldn't ever look forward to taking another life, no matter how evil, she sincerely hoped that she handled the aftermath better. It hadn't been her finest moment.

"All right. Let's start talking scenarios, problems and solutions."

With those words, the OZ leader was giving everyone a chance to voice their opinions and suggestions. As Jules listened, she became even more energized. No matter what happened in the future, she couldn't help being glad that she was involved with this project and with the OZ team. They were going to apprehend one of the world's most dangerous monsters. That, if nothing else, made the future pain worthwhile.

# CHAPTER TWENTY-NINE

**Washington, DC**

Her mouth bone-dry, Nora stared at the caller ID on her ringing phone. Chewing her lip, she hesitated, her finger poised over the answer icon. She could let it go to voice mail. Not only was she preparing an important speech before the entire Senate, she was on numerous committees. She was an extremely busy woman with little free time. Not answering a call should be the norm, not the exception.

Unfortunately, the person on the other end of this call likely knew her schedule better than she did. Even knew about her meetings before she did and what she would say. If she didn't answer, there would be a discussion. Speculation. Concern. That was the last thing she wanted.

Knowing she had no choice, Nora swiped the answer icon and said, "Yes?"

"How are things on your end?"

There was never any unnecessary chatter, no lead-in to the reason for the call. Though her profession required her to be verbal, sometimes to the extreme, Nora had no problem reverting to this type of pointed conversation.

"Nothing as of yet. I'm hopeful I'll hear something soon."

"Hopeful?"

Nora winced at the question. *Hopeful* was not a good word in this situation.

"Confident. I'm confident I'll hear something soon."

"I don't need to reiterate the importance of this matter."

The statement was rhetorical, but Nora knew to answer anyway. "I understand completely."

"Then, considering what lies in the future, don't you think it's time to take things to the next level?"

Again, this was not a question, nor a suggestion. Arguing would do no good. Besides, getting the go-ahead was a relief. This thing with Asher Drake had been hanging over her head for much too long.

"The problem will be handled."

"It can be handled for you."

She knew exactly what that meant. The consequences would be catastrophic. If she couldn't handle this one small problem, how could she handle future, larger issues?

"No. No. I will take care of it."

"Soon?"

"Yes. Soon."

"And you believe your employee can handle this matter without implicating you?"

"Without a doubt."

"Excellent. You have a committee meeting in ten minutes, so I won't keep you."

The statement wasn't said out of politeness or generosity. It was a reminder that everything she did, no matter how minute, was monitored.

"Goodbye, Nora."

Nora didn't bother with a farewell. She dropped the

phone onto her desk and drew in a ragged sigh. She did indeed have a meeting to attend, and two more after that. She wouldn't be able to communicate with Jessie Diamond until late tonight. And when she did, it wouldn't be to ask for an update. Her orders had changed.

Asher Drake must die.

# CHAPTER THIRTY

**OZ Headquarters**

S haking the last of the dampness from his head, Ash walked into the main house, noting the silence. Yesterday afternoon, Mother Nature had dumped a foot of snow on half the state. All OZ employees would be working from home for the next couple of days at least.

Fortunately they were ready for their next op. For the past nine days they'd worked their tails off preparing for the auction and the takedown of Carl Lang. Every scenario had been discussed and practiced numerous times.

He'd used his new Polaris snowmobile to get here from his house and had enjoyed every moment. One of the reasons he'd wanted to move here was winter. With snowfall averaging about forty-five inches a year, the amount was almost enough to satisfy him.

A noise in another room reminded him that the building wasn't completely empty. As if he needed the reminder. There were very few waking moments that he wasn't aware of Jules. And lately, she'd appeared in a couple of his dreams.

Telling himself he couldn't get involved with an OZ employee hadn't made much impact on his libido. Good thing he was old enough to control those urges. Any relationship between him and Jules Stone would never work. She had too many secrets, and he went from one viper nest to the next. Neither of them was a candidate for anything stable.

"Ash?" Jules said behind him. "How did you get here?"

"Snowmobile."

Turning, he got his first full view of Jules and had to work to keep a straight face. How anyone who was wearing at least four layers of clothes could still be so enticing was a mystery. She wore a thick navy sweatshirt over a flannel shirt over a turtleneck sweater. Getting a jacket on over all of that must've been a struggle. She wore sweatpants, but beneath those pants he caught a glimpse of jeans. Her head was covered with a ski cap, and she was carrying a pair of heavy boots in her gloved hands. She would quite likely have difficultly getting them on over the thick socks she was wearing.

He nodded at her apparel. "Feeling a little chilly?"

She grinned and tried to shrug, but the multiple layers kept her from being able to move much. "I know I look ridiculous, but this is the first time I've been warm all morning."

Noting that the temperature in the house was warmer than usual, he said, "It feels warm in here to me. Are you getting sick?"

"No, I'm just trying to thaw out. I had to get something out of my car, so I just threw on a jacket, thinking it wouldn't be that bad. I slipped and fell into a snowdrift. By the time I got back into the house, I was soaked."

"You okay?"

"I'm fine. Just decided wearing everything I own was the best way to warm up."

"Is it working?"

"Think so, but I'm not taking anything off until I'm completely sure."

"I take it you're not a cold-weather fan?"

"It's one of the reasons I moved to Arizona."

Ash frowned. "Jules, you do know that the area of Arizona you lived in gets a lot of snow, don't you?"

Her face lighting up with laughter, she shook her head. "I didn't until I moved there. I visited during the summer and impulsively decided to move there. I ended up falling in love with the area and decided I'd learn to live with the snow."

"It can be fun if you're dressed right. I'll take you out on my snowmobile sometime."

She smiled again but didn't answer. He got the feeling it would take a lot of encouragement to get her to enjoy snow the way it was meant to be enjoyed.

"What about breakfast? You have any yet?"

"I was just headed to the kitchen for some cereal."

"You can't have cold cereal on a day like this. Especially after falling into a snowdrift. Come keep me company while I whip us up a hearty winter breakfast."

Not waiting for a reply, Ash headed to the kitchen. He hadn't planned on cooking breakfast. He wasn't hungry… he'd had some cereal and a bagel at home. But he hadn't been able to turn away from her and go to his office. The thought of her eating cold cereal alone in the kitchen while he worked in his office didn't sit right with him. He didn't try to analyze why.

The kitchen was one of the largest rooms in the place. The original owner had been a rancher with dreams of filling the house with a large family. Instead, his wife had died young, and the brokenhearted man had never remarried. Ash had read about the man before he'd seen this place. Didn't take a psychiatrist to explain why he'd identified with a man he'd never met.

Jules stood in the doorway as he went about his work. From time to time, he glanced at her, wondering if she would ever sit down. Then a thought came to him. "Can you sit down in those clothes?"

She flushed a perfect pink and shook her head. "Not well."

"The oven is heating the kitchen up. Why don't you discard a few layers and see if you'll be comfortable?"

When he turned back around, he was pleased to see she'd discarded the jacket, cap, scarf, and sweatpants and looked a lot more comfortable. He nodded toward the table. "Have a seat. It'll be ready in about five minutes."

"I can make coffee." Showing she was familiar with the kitchen, she grabbed the canister from the cabinet. They worked in companionable silence for several minutes. Once the coffee was brewed, she poured two cups and set them on the table.

"Where did you learn to cook?" she asked.

"My mom. After my dad left home, it was just her and me. We took turns."

"Your father abandoned your family?"

"Not exactly. I finally got big enough to kick him out."

"He was abusive?"

"Oh yeah."

"I'm sorry."

"We got through it. We had each other. And good friends and neighbors."

"Is he still alive?"

"No." Ash didn't elaborate. The old bastard wasn't worth the breath required to tell her how he'd died.

Apparently sensing a change in subject was needed, she said, "Does the team use this kitchen often?"

"On occasion, we'll pull an all-nighter. Rose has fresh

food delivered weekly, so we always have something on hand. What food we don't use goes to a food pantry in Missoula."

"Whatever you're making smells delicious."

"Cold-weather food is the best."

"I agree. My mom used to make the best vegetable soup."

He glanced over his shoulder. "You don't talk about your parents. They died in a car accident a few years back?"

"Yes." Her eyes met his. "It was horrific."

"I'm sorry. Losing a parent is rough."

"Your mom's gone, too?"

"Yes, about seven years ago. Cancer."

"We've both lost a lot."

"Yeah." Hoping to dispel the grim silence, Ash placed two plates loaded with eggs, bacon, fried potatoes, and biscuits on the table. "Maybe this'll warm you up."

"Oh my." Her eyes wide, she shook her head. "I'll never be able to eat all of this."

"Eat what you can."

Suddenly ravenous himself, Ash sat down and dug in. After a few moments, he looked up, pleased to see that she'd done a decent job on her own plate.

Catching his eye, she grinned. "I've never eaten that much at one sitting. It was delicious. Thank you." She sat back in her chair with a pleasure-filled sigh. "And I think I've finally warmed up, too. Not sure I've ever been that cold."

"It can get dangerous out there. Best not to go out there without telling someone."

"Did you grow up in Montana?"

"No. Little town in Wisconsin. We got plenty of snow there, too, but I like the combination of the mountains and snow."

"Kate told me that you're an avid skier."

"Used to be. Haven't had the chance in a while."

"OZ doesn't have much downtime, does it?"

"Yes and no. We're not on ops every day but enough so that finding time to go on an extended trip isn't easy."

"The other day, during our initial meeting about the Lang op, you said something about special projects. What does that mean? Do your people work ops on their own?"

"Sometimes. They have a lot of leeway, so if they see something they feel needs attention, they're free to do so. Our main priority when we set up OZ was the autonomy of each individual. When we have a major mission, like the Lang op, everyone drops what they're doing. Once this is over, they'll go back to their individual projects. If they need a team member or the entire team to step in and help, that's what we do."

"That takes a lot of trust."

Taking one last bite of his meal, Ash took a long swallow of coffee before he pondered her statement out loud. "We're all in this together. Just because I'm team leader doesn't mean my opinion is more important than anyone else's. I took on the task of leading OZ because I had the contacts, but any one of the team is fully capable of running an op."

"How did you get the contacts?"

"Kate was instrumental at the beginning. She helped me make some connections. From there, it grew."

"I know you've been friends with Xavier, Liam, Gideon, and Sean for a long time, but how did Eve, Serena, and Jazz come to OZ?"

"Jazz was like you—one of Kate's recommendations. Eve and Gideon have known each other for years. They were partners in a similar line of work. When Gideon came on, he brought Eve with him.

"Serena was working for the State Department when she started dating Sean. When OZ started up, he brought her over."

"And Hawke…you lost him a few years back? Was that on an op?"

"Yes." Since discussing that particular op and what had happened between Hawke and his wife, Olivia, was definitely on a need-to-know basis, Ash stood and began to clear the table.

"I'm sorry you lost your friend."

"I am, too."

"I can clean up. It's the least I can do after that delicious meal."

Appreciating the out, Ash nodded. "Thanks. I've got some work to do in my office. Once you're finished, we can review some notes Gideon sent over."

"Sounds good."

Jules watched Ash leave. Having done the same thing many times herself, she easily recognized his excuse to work for what it was. He needed to get away. They'd been talking about losing his friend and a fellow OZ operative. Were the wounds still too fresh to talk about them, or was there more to Nick Hawthorne's story?

Kate had briefly mentioned Hawke not long after OZ lost him, but she'd known few of the details. Just that Nick Hawthorne and his wife, Olivia Gates, both OZ operatives, had been on an op together. The mission had ended badly, with Hawke dead and Olivia leaving OZ. Whatever had happened was obviously still painful for Ash.

It was becoming apparent that Ash and his OZ team had almost as many secrets as she did.

As she cleaned up their breakfast dishes, she thought about the decision she'd come to last night. She was going to tell Ash everything. She owed him the truth. Yes, her reasons for not being truthful at first had been valid, but as she had worked with Ash and his team this week, she had realized something: If she was going to trust these people with her life and expect their trust in return, then she needed to be honest about her reasons for being here.

Kate had believed that once he learned what Turner was trying to do, Ash would go after her full force.

Having gotten to know Ash, Jules disagreed. He was too levelheaded to do anything rash, so she no longer had a reason to keep secrets. She trusted Ash to do the right thing.

What that would do to their working relationship remained to be seen. Though she would love to stay at OZ, he would probably tell her to leave. She wouldn't blame him for that. Trust came hard for people who had been betrayed. Learning she had lied about her past would be hard to forgive. Finding out why she'd lied would be even more so.

On a personal level, she didn't want to leave him, ever. These few weeks with Ash had been almost dreamlike. The spark of attraction she'd felt at their first meeting had grown into a wildfire. She'd liked and admired Asher Drake long before she met him, and now that she'd gotten to know him, she knew without a doubt that she was in love with him. How it had happened…why it had happened was inexplicable. She only knew that if he told her to leave, her heart would break into thousands of pieces.

She couldn't let that stop her. Ash deserved the truth.

Now that she had made that decision, she wanted to get it done. Come clean with everything. But she couldn't, not yet. The mission to capture Lang had been in the works for months. It was much too important to let personal issues get in the way now. She and the OZ team had built up trust this week. Throwing a wrench into that trust at this point could cause major issues. She couldn't take the risk.

When the op was over, she'd tell Ash everything, and then if he wanted her to, she'd tell the team together or individually. However he preferred. And since the mission was scheduled to begin four days from now, she would use any free time to come up with the right way to tell her story.

She headed toward Ash's office, thinking about the words she'd need to explain things. Confessing that she had fooled Turner into believing she would get intel on Ash to ruin him wouldn't be exactly easy, but she believed she could make him understand before he threw her out the door. The other part, the part where she told him who she really was and why she felt indebted to him, would be one of the hardest conversations she'd ever had—maybe even more difficult than telling him of her parents' murders and her abduction by a serial killer named John Leland Clark.

CHAPTER THIRTY-ONE

They worked through the day into early evening, reviewing the differing scenarios and making alternative plans in case things went awry. Ash always enjoyed coordinating an op. The best planning had to allow for human error and the FUBAR factor, but when it all came together and worked perfectly, there was nothing like the rush.

The gleam in Jules's eyes matched his own enthusiasm. She had made some excellent suggestions and offered some insight into Omar's thinking that he hadn't considered.

"So you think Omar is intimidated by Humphrey?"

"I do. When we were at his house, he did everything he could to try to impress you. From showing you his home, to the meal he had prepared for us. And when he announced his special guest, his excitement was more than being able to pull off a surprise. I think he wanted to please you."

"That's a keen observation. Makes me wonder how Humphrey can use it to his advantage."

"Perhaps he can suggest that, as a special favor, Elsa could attend the auction as well. She's already going to the gala. Seems only fair she get to see the other part, too."

Ash grinned, seeing through her ruse. "You worried about me, Stone?"

"You'll be surrounded by some of the most evil people on earth. Any one of them wouldn't blink an eye to kill you if given the slightest hint that you're not who you say you are. Having me right there with you, watching your back, keeping eyes and ears open to any nuances, would be helpful."

She had a point. "I'll see how Humphrey can work that into the conversation." He glanced at his watch. "It's getting late. I'd better head home."

"Why don't you stay for dinner? I'll cook this time. You can clean up."

He had to admit that going back to an empty house and eating alone held no appeal.

"You've got yourself a deal."

He told himself having dinner with her was nothing. They were two grown adults who needed to eat. They could keep discussing the upcoming mission. It would be a working dinner, nothing more.

Ash set the table and then, at her request, sat down and let her work. Jules cooked the way she did everything else, with efficiency and imagination. He watched, intrigued, as she sprinkled different spices with what seemed like liberal abandon into a skillet, then added cream, some kind of shredded cheese, and a couple more surprising ingredients. He had no idea what she was making, but by the time she set the meal on the table, the fragrance was almost overwhelming, and he was starving.

Ash attacked the meal like a ravenous lion and didn't look up for several minutes. Once he did, he couldn't contain his awe. "What is this?"

"Pasta carbonara." She shrugged. "My version of it anyway. Do you like it?"

"Yeah…a lot. Where did you learn to cook like this?"

Her delight was obvious. "I've always loved creating different dishes. I took some classes and discovered I have a talent for combining spices. I never realized it was an art form…I just like experimenting."

"Feel free to experiment on me any time you like."

He hadn't meant the words as a come-on, but they'd sounded that way all the same. Jules's eyes widened slightly, and she blushed a pretty pink.

"Sorry, that sounded weird."

She laughed, not taking any offense at his unintended sexual innuendo. What she said next totally destroyed any errant sensual thoughts. "Tell me about Meg."

SHE WATCHED the smile slide from his face and the light go out of his eyes. She had spoiled the lighthearted mood and wanted to kick herself for her ill-timed question. But it was out there, and she couldn't call it back, so she waited for his reply.

"What do you want to know?"

"What was she like? Where did you meet?"

"She was sweet, funny, intelligent. We met when we were ten years old. Her family moved next door. Our mothers became best friends, so we got thrown together a lot."

"You were childhood sweethearts?"

"Not until our sophomore year of high school. Her dad died, and I don't know…I guess we realized how short life is. We started dating and never dated anyone else after that.

"I joined the Marines right after high school. We got married right before my first deployment. Meg went to college, got her nursing degree."

"How long were you married…before…" She trailed off. She couldn't even make herself say the words.

Ash had no such problems, but the anger was evident in his voice. "Before she was brutally murdered by a serial killer? Thirteen years."

"I'm sorry."

Letting her know he was done sharing, he stood and began to clear the table. Jules sat still for several moments, wanting to say more. Wanting more than she'd ever thought she could want. If she could only work up the courage to take that final step.

"I'd better get out of here."

Surprised, she glanced around the kitchen and saw that while she'd been lost in thought, Ash had cleaned and straightened up the kitchen.

"Don't go." The words sprang from her mouth before she could stop them.

"What?"

"It's late and unimaginably cold out there. There's plenty of room here." She shrugged, hoping she looked nonchalant. "Why not stay the night?"

Instead of answering immediately, he surprised her by holding out his hand. Her heart pounding, she put her hand in his and allowed him to pull her up. They were standing toe-to-toe, inches from each other. She could feel his breath on her face, the heat from his body.

Raising her eyes to his, she took a huge risk and whispered, "Stay with me, Ash."

He gave a low, growling groan. Lowering his head, he touched his lips to hers, softly, gently, testing, teasing. Pressed against his hard body, Jules returned the kisses, telling him things she couldn't say aloud.

"What the hell are we doing, Jules?"

"I don't know, but please don't stop."

"This is crazy." He punctuated every protest with a brief, hot kiss. "Insane." Another hot kiss. "Out-of-this-world wrong."

"Can't be." Breathlessly accepting every kiss, she gloried in the feelings surging through her. Never in her life had she felt this way. Heat and need surged through every pore. "Nothing this good could be wrong."

ASH GAVE UP THE FIGHT. Responsibility and clear-minded focus had always been his mainstay. Loyalty, honor, and doing the right thing no matter how difficult had been his beacon in the darkest times. For tonight, just for tonight, he shoved all of that aside and took what he wanted, what he had been craving from the moment he'd met Jules Stone.

Holding her slender body against his, Ash devoured her mouth, relishing the soft, lush sweetness. His tongue plunged into the depths of that sweet heat, dancing, mating with hers. Waves of need rolled through him, and wanting to take Jules with him, he skimmed his hands over her body, taking her clothes along the way. When his fingers reached silken skin, they paused, tested, aroused, then soothed.

"Ash, please…"

The whimper did something to him, destroying any hesitation. Scooping her into his arms, Ash left the kitchen and headed for a bedroom. He stopped at the one Jules was using. With one hand, he opened the door, strode through, and then closed it behind him with a kick. Instead of placing her on the bed, he dropped her feet to the floor. He wanted to see her…all of her.

She was beautiful. Her eyes glittered with need and heat, her face was flushed a light pink, and her mouth curved up into a sensuous invitation. One he couldn't resist. Lowering his head, he pressed his mouth to that smile, loving the way her lips curved even more.

"Just so you know," she whispered, "it's been a long time for me."

"It's been a while for me, too. I don't think anything's changed, though."

She laughed softly. "Good to know."

"You're absolutely sure about this? We don't have to if you—"

Her fingers pressed against his mouth. "I can't think of anything I want more. I feel like I've waited a lifetime for this."

"Then let's not wait any longer." He barely remembered taking his clothes off, but he remembered every second of Jules removing hers. When they'd showered together, he had forced himself not to look at her, but now his eyes made up for what he had missed. She was slender without being thin, strength and courage hidden beneath beautiful, silken curves. When he'd first met her, he had thought her body was likely covered in tiny freckles like those on her face and shoulders. He'd been right. Suddenly, he couldn't think of anything he'd rather do than to kiss each one of them.

Holding out his hand, he led her to the bed.

# CHAPTER THIRTY-TWO

Wrapped in Ash's arms, warm and safe, Jules couldn't imagine a more perfect place. Making love with a man like Asher Drake demolished any other sexual pleasure she'd ever experienced. Those other times, few though they were, were like vague, insipid apparitions of the real thing. Both tender and fiercely passionate, Ash had given her the kind of pleasure one only dreams is possible. She had never believed it would be possible for her.

Her brutal experiences years ago had rotted any good thoughts of a healthy physical relationship for a long time. It was only after years of therapy and meditation that she was able to stomach a man's touch. And when she had reached the point where passion overcame fear, there had been no feelings or emotions behind the actions. It had been a physical release and nothing more. Meaningless.

With Ash…everything was different. Before she had met him, she had admired him greatly. After meeting him, working with him, getting to know him, that admiration had grown a thousandfold. The man, even with his autocratic ways and stubbornness, was the hero of her dreams.

The optimism she'd felt earlier was slowly dwindling beneath the doubts and fears. With so many lies between them, how could there be any hope for a good outcome?

"Hey, what was that heavy sigh for? You bored already?"

She nuzzled his neck, loving his scent, the warmth of his skin. "Never."

"Sorry about the condom thing. When I was younger, I was never without one. But the last few years, it seemed pointless to carry one around."

That had been one of the sweetest, funniest moments of the night. In the midst of a need so heated she'd felt as if the world could explode, he'd lifted his head and confessed he had no protection. The look on his face had been both comical and incredibly touching. Even though it would have been painful for him, she'd known without a doubt that he'd been willing to stop.

She had been more than happy to explain that it was not a problem.

"My birth control is sufficient. Besides, I think we were doing quite well without one. You're very good at improvising."

"Thanks. I was motivated."

She laughed softly and then cut her eyes up to look at him. "You said it had been a while for you, too."

"Yeah." He grinned down at her. "You could tell?"

She shook her head. "It was perfect in every way."

He rewarded her compliment with a kiss, and Jules gave herself up to the beauty of the now. Worrying about the future could wait.

Several long moments later, she settled back into Ash's arms. They were quiet, peaceful, and then Ash began to talk.

"Meg died saving my life."

She pulled her head back and looked up at him, genuinely

shocked. She had thought she knew everything about that night.

"How?"

"We were supposed to go to the lake together. I got called into a late meeting. She decided to go on without me, said she'd set things up and get dinner started. I called her from the office to tell her I was on the way. She picked a fight with me. Told me she was tired of my late nights and excuses. Of me always putting my work first. That she wanted some time to herself. Told me to stay away.

"I hesitated. Dammit. I hesitated. Maybe if I hadn't…" He shook his head. "Meg and I had been having some issues. Having an argument with her about my long hours didn't seem that much of a stretch. It wasn't the first time, but I should have realized something was different about this one. We had agreed to go away together…to try to work things out, and then she told me not to bother.

"The coroner figured Clark probably killed her right after she spoke with me." His voice went emotionless, and she knew he was fighting back the pain. "She had forty-two stab wounds. He was in a rage, no doubt because she had tried to keep me away."

"But you left for the lake immediately after talking to her."

"Yeah. Not that it did any good."

"You couldn't have saved her."

"If I had been there when he arrived, I could have. I put my work before my marriage. Before Meg."

"Ash, you know in your heart of hearts that's not true."

"If I hadn't pursued Turner, Meg wouldn't have died."

As if he couldn't handle having this conversation while she was in his arms, he released her and sat up in the bed. Jules moved away slightly, but unable to bring herself to totally break their contact, she kept one of her legs inter-locked with his.

Ash stared into space, and she could easily imagine the hell he was seeing in his mind.

"I should have let it go."

"You had every right to demand justice for those men."

"It was a long, bloody battle. I don't know if that was their plan—that we all die or if they literally never thought about us again."

"How many died there?"

"Five. I was the only survivor. Although there were plenty of days I wished I'd died with them."

"What happened?"

"I was captured, questioned. They were excited to have an American. I didn't tell them I was a Marine. That would've made them way too happy. They had some fun with me. I lost consciousness. Next time I woke up, I was in Syria."

"Syria? But how?"

"Cartel had no interest in me other than the money I could bring them. They sold me to some terrorists, who had their own agenda."

She knew there was much more to the story. Knew that he'd been questioned, beaten numerous times. He had barely survived. They had planned to use him as propaganda, a bargaining chip.

Pain and anger dripped from every word he'd shared, but she let him tell the story the way he needed to.

"Liam and Xavier were being held hostage in a prison there. Hawke, Sean, and Gideon broke in and got us out."

"They knew you were there, too?"

"No, I was a stranger to them. They came to rescue Liam and Xavier. I was lucky enough to be in the right place at the right time."

Kate had given her a few of the details. The men had barely made it out of Syria alive. The mission had been a covert, undercover op to rescue two Americans who had been given up for dead. If things had gone sideways, they all would have died. Instead, they'd fought their way out of hell together.

"When I returned home, I was determined to find the people responsible for what went down in Colombia. I searched everywhere and could find no evidence of the meeting ever taking place, much less find the people involved. I looked up the guy we were protecting, and it wasn't the same man. These people used fake names, fake everything. I was at a dead end. I finally gave up looking, until one day I turned on the television and saw one of the people who was at the meeting."

"Nora Turner?"

"Yeah. She wasn't a US senator yet…still a state representative. The thing in Colombia would've happened before she even got into politics. At that time, she was CEO of a tech company."

"Tech Now."

"You know it?"

"Yes, it's a huge company. From my understanding, she spring-loaded her political career through the company and her success in running it."

"Yeah, she's a smart businesswoman. She's also rotten to the core."

"What did you do when you found out who she was?"

"I made an appointment with her, told her I knew she was there in Colombia. She denied it, of course. Told me I was delusional."

"But that wasn't when you had to leave the FBI, was it?"

"No. That was after Meg's death. I did back away for a while though. We were finally closing in on finding a serial killer."

She didn't flinch and even managed to calmly murmur, "The Dear Lucy killer—John Leland Clark."

Odd how she could feel no emotion in using the moniker the press had given the bastard. She could even say his real name without flinching. Without revulsion or pain. She had separated herself from that ravaged, damaged person so well that she could discuss the case as if it was just that…a case.

Some would call it denial. She called it survival.

Ash blew out a long breath. "The son of a bitch had been killing for almost five years, eluding authorities at every turn. I'd been working on the case a few months and then got tapped to head it up after Kate left. We finally found Clark, took him down. I thought it was all behind us."

"And then he escaped."

"Yeah."

"And you believe it was Turner who arranged his escape."

"I don't think it…I know it. I just can't prove it…at least not yet."

"How can you be sure it was Turner you saw in Colombia and not just someone who looked like her?"

"Because right before the building exploded, I picked her up and carried her out the door. She was being trampled. I got a close-up of her. And if that didn't convince me, as I was carrying her out, I saw she had a cut on her left arm. The scar is still visible today."

Yes, she had seen the scar. It would have been a nasty cut, but it could have been so much worse. How ironic that Turner wanted to destroy the man who'd saved her life.

"Kate was one of the few who believed me. She's been working behind the scenes, looking for the other people who were at the meeting. Trying to find out what the meeting was about. We're doing the same on our end. We won't stop until we get justice for those we lost."

"What about the men's families? The ones who died? What explanation were they given?"

"They were told different accounts. The family of Yeager Bates, the friend who hired me for the job, was told he died in a car crash. There are records of the accident. If I didn't know for a fact that it was all a lie, I'd believe it, too.

"But I do know what happened. I was there with him when he took his last breath."

Though she longed to give him assurances, promises, she couldn't. Not yet. All she could do was hold him close and hope that it brought him some comfort.

"After I recovered, I went back there...to the meeting site. There was nothing left. The building was razed. It was like it never existed. I could prove nothing."

"Turner went to an awful lot of trouble and expense to cover everything up. Do you think she did it alone?"

"Absolutely not. Every one of those people knows what happened. Problem is, Turner is the only one I've ever found."

"How can I help?"

"You help just by listening. It's been a while since I've been able to talk about this without rage taking over."

A rush of nausea went through Jules as she realized something monumental had happened here. Ash had told her all of this because he trusted her. If she were truly working with Turner, she could ask a few more pointed questions and get what she needed to destroy Ash and maybe OZ along with him.

But she wasn't working for Turner. She was working against her.

Never had Jules been so torn. Would it be selfish of her to tell him everything now? Locked in his arms, she could explain everything she'd done and why. Could she make him understand? Or would telling him ruin everything? In a few days, the entire OZ team would be involved in their biggest takedown to date. If Ash was unable to get past her lies, he might push her off the op, jeopardizing the entire mission.

As much as she wanted to spill her guts, she couldn't. Not yet. But she swore to herself that the moment Carl Lang had been taken into custody, she would come clean with everything.

Since she could do nothing about it now, Jules turned in Ash's arms and showed him how very much she appreciated his trust in her.

# CHAPTER THIRTY-THREE

A snowball slammed into the back of his head, exploding on impact. Ash turned just in time to see the triumphant expression on Jules's face before she zoomed another icy projectile toward him. Laughing at her antics, he dodged it at the last minute. She was good.

But he was better.

Running for cover, he grabbed a handful of snow on the way. By the time he made it to the giant aspen tree, he had a hand-size, frozen missile. Peering around the tree, he spotted his target and launched. The snowball landed on her shoulder and exploded, covering her in snow.

Delighted laughter pealed through the forest as they lobbed snowballs at each other, often sending taunting remarks as a shot landed.

A snowball fight hadn't been on his agenda this morning. When he'd woken, Jules had been snug and warm in his arms, still asleep. He'd lain there for a long while, contemplating one thing: Everything had changed last night.

Waking up with a warm body beside him had been a long-forgotten pleasure. He hadn't shared that kind of intimacy with anyone but Meg. After he'd lost her, he hadn't wanted to be with another woman for a long time. Yeah, the physical need was there, but squashing those desires had been easy. Being with anyone other than his wife held no appeal.

It had been years before he'd been able to even share the slightest intimacy, like a kiss, and even then he'd felt as if he were betraying Meg. When he'd finally slept with another woman, he walked away after the deed and never saw her again. He had enough of a heart to call and apologize, but that had been all he could offer.

Now, with Jules, he felt like a new person. He really, sincerely liked this woman. Liked being with her, talking with her. Liked working with her. He enjoyed seeing her eyes light up when she was talking about an op. She had a dry sense of humor and a sometimes unique way of looking at the world.

And he especially liked the way she felt in his arms.

"Hey, Drake! You ready to surrender?"

The taunting question was followed by a giant, thankfully loose snowball, which splattered over his face like an ice-cold shower. A good wake-up.

A battalion of snowballs leading his way, Ash went after her with everything he had, hurling snowball after snowball as he strode toward her. She was so busy dodging and giggling, he was on her before she could retaliate.

When he reached her, she looked both surprised and irritated that he'd managed to outwit her. Though the snowsuit covered her from head to toe, he figured she was beginning to get a chill. They'd been out here for over an hour.

"You don't fight fair."

Ash laughed at the childish words and the lovely little pout of lips. Pulling her into his arms, he covered that beautiful mouth with his in a fiery kiss. When she wrapped her arms around him, he tumbled them both into the snow.

Devouring her lips, Ash felt a peace he hadn't believed he'd ever feel again.

Squealing and laughing at the same time, Jules rolled over in Ash's arms. Looking down at his smiling face, she couldn't remember when she'd been happier. Last night had been a dream come true, and today was pure magic.

After breakfast, Ash had persuaded her to go with him to his house. She had resisted at first. She was so not a snow person. Finally, she had relented and was glad she had. Riding with him on his snowmobile had been a blast. In fact, she was hoping he'd let her drive it back to headquarters.

Ash's house had been another surprise. She had expected a small cottage, maybe even a cabin. She was thrilled to see it was a traditional-style two-story red brick house with a large wraparound porch, complete with rocking chairs and a porch swing.

The décor was basic. Nothing extravagant or fancy, but extremely comfortable all the same. The oversize leather sofa, large fireplace with a giant flat-screen TV hanging above it, spoke of comfort and not a lot of flash. Definitely her style of living.

She could see herself staying here with him forever. The minute the idea flashed in her head, she squashed it. That kind of thinking was too dangerous to even contemplate. She knew what she wanted and where her heart lay, but she had no idea about Ash.

Not wanting to ruin what had so far been a truly spectacular day with what might happen in the future, she focused on the here and now, giving him her brightest smile.

"What are you grinning about?" Ash asked. "I won the battle."

Pulling him down to her for another kiss, she whispered softly, "That's because I let you."

He raised his head. "Excuse me?"

"Ha! Gotcha!"

Laughing, he rolled her over onto her back again and kissed her. Ignoring the cold, ignoring the problems that faced her, Jules gave herself up to the sheer beauty of being in love for the first time in her life.

"That's not even a word!"

Ash grinned at Jules's indignation. When he was a kid, he and his mother had spent hours at the Scrabble board. It had been her favorite game. After his dad had finally gotten out of the picture, there had been a lot more laughter in the house. Playing word games had been one of her favorite ways to unwind after a long day at work. Ash would have done anything for her. She had sacrificed so much to keep him safe.

"It's definitely a word." He slid the dictionary across the table. "Read it and weep."

Eyes narrowed with suspicion, she grabbed the dictionary and began to turn pages. Ash watched her face as she found the word. He'd noticed when she was concentrating, she got the cutest wrinkle right at the bridge of her nose.

Sighing, she slammed the book closed. "How on earth does anyone know that word?"

"What? I use it in conversations all the time."

"Oh yeah? Give me a sentence using it."

"No problem. I'm surprised to learn that, despite Juliet

Stone's obvious intelligence, she's never heard the word absquatulate."

Jules sputtered. "That's cheating."

"Hey, you asked me to use it in a sentence."

"Very well." She rearranged some tiles on her Scrabble tray and then placed them on the board. "I hate to get rough with you, Mr. Drake, but here you go."

"Wabbit?" He eyed her carefully. "Isn't that what Elmer Fudd calls Bugs Bunny?"

"Maybe." Her lips twitched, telling him she was working hard not to laugh. "But it's an actual word, too."

"Okay, then you use it in a sentence." He raised his hand. "And don't use my sentence. I own that one."

"After a long day of hunting down bad guys, Asher Drake was wabbit."

"Like, I actually turned into one?"

She rolled her eyes. "It's an adjective, not a noun."

"Give me that dictionary."

Glee twinkling in her eyes, she slid the book back across the table. "Now you read it and weep, Mr. Drake."

He found the word easily enough. It was a Scottish word meaning exhausted. Putting the book down with one hand, he used his other hand to grab Jules's wrist and pull her around to sit on his lap. "Asher Drake is not too wabbit for this."

"Good, because I'd hate to have to absquatulate."

"We've got three feet of snow at the door. No way could you absquatulate."

"Maybe if I turned into a wabbit, I could."

Shouting with laughter, Ash kissed her smiling mouth. She was sassy, sweet, and so damn appealing.

OZ headquarters had been closed for three days. A second snowstorm had come a day after the first one and added another half foot of the white stuff. All OZ personnel and operatives were still either working from home or taking time off. The snowstorm might have come at an inconvenient time, but it had also offered an unexpected and delightful consequence. Even though Ash had worked in his office, and he and Jules had reviewed the upcoming op ad nauseam, he'd still taken time for himself. Time to get to know Jules.

He'd learned she hated blueberries, but loved blueberry-flavored everything. She was an avid runner, could almost outshoot him, and could swim like a fish. She also had a quirky sense of humor. He'd laughed more over the last three days than he had in years. She made him happy, and if that wasn't one of the most shocking things he'd thought in a long time, he didn't know what was.

Without a doubt, or even an ounce of fear, he knew he'd fallen in love with her.

JULES RELEASED a sigh of sheer contentment as she sank into Ash's arms. If she could wrap up a period of time and hold on to it forever, she would choose these last few days. They had been as close to perfection as she had ever known. Every morning, she'd woken in Ash's arms, and every night she had gone to bed with his arms wrapped around her.

Getting to know Ash—the real Ash—had been sheer magic. The problems that lay before her had been put on the back burner. She had forced herself to let her worries go and live in the moment.

"What was that sigh about?"

She shrugged. "I really enjoyed these last few days being alone with you."

The team would be back tomorrow, and the next day they would be flying to Slovakia for the auction. As much as she anticipated the mission that would put an end to Carl Lang's evil, she couldn't help but feel regret that these idyllic days were almost over.

"We'll just have to make sure we find time to be alone again after the auction."

Warmth rushed through her blood. This was the closest he had come to telling her that these days together weren't an anomaly. That he wanted something more.

But there was a huge hurdle he didn't know about. One she had to cross before anything permanent could happen. The lies she'd told, though necessary at the time, stood between them like an invisible wall, blocking the way. Until she gave him the truth, nothing remotely resembling a future for them was possible.

The text she'd read last night was burned into her brain. Turner had apparently sent it a few days ago, and Jules had been lax in checking for messages. When she'd read it, fury had clashed with an overwhelming nausea. She had wanted nothing more than to call the woman and tell her exactly how vile she was. Instead, she had gone to the bathroom and thrown up. Then she had returned to her room and answered the text. Even though her hands had been shaking, she had managed a one-word answer. One that Turner would be happy to see. She'd then hidden the phone again and calmly returned to Ash as if nothing untoward had happened.

Jules didn't yet know how or when, but Nora Turner would regret every ounce of pain and misery she had caused Ash. That, she swore.

# CHAPTER THIRTY-FOUR

**Omar Schrader's Estate**
**Slovakia**

With the glitz and glamour that would rival any Hollywood event, Omar's gala was in full swing. Women wore gowns in a variety of colors that glittered beneath the giant chandeliers, making them look like brilliant, sparkling flowers. The tuxedoed men were a stark contrast to their vibrant beauty.

Once again, Ash's eyes veered over to his companion. Jules was a vision in sequins of silver blue and in his opinion outshone them all. Her gown's neckline was modest and gave only a small hint of cleavage, but the back of the dress had him catching his breath each time she turned from him. Creamy, golden skin with just a slight sprinkling of cinnamon-colored freckles glowed under the blazing lights. Several men had sent her searing glances. Ash had gladly sent a different kind of searing glance right back at each of them. He was playing the role of a cold-blooded arms dealer.

Humphrey did not take kindly to people trying to poach his property.

For the first time ever, he and Humphrey were of the same mind. Asher Drake didn't like the leering glances either.

Ice princess Elsa Olsen was back in full force, but Ash saw Jules as she was last night in his arms. The warm-blooded passionate woman had nothing in common with the coldly composed person beside him, except for one thing: They were both incredibly beautiful.

"Have I told you how lovely you look tonight?"

"Of course you have, darling. Several times."

Elsa's answer was cool, as if she was slightly bored with life in general.

"Not having a good time?"

"As much fun as anyone has at these events." Her eyes lit up as she turned to him. "I am looking forward to the event later tonight."

His smile was as cold as hers. "You're a bloodthirsty wench, aren't you?"

"Just the way you like me."

"That is true."

Omar had surprised him by agreeing to allow Elsa to attend the auction. Ash had thought he'd have to do more convincing, but it was apparent that Schrader was quite a fan of Elsa Olsen.

He subtly nodded to a corner across the room where they could talk without being overheard. Weaving through small pockets of people, Humphrey made little acknowledgment of speculating eyes. And Elsa stared through the others as if they didn't exist, showing that, without a doubt, they were a perfect match.

Stopping at the small alcove, he heard Jules inhale slightly and looked at her sharply. "You okay?"

"Yes," she said softly. "Neither Elsa nor Jules is a fan of large crowds."

"Humphrey and Ash agree with you both."

Taking a sip of her champagne, Jules asked, "Do you think everyone knows what's going on here?"

"Doubtful. Omar has a reputation for throwing lavish parties. He probably thinks it's amusing to have all these people out here enjoying themselves while people in another part of the house plot death and destruction."

"I hope you're right. Two of my favorite actors are over there, happily gobbling caviar."

Ash followed her gaze and though he recognized the young woman as the star of a television detective series, he didn't recognize the man.

"Who's the—"

His earwig dinged once. He had worried that they wouldn't be able to use their comms inside the house, but so far they hadn't had any issues. Once they entered the auction, he expected to lose contact.

"Ash, can you hear me?"

He glanced over at Jules and saw no indication that she'd heard Serena's voice. The ding had been his notice that all comms had been cut but his. He gave a grunt to let Serena know he'd heard.

"We've got a problem. Can you walk away from Stone for a moment?"

More confused than concerned, he asked Jules, "More champagne?"

Jules shook her head. "Ice-cold water would be heaven, if you can find some."

"Be right back."

Turning away from her, he headed toward the large double doors leading to a balcony. He stepped out, barely noting the cool, crisp night. "What's going on?"

"Something's come up on Stone's background."

He had told Serena to stop looking. He trusted Jules. Any other secrets she had, he wanted her to feel comfortable sharing with him. And while he could tell his communications specialist to forget about any further intel, he wouldn't. This mission was too important to risk not knowing anything that could ruin it.

"What is it?"

"The monthly tracker analysis came in a few hours ago. I didn't pay much attention to it since we're all accounted for, but since we had some downtime between the party and the auction. I just thought I'd—"

She was rambling, and that was uncharacteristic. "Get to the point, Serena."

"An anomaly came up on Jules…the day before she arrived at headquarters that first day."

That would've been the day after she'd received the tracker.

"Okay…so what is it?"

"She flew from Arizona to Ohio."

Dread began to trickle in. "Where in Ohio?"

"She flew into Cleveland and then went on to Brooklyn from there."

Okay, that was a surprise, but not necessarily notable. Ohio was a big state. Maybe she had friends who—

"She went to a hotel there."

"And?"

"Senator Turner was staying at the hotel. I did some more digging. I've got camera feed of Stone going into her room. She stayed there approximately ten minutes."

In seconds, a dozen reasons why Jules would have met with Turner zoomed through his mind. He discarded all but the one that made the most sense. The blow was harder than he'd thought possible. Hell, he'd suffered plenty of them. But he had trusted her. Dammit, he had trusted her with everything.

"Have Xavier and Liam wait at the stairway at the back of the house. I'll send her out. Tell them to hold her at the safe house. I'll handle her when the op is done. Also, tell Rose to search Jules's room at headquarters."

"Will do. And, Ash, I'm sorry."

He didn't reply. What the hell could he say?

He made it back to Jules in record time. When she sent a questioning look at his empty hands, he shrugged. "Couldn't find water. We've got an issue."

"What's up?"

"Meet Xavier and Liam at the stairs off the kitchen. They'll fill you in."

A slight frown of confusion flickered, but he saw no alarm or real concern.

"Okay." Then, in a very un-Elsa-like way, she winked and said, "See you soon."

He watched her walk away, his heart so heavy with bitterness he could barely breathe. Turner had struck once again. Stupid to be shocked. The woman would do anything, use anyone to destroy him.

He had known all along he was playing a dangerous game with Jules. The secrets he'd detected in her, the lies she'd started out with, the way she kept herself separate from the team. They were all signs that he had ignored. All because he'd fallen head over heels in love with her. He had seen what he wanted to see, and because of that, this op could be compromised.

Ash pulled his head out of his ass and refocused. How this had happened—how Jules had not only fooled him, but fooled Kate, too—would have to wait. This op was too important to let anything or anyone derail it.

As painful as it was, this was a good reminder that he did

much better on his own. Not getting involved with an OZ operative had been a self-imposed rule for a reason. When emotions and libido got in the way, shit like this happened.

For right now, he had another priority. A major one. This op could not go sour. Way too many lives were on the line. He would have to deal with his fury and the hurt when this was over.

JULES HEADED TO THE EXIT, nodding a cool greeting or a frigid smile as she went. Playing Elsa was an easy transition for her since the character was so standoffish. Keeping people at a distance was as natural as taking a breath. Except when it came to Ash.

Asher Drake had changed her life in more ways than one. Tonight, she would tell him the truth. She knew he would be angry, probably hurt that she'd not been truthful about her real identity, but she believed she could make him understand. She had to…there was no other choice. She loved him with all her heart, and she could no longer keep the words to herself.

Ash was one of the most loving, supportive people she'd ever known. She told herself he would understand why she had kept the truth from him. Working together, they would bring Turner down. Whether he shared her feelings was another matter. The thought of revealing herself, her emotions, was both a frightening and exhilarating feeling. She didn't open up ever. But with Ash, she would reveal all.

She walked through the busy kitchen, thankful that everyone was so focused on their own tasks, they barely glanced her way. She went to the door leading to the back stairway and slipped through. Both Xavier and Liam were waiting for her with expressions so bleak the grim reaper might find them depressing.

It suddenly occurred to her that she hadn't heard any communication in her earwig, so how had Ash known that there was an "issue"?

She flashed them a curious smile. "What's up?"

"You need to come with us," Liam said.

"What? Why?"

Xavier shook his head. "Don't make this harder than it needs to be, Jules."

"Make what harder? I don't understand."

Surprising her, Liam moved behind her and put a gun to her back. "Move."

Her heart thudding with dread, she said calmly, "I want to talk to Ash."

"When this op is over, you'll get your chance. Until then, you're coming with us."

They had found out about Turner. There was no other explanation. And there was no point in asking how. It didn't matter. She had known this could happen, but dammit, why now? This mission was too important for Ash not to follow through.

"All right. Okay. I understand. But if I could just have one minute with Ash, I could—"

"Yeah, you could screw everything up like you were hired to do," Xavier snarled.

"No, I promise I'm not—"

Grabbing her arms, Liam pulled them behind her back and zip-tied her wrists. She could escape. She had practiced a thousand times how to get out of restraints. She would suffer some injuries, but she knew she could get away. But at what cost? If she did…if she created a distraction, this mission would fail. She could not take the risk.

"Fine. Fine. I'll go with you."

With Xavier behind her and Liam in front, they walked down to the first floor and went through a side door. One of the large, modified SUVs they'd arrived in was waiting for them. They moved Jules forward so quickly she got only a glimpse of the person driving. Jazz. And the sheer hatred on the woman's face made Jules want to scream.

Liam opened the back door and shoved her inside. The door slammed, and the SUV sped away.

Jules took a shaky breath. She had made a mess of things and had only herself to blame. She should have come clean with Ash long before this. He had given her so many chances, and she had blown every one of them.

Did he really believe that she would work with Turner? Since they'd become intimate, grown so close, it was hard for her to comprehend that he believed she would do something so heinous. Yes, apparently there was evidence that she and Turner knew each other. Despite that, whatever evidence they had to the contrary, he had to know in his gut, in his heart, that she could never work against him.

"You want to talk now, or wait till we get to the cabin?"

With a gasp, Jules realized a man was sitting across from her. How had she missed that? The overhead light flashed on, and the moment she looked into Gideon Wright's glacier-cold eyes, she knew she was in huge trouble. She barely knew this man, and he certainly didn't know her.

"I'll talk when I can see Ash."

"Ash is busy."

"I'm aware of that. I can wait."

"Can you?"

"Yes. And would you please remove these ties from my wrists? They're cutting into my skin."

"You can wait." The sarcasm as he used her words was infuriating but also helpful. If she concentrated on the anger, then she wouldn't think about how she was tied up and help-less. She had sworn never to feel helpless again, and she had kept that promise. Damned if she would allow that fear to creep in and strangle her.

She reminded herself that OZ was made up of good people. They didn't rape and torture. They didn't kill for evil reasons. They fought for good. They wouldn't hurt her. Ash wouldn't let them hurt her.

Now if she could only get her volcanic emotions to accept the reassurances. Because no matter how much she tried to reassure herself, they all sounded like lies to her.

# CHAPTER THIRTY-FIVE

Maintaining a bored, frozen expression, Humphrey surveyed the auction attendees. Though his formula wasn't the only product for sale, the majority of the people were here for that specific item. Not all of them could afford to bid, but they definitely wanted to know more about it, possibly get a glimpse of its possibilities.

The weapon was such that wars could begin or end with its use. It was designed for one purpose, and whoever won the bid would want the weapon for only one thing—to destroy. If there was one commonality among all of these people, it was the need for power. From the sick and the twisted to the soullessly evil, in this they were of one mind.

Ash wished he could take them all down. If destroying everyone in this room would take care of the problems of the world, he'd do it in an instant. Destroying them would solve nothing. He had long ago accepted that, no matter what he did, evil would never go away. But as long as he had breath, he would continue to fight against it. Yeah, some people thought he was just as evil as what he fought. Other people's opinions had stopped mattering to him long ago.

They had been working on this op for months, and while the determination to bring Carl Lang down was as strong as ever, the excitement had dampened considerably.

As more people continued to fill the room, Humphrey sat stoically in the back, waiting, his expression never altering. Anyone looking at him would likely think he was ruminating on the millions he would make tonight. That would be the furthest thing from the truth. It was a rarity for him, but while Humphrey maintained his cold demeanor, Asher Drake was doing something he hadn't done in years. He was thinking about heartbreak.

Allowing personal feelings to get in the way of a mission was a mistake only a neophyte would make. He could operate with a shattered heart. Wasn't the first time, but he damn well promised himself it would be the last. Never again would he care for someone who could rip out his guts.

Jules had been the most refreshing and loveliest woman he'd met in years. The impish smile with the delightful dimple on her left cheek, the gray-green eyes that sparkled with laughter, the scent of strawberries and something citrusy in her perfume. Her sense of humor, the unique blend of vulnerability and incredible strength he'd sensed in her. All of those things and a thousand more had intrigued him, fascinated him.

The explosive passion that had seemed to match his so perfectly had been a lie.

Everything had been a lie.

Once this op was done, he needed to talk to one person in particular before he faced Jules. How had Kate been fooled by her, too? Kate Walker could spot a liar a mile away. She was the savviest person he knew. No way could she have been taken in by Jules's lies. Which brought to mind the possibility of another blow. Could Kate have fooled him, too?

Anger washed through him, and he shoved it away. If he

started questioning everything, everyone, he would get nowhere. Concentrating on the here and now had to be his priority. Whatever came next could wait.

"Humphrey, my dear friend." A beatific smile on his face, Omar Schrader appeared before him, holding out his hand.

"Impressive turnout, Omar."

Schrader practically preened with delight at the compliment, reminding Ash of Jules's observation about the man. She'd said that the weapons broker had a deep need to please Humphrey, and Ash could see she was right on the mark. Omar was practically glowing.

"I'm thrilled you approve. I've worked extra hard on making this a night we can both remember with great fondness."

Ash wasn't surprised that Omar didn't mention the monumental screw-up he'd been responsible for weeks ago. All of that was water under the bridge to the weapons broker, but it likely did increase Omar's need for this night to go perfectly.

"How many products will you be auctioning tonight?"

"Only five, but yours will be last. The pièce de résistance, if you will."

On one hand, that was good news. Though the other products wouldn't be nearly as destructive as Humphrey's offering, they could still cause destruction and chaos. He would pass along this vital intel to his contacts and hopefully prevent the products from reaching intended targets.

On the other hand, having his product as the last one to auction off meant he could not participate in Lang's takedown. The man would leave after he won the bid, and three miles from this location, he would be apprehended. They had practiced such a scenario. His team would have no issues. Yeah, he'd like to be there but if he rushed out of the auction, there could be speculation. If it leaked that

Carl Lang had been apprehended after the auction, he wanted no suspicion that Humphrey could have been involved. Getting Lang out of circulation would be reward enough.

"Where is the lovely Elsa? Since you specifically requested her presence at the auction, I had hoped to spend some time talking with her."

"She left. Said she wasn't feeling well."

"Oh dear, I hope it's nothing serious."

It was as serious as hell, but Humphrey, being the cold-hearted bastard he was, only shrugged and said, "The bitch was beginning to bore me anyway."

A glimpse of amused sympathy in his eyes, Omar nodded understandingly. Having the man believe Elsa had dumped Humphrey was Ash's best bet. That she had left him on the same night Humphrey was to receive a monumental amount of money would hopefully be overlooked. After all, Elsa was young, beautiful, and seemingly years younger. Finding another wealthy benefactor should be no problem for her.

"Ah, I understand. Fickleness often accompanies extreme beauty." He lowered his voice slightly. "I have several lovely young ladies in another part of the house. Once our business is concluded, I would be happy to arrange a room and a night of unimaginable bliss."

Ash eyed Omar speculatively. Was the man into more than weapons now?

"Willing young ladies?"

"But of course. When I have a gala, I always have one of the more exclusive pleasure houses send over their finest and loveliest professionals for special guests."

That was good to know. Having to rescue a group of human-trafficking victims on top of everything else would've put a major strain on the team's resources.

"The offer is appreciated, but I'll be leaving directly after the auction is concluded and my payment is confirmed. As to the night of bliss, that's been taken care of already."

"Excellent." Omar turned away, his gaze wandering over the rest of the room.

From Ash's count, there were twenty-nine people. He recognized several faces, but didn't see the one he was looking for. There was still time, but if Lang didn't show up, this entire op would be a bust.

"Is everyone here?"

"No. We have a couple more coming. One of them wanted to wait until all the others arrived. He's a bit of a recluse and dislikes crowds immensely. He's not happy with being required to be present to bid." Omar rolled his eyes. "Some clients can be such prima donnas."

Psychopaths had a tendency to want things their own way. He didn't bother to remind Omar that his last client had been very much in that category, too.

A low chime sounded, indicating that the attendees should take their seats. As several people began to do just that, Omar said, "I must take my leave now. I likely won't get to talk with you in private for a while." He held out his hand for another handshake.

With a grim smile, Humphrey complied. "A pleasure doing business with you, Omar."

"And you as well, my friend. Please don't be a stranger."

Ash watched as Omar made his way toward the stage. The room had grown steadily quieter. The sound of a door opening and closing, followed by a small twittering of whispered voices, caught Ash's attention. Barely allowing himself to breathe, Ash turned. Making his way toward an empty seat in the back was the man he wanted to see.

Carl Lang was an impressive-looking individual. Well over six feet tall, he had a silvery mane of thick hair, lightly tanned skin, and the physique of a professional athlete. Any one of the movie executives at the gala would likely be thrilled to cast him in a variety of movie roles. He had the kind of face and presence to play anything from a distinguished scholar to a Mafia kingpin. But Lang didn't desire the adoration of millions of fans. He liked to kill. Period.

Ash had first learned of Lang several years ago when an entire village in West Africa became ill with a mysterious disease. By the time the virus had been identified, half the villagers had died. Carl Lang had not taken credit, but Ash's sources in the intelligence community had no doubt that he was solely responsible. It had been Lang's first major kill. Some speculated that the entire act had been an experiment to determine whether he'd enjoy watching people suffer. Unfortunately, he had.

Lang was suspected of a half-dozen more mass murders since then. All had been the result of bioweapons, but no law enforcement agency had any direct evidence to link Lang to the massacres. This would be the first time Lang would be caught red-handed purchasing a biological weapon.

"Thank you all for attending tonight's special auction." Omar's slightly rushed words made Ash think he might be a bit nervous. Since he was standing in front of more than two dozen people who would kill without an ounce of compunction, Ash thought the nervousness understandable.

It was a crazy world, but at least, despite the heavy burden his heart carried, he was doing something to make it a little safer. That had to be good enough for now.

# CHAPTER THIRTY-SIX

The instant they pulled up to the cabin, Jules knew she was in even more trouble than she'd feared. Only a few things triggered flashbacks for her. She had worked through the most obvious ones, but this was one she'd never been able to overcome. The additional facts that her hands were bound and she was at the mercy of a man she didn't really know was causing all sorts of panic to race through her bloodstream.

"Listen"—she spoke fast because she didn't know how long she had—"I'll tell you what you need to know right here. Just, do not take me into that cabin. I won't be able to handle it."

"You handling anything is not my concern, Stone. Or would that be Jessie Diamond?"

Jules closed her eyes, concentrating on her breathing. They knew a lot more than she'd thought. Stupid not to realize that they'd gone through her room at headquarters. It would take an OZ tech person little time to crack her password and read her texts—specifically, the last one she'd received, which had given her the go-ahead to kill Ash.

Her response to the order would definitely not help her case.

"My name is Jules Stone. Jessie Diamond is an alias I used to manipulate Turner into giving me the job of infiltrating OZ to hurt Ash. But I would never hurt him."

"Well, thanks for explaining everything so clearly, Jules. Now, let's get inside and hear more of your lies."

"I told you, I cannot…will not go into that cabin."

"And I told you, I don't care what you want."

"Gideon." Jazz's worried voice caught her attention. "Maybe we can question her out here."

Jules grasped the suggestion like a lifeline. "Yes. I'll answer whatever you ask me right here."

A man she didn't recognize opened the door of the vehicle. "You need help?"

Jules's heart rate sped up even more. They were going to let strangers question her? Take her inside a cabin, tie her up so that she was helpless, and…and…

Panic surged like an out-of-control wildfire. A scream erupted before she could suppress it. Pulling and tugging at the ties on her wrists, Jules screamed and cursed at the top of her lungs.

Hands grabbed her, pulled her out of the SUV. She broke the ties at her wrists and whirled around, kicking whomever was in her way. She felt an impact, knew she'd gotten someone. She didn't care who or why. She only knew there was no way in hell anyone was getting her into that cabin.

Hands reached for her again. Jules kicked, punched, slapped, and bit, doing everything she could to protect herself. This couldn't happen again. It couldn't. She couldn't breathe, couldn't think. Survival was her only focus.

People shouted, cursed. And then, as if she'd gone completely deaf, everything went silent. Out of that dark emptiness came laughter…that evil, evil laughter that penetrated her nightmares and taunted her. He'd said he'd never let her go, and he was right.

She was running, running. People were shouting again, but it was his laughter she had to escape. She heard a screeching squeal, like an animal in severe pain.

Hands pulled at her, pain pierced her arm, and then her world dissolved into blessed, peaceful darkness.

# CHAPTER THIRTY-SEVEN

Ash stepped into the limousine and began to rid himself of Humphrey. His driver, Finn Sullivan, was a trusted associate with a private security firm. Since every OZ operative was otherwise occupied, Finn was his backup in case something went sour after the sale.

With one hand, Ash removed the veneers from his mouth and used his other to grab the earwig from the case in front of him.

"It's done, Ash," Finn said.

"No one hurt?"

"A few of Lang's men got roughed up a little. None of your people or mine was injured."

"And Lang…he's healthy?"

"Oh yeah, cursing like the devil on Judgment Day, but not a bruise on his scummy ass. He's plenty healthy to go to prison."

Finn grinned at him in the rearview mirror. "It was a beautiful thing to hear. Wish I could've been there."

Ash nodded his thanks and turned his earwig on. He had

more than one op going tonight, but first he needed to check in with the team.

"Xavier, you copy?"

"Hey, boss. Glad you could join us. You missed all the fun."

"Heard it went well. Everyone okay?"

"Oh yeah. Couple of Lang's men got their asses kicked, and I had to shoot a hole in one of them, but it's nothing that won't heal."

"And Lang is…"

"On his way with the bigwigs for a fun Q&A."

Relief flooded through him. They'd planned this down to the minute, but there was always the possible shit factor to contend with. Learning at the last minute that one of their own was a traitor could have derailed everything. In spite of that, the op had worked.

Xavier's tone went from pleasant to grim. "You talk to Gideon?"

"Not yet."

"Might want to give him a call ASAP. I think they had some trouble."

"Will do."

His entire body pounding with a new kind of dread, Ash grabbed his phone and punched a number. Gideon answered immediately.

"Hey, man, you headed this way?"

"Yes. What happened? Xavier said you—"

"We've got a problem, Ash. I don't know who Jules is or her agenda, but she's had some kind of mental break. You need to get here now."

"What happened? How…"

"She's secure right now. I had to give her a sedative."

"Did she tell you anything?"

"Haven't had a chance to question to her. She flipped out as soon as we got here. You talk to Serena?"

"Just the one time before the auction. Did she find something else?"

"Rose found a burner phone. Not much on there other than several voice messages, all from Turner."

If he'd had any doubt that Jules was involved with Turner, that sealed the deal.

"Anything else?"

"A text message." Gideon paused for a second, then said, "Apparently, Turner told Jules to kill you."

Jaw clenched with tension, Ash ground out, "And her response?"

"She replied, 'Okay.'"

"I'll be there in ten."

He wanted details. The thought of Jules having some kind of breakdown tore his insides to shreds. What the hell had happened? Or had that been an act, too? Gideon was an expert in interrogation. Could Jules have fooled him? Ash didn't think so.

Even though she had betrayed him, there was a helluva lot more to the story. If Jules had been hired to take him out, why hadn't she? She'd had plenty of opportunities. Those days they'd been alone at OZ, he'd been at his most vulnerable. He had slept right next to her. She could have killed him in his sleep and he never would have seen it coming. She'd had access to plenty of weapons. So if her answer to Turner's order to kill him had been an affirmative, why hadn't she carried out the deed?

There was one person he needed to talk to before he confronted Jules.

He punched Kate's number, and before she could get her usual warm greeting out, Ash barked, "What the hell is going on, Kate? Why did you send one of Turner's employees to spy on me?"

"What are you talking about?"

"You know exactly what I'm talking about. Who is Jules Stone? Have you been lying to me all along, too?"

"Ash…no. Oh dear, I was afraid this would happen. Where is she?"

"No. I ask the questions. What the hell's going on?"

"Ash…all I can say is that in no way would Jules ever try to harm you. She was there to protect you."

"Protect me? From whom?"

"Turner."

"Oh yeah? Is that why she has a text on a burner phone from Turner telling her to take me out?"

"Oh damn, I knew she was close, but not…"

Ash spoke through clenched teeth. "Tell me what the hell is going on here."

"That's Jules's story to tell, Ash. What has she told you?"

"Nothing yet. I'm on the way to the cabin to talk to her."

"What cabin? Where?"

"The bioweapon auction was tonight. We're in Slovakia. When the call came in about Jules, I had Gideon take her to a safe house."

"But it's a cabin…in the woods?"

"Yeah. So? We always have one available to—"

"Oh, Ash, no. You have to get her out of there. Now."

"Why? If this is some kind of trick to—"

"Listen, I know you're angry, and you have every right to be, but you have to get Jules out of that cabin. That's a huge trigger for her. She's not going to deal well with being held prisoner."

Though taking any advice from Kate right now was the last thing he wanted to do, the urgency in her voice matched with Gideon's assessment.

"She's with Gideon. He said she had some kind of breakdown. He had to give her something to calm her down."

"I'm getting on the plane. I need to be there for her."

"No. You don't get to run this your way, Kate. Apparently, I've put too much trust in our relationship."

"Ash, I promise you it's not what it looks like."

"Then tell me what it is. Who is Jules Stone?"

There was a second of silence and then a ragged sigh. "She's someone who has admired you for years. That's all I can say for now. Let her tell you. Just promise me you'll be gentle with her. She's come a long way."

Kate's words were a jumbled mass of confusion for Ash. He had no context for them. It had been a long time since he'd felt so out of touch with reality.

"Very well. I'll talk with Jules. After this is over, you and I are going to have a face-to-face discussion. Understand?"

"Yes, I understand. I'm sorry about this. Please make sure she's okay."

Ash ended the call and slumped down in his seat. Hell, he hated being out of the loop, but he'd be the first to admit he was completely confused. Just who the hell was Jules Stone? And why had she "admired him for years"?

"Should be there in a couple of minutes, buddy."

The sympathy in Finn's voice barely penetrated Ash's thoughts. He nodded an acknowledgment, his mind filled with more questions than answers.

Everything was upside down. The op that could have gotten complicated and messy had gone as smoothly as any they'd ever run. The auction had gone off without a hitch. Ash had taken note of the other items being sold and their buyers. A cache of weapons, a modified drone, a couple of particularly nasty viruses that could cause havoc—all had been purchased by individual buyers. He would send that intel to various agencies that would handle each one accordingly.

The finale of the night had been Humphrey's offering of a biochemical weapon that could wipe out hundreds and, depending upon the financing, possibly thousands. The opening bid had been a measly five million, but that hadn't been a surprise. What had concerned him was the number of people who'd ended up bidding. He had believed it would be a runaway between Lang and perhaps one other terrorist organization. Instead, there had been a bidding war between five of them. In the end, Carl Lang was the winner, with his bid of just under three hundred million.

Even though he'd had other plans, Ash had been left with no choice but to stay awhile after the auction ended. Omar had been in a jovial mood and had insisted that Humphrey join him in a celebratory drink. That had been the hardest part. While he'd been making nice with Omar, his team had been taking down Carl Lang.

Humphrey's cover was secure, as was his relationship with Schrader. In a few months, depending on which country won the right to do so, news would be released that Carl Lang, the terrorist much of the world was searching for, had been apprehended. Ash and the people of OZ would never be mentioned.

When Schrader learned of it, he would, like everyone else, assume that fate had finally caught up with Carl Lang. He would never know that Humphrey was the reason and that Omar himself played an integral role in his capture.

Usually after a successful op, the OZ team celebrated their victory at a watering hole. There would be no celebration this time.

The triumph Ash usually felt at the end of a successful op wasn't there. How could it be when everything was so messed up? If he had needed a reminder that getting involved with an OZ employee was a very bad idea, this one was a spit-in-your-face, kick-in-the-balls doozy.

The limo stopped in front of the cabin. "Need me to stay?" Finn asked.

"No. We're good. Thanks for your help."

"Anytime."

Ash got out of the car and headed to the steps. Finn called out behind him, "Good luck."

Waving him a thanks, Ash took the steps two at a time. The minute he reached the door, he paused. Weariness sat like a boulder on his shoulders. They'd found this place a few months back to serve as their fail-safe if they needed to lie low or interrogate an enemy. Never had he considered that the enemy would be Jules.

Disgusted with his thoughts, Ash pushed the door open. Delaying the inevitable never solved one damn problem.

Gideon was standing in the middle of the room, his back to Ash. When the door opened, he whirled, gun in hand.

"It's just me."

"Sorry. This thing has got me twitchy."

"What happened to you?"

Gideon touched a finger to a busted lip and a rapidly blackening eye. "Jules happened."

"She did that?"

"And a lot more." Gideon shook his head. "She went berserk on us, Ash. Jazz had to take Lowell to the emergency room. He's got a nasty hole in his side where she kicked him with one of her heels."

"Where's Jenkins?"

"He's in the kitchen, icing his balls."

There was no explanation needed for that.

"Where is she?"

"In the bedroom. She's awake but probably a little loopy. Not sure you'll get much out of her for a while."

"How the hell did this get so messed up?"

"There's more to your girl than meets the eye. She's definitely hiding all kinds of shit, but you're going to have to dig deep to get to the truth."

"What did she tell you?"

"Just that things aren't what they seem. That she would never do anything to hurt you. Said she wouldn't talk to anyone but you about it, though."

Determined to get to the truth, Ash opened the bedroom door.

# CHAPTER THIRTY-EIGHT

Ash halted in the doorway and took in the scene. Jules lay on the bed, her eyes were closed, but her breathing was slightly rapid. She wasn't asleep.

Closing the door behind him, he walked to the middle of the room and said quietly, "Talk to me, Jules."

"Knew you'd find out the truth." Her voice was gravelly and lifeless, sounding nothing like Jules. "Just didn't expect it to be like this."

"Look at me."

When she opened her eyes, the misery in them gave him pause. Reminding himself that she was a good liar wasn't helping. She looked totally defeated.

Pulling up a chair, he placed it beside the bed and sat. "Gideon said you would only talk to me. So…talk."

"My name is Lucy Carson."

What had been crooked and off-kilter before began to adjust itself. Just those few words gave him answers to so many questions. And instigated a dozen more.

"You were John Leland Clark's first victim."

"Actually, no. That would be my parents."

Feeling as though he'd entered another dimension, he could only shake his head. Where the hell was this going, and why hadn't she told him before this? Hell, they'd talked about Clark. Discussed his capture. Why hadn't she said anything?

So many clues he'd missed came flooding to the forefront. When they'd been headed to Washington to assist Liam, he had known something was bothering her, but he had allowed himself to ignore the signs of distress. When they'd been in the shower in Schrader's house, she had almost slipped up. He had asked her about sign language, and she'd started to say something about her mother and then stopped. Lucy Carson's mother, Gail, had been hearing impaired. It made sense that her daughter would be fluent in sign language.

And the scars. He had seen and kissed every inch of her body. Jules had some significant scarring on her arms, legs, and torso. With seeming ease, she had explained each one away with various reasons—dangerous jobs, her story of abduction in Europe, a bicycle accident when she was a kid.

He was trained to detect lies. Instead, he'd let his libido— and yes, dammit, his feelings for her—get in the way of seeing the truth. Plus, Jules Stone was without a doubt one of the best liars he'd ever met.

"Could you unlock the cuffs, please?"

Ignoring the plea in her voice wasn't easy. She was suffering, but he knew as well as he knew anything that if he unlocked the cuffs, she'd be out of here in a second.

"Later. Right now, I want answers. Why didn't you tell me your real identity?"

"It wasn't pertinent to my mission."

"And what exactly was that mission? What did you promise to do for Turner?"

"She hired me to find incriminating evidence to ruin you and destroy OZ. And if that didn't work, I was supposed to murder you."

Even though he'd already known that was the most likely reason, the stab of betrayal was there.

"Why did you take the job?"

"Ash, please. I won't leave until you know everything, I promise, but I need to get out of these handcuffs."

The words wouldn't have worked, but the tears behind them did. Sighing, Ash stood and unlocked the cuffs. She lay still for several seconds.

Watching for a sign that she would try to run, he waited.

JULES SAT up carefully in the bed. One wrong move, and Ash would handcuff her again. She would do almost anything to avoid the humiliation. Not that she hadn't already humiliated herself enough for a lifetime. Having a meltdown in front of friends was one thing. Friends understood you, cared about you. Wanted good things for you. Experiencing a meltdown in front of people who hated you was altogether different. She was lucky they'd sedated her instead of shooting her.

"I'm very sorry about hurting Gideon and the other two men. I don't even know who they are."

"They're from a team of mercenaries we use from time to time if the job is too large for our small group."

"How…how did the mission go? Did you get Lang?"

"I don't discuss OZ missions with outsiders."

The barb went straight through her heart, just as he intended. If she had been standing, she was sure she would be on the floor now.

Swallowing past the huge lump in her throat was impossible. If she spoke now, her words would be a garbled mess. Jules nodded, waiting for her composure to return.

"All right, Jules. You've delayed the telling long enough. I know your real name is Lucy Carson. I know what happened to you, before and after you escaped Clark. And I have no problem understanding why you faked your death and started a new life."

Hearing him gloss over the most painful events in her life might have bothered her if the words had come from someone else. But she knew Ash's heart, his compassion. Besides, she didn't need sympathy from him now. What she needed was for him to have an open mind.

"I'm assuming you had major plastic surgery. You look nothing like your photos."

"The scars were significant. Plastic surgery was the only way to remove them. I could have just had them repaired, but I was too recognizable to be able to disappear completely with the same face I was born with. I wanted a new look and a new life. I got both."

"Later, we'll get to why you didn't tell me the truth. Right now, what I cannot comprehend…cannot begin to fathom, is why you would work for Nora Turner."

"I did it to protect you."

"Protect me how?"

"Kate told me what Turner did to you. The incident in Colombia. How she betrayed you and the other men. Then she told me about how you were both sure that she arranged for John Leland Clark to escape.

"By the time she finished, I hated Turner almost as much as you do. I wanted to do something…to help. Kate said that you were close to finding the evidence against her, but that Turner was looking for a way inside OZ to destroy you from within your organization.

"We created a mercenary…Jessie Diamond…a hired gun. Diamond had a reputation for such things. Kate spread the word, dangled the bait. Took a while, but Turner finally bit."

"It must've been a good cover. Turner is not only savvy, she's as paranoid as hell."

"Kate's very good at creating people."

"I'm assuming she's the one who helped you create Jules Stone. Who arranged your new life."

"Yes."

When Lucy Carson had escaped that day, she had believed her nightmare had ended. That Clark could never hurt her again. Nothing could have been further from the truth. Instead, she had learned there were all kinds of nightmares. Being accused of taking part in her parents' murders and then being blamed for every kill that John Leland Clark committed had been a different kind of hell.

Law enforcement had found no evidence to implicate her as a person of interest. That hadn't mattered to some. Clark had used the media to start the rumor, and that false narrative had bloomed like a wildfire.

Kate had argued for her, fought for her, and then had arranged a new life for her.

"So as Jessie Diamond, your assignment was to infiltrate OZ and find a way to discredit me?"

"Yes."

"I'm surprised Turner didn't hire you to just kill me right off the bat."

"Ruining you...destroying OZ was her goal. She said you have too many powerful friends to just take you out without trying this method first. Killing you was a last resort."

"Did you give her any intel?"

"Of course not, Ash. I did this to protect you, not harm you."

"You'll excuse me if I find anything you say questionable. Lying convincingly seems to be one of your best talents."

This barb stung but also was so true that she couldn't work up the energy to be offended. She *was* extraordinarily good at lying.

"You're right. I am a good liar, and you have every right to hate me and not trust me. But I know you trust Kate."

"Not anymore."

"Don't do that, Ash. Don't push away the one person who can help you bring Turner down."

"How long did you think you could hold Turner off without giving her something?"

"I did give her something...only none of it was true. I gave her some vague information, and she believed she could build on it to create suspicion of treason."

Ash nodded his understanding. "Just the question of something like that would cause major problems for OZ. People would stop sharing intel with us, stop trusting us. That would definitely work, but it would take some time."

"She mentioned another option—one she felt she could use without killing you. I convinced her to let me try for the intel first. Since having you killed held some risk for her, she agreed."

"What was the other option?"

"She wanted to target your team."

"She thought she could get away with having my people murdered?"

The fury in that one question swamped his previous anger. Ash had discussed his possible murder as if they were discussing a mundane topic. The thought of having his team targeted was altogether different.

"I convinced her to wait."

"But why the subterfuge with me? If you and Kate had told me, I could've provided you with intel that would have had her running all over the place. Digging for stuff that would amount to nothing."

"Because Turner is running out of time. She's got ambitions well beyond being a senator. She wants all obstacles out of her way. You're one of her biggest."

"Still doesn't explain why I was kept in the dark."

Suddenly feeling so weary and sad, she let her shoulders

slump. "Kate believed you'd go after Turner with all you had. If you'd done that before you got the evidence you needed, you would have lost."

Surging to his feet, Ash began to pace around the room. Anger pulsed from him in palpable waves. No one liked to be lied to, no one like to be used. She imagined he felt betrayed and hurt. Causing Asher Drake pain was the last thing she wanted. She had uprooted her whole life for this mission, and it had been a complete and utter failure.

"I really thought I was doing the right thing, Ash. Instead, you're no closer to getting the intel you need, and Turner won't hold off much longer. When she learns I didn't follow her last order, she'll find someone else to do it."

He didn't offer her reassurances or anything remotely encouraging. She didn't expect anything. She had lost her job with OZ, lost her credibility with the team. Lost the right to give her advice.

And she had lost Ash. There was nothing left for her.

"So what now?"

"Is Turner having you watched?"

"At first, she was. I don't think she is any longer."

"Just in case, it'd probably be best if you stay holed up somewhere until we can figure this out."

"All right."

"I'll send a doctor to remove the tracker."

Her devastation was complete. What she had so strongly objected to only a month or so ago was suddenly something she wanted to hang on to like a security blanket. Having the tracker removed would destroy the last link she had with Ash.

She cleared her throat, determined to sound as strong as possible. "Okay if I stay somewhere else? I'm not a fan of cabins in the woods."

His recognition of why was almost her undoing. The pity in Ash's eyes was something she absolutely could not abide.

Throwing her feet to the floor, she waited for him to back away so she could stand.

He seemed to hesitate, as if he wanted to say something else. She hoped he didn't. She was a hundred degrees past her limit and needed to find someplace to crash. Falling apart in front of Jazz and Gideon had been beyond humiliating. Doing so in front of Ash would be so much worse.

Keeping her gaze focused on the small abstract painting on the wall across from her, she waited him out. Surely he would let her go now. He knew she was no threat to him or to OZ.

It seemed to take an eternity, but he at last stood and stepped back. Willing her legs to hold her, she pushed herself to her feet.

"Your dress…"

She looked down at what had once been a stunning silver-blue gown. It had been the prettiest thing she'd ever worn. When she'd slid into the dress, she had felt like a princess. The material was now ripped in several places and stained with dirt and blood, a perfect complement to how she felt.

She grimaced and tried to rearrange the material to cover a particularly large hole on the left side of the dress. "I'm sorry. I don't think it can be repaired."

"It's not important. Here, it's cold outside."

He held his tuxedo jacket out for her, and she gratefully took it and slipped her arms into its luxurious warmth. Even though the jacket swamped her, the comfort of being covered went a long way in making her feel whole again.

"I'll have Gideon take you to a hotel."

"Thank you."

She didn't bother to protest that Gideon would be her

ride. Getting out of here was her number one priority. If she had to ride with the devil himself to get out of here, she would.

She didn't look at Ash again. She couldn't. Escaping was her only focus. She got to the door, but stopped when he said, "Was everything a lie?"

"No, not everything," she whispered. Her lips formed the words that her love wasn't a lie, but she couldn't bring herself to say them. He wouldn't want to hear them.

"Why you?"

"What?"

"Kate said you admired me from a distance for a long time. Was it gratitude that I caught Clark and put him away? There has to be more than that. Why would you give up your career, put your life on hold and yourself at risk to do this?"

A part of her had hoped he wouldn't ask, but another part wanted to get everything out in the open, once and for all. Even as ashamed as she felt, she just wanted to get it said.

If she held herself very still, if she concentrated on saying the words and not the pain, she could get through this. "The day I escaped from Clark…I stood over him. I had a knife. He was unconscious, passed out from drinking. I could have killed him. He never would have known it was happening until it was too late. But I chickened out at the last minute and didn't do it."

Forcing herself to face him, telling herself she owed him this, she whispered the last painful secret. "If I had killed him that day, I could have saved twenty-five lives…including Meg's. Your wife is dead because of me."

She didn't wait to see his reaction. Turning, she walked into the living room and, in a toneless voice, told Gideon, "I'll be in the car."

## CHAPTER THIRTY-NINE

Jazz slid the keycard into the hotel door. When Ash had asked her to come here to check on Jules, she'd had no problem agreeing. She wanted answers, and she wanted them now. The only people Jazz trusted belonged to OZ. Jules had not only betrayed that trust, she had done something no one to her knowledge had ever done—she had broken Ash's heart. If she hadn't known that Jules could easily kill her, she'd try to beat the answers out of her. But she had seen what Jules had done to Gideon, Lowell, and Jenkins. No way was she making that mistake.

Jules was sitting on the sofa, facing away from her. Jazz hadn't been exactly quiet, so she had to know that she was here, but Jules made no effort to turn around.

"We need to talk."

"I've said everything I need to say."

The voice didn't even sound like it came from the same woman. Ash had told her that Jules was not a threat, that she was working against Turner, not for her.

Even though she trusted her boss more than anyone else

on earth, she couldn't help but wonder if he was letting his
heart call the shots on this one.

Refusing to be deterred, Jazz went around the sofa and
sat in a chair across from Jules. Her breath caught in her
throat at the changes in Jules Stone. Gone was the lovely,
composed woman who'd fooled them all. In her place was a
pale, hollow-eyed young woman with shoulders slumped
from what must be a mountain of pain weighing her down.

Anger began to dwindle as doubts soared. This was not
guilt, nor was it defiance. This was grief. An emotion that
Jasmine McAlister had more than a passing acquaintance
with.

"Talk to me, Jules. What the hell happened?"

A slight smile twitched at Jules's mouth. "You and Ash
have the same opening lines."

When Jazz didn't respond, a ragged sigh rattled through
Jules. "What did Ash tell you?"

"Almost nothing."

"Very well. What do you want to know?"

"Everything, but start from the beginning."

JULES TOOK A BREATH. Perhaps this was what she needed.
Maybe a full cathartic cleansing would ease some of the pain.
She had barely spoken to anyone since she'd left Ash and the
cabin behind. Gideon hadn't tried to talk to her, and she had
been grateful for his silence. Having to discuss anything with
the man who'd witnessed her embarrassing breakdown had
been well beyond her.

He had driven her to a quaint little town close by and
walked into the hotel with her as if he was used to escorting
traumatized women with ripped gowns and ill-fitting tuxedo
jackets into elegant hotels. Who knew? Maybe he was.

After arranging for her indefinite stay and escorting her to her room door, he had given her a sharp nod and left.

The only surprise after that was the doctor who'd shown up an hour later. He had explained that he was there to ensure she was all right. He had checked her vitals, encouraged her to get some rest, and then he had left. The OZ tracker she had thought he would remove was not mentioned.

Silly, she knew, but that one small omission had created a tiny kernel of hope inside her. The longer she stayed here alone, though, the smaller that hope became. It must have been an oversight on the doctor's part, nothing more. The idea that she could still be a member of OZ was a useless fantasy. If anything, Ash had chosen to wait to have it removed because he wanted to know where she was at all times. Not because he cared, but because he didn't trust her.

Why would he?

She hadn't had the courage to talk to Kate yet. She had texted her and told her she would talk to her soon but she hadn't yet reached that point. Not only had she hurt Ash, she had failed in every objective Kate had expected of her. Dealing with the guilt and a broken heart as well as letting down her best friend was all a little too much to deal with right now. Discussing things with Kate would have to wait until she could speak without falling apart.

Kate had responded immediately, wanting to come to Jules and whisk her away. She had thanked her but requested she not come. For right now, she would deal with this heartache on her own.

"Jules?"

Shaking herself out of her stupor, she turned her attention back to the woman across from her. Even though she doubted anything would help, Jazz deserved an explanation. They had been becoming friends, and Jules mourned that loss. She recognized a kindred soul in Jazz McAlister—a woman who trusted few and would give her life for those she did trust.

Jules took a breath and said, "My real name is Lucy Carson. My parents were murdered by John Leland Clark. He abducted me, kept me prisoner for several weeks. I managed to escape."

She saw the recognition of Clark's name in Jazz's expression and appreciated that she didn't ask what Clark did to her during that time. Reliving that was beyond her. Just getting the bare facts out was going to take every ounce of energy she had left.

"When I was found, I thought the nightmare was over. I was wrong. Clark continued to kill. At each kill, he left a letter saying that if I returned to him, the killings would stop.

"At first, everyone sympathized. I was a victim, and he was continuing to torture me. But the longer it took to find him, and the more he inferred that I wanted him to kill my parents, the more angry people became. They needed a scapegoat, and I was the only available target."

Jules lifted her shoulder in a helpless shrug. "I had never seen Clark before that night. Turns out, he was a busboy at the restaurant where my parents and I ate dinner. My dad and I had an argument. Clark, for whatever reason, became fixated on me.

"People started speculating that perhaps I did know him before. That maybe I did help him kill my parents and then ran away with him. That my escape was nothing more than a lovers' spat."

"That's ridiculous."

Despite the deadness she felt inside, Jules felt something like hope blossom within her. She shoved it down.

"At first, it was only a few whispers, but the more Clark killed, the more people wondered if it could be true. Social media wasn't at a frenzy then the way it is now. It was new enough that people could say all number of things and not have their opinions questioned. Before long, there were groups devoted to creating all sorts of theories about my involvement. People even created blogs about it. Clark became known as the Dear Lucy killer—in reference to his letters to me."

"How did people know about the letters? Seems like that's something law enforcement would keep under wraps."

"The FBI tried to keep a lid on them, but there was a leak in local law enforcement in one of the towns where Clark had killed a young woman. A deputy sheriff who believed the rumors of my involvement told the local press about the letters. The news went viral. The Dear Lucy killer moniker came after the leak."

"Kate was the FBI agent in charge of the Clark case. That's how you met her."

"Yes. She was my saving grace. If it hadn't been for her, I would be dead."

"You don't have any other family?"

"My mother and father had no siblings. I was an only child. My grandparents are dead. My father's law partners were kind at the beginning, but I think they began to question my innocence, too."

"You had no friends to help you?"

"I had a boyfriend. He didn't stick around long, though." At the time, Rob's defection had hurt. She had thought he loved her. It had been one more bruise to a soul that was already defeated. Now she could be glad that he hadn't stuck around. She hadn't known what real love was then…she did now.

"So Kate arranged a new life for you?"

"Yes."

But the new identity and new face were just the surface

stuff. Kate Walker had quite literally saved her life. Not only had she still been dealing with her parents' deaths and the brutality of what she'd endured during her weeks of captivity, she'd begun to believe what people were saying about her. That, in some way, she *was* at fault. If she hadn't argued with her father at the restaurant, Clark might never have noticed her. Had he taken that argument as some kind of sign that she wanted her parents dead? She began to question everything about that night. Had she done something, said something, that had sparked his insanity?

All of that, plus the knowledge of all the lives she could have saved if she had just killed Clark when she'd had the chance, had put her over the top.

Her one thought was to end it all. If Clark was killing just to get her back, as he claimed, her only choice was to no longer exist. If she were dead, he would stop. She had thought to make that a reality. Her depression had been so deep, her guilt so all-encompassing, suicide had looked to be the only way out. Kate had convinced her that she had survived for a reason. She'd made her realize that living would be the best revenge.

And then Kate did something she'd never done before. She broke the law, not once, but many times over. Not only did she fake Lucy's suicide, but she created a new identity and new life for Jules.

"Was that when Kate left the agency?"

"Not then but it wasn't long after. Her husband had been diagnosed with early-onset Alzheimer's around that time, too. She wanted to spend as much time with him as she could."

"I never got to meet him."

"Lars was an amazing man. Without him and Kate, I never would have made it."

"So once you became Jules Stone…what did you do?"

"I had some scarring on my face so I had to have a lot of plastic surgery. Plus, thanks to the media's obsession with Clark, my face was everywhere. Once I recovered from the surgeries, I began to train. I still didn't know what I wanted to do, but one thing I swore: I would never be helpless again."

"How does Ash fit into the picture?"

That was both easy and hard to answer. Helping the man who'd singlehandedly taken down Clark, not once but twice, was a no-brainer. He had become her hero the moment he captured Clark. But when Clark had escaped and murdered Ash's wife, a new emotion had been added. Jules felt a massive amount of guilt.

Kate tried many times to talk her out of it, claiming that she was allowing the people who blamed her before to influence her decisions. And while some of that might be true, she knew she was partly to blame. Megan Drake would not have died if Jules had killed Clark when she'd had the chance. Some things were undisputable. Facts were facts.

"When Kate told me about Turner, about what she did to Ash, I was infuriated but knew I could do nothing to change that. I continued to train, to find my path. I started a security agency, began to establish a reputation for being able to suss out traitors and spies. It was lucrative, but ultimately not what I wanted to do."

"Is that when you started hunting serial killers?"

Jules winced. Apparently, there were no secrets left for her. "Yes. The first one was a fluke, but it made me realize that I could do more."

"How did you get involved with Turner?"

Weariness began to tug at Jules. For the past twenty-four hours, she'd barely slept. Every time she closed her eyes, Ash's face would appear. The hurt in his eyes, the disappointment in his expression had torn her heart to shreds.

Talking with Jazz helped. The load of shame and remorse

didn't seem as heavy, but exhaustion was taking a toll. Determined to get everything out in the open, Jules gave her the condensed version of how she and Kate created Jessie Diamond and why.

"And then Turner decided that Ash needed to die instead?"

"Yes. I don't know why she's suddenly in a hurry. The last time I talked with her, she seemed set to wait until I could give her something substantial."

"You haven't talked to her since she texted you to kill Ash?"

"No."

"So you don't know what's happened?"

The dull thud of her heart spiked to rapid. "No. What happened? Is Ash okay?"

"Ash is fine. Much better than Turner will be soon. They found the helicopter pilot that left them in Colombia. He should be able to place Turner there. Ash and Kate are on their way to interview him now."

# CHAPTER FORTY

**Key West, Florida**

Kate Walker stood on the tarmac of the private airfield and watched Ash come down the steps of his plane. He looked tired. After what he'd been through, he had earned every one of the shadows beneath his eyes. She knew he was furious with her, and there was little she could say to defend herself. She had believed, and still believed, she'd done the right thing. Getting Ash on board was another matter.

They had agreed to interview Pete Lawrence together. The former airline pilot turned helicopter pilot for hire had agreed to meet with them, but that didn't mean he would spill his guts. Ash had asked Kate to assist with the interview. At the FBI, they'd interviewed numerous suspects together. They complemented each other and should be able to use those skills to get what they needed. She knew there was another reason he'd asked for her help, and despite his anger at her, she was grateful he'd seen past his fury.

Asher Drake was one of the most controlled men she'd ever known, but he did have triggers. Cowardice and greed were two of them. Lawrence was guilty of both. He had left those men to die. Instead of doing the right thing, the brave thing, he'd kept his mouth shut, taken a payoff of two hundred and fifty thousand dollars, and disappeared.

"Hello, Ash."

Ash nodded. "Kate."

"I'm assuming you want to talk before we go see Lawrence."

"You assume correctly."

"I've got a private room in the hangar. Let's go."

Ash raised a brow, but didn't ask how that'd come about. Kate had to admit that being wealthy had its advantages. The money was nice, but she'd give up every penny for just one more day with the man who left her a brokenhearted but very wealthy widow.

They were silent as they walked together toward the hangar. Waves of tension were coming from Ash. So much so that she wondered if he'd be able to control his temper until they got into the hangar. He did, but barely. They entered the small office, and the instant the door closed behind him, he exploded.

"What the hell, Kate?"

"That's what I like about you, Ash. No preliminaries."

"Cut the bullshit and tell me why the hell you kept all of this from me."

"First things first. How is Jules?"

"I figured you would have already talked to her."

"She texted me…asked me to wait. She assured me she was fine, just needed some time."

"There you have it. She's fine. She's holed up in a hotel room until we can get this figured out."

"I mean emotionally, Ash. You said she had some kind of mental breakdown."

"I sent a doctor to see her. Other than exhaustion, she's physically sound."

"And emotionally?"

"That remains to be seen."

"All right. And I'm assuming she told you her real name? And what she was doing working for Turner?"

"Yes. But I want to hear it from you."

"I knew Turner was looking to infiltrate OZ. I mentioned that to you at one time, and you blew me off, saying there's no way you would bring someone into OZ that you didn't fully vet."

"And so you, what, decided to prove me wrong by sending Jules to me?"

"Of course not. You know me better than that. I did it because I knew that Turner was going to get to you no matter what. If she couldn't do it by infiltrating OZ, she was going to take you out. By creating Jessie Diamond, we bought you some time."

"Why Jules? Why not someone else?"

"For two reasons. First, Jules is incredibly talented at undercover. I trained her myself, and she's exceeded every expectation."

"You trained her?"

"Yes. After she recovered from her surgeries, I thought she could move on. She couldn't. She was determined to never be vulnerable again, and she was determined that, no matter what, her life would mean something. I helped her focus that anger into becoming the best.

"She's the one who decided to open a security agency. I backed away then. She needed the independence, not me hovering over her every decision."

"So I'm assuming it wasn't your suggestion that she hunt down serial killers."

Kate visibly shuddered. "Absolutely not. But it didn't surprise me. Jules has always gone her own way."

"Okay, so Jules is good at undercover. What's the other reason you sent her?"

"Because she wouldn't have it any other way. I don't know if you know it or not, Ash, but Jules Stone has a backbone of solid steel and a stubbornness to match yours."

"Don't give me that, Kate. You could teach stubborn to a mule. If you had told her you were going to use someone else, she would have backed off."

"I think you underestimate our girl, but okay, yes, there is another reason. When Jules was found, she was so damaged, so hurt, but she was rallying. She could have gone on to have a normal life if it wasn't for that bastard Clark. He continued his torture by leaving those letters, and then mob mentality ensued."

"I know the story, Kate. I was there."

"But only later. You read the file, knew the case, but you never met Lucy. She was already gone by the time you came on the case. You didn't see how each day she blamed herself more and more. At some point, it was going to drive her to suicide. No matter how much counseling she received, it would have happened someday. I arranged her new life, but that didn't alleviate her guilt. Then something miraculous happened. You found Clark, and you brought him to justice. You were her hero. You took down her boogeyman. She wanted to know everything about you. I told her what I could.

"That was the first time that I saw real recovery in her eyes. Genuine peace. And then that bitch somehow helped Clark escape, and he killed Meg."

"She took a downward spiral?"

Kate smiled, remembering. "Not so much downward as

sideways. She got pissed. And as we both know, getting pissed is a good motivator."

"She felt like she owed me."

"Absolutely."

"She told me she had the chance to kill him and didn't. Can't believe she blames herself for that."

"She's gotten better at putting the blame where it belongs, but when this opportunity to help you came along, she was the one I went to with it."

"And you didn't tell me because…?"

"One reason is because it's her story to tell, not mine."

"All right, but why didn't you at least let me in on the Jessie Diamond angle?"

"Ash, if I had told you that Turner was putting out feelers for someone to infiltrate OZ, what would you have done?"

She saw the knowledge in his eyes before he said the words. "I would have confronted her."

"For years, you have followed Turner around, basically stalking her, daring her to do something. If you'd found out she was not only targeting you, but also your team, nothing would have stopped you from going after her full force. I thought this was the best way to keep her in line until we got what we needed."

"And keep me out of prison."

"Prison or worse." Kate shook her head. "I saw what you did to Clark. The man deserved every broken bone and laceration he received, but going after a US senator with that same kind of mercilessness wasn't going to fly."

"I'd like to think I would have been a bit more subtle than that."

"Normally, yes, you are, but not when it comes to those you care about. The people of OZ are your family. I couldn't take the chance that you'd go after her. We were too close to getting what we needed." She shrugged. "I'm sorry it got so screwed up. And I'm very sorry you and Jules got hurt."

Before he could respond to that, she added, "If it makes you feel any better, it was never my intent that Jules should work for you. She was supposed to tail you and feed Turner basically junk that we manufactured to keep her satisfied."

For the first time, she saw the beginnings of a smile in his eyes. "Jules told me she has a problem with following orders."

"She told the truth there." Kate sighed. "And I certainly never anticipated there would be an attraction between you two."

"So you don't think that was a ploy, too?"

"That would be a one-thousand-percent hell no."

Ash shoved his fingers through his already shaggy hair, making Kate want to smile. The first day she'd met him, she'd advised him he didn't look like an FBI agent. Instead of being insulted, he'd thanked her for her kind words. She'd sputtered out a surprised laugh, and they'd been friends ever since.

"You're in love with her, aren't you?"

"I don't know what I am anymore. I don't know who she is."

"Yes, you do. There may be secrets between you, but not in that. Don't lose the best thing to have happened to you in years by letting your pride get in the way."

Ash nodded and then checked his watch. "We'd better go. Lawrence is expecting us in half an hour."

"So are we okay, here?"

"Yeah, I'm still pissed, but we're okay."

Relieved, she headed for the door. "Pissed, I can handle. Now let's go get some answers."

# CHAPTER FORTY-ONE

**Flagstaff, Arizona**

A sh stood at Jules's door and knocked. He still had questions, and yeah, he was still angry, but he needed to make sure she was okay. Whether she would let him in was anyone's guess.

He had given a lot of thought to what she had done and why. He knew more than most about what John Leland Clark had done to her. He had read her file, seen the photos, read her testimony of the events. Clark had brutalized and tortured her for weeks. And when she'd finally been able to escape, she had returned home to face a new nightmare. The bastard had used social media like a master, keeping her in the limelight and making her look like an accomplice. It hadn't been enough that he'd killed her parents and taken her innocence. He had almost taken her sanity.

Comparing the broken, defeated young woman she'd been then to the warrior woman Jules Stone was today was almost impossible. They were two different people. What she had been able to overcome and accomplish was nothing short of a miracle.

The doctor Ash had sent to her had reported that other than exhaustion, she was physically sound. And Jazz had said that though she seemed sad and sorry for how things had turned out, she appeared to be emotionally well.

But he needed to see for himself.

After he'd left Kate in Key West, he'd been set to fly back to Slovakia when he'd learned that Jules had taken a flight back to Arizona. Even though he'd told her to stay out of sight, he couldn't blame her for wanting to go home.

The interview with Lawrence hadn't been the major breakthrough they'd hoped for. The answers they were seeking hadn't been there, at least nothing concrete that they could take to the Justice Department. But Lawrence had given them leads, and that was more than they'd had before.

While Lawrence claimed to be all sorts of sorry that he'd left men to die that day, Ash couldn't help but believe that the man was just all sorts of sorry that he'd been found.

He raised his hand to knock again when the door opened, and Jules stood before him. Though her attire of jeans and sweatshirt were casual, there was nothing relaxed about her demeanor.

"Hello, Ash."

"Can I come in?"

Still holding the door open, she took a step back. "Of course."

She had once described the house as an old Victorian fixer-upper. The description was apt, but it was obvious she'd put a lot of time and money into making it into a home.

As the door closed behind him, he turned to face her. There were a lot of things he wanted to say, so many questions he still needed to ask. Instead of doing either, he held out his hand.

Tears pooling in her eyes, she took his hand, and Ash pulled her into his arms and held her. Yeah, it was a stupid-ass thing to do, but he couldn't think of anything he wanted more. She felt perfect in his arms, and for the first time in days, Ash drew in an easy breath.

"I'm so sorry, Ash."

"Don't, Jules. Not yet. Let me just hold you. I haven't slept in two days, and don't take this the wrong way, but you look like hell."

Burying her face against his chest, she gave a laughing sob.

"Where's your bedroom?"

"Upstairs."

Releasing her, he held out his hand to her again. When she took it, he knew she was giving him more than her hand. She was giving him her trust, telling him she knew he wouldn't hurt her.

Letting her lead the way, he followed her up the stairs and into the bedroom. He paid no attention to décor. His only focus was Jules and the king-size bed in the middle of the room. He stripped off his clothes, and though she did nothing but just stand there and watch him, he knew it wasn't because she was shy. She was waiting. Naked now, he moved to her and pulled the sweatshirt over her head. She unzipped her jeans. When she was nude, he led her to the bed and pulled back the covers. She got in, Ash followed. Wrapping his arms around her, he kissed her forehead and whispered, "Sleep."

Ash waited until he felt her relax in his arms, and then he followed her into sleep. Their problems would still be there when they woke, but for now, he had everything he needed.

WAKING in Ash's arm was a surreal moment that she never

wanted to end. Of all the things she'd thought he would do when he saw her again, this hadn't been one of them. But she'd seen in his eyes that he was at his limit. Since she'd hit hers days ago, falling asleep in each other's arms was exactly what they'd both needed.

The last couple of days had been an exhausting whirlwind of emotions. From devastation to grief and now to elation. Maybe she was reading too much into this, but a man didn't fly halfway across the country, strip you naked, and let you fall asleep in his arms if anger was the only thing driving him.

Okay, yes, Ash was a sexual, sensual man, and lying naked in each other's arms would likely lead to other things, but that wasn't what she'd read in his eyes last night. Need had been there, but not in the usual way. He'd been hurting, and instead of staying away from her, he'd come to her. That had to mean something.

"Loud thoughts for this early in the morning."

She turned her head slightly and looked up at him. His eyes were half closed, his sensual mouth slightly turned up. It would take a stronger woman than she to resist the temptation. Stretching slightly, she pressed a soft kiss on his mouth. "Good morning. I didn't mean to wake you."

"You didn't. I've been awake for a while."

"Feel better?"

"Some." Startling her, he rolled on top of her and slid into her with one smooth move. "That's much better."

Her brain might have had questions about what was next for them, but her body had no such problem. She was slick and ready for him, the man she loved and adored with all her heart.

Wrapping her legs around his hips, she looked up at him. "What now?"

"Now we show each other that, no matter what, we are one."

"Ash," she whispered, "I love you."

Tears poured from her eyes and Ash wiped them away. "And I love you. I didn't realize how much until I thought you betrayed me."

"I'm so—"

He pressed his fingers to her lips. "No more apologizing. We're on the same page now. That's all that matters."

Her heart so full it could burst, Jules pulled his head down and kissed him, showing him the love she'd held in her heart for so long.

They made love the way it was meant to be made, their bodies moving as one. One heart, one mind, one body.


"IF YOU EVER DECIDE YOU don't want to be an OZ operative, you could open up a pancake house and make millions." Ash said this as he shoveled another giant forkful of pancakes into his mouth.

Beaming, Jules glowed with happiness. If he had wondered what all the secrets she was keeping from him had been doing to her, her expression answered his question. Never had he seen her so relaxed and at peace.

When he'd arrived on her doorstep, none of this had been on his agenda. He'd wanted to make sure she was okay, and then he'd wanted answers and explanations. All of that had changed when he'd seen her face. If there had been anyone who felt more miserable than he had, it was Jules. And in that moment, he had wanted nothing more than to make her stop hurting.

This strong, beautiful, vulnerable, incredible woman with a mountain of secrets and a spine of steel had captured his heart. Seeing her in pain was something he could not abide.

Love had happened quickly this time. With Meg, it had grown through the years, first with friendship and then love. Back then, they'd had everything in common, and it had worked. But after Colombia and Syria, nothing had been right. Meg had still been the same person. She'd had every right to expect Ash to be the same, too. But he hadn't been.

In Jules, Ash recognized a soul mate—the other part of him. The hurt she'd suffered matched his own, and his soul reached out for her. He wasn't much into woo-woo stuff, but his feelings for Jules were about as magical and mystical as he'd ever gotten.

"You want more pancakes?"

Ash shook his head. "Twelve's my limit."

"When's the last time you ate?"

He shrugged. "I actually don't know."

Looking down at her half-eaten pancake, she sighed. "Guess you had other things on your mind."

The mood had shifted from light to dark in seconds. As much as he'd like to continue talking lighthearted gibberish, he couldn't. They still had a ton of things to get through. Their connection had been reestablished, and their foundation was firm. They would start from there.

Grabbing her hand, Ash pulled her with him into the den. Settling on the sofa, he tugged until she sat down beside him. "Let's get it all out in the open, the good and the bad."

"Ask me anything."

"Maybe you could just start from the beginning."

"You probably know most of that already. Kate helped me start a new life."

"Yeah. And it all makes sense now. You were being tortured not only by Clark, but by people looking for someone to blame."

"I couldn't go anywhere…even another state. My face was all over the national news."

"You could have just disappeared. Changed your name, your face, and gone on with your life."

"That's what Kate suggested, but I thought if Clark believed I was dead, he would stop killing."

"I'm sure Kate told you that wouldn't work."

"Yes."

"Clark got off on killing. You had nothing to do with it. He was going to kill whether you were alive or not. Blaming you was just another way of torturing you."

"I know that now. A part of me knew that then, but I had to try."

"So Kate helped you fake your suicide."

"Yes. If not for her, it probably would have been a real one. I just couldn't take it anymore."

Ash held her close, understanding exactly what she meant. She had endured hell at the hands of John Leland Clark. In Ash's estimation, there was no hell hot enough for the bastard.

"So once you had your surgeries, you could've done anything. Instead, you became a badass."

She released a laughing sob. "Not feeling too badass at the moment."

"That's okay. Even badasses need to mellow from time to time."

She pressed a kiss to the hollow of his neck in appreciation.

"So you and Kate cooked up the scheme of Jessie Diamond. I'm still not sure what you hoped to accomplish."

"Kate learned that Turner's ambition stretched much further than a Senate seat. She's made several enemies over the years, and one by one they seemed to be fading away. The man who took over her tech company trash-talked her to the media. She never responded to his insults, and they basically died down. He was killed in a one-car accident while on vacation in Miami."

"I remember that, but people get killed in accidents all the time. Kate and I discussed it. We both agreed it could be a coincidence."

"That's true, but three other people with varying grudges against the senator all suffered a major loss in the last year. That's more than a coincidence. That's a pattern."

"I'm aware of all of them. I knew she was coming after me. That's why we were scrambling to find something."

"And that's where I came in. She was looking for a way to ruin you. Infiltrating OZ was the next step. Kate and I agreed that if we got there first, we could control the intel."

"Kate said you were supposed to tail me, not ask for a job."

"Yeah, well… That was the plan, until I met you."

"Oh yeah? Why's that?"

"For a lot of different reasons, but one of the biggest was because I knew Turner would be impressed. She knew infiltrating OZ would take time. I wanted to show her how talented I was. If she believed I was that good, that might buy us a little extra time. Also," she threw him a wry grin, "I didn't expect you to confront me about following you. I had to regroup and roll with the moment."

"That was a dangerous thing for you to do."

She shook her head. "Turner wouldn't have hurt me as long as she didn't find out the truth."

"I'm not talking about Turner. I'm talking about OZ. You infiltrated an organization filled with elite spies who could kill you in a thousand different ways. You took a hell of a risk."

"I needed to do something to help."

Remembering the conversation he'd had with Kate, Ash shifted Jules in his arms so he could see her face. "Why? You felt guilty about Meg, or you were grateful that I'd caught Clark?"

"Both reasons and a million more."

"First, you have no reason to feel guilty about Meg. We've already established that Clark enjoyed killing."

"But if I—"

"You were a traumatized young woman who'd lost her parents in a horrific way and had been brutalized and tortured for weeks. I do not blame you. There is no sane person in this world who would ever blame you."

"Intellectually, I know that, but there's still the what-if factor."

"What-ifs are bullshit. It's the what's next that matters. You turned your life into something remarkable."

She pressed a palm to his face in a gentle caress. "Thank you, Ash."

He kissed her forehead. "Kate told me you were grateful that I captured your boogeyman."

"I was…I am."

"I'm no hero, Jules. I'm just a man who does what he has to do."

"Forgive me if I disagree."

"This thing between us…it can't survive if you put me on some kind of pedestal. I'm about as far from perfect as a man can get."

Understanding dawned in her eyes, but instead of denying his words, she smiled her delight and said, "You're as stubborn as a whole team of mules, you hog the bedcovers at night, you snore like a locomotive, you desperately need a haircut. And you like snow and cold weather way too much."

He laughed, but stopped when she placed her hand over his heart and said softly, "And you have the heart of a lion and the soul of a warrior. I love your strength, your courage, your determination. I love that you want to right wrongs. I don't see you as perfect…I just see you as you are."

Unable to speak for the lump in his throat, Ash kissed her, letting his lips speak for him. How life had brought them together was still a mystery. Linked by nightmares he wouldn't wish on anyone, they'd still found each other. If that wasn't a modern-day miracle, he didn't know what was.

She pulled away from his kiss and said, "So what now?"

"We keep digging."

"I have a suggestion."

"Oh yeah? Then I'm all ears."

"I'm going to follow her orders. I'm going to kill Asher Drake."

# CHAPTER FORTY-TWO

**OZ Headquarters**

J ules stood in front of the people she'd come to know
and trust. These people risked their lives every single
day for people who would never know they even
existed. They worked hard, felt deeply, and trusted few. She
had been the recipient of that rare trust, but it had been
broken. She had to fix what she'd damaged.

Ash had offered to stand with her, had even offered to
explain for her. She couldn't allow that. This was on her. If
even one of them couldn't get past the betrayal, she'd already
decided she would bow out. The OZ team worked so seam-
lessly together because of the mutual trust and respect they
had for one another. If that was irreparably damaged, then
she owed it to the team to leave.

She and Ash had discussed this beforehand. They both
knew what could happen. But there was one thing they had
assured each other—she would still have Ash, and he would
still have Jules. Nothing was going to keep them apart. That
would be more than enough for her.

Her eyes met his, and the love, compassion, and acceptance she saw in them gave her the courage to begin.

Jules took in a bracing breath. They knew the basic facts of why she'd lied and deceived them. Now they needed to know the rest.

"First, I want to apologize for the deception. I believed, still believe, I was doing the right thing. Protecting Ash and OZ, all of you, was my primary goal. Turner was not going to stop. We knew she had aspirations beyond her Senate seat, which meant she would want to rid herself of any threat against those goals. Ash has mercilessly pursued her, seeking answers.

"She was getting desperate. And we know desperate people do desperate things. We…Kate and I…believed we could not only buy some time by creating the mercenary Jessie Diamond, but we could control whatever threats came at Ash."

She took another breath and added, "I'm just very sorry it involved lying to all of you. Causing problems for OZ, for any of you, was the last thing I wanted to do."

She deliberately looked at each person before moving on to the next operative. She had shown them she was a good liar and could only hope that she could prove that she had the honor and integrity of truthfulness as well.

Jazz gave her a quick smile and a thumbs-up. Though she was sure the operative had kept most of the things Jules had told her to herself, she felt certain Jazz had been advocating for her.

She shifted her eyes to Serena, who gave her a nod and a smile. Sean was seated beside his wife, and though there was no smile, he did give her a nod as well. Okay, three out of three.

Taking a breath, she shifted her gaze and faced the man who had seen her at her worst. Gideon Wright wasn't smiling, and there was no nod. What she did see brought a lump to her throat and a wash of tears to her eyes. She saw compassion.

Grateful for the peace offering, she moved her gaze again and came to an abrupt stop. Eve Wells was not going to be so easy to persuade. That wasn't a surprise. They'd barely exchanged a word with each other. All Eve knew was what she'd observed.

"Eve, you have questions?" Ash's voice broke through the staring contest Jules and Eve were waging.

"Questions? No. Reservations? Yes. Lying is our business, and while I'm damn good at it, I draw the line at lying to my teammates. You crossed that line, Jules."

"Yes, I did."

"Your reasons were just, but the outcome could have been catastrophic."

She couldn't argue with the statement, so she just waited for Eve's judgment.

"Very well. We don't know each other yet, and we'll remedy that soon. However, I trust the people in this room more than I've ever trusted anyone in my life. Their judgment has always been sound. If they believe in you, then so do I."

Jules nodded her thanks and continued to the other team members, waiting for each one's judgment before moving on to the next. No one else objected, and Jules knew a peace she'd never experienced. This was her team…her people… her tribe.

She was where she belonged.

Ash blew out a silent sigh of relief. Even though he'd been certain of the outcome, he hadn't been sure what questions might be thrown at Jules before the team agreed to accept her explanation. Having her go into detail about what she'd gone through was not something he would allow. She had explained herself enough, but she did need to make peace with the team. As much as he wanted to shield her from any more pain, he knew she needed to do this on her own.

He was proud of her and his team for making the right decision.

"Now that we're all together again, let's take a moment, belated though it is, and give each other a big *oorah* for the op in Slovakia. It might not have gone completely as expected, but it worked all the same.

"Carl Lang is being held at an unknown detention site while several countries vie for the right to decide his punishment. Not only that, we were able to identify two other up-and-coming organizations we need to keep an eye on. Plus, both the CIA and MI6 were appreciative of the intel on the winning bidders for the other weapons that were auctioned."

"In other words, we done good," Jazz said.

"Hear, hear," Xavier added.

"What about Turner?" Sean asked. "What's going on there?"

"Right now, we're in a holding pattern. Even though we have more intel from the helo pilot, we're still a long way from being able to make anything against Turner stick."

"Does he have any idea what the meeting was about?" Serena asked. "Who was involved?"

"No. He was hired and paid through an anonymous source. Swears he never met anyone until he picked them up that day."

"How did he know to pick them up?"

"He said he'd been told to fly to a certain location and wait for further instructions. He was about a mile from the meeting site when the attack came. He got a text telling him the coordinates. He picked up Turner and the others and flew them to an abandoned airstrip about twenty miles down the road. They got onto a waiting plane, and he was told to tell no one about what went down."

"And that's it?"

"Basically, yeah. He did remember a few snippets of conversation he overheard. Seems everyone was surprised at the attack, but one or two of them made accusations against each other for picking such a dangerous location for the meeting. He also said they didn't seem to like or know each other very well. They were wary…distrustful."

Gideon issued a disgusted snort. "You're right. That's not a lot to go on."

"We've come this far. We found the pilot after all this time. We'll keep digging. I've focused on Turner because she's the only one we've been able to find. Hopefully, with this new intel, slight though it is, we can identify some of the other players. There are more out there, and we're going to find them all."

"And in the meantime, what happens?" Eve turned her gaze to Jules. "Aren't you supposed to carry out Turner's orders of termination?"

"Yes." Jules met Ash's eyes and smiled. "But we know how I am about orders."

"What will you tell her, then?" Serena asked.

"I'm going to tell her what she wants to hear. That I followed her orders."

"What?" Xavier glared at them both. "How the hell is that going to help?"

"Even though it pains me to say this, looks like…at least for a little while, Asher Drake is going to have to die."

Ash sent his friend a tiger-like smile and added, "Congratulations, Xavier, you are my successor."

# CHAPTER FORTY-THREE

**Washington, DC**

"Drake is dead."

"So I've heard."

Clutching the phone in her hand, Jules met Ash's eyes. Just those three words told them so much. Only a handful of people had been told that the leader of OZ had been killed. Which one of them told Turner?

"Do you have proof of death?"

"Photo work for you?"

"Absolutely."

"Good. I'll be there in ten minutes."

"What? You're here in DC? Why? Can't you just send it to me? Why do we need to meet?"

"Because I have a proposition for you."

There was a long pause, and Jules held her breath. Their plan depended on her meeting in private with Turner. If that didn't happen, the whole thing would go up in smoke.

"Very well, but not at my office. There are too many eyes

and ears. There's a private club called Millie's Spot on K Street. Meet me there in an hour."

"See you then."

Jules returned her phone to her pocket and turned to Ash. The difference between the photograph on her phone and the man standing, healthy and whole, beside her was like night and day.

Rose Wilson's talents were numerous, and makeup artist was one of them. After working on Ash for over two hours, Rose had called Jules in to see the results. Just thinking about it caused her to shudder. It had been much too realistic looking.

But now she had several photographs showing Asher Drake lying in a filthy, damp alleyway in Madrid. Two holes in the middle of his forehead and one in his chest had ended the life of the OZ leader.

Rose and Ash had done their jobs. Now it was up to Jules. She would weave a tale of how a cold, cunning killer had gotten the drop on Asher Drake and destroyed Turner's archnemesis.

"Turn around. Let's check you out again."

At Eve's words, Jules dutifully turned. If there was anyone who knew about undercover and subterfuge, it was Eve. Since learning of Jules's plan to trap Turner, Eve had been her biggest supporter. And while she sincerely appreciated the help, as well as the turnaround in her attitude toward Jules, it wasn't always comfortable. Eve Wells was a perfectionist.

Jules withstood the scrutiny. Eve's experience as a former CIA operative was invaluable. Fooling Turner would take every ounce of acting ability she possessed, and she would gladly take all the help and advice she could get. If this didn't work, and Turner suspected she was being manipulated, Jules could be dead the moment she walked out the door of the meeting place. It was a risk she was willing to take.

"Remember, don't get too close to the woman, or the sound could get distorted."

"I'll remember."

"Also, try not to touch the front of your blouse. The bug is a delicate device and will pick up even the slightest sound."

"Okay."

"What's your distress word?"

She sent a smile to Ash and said, "Snow."

"Eve, I need a moment," Ash said.

"Okay, but don't muss her makeup, and for heaven's sake, don't dislodge the camera button."

Ash laughed and pushed her toward the door. "Yes, ma'am."

Before going out the door, Eve turned and gave Jules a brilliant smile. "Welcome to the team, Jules. Proud to have you."

Her heart swelled with gratitude. Even though Eve had given her approval, Jules had still felt like there was distance between them. Those words gave her the assurance that, no matter what, Eve accepted her as a trusted team member. "Thank you, Eve."

The instant the door closed, Ash grabbed her hand and pulled her to him, but took care not to touch her anywhere else. "We can find another way. You can still change your mind."

"Not going to happen. This is going to work, Ash. I feel it in my bones."

"Yeah, well, if you feel anything else in your bones, like danger, then you say *snow*, and we'll be there."

That couldn't happen. The OZ team storming into the club could have dire consequences, ruining everything. This had to work. There was no other option.

"I'll be fine. I promise."

"Promise me something else."

"Anything."

"When this is over, we'll go away for a few days. Just the two of us."

"Someplace warm?"

Ash laughed and kissed the hand he held. "Someplace so hot you'll want to run around naked all the time."

"You got yourself a deal, Mr. Drake."

The door opened, and Eve peeked in. "Ash, she needs to get going."

Ash nodded, and with one more kiss on her hand, he whispered, "Go kick her ass."

Jules walked out of the hotel room and to the elevator. A taxi, driven by a man Ash trusted, would be waiting at the front door. She wasn't surprised at the meeting location. Turner had been seen at the club several times. Many politicians had favorite private meeting places. As far as she knew, Turner was the only one who used Millie's Spot, which made sense. Having clandestine meetings about murders and cover-ups required extreme privacy.

She got into the waiting car, and it took off. If this plan worked, and she planned to make sure that it did, it would be one of the most worthwhile things she'd ever done. She would get justice for the men who had died, justice for Meg. And justice for Ash.

And when this was over, she and Ash would be together. This might not be the fairy-tale ending most people were used to, but for Jules, it was as close as she could imagine.

# CHAPTER FORTY-FOUR

Ash adjusted his earwig once more. He could hear Jules breathing, hear and see the traffic surrounding her. He wished he could talk to her, reassure her that he was right there with her. He couldn't. They had agreed that Jules wearing an earwig was too dangerous. If Turner suspected a setup, the consequences would be fatal.

Having Jules put herself at risk was one thing. He trusted her skills. Putting herself at risk specifically for him was another matter. If anything happened to her, he'd never recover. Losing Meg had almost killed him. She'd been his best friend for years, and even though their marriage had been on shaky ground, he had still loved her. Being responsible for her death had put him in a black hole for a long time. If he lost Jules, he'd go back down that hole again, and Ash was pretty sure he'd never come back up.

This had to work!

"Okay, we're stopping in front of the club. Wish me luck."

Ash closed his eyes and, instead of wishing her luck, prayed for a miracle.

❧

REEKING of wealth and clandestine happenings, Millie's Spot was a small and elegant private club. Jules could imagine that while sipping expensive liquor or the latest fancy cocktail and munching exotic hors d'oeuvres, bad people had conceived many illicit deals here. How many had Turner been responsible for? And how many deaths had resulted from those deals?

Following Turner's directions, Jules knocked on a side door. It was immediately opened, revealing Turner.

"I hope you understand that not only is this an inconvenience, but it's incredibly dangerous."

"I'll be brief."

"Very well."

Turner backed away, and Jules walked inside. The interior was dark, allowing only glimpses of light from the low-glow light fixtures above each table. For their plan to work, the conversation required light.

"Interesting place. Does it have to be so dark? I can barely see where I'm going."

Surprising her, Turner adjusted a lamp over one of the tables and said, "Have a seat."

Though the rest of the room remained dim, she was pleased that the small area was lit up quite nicely. Relieved, Jules settled into a chair.

The instant Jules was seated, a man came out of the shadows.

"What the hell?"

"Did you think I'm going to talk with you without making sure you're not wired or armed? I've been around too long to fall for that trick, Ms. Diamond."

"Stand up," the man growled.

Jules released an exaggerated sigh and stood. The man

was only slightly taller than she was and on the thin side. However, he had the look of an experienced killer. Since she had no reason to fight him, Jules raised her arms and allowed him to pat her down. He removed her phone from her pocket and the gun strapped to her ankle.

He placed the items on a nearby table and then took something from his pocket. Jules showed no outward sign of fear, but her heart rate sped up a bit. The cam/mic inside the button on her shirt was the most modern and sophisticated one in existence. It wasn't yet on the market, and so far no scanner had been designed to detect it. Still, there was the worry.

Seconds passed as he waved the scanner around her body. When he nodded at Turner, she smiled and said, "Wait outside for me, Ted. I'll only be a few moments."

Without a word, he nodded and left the room.

"Have a seat, Ms. Diamond."

Jules settled into her chair and said, "I have a proposition for you."

"First, show me the photographs."

Jules reached over and grabbed her phone from the table. "I was in a hurry so could only take a couple." Clicking the icon, the image of Ash appeared. No matter how fake it was, the photo looked altogether too realistic to Jules.

Apparently, Turner agreed. She let loose a delighted little laugh. "How wonderful. If I thought I could get away with it, I'd have an eight-by-ten made for my credenza."

Resisting the urge to punch the woman in the face, Jules smiled. "Photography has never been my thing, but I must admit, the picture does highlight my work."

"How did you get away with it?"

Jules gave a casual shrug as if it was all in a day's work, but she added a smug smile. What killer wouldn't be proud of such a scheme? "We were on an op in Madrid.

Drake and I were chasing a slimy informant. I pretended to pull a muscle and held back a little. We got separated. He lost the suspect and came back looking for me. I was standing behind a dumpster. I came out, took the shots. Radioed in that the suspect had shot Drake and gotten away."

"Did he know I was responsible?"

The gleam in Turner's eyes was hard to stomach, but Jules held back her revulsion. "I doubt it. He was dead before he hit the pavement."

"Ah, well, can't have everything." She pushed the phone back to Jules's side of the table and took out her own phone. Her finger clicked a couple of keys, and then she said, "Your money is in your account. That should end our business transaction."

"Not so fast. I have a proposition for you."

"Yes, so you said. However, I'm not interested in doing more business with you, Ms. Diamond."

"Then you don't care that Xavier Quinn has taken over OZ and has vowed to keep the investigation on you going?"

"Quinn? Hell, he wasn't even there that day. Why should he care?"

Warmth ran up Jules's spine. It wasn't exactly a confession, but hearing Turner indicate she knew something about the incident was definitely progress.

Jules didn't bother to respond to the question, allowing Turner to adjust to the new threat. Had she really believed that taking out Asher Drake would be the end of her troubles?

"Very well, Ms. Diamond. Tell me what you know."

"Quinn and Drake were close…apparently like brothers. At the op meeting after Drake's death, Quinn and the others vowed to continue the investigation. They won't stop until you go down."

Turner's eyes narrowed speculatively. "What do you know about Drake's vendetta?"

"Enough."

"If you want to continue doing business with me, Ms. Diamond, I suggest you be a little more forthcoming in your answers. What do you know?"

Thoroughly enjoying herself, Jules drawled, "I know that you were in a meeting with some people in Colombia. A drug cartel attacked the building. You and your meeting attendees escaped by helicopter. Drake and several others were left behind to die. Drake was the only survivor. He's been working for years trying to find out why you were meeting and the names of the other attendees."

Jules waited for the denials. Waited for Turner to come up with lies or accusations against Ash.

Instead, Turner waved her hand as if the events Jules had just described were nothing more than a bothersome gnat. "It wasn't my fault. How was I to know a cartel had taken over that area? I was the one who called for more security. How is it my fault that they failed to protect themselves?"

"What was the meeting for?"

"Careful, Ms. Diamond. I would hate to give you intel that would get you killed."

Jules shrugged. "That's okay. I don't have any skin in this game. But if you don't take care of Quinn and his friends, you'll never be able to relax."

"You can't just kill them off. As much as I would like to see that happen and as good as your skills are, you won't be able to get away with killing all of them."

"I could if they all died in the same explosion."

The doubt disappeared, and a gleam appeared in Turner's eyes. "And just how do you propose to do that?"

"Simple. Remember, I have infiltrated the organization. I know where the rats sleep."

"So they have a barracks or some such?"

How much did Turner know about OZ? Since the woman had proved she knew more than the average citizen, Jules could take no chances.

"Not barracks, but when they've got a big case, they stay in one place. It'd be easy to arrange a bit of a gas leak during the night. Take out the entire organization in one fell swoop."

"When?"

Jules wagged her finger at Turner. "Uh-uh. Not till we talk terms."

"All right. I'll pay you the same amount I paid for Drake times four."

"Make it five. There are a couple of other operatives that'll go up with them. They've got to be worth something, too."

"Very well, but that's all I'll authorize."

"You've got yourself a deal, Senator."

Turner stood. "Can you do it soon? I have some plans for the future and would like to have this nasty business far behind me before I announce them to my constituents."

"I'll take care of it within the next couple of weeks."

"All right. Text me photos as soon as it's done. I'll deposit your fee the same way I did for the Drake job."

Her eyes as cold as ice, Turner added, "And for the record, Ms. Diamond, let's not see each other again."

"Not a problem."

Jules walked out the door and got into the car waiting a block away. Her expression never changed, but her heart was pounding like a jackhammer in her chest. They had done it. They'd actually done it. Senator Nora Turner had just been recorded ordering the murders of several American citizens.

She was going down, and she was going down hard.

∼

Ash opened the door to the hotel room, and Jules flew into his arms. "We did it. We actually did it."

"No, baby. You did it. I've never been so proud of anyone in my life."

Pulling from his arms, her eyes twinkling with happiness, she said, "Pretty damn good if I do say so myself."

"I'd say incredible." Covering her mouth with his, Ash kissed her. Longing, pride, relief intermixed with a love so profound he couldn't comprehend his next breath without her.

"I would tell you guys to get a room, but you already have one."

Laughing, Jules pulled away and peeked around Ash's shoulder to see her fellow OZ operatives all grinning at her. "Wow, the gang's all here."

"We are." Holding up a glass filled with something sparkling, Eve smiled at her. "You done good, newbie."

"High praise coming from the queen of undercover," Jazz called out.

Drinks were poured, and more toasts were made. It occurred to Ash that this was the first time in years they'd actually celebrated anything. Sitting around a local watering hole rehashing an op was a far cry from an actual celebration. The fight wasn't over, but for this moment, they needed to feel good about what they'd accomplished.

Ash took a swallow of champagne and watched Jules with the rest of the team. When she'd first arrived at OZ, he'd been concerned that she would continue to hold herself separate. He now understood why she had done that. The lies she'd told had driven an invisible wedge between her and the others. But now the secrets were out, and the OZ operatives were all on the same page.

"She's a natural."

Ash sent Gideon a small smile. "Remind you of anyone?"

"Yeah. In fact, she might be better than Eve. And if you tell Eve I said that, I'll shoot you."

"It'll never leave my lips."

"So what now?"

"It's already in FBI hands. The moment Jules was safe, I sent the recording to a trusted friend there. I'd say Turner has about an hour or so to feel smug. Then life as she knows it is over."

"Think she'll give up the names of the others?"

"Doubt it. At least not at first. She's got too much to lose to admit to anything. Down the road, though, I think she'll sell out for a deal."

"You good with that?"

"Am I good with cutting a deal with the woman responsible for letting Clark go so he could kill my wife? Hell no. But I've learned to compromise. It'll be good enough to know her career is over and that she'll serve some time. Maybe not as long as she deserves, but again, good enough."

The bitterness in his tone belied his words. No, he wasn't all right with Turner getting a light sentence. He knew to his soul she was directly involved in arranging Clark's escape. Meg's death was on her. Problem was, he couldn't prove it. What he could prove was her presence in Colombia.

Thanks to Jules, the men who'd died that day would finally get justice. So yeah, it'd have to be good enough.

# CHAPTER FORTY-FIVE

**Three Days Later**
**Alexandria, Virginia**

Ash stood before the woman he'd spent years trying to bring down. The satisfaction was still there, but it had been tempered by frustration. Turner wasn't talking. She knew she had been had, knew she was finished. The allegations, along with the recording of her meeting with Jules, were classified, but soon everyone and their neighbor would know that Senator Nora Turner was both corrupt and evil.

No way would a helicopter come swooping in to save her hide this time.

To avoid a media frenzy for as long as possible, the FBI had placed her under house arrest. So far she'd been closed-mouth and refused to answer any questions. This meeting at her home—one he was surprised she'd agreed to—was to try to change her opinion about talking. There was a ton of intel in her head.

"I must say you look quite healthy for a dead man."

Ash had to give her credit. Turner was as cool as any

cold-blooded killer he'd ever faced. But behind that bravado, there was fear. She looked a full decade older than she had in her meeting with Jules. She knew she was beaten.

"I'm feeling better. I'll be even better when you're behind bars where you belong."

She tilted her head slightly as if trying to figure him out. "I'm assuming you wanted this meeting for more reasons than to exchange insults with me."

"You know exactly why I'm here. I want answers."

"I agreed to this meeting as a courtesy, but I'm under no obligation to tell you anything. In fact, my attorney strongly urged me not to see you."

"Then why am I here?"

"I guess since we've been in each other's lives so much over the last few years, I thought it only fitting that we have a face-to-face."

"In each other's lives? That's how you're going to play it? Turner, you not only left a half-dozen men to die that day, you arranged for John Leland Clark to escape and murder my wife."

"You don't have proof of any of that."

"I noticed you didn't bother to deny your involvement in either incident."

"What's the point? You can't record anything in this room. I fell for that once. I won't again. It's your word against mine. And no matter what you might think, mine still holds a lot more weight than yours."

That wasn't true, but he didn't call her on it. He had come for answers, not to gloat. She had resigned her Senate seat, and every reporter in the country wanted to know why. She had given no answers to their questions, and speculation was running rampant. She could keep up the illusion of control if she wanted. He knew what a person who was on the edge of losing everything looked like.

"If it's just your word against mine, why not tell me the truth?"

"Good try, but no. Ms. Stone got everything you're going to get from me the other day. You'll not get anything more."

Jules's real name had not been revealed, but Turner had already proved she had connections. Just how far those connections went was something he intended to find out.

"You'll have to tell the truth at some point."

She smiled almost pityingly. "So naïve for one of such experience. I will say that no one was supposed to get killed that day. We had no way of knowing we would be attacked."

"Maybe not, but you worked hard to hide what you were doing. And you've spent a boatload of money covering up the aftermath."

"The meeting was supposed to be a secret. No one, including that cartel, should have known anything about it. The attack caught us all off guard."

"And you ran like a coward."

"I'm not trained to fight."

"Fighting is one thing. You could have sent someone in to save us, but instead, you've spent more than a decade trying to bury it."

She shrugged. "Casualties of war."

Fury surged, and he ground his teeth to keep from going after her with his hands. That would solve nothing. "This was no war, Turner."

"Life is a war, Mr. Drake. We're all fighting for one thing or another. You and those other men lost that day. And now you think you've finally beaten me. That you're going to get what you want. You think you're going to make me pay. Are you happy about that?"

"Happy? No. Relieved? Yes."

"You probably don't agree, but I was a victim, too."

"You're right about that…I don't agree."

"Look, I wasn't even in politics then. I was a—"

"You were the CEO of a very successful tech company. Yeah, I know exactly who you were. You think that absolves you somehow? You were a human being abandoning other human beings to die."

"I didn't know they were just going to leave you. How could I? We were all in shock."

"And when did you find out we were left behind?"

Her eyes slipped away from his for just an instant. "It was a couple of days. I assumed you were dead. We all did."

"And you didn't give enough of a damn to find out."

"I just wanted to put it behind me. I don't see why you can't do the same. You lived. You should be happy."

His jaw clenched, Ash ground out, "Yeager Bates, Jeff Mason, Cort Dunley."

Her frown of confusion was real, and then he saw the recognition in her eyes. She knew those names.

"Yes, those are the names of the men you left to die. The other two were locals. I never knew their names. They got covered up like everything else. Swept under a rug like they never mattered. Each one of them mattered. They had hopes, dreams, aspirations."

Ash had sworn to himself that if he ever got the chance, she would at least know their names, know them.

"Yeager was twenty-eight years old, still single, but he had a mother who loved him. Neither Cort nor Jeff had families, but they had people who cared about them. They mattered."

Instead of remorse, he saw something like exasperation in her expression. Hell, had he really expected her to care?

"Again, it's not like I was the one responsible. I don't even remember you."

Of course she didn't. "I am the one who saved your life."

Her eyes widened as realization dawned. "I was being

trampled, and you picked me up and carried me out. I knew somebody did. It was a horrific experience for me."

"It was no picnic for the men you and your people left behind."

"So where do we go from here?"

"I would think that's obvious."

"Not really. Do you think I'm going to just sit back and let you ruin my career?"

"Your career is the least of your worries, Senator."

"Ah, I see. You think I'm going to be indicted and put in jail. My sources told me you're an intelligent man."

"How do you think you're going to get out of this?"

"You really have no idea how big this thing is, do you?"

"You're a good start."

"So smug, yet so stupid."

"You can make it easier on yourself if you tell me who else was involved."

The self-satisfied smile remained, telling him there was no point in staying any longer. He'd come for answers and wouldn't be getting any. He had at least reminded her of the men she'd let die. For now, that had to be enough.

"In case you're thinking about skipping town, be aware that the FBI is right outside your door. No helicopter is going to swoop in and save your ass this time."

"Get out of my home. Now."

With a nod, Ash left through the backdoor, the way he'd come. No way was Turner getting away. He hadn't been able to persuade her to give up names, but she had confirmed something he had known all along. This thing was a whole lot bigger than just one person. Turner would be only the first to fall.

But how many more were there? And who was at the top?

. . .

ON LEGS that were much too shaky, Nora went to the bar in the corner. The brandy and Scotch she served guests were on the counter, but this called for the good stuff. Opening the cabinet, she took down her prized bottle of brandy and poured herself a generous portion. Holding the bottle in one hand and her glass in the other, she headed to the leather recliner she'd bought a few years ago. It was her favorite thinking chair, and she had much to think about.

Easing down into the chair, Nora took a sip and allowed the liquor's warmth to permeate her body. She took another sip, then another, before the worry pounding within her began to ease.

Drake thought he had her. Believed he had won. And though she could admit things didn't look good for her, they looked even worse for Drake. He just didn't know it yet.

As for Jessie Diamond, or rather, Jules Stone, things looked downright deadly.

Nora had to give the other woman credit. She had fooled her, and for a crafty woman like herself, that wasn't easy to do. But Nora would have the last laugh. While Drake and Stone were scrambling to stay alive, Nora would be on a private beach drinking mojitos.

Yes, her career was trashed. She wouldn't recover from this debacle. The presidency had been on her radar. She'd been working for that all her life. Others would take up the slack now. This wasn't the way she wanted things to end, but that was life—you rolled with the punches. She had learned to roll from the best.

When she'd told Drake there were more powerful people than Nora herself involved, she hadn't been blowing smoke. No way this man could ever fathom just how high or how far all of this went.

They would be disappointed in her, that was a given. But she had done everything they'd asked of her. She'd given up any kind of life of her own to follow their edicts. They should have protected her better.

Certainly the debacle in Colombia was a black mark on her record, but she had done everything she could do to rectify her mistakes. Was it her fault that Drake had survived? Was it her fault he was as slippery as an eel, escaping death time after time?

No, they were the ones who'd screwed up. If they'd wanted to help, they could have taken Drake out years ago, before she'd started her political career. All of this was on them.

They knew she would never talk. Why would she when she would go to prison? Plus, she knew better than to betray them. They knew she was loyal. They knew they could trust her.

So why was she suddenly terrified?

Nora took another sip of her brandy. They would have to sort it all out without her. She had plans nobody knew about. They thought they knew everything, but there was no way they knew this. Even now, her private plane was being readied. Her luggage had already been transported. She had picked up many skills in her career, and hiding money, huge amounts of money, was one of them. She would never want for anything ever again.

They would never find her. No one would. A private little island in Greece. A couple of loyal staffers who would die before they betrayed her.

Maybe she would have plastic surgery. In a few years, she could be seen in public again. No one would know who she was. Maybe she would start dating. Finally have a social life, have some fun.

She would indeed have the last laugh.

Noting that her glass was empty, she reached for the bottle from the side table. How odd. Why were her fingers numb? Why was her mouth so dry? Why did she feel so dizzy?

Why…?

She slid to the floor, knocking against the expensive bottle of brandy, which teetered, almost falling to the floor. A gloved hand reached out to stop it.

Looking up into a familiar face, she tried to form words but couldn't make her mouth and brain connect.

"Go to sleep, Nora. You failed your mission. Your service is over."

She lay on the floor, her body frozen, but her eyes were open, watching as the man took the bottle and glass. It took less than a minute to remove the evidence, and though Nora's eyes were still on him, she was long past being able to see.

Thousands of miles away, a phone chimed. The owner read the encrypted text. After years of decoding such messages, the words were easy to understand. It was done.

Five minutes later, a series of texts went throughout the world. One text was different from the others. That text was read with resignation and then resolve.

A life was over. A new life would begin.

# CHAPTER FORTY-SIX

**Tahiti**

Ash closed the door to the bungalow and headed back to the beach, where Jules was waiting. Today, he felt like he had it all—sun, sand, and the woman he loved. An hour after his meeting with Turner, he and Jules had hopped on a plane. They had arrived last night and fallen into bed, exhausted. For the next ten days, they would put the evils of the world behind them and concentrate on being a normal couple on holiday.

Unless something major came up, the entire OZ organization was lying low, running down leads, and working assets. They all needed the break.

When they returned, they'd hit the ground running, as several ongoing cases were about to heat up. But for a while, he and Jules would disconnect from the world and connect with each other.

Ash grinned like a fool at the silly euphemism. Nothing like a man in love to bring them out.

A loud, distinctive bleep told him he had a text message

from Kate. As much as he wanted to ignore the world and its worries, his gut told him to read it now.

The minute he read the terse, three-word message, that feeling of optimism and anticipation turned to ash.

**Turner is dead.**

Skidding to a stop, he punched Kate's number. She answered with, "I don't know how yet."

"No way in hell was this natural causes."

"I agree. Coroner will have to give the final say."

"The FBI was right outside her door. How did anyone get in or out without being seen?"

"Another question for which I don't have an answer."

Ash didn't know what infuriated him more. That Turner had escaped the punishment she deserved, or that she had been killed to keep her silent.

"Who the hell is behind this shit?"

"I don't know, Ash. My contacts are getting more close-mouthed. What about yours?"

"Yeah. I've seen some signs, but we still have leverage over most of them. At least for now."

"If you get anything, let me know. I'll get back to you with the autopsy results."

"Will do. And, Kate?"

"Yeah?"

"Watch your back. The people we can trust are getting fewer and fewer."

"Back at ya, pal."

Resisting the urge to throw his phone into a nearby lagoon and curse a blue streak, Ash reined in his anger. Turner had told him this was bigger than he could even imagine. He had known there were more people involved. What he hadn't considered was that Turner might have been a pawn. She was no longer useful, had become a liability.

They had taken her out of the equation before she could destroy their plans.

Three questions pounded in his brain: What were those plans? Was a new pawn already set to replace her? And just who the hell were *they*?

JULES MOANED in pleasure as Ash applied sunscreen to her bare back. The hot sun beat down in glorious warmth, and the snow of Montana although exquisitely beautiful, was a distant memory.

"Feel good?"

"Cannot imagine anything feeling better."

"Is that right?" He leaned closer and whispered, "Then I guess I'd better step up my game tonight."

"Oh, your game is just fine, Mr. Drake. In fact, your game wore me out this morning."

He pressed a kiss to the back of her neck, causing all sorts of tingles throughout her body. This man, with one caress, could cause the most amazing chain reaction.

"Ash?"

"Yeah?"

"Are you sure you wouldn't rather be back home, working to find Turner's killer?"

When Ash had returned from grabbing the novel she'd left in her suitcase, she hadn't expected the news about Turner. The knowledge that someone more evil, with more power than Turner, was still out there calling the shots was unsettling. They had known there were more, but to what end? For what purpose did they exist?

"We've done all we can for now. It could be weeks before the coroner determines cause of death."

"You know as well as I do that she was murdered."

"Yes, and I also know that whoever is responsible will still be around when we get back."

"But…"

Ash pressed a finger to her lips. "Serena and her team are digging. Until we have intel to go on, all we'll be doing is running around in circles."

She sighed. "You're right."

"If you're bored, I can give you a special OZ assignment."

Rolling over, she propped her head on her hand and grinned at him. "Oh yeah?"

Ash pulled her on top of him and whispered an order she was more than happy to comply with. Laughing with both joy and delight, Jules gave herself up to the wonderful moments of being in Ash's arms. Even though sadness, wars, and evil still existed, these pockets of happiness were what made life worth living.

TEN DAYS **later**

"Can't believe our vacation is over. Sure you don't want to move OZ to Tahiti?"

The glowing, golden woman with the cinnamon freckles sprinkled across her nose was the most beautiful sight he'd ever seen. Their time together had been exactly what they'd needed. Not only had the haunted look completely disappeared from Jules's eyes but Ash felt a peace he'd didn't think he'd ever experienced.

"I think we could get a few operatives onboard, but it would take a bulldozer to get Rose to move."

"Why's that?"

"Five grandchildren within an hour of her house."

"You're right. OZ can't do without Rose."

"If I promise to take you somewhere warm once a quarter, will you go home with me now?"

Wrapping her arms around his neck, she beamed up at him. "I'll go anywhere with you, Asher Drake."

"Even where temperatures are subzero?"

"Absolutely. But just so you know, if you do, I won't be taking my clothes off. Ever."

"Then we're definitely not going anywhere that cold."

The teasing and silliness were something new. Jules made him feel happy and carefree. For a man who hadn't believed he'd ever have an ounce of happiness again, it was an exhilarating and frightening experience. What if he lost it all again?

The gut-deep feeling he sometimes had when an op was about to go sour hit him like a sledgehammer. Something was off.

"I'm going to the lobby for some gum," Jules said. "Want anything?"

"I'll go with you."

She nodded toward her open suitcase on the bed beside his duffel bag, which was already zipped and ready to load onto the plane. "How about you stay here and finish my packing? I tried three times to close the suitcase. Something's got to come out."

That was because she'd gotten every OZ employee a souvenir. Even though he'd insisted no one expected a gift, she had ignored him and bought them anyway. She'd enjoyed buying them so much he hadn't had the heart to tell her their suitcases would likely burst open.

"I can put a few more things in mine."

"Thank you." She turned to grab her wallet. "I'll be back in a sec."

Telling her he didn't want her out of his sight would be so completely out of the norm, he pushed aside the dread. They'd been here ten days. No one, other than OZ employees, knew their location. Nothing even remotely threatening had taken place. There was no danger out there.

"Okay." Unable to watch her walk out without giving her some kind of warning, he tried to make it sound normal. "Be alert. Okay?"

"What? Why?"

Being subtle was apparently not in his wheelhouse today. As he reminded himself they had agreed to share everything, he said, "Sounds stupid, but I just got this pit-deep feeling that something bad is going to happen."

Frowning, she went into his arms and looked up at him. "No matter what, we're together. We can face anything. Right?"

She didn't question his feelings, didn't blow them off. If he hadn't known it before, he knew it deep in his soul now. Jules Stone was meant for him.

After showing her for several breathless moments just how much he loved and appreciated her, he raised his head. "I'll get the packing finished. You get the gum."

"I love you, Asher Drake."

"And I love you, Jules Stone."

With the knowledge that she was right, he watched her walk out the door. No matter what, they would face any threat together.

He was hip-deep in T-shirts, tote bags, and scarves when his phone gave a familiar chime. Pulling it from his pocket, he answered with a smile in his voice. "Feeling better?"

Two days after they'd left, Serena had come down with the flu. Though her voice still sounded hoarse when she said his name, it was the urgency in her tone that caught his attention.

"What's wrong?"

"We've been hacked."

"What? How?"

"I don't know. I came in this morning and discovered it. Somebody broke through our firewall."

His mind raced with a thousand suspects and a million scenarios of how any stolen intel could compromise the lives of thousands.

"Did they get everything?"

"Thankfully, no. We change our passwords daily and have multiple security measures in place. It's what they did get that has me concerned."

"Such as?"

"They hacked the files on Turner."

Ash closed his eyes. He wasn't surprised, but it did increase his concern. When it came to technology, OZ had the tightest, most sophisticated security. Whoever had hacked them was no amateur.

"There's something else. They got into your personal file. They know where—"

*Jules!*

Ash was out the door before Serena finished her sentence.

JULES WALKED along the pathway that led to the gift shop. She needed to remember to buy gum before she went back to the room, but that wasn't why she'd wanted to come to the gift shop. Yesterday, she'd seen a suncatcher in the window, and she couldn't resist getting it for Ash. He had a tattoo of a phoenix on his arm and had explained that when he had started OZ, he had looked at it as a new beginning. A new life. A phoenix represented reinvention, rebirth. She knew the symbol meant a lot to him. The suncatcher had the exact same emblem on it. When they were alone tonight, after they returned home, she would give it to him.

She smiled at the people she passed by, marveling at the sheer beauty they'd enjoyed the last ten days. It had been a glorious experience, and while she would definitely miss the warmth of the sun and the beautiful ocean, she couldn't wait to get back home and start her life with Ash. When she and Kate had cooked up this plan months ago, never had she believed this would be the outcome. She was in love with a man of strength, honor, and incredible courage. They hadn't talked marriage or anything permanent really, but she wasn't concerned. She trusted him with her heart. They would reach that point, but for now she was relishing each day as it came.

With Ash and his beautiful smile on her mind, Jules didn't see the man until he was right on her. A gun was shoved into her side, and a voice growled in her ear, "Get in the van."

Training took over, and Jules turned away from the man, whirled, and kicked. The kick never landed. A sharp pain slammed into her face. Momentarily stunned, she fell face first into the arms of someone extremely strong. The arms threw her into the back of a van, and the vehicle sped off.

Jules shot up from the floorboard, ready to fight. A needle jabbed into her arm. She got in one good punch to her faceless attacker before darkness swallowed her.

BLINKING HER EYES OPEN, Jules tried to move and found she couldn't. Her hands and feet were tied together in an awkward position. She couldn't move a muscle. How long had she been out? And where was she? The air smelled stale, damp…slightly moldy. She was in a container of some sort. The outside sounds were indistinguishable but sounded hollow, as if she were in a drum.

Ash! He would be tracking her. He would know within minutes that something was wrong when she didn't return from the gift shop. He'd check her tracker and be on his way. She needed to be ready when he arrived. Together, they would take these men on and find out who was behind it.

She had that confident assurance up until she heard a massive engine start up, and the vehicle that held the compartment she was in began to move, faster and faster. Seconds later, she felt the lift of takeoff. She was in the air.

Calm spread over her mind. Ash could track her anywhere in the world. He and the OZ team would find her. Whoever these people were, they didn't know Asher Drake or the Option Zero people. They thought they were dealing with average, ordinary people. They were wrong. There was nothing average or ordinary about the OZ team. For the first time ever, Jules realized what it was to be a part of something bigger. She had always been a loner. Even before she was taken and her parents were killed, she had often gone her own way in things, even when others disagreed. Her mother had called it marching to the beat of her own drum.

Then, after everything happened, there had been no other choice. Being alone meant not getting hurt.

All of that had changed. She was a member of an elite team of warriors. Ash had told her that no one would watch her back like OZ would. They depended on one another. They would find her, there was no doubt. But that didn't mean she would sit back and just wait to be rescued. She was no victim…never would be again. Whoever was responsible for this was in for a rude awakening.

SURROUNDED BY OZ OPERATIVES, Ash sat in the rear of the helicopter. The whir of the blades drowned out even the loudest of shouts, but he'd said all he'd needed to say when they'd been on the ground. They were going to do whatever they had to do to save Jules.

Ash had been stunned when he'd lost her tracker signal. When he'd found a small abandoned airstrip a few miles down the road, his question was answered. She had to have been flown off the island—there was no other explanation. Unfortunately, not a soul around could confirm a flight had taken off.

He'd called the team and given them the details. Serena was able to pull up Jules's signal. It was weak and went in and out frequently, but when the plane she was on landed, the signal was crystal clear. The instant he learned the location, he'd had no trouble connecting the dots.

That someone had leaked Humphrey's real identity was no surprise. Ash had known that would happen someday. But what infuriated him was that Jules's identity as Elsa Olsen had also been discovered. Few people outside of OZ knew about the op that had brought Carl Lang down, but someone in that inner circle had given the intel to the one person who had cause to hate both Ash and Jules. Nora Turner had gotten her revenge after all. Her final vengeful act before she died had been a call to Omar Schrader.

Schrader was not a killer. Not that he wasn't evil. He was just on a different level of evil. Money was the weapons broker's number one motivator. This was a different scenario, though. Learning that he'd been deceived and used might bring out other tendencies. Would his pride turn him into something more dangerous?

Ash had three choices. He could go subtle—call the man and find out exactly what he wanted.

He could go in soft—sneak in and take her without Schrader even knowing he was there until it was too late.

But the time for subtlety or softness was gone. He was going in hard and fast, with the full force of OZ at his back. Arriving with his entire team, they would sweep through the place like rockets. What happened to Omar was up to Omar.

Ash had chartered a flight to Slovakia. On the way, he'd called in a couple of favors. When he'd landed, he'd been pleased to find exactly what he'd asked for waiting on him. The Black Hawk helicopter would make the kind of statement he needed. The team had arrived in the OZ jet not long after, and it'd taken less than five minutes to review the op details and get them back up in the air.

Jules had been at Schrader's house for almost twelve hours. He told himself that she was one of the smartest, savviest, and most skilled operatives he'd ever known. He trusted her with his life, and he trusted her with her life. She knew how to survive.

His biggest worry was the fact that Omar had not called with any kind of demand. There was a reason he'd taken Jules and hadn't gone after Ash. But why hadn't he called and at the very least taunted him?

Ash knew he could make the call, but that would take away the surprise. Schrader believed he'd gotten away with taking Jules. He was likely enjoying the thought of Ash trying to find her without any idea about who had taken her or why.

He was wrong. In less than an hour, Omar Schrader was going to get the shock of his life.

# CHAPTER FORTY-SEVEN

**Slovakia**
**Omar Schrader's Estate**

"Omar, just what do you think you're doing?"

The smirk on Schrader's face would have been comical if Jules wasn't so infuriated. Did the idiot really think this was going to end well for him? Did he not realize whom he was going up against?

"You do not get to call me by my given name. That privilege is given only to people who don't deceive me."

"In your line of work, I don't imagine you get called Omar very often, then."

"Trust doesn't come easy for me. Considering what you and your partner perpetrated, you're fortunate I'm willing to negotiate your release."

"Negotiate?"

"Your freedom for the money Mr. Drake made off my auction."

That confirmed her suspicions. No way did this man

realize the hurt that would come down on him if he didn't release her.

"Listen, Omar, I don't know how you found out about Drake or me." Although she had an inkling it involved Turner, there was no point in asking. There was only a limited amount of time before Ash arrived. And knowing him, he'd be bringing the team and a whole lot of firepower. "But you need to understand he's not going to be in the mood to talk."

"There will be no need to talk for long. I may, in fact, wait for several days. By the time I contact him, he'll be desperate and will give me what he owes me."

"And if he refuses? What then, Omar? Are you going to kill me?"

"It won't come to that. I saw how he looked at you. He'll do whatever is necessary to get you back."

Yes, he would. Unfortunately, that would involve a lot of blood and possibly a few deaths. While she couldn't say she was fond of Omar, watching him get killed out of sheer stupidity didn't sit right with her.

The flight had been a long one. Jules had somehow fallen asleep and had woken to a pounding headache and an all-over body ache. Though her hands and legs were still tied, she'd realized she was too angry to worry about having a flashback. The anger had increased when she'd been hauled out of the plane and tossed into a cargo van. No one spoke, and she didn't bother asking questions. They obviously had an agenda.

When the van had stopped, the door had slid open, and Omar had been standing in the drive in front of his mansion. The instant she'd seen him, she'd started yelling.

Looking somewhat startled at her anger, Omar had given a few quick orders to his men. Jules had been untied and allowed to use the bathroom. A guard had then led her to a living room. The same one where she had ended Renee Kirkson's life. The memory of that night might have made an impact, but seeing Omar sitting on the sofa with a grin of triumph on his face had erased the worry.

She glanced at the window, noting the darkness. "What time is it?"

"Almost nine." He gave her an almost kind smile. "I don't want to hurt you, Ms. Stone. The man who hit you has been reprimanded. Once I have the money owed to me, you'll be released. In the meantime, I really do wish you would accept my offer of a meal. It's been hours since you've eaten and you're looking a bit peaked. My chef can make you any dish you desire."

More exasperated by the minute, Jules snapped, "Make the call, Omar. Let's get this done with."

"Very well." He took a phone from his pocket, pressed a few keys, and then placed the phone on the table in front of them. "I put it on speaker so we can both discuss the terms with him."

As Jules figured, the call went to voice mail, and Omar frowned in confusion at the phone. "I'm sure that's the number I've always used to reach him. He's never not answered."

That was because Ash was not in the mood to talk. Before she could explain that to the idiot across from her, Jules heard a loud *thump...thump...thump.*

"What is that noise?" Omar asked.

A month or so ago, she had pretended to hear a helicopter to cause havoc. There was no need for pretense this time. Havoc in the form of Asher Drake had arrived.

"That is the sound of an actual helicopter, Omar. Your time has run out."

"How is that possible? Your phone was dismantled within

seconds of your abduction. There's no way to trace your location."

She didn't bother to explain the tracker to him. It wasn't his business. She needed to spend the next few moments, or however long they had, convincing Omar to stand down.

"Listen, we don't have much time. You need to understand something. Asher Drake is not like other men. You took something of his, and he will not come in to talk to you about getting it back. He'll be extremely pissed."

"My men will stop him."

"Your men will be killed. And so will you."

"Don't be ridiculous. He—" The sound of a gunshot stopped him in midsentence.

"Omar, listen to me. Let me walk out of here. That's the only way to save your life."

She thought she had him convinced. His face was three shades whiter since the sound of the gunshot, and there was the slightest sheen of sweat on his brow.

But then pride reared its ugly head. "I have several men surrounding the mansion. There's no way he can get inside."

"Is that what you want, Omar? Do you want to hurt him because he lied to you?"

"I just want what's owed to me."

The sound of the front door crashing open had both of them standing. Less than ten seconds later, Ash stood at the entrance of the room. An M16 rifle hung from his shoulder, a SIG Sauer P320 was holstered at his thigh, and a sheath with a KA-BAR knife was attached to the belt at his waist. Wearing camo pants, a long-sleeved black T-shirt, and a Kevlar vest, Asher Drake was dressed like the warrior he was.

To Jules, he was the most beautiful sight she'd ever seen. To the man standing a few feet away from her, he was Omar Schrader's worst nightmare.

His beautiful eyes roamed over Jules, and she felt the heat

to her soul. Only Asher Drake could melt her into a puddle of goo in the middle of a hostage negotiation.

"You okay, Jules?"

"I'm fine." Recognizing the fury behind his mild-sounding question, she added, "He's not worth killing, Ash."

"We'll see about that." Fury on his face, Ash stalked toward Omar, not stopping until he was right in his face. "You went too far, Schrader."

The bewilderment on Omar's face was almost comical. "You look nothing like Humphrey."

"That's the point."

Omar backed away slightly, and Ash followed, keeping him close.

"Listen, I can see you're angry, but you must see this from my perspective. You took—"

"Shut up and listen to me. I'm going to give you a chance. An offer few people get. If you don't take it, you're going to spend the rest of your life in prison."

"I don't know what you mean. You have no authority. How can you—"

"Just know that I can."

A noise at the door had Omar's gaze shifting away from Ash. What he saw caused his eyes to go considerably larger. The OZ team stood at the door. Every one of them was armed to the teeth, their expressions ranging from deadly cold to lethal. Even Jazz, who when dressed in street clothes, looked as dangerous as a kitten, looked like she could take on an army and win.

Omar swallowed audibly and asked in a wavering voice, "Where are my men?"

"Tied up and piled up," Liam answered. "We're ready for the last one, boss. You want me to take care of him for you?"

Omar's eyes zoomed back to Ash's. "What kind of deal are we talking about?"

. . .

THOUGH ANGER CONTINUED to pound through Ash, just
seeing Jules and knowing she was okay had gone a long way
in cooling his fury. The offer he was about to make to
Schrader was given to only a select few. He had come here
ready to take the bastard and his men down. The minute the
helicopter had touched down, Ash had begun to think of a
new plan.

Omar had no idea what he had stepped into. Two men
had been in front of the house, smoking. When they'd
spotted the helicopter, they'd stared for a full minute before
they'd pulled their weapons. Xavier had been the first out of
the chopper. He'd fired one shot into the air, and both men
had dropped their guns and held up their hands. No one else
had even approached them.

"You will not go to prison…you won't even be arrested.
What you will do is retire."

"What? Why would I—"

"Stay quiet till I finish. You have contacts inside the ille-
gal-weapons world. You hear things. When you do, you will
call me."

"What kinds of things?"

"That's a stupid question, and I'm about at the end of my
very limited patience with you, Omar."

"But I—"

Ash held up his hand. "I'm going to leave a couple of
people here with you. They'll help you understand what is
expected of you. If you at any time divulge Humphrey's or
Elsa's identity or try to make a profit from any illegal deals,
you will be arrested, and you will never see freedom again."

"Who are you, Drake?"

"I'm a man who can make your life miserable. Remember
that."

Turning away, he held out his hand to Jules, who ran into his arms. Holding her close, he whispered, "You gave me a scare."

"That makes two of us."

"You're really okay? You weren't hurt?"

"I'm really okay."

Lifting her chin, he growled, "You have a bruise on your cheek."

"It'll heal."

Still holding her, he turned to Omar. "You ever hurt anyone I care about again, prison will be the least of your concerns. Understand?"

"I didn't intend for anyone to get hurt."

Jules had said that Omar had a deep need to impress Humphrey. Learning that he had been hoodwinked had apparently scrambled the man's brain.

Ash looked down at Jules. "Ready to get out of here?"

"Yes."

Not bothering to speak to Schrader again, he ushered Jules out the door. On the way, he gave Gideon and Eve a look. They would stay behind, explain Schrader's new responsibilities, and describe in vivid detail what would happen to him if he did not follow the rules.

Stopping in the foyer, Ash asked again, "You're sure you're okay?"

"I'm fine. Really."

"No bad moments?"

He knew she'd been tied up, possibly drugged. Not only that, she had been returned to the place where she'd killed someone. If those things hadn't triggered a panic attack, how had she prevented one?

"Believe it or not, I was too angry to panic. And…" She glanced over her shoulder. "He really didn't know what he was getting into, Ash. I figure Turner spilled the beans, but she must not have told him much."

"You're right. He wasn't remotely prepared to handle us."

His hand swept through her hair, caressing the silkiness. "I don't want to ever go through that again." Cupping her head in his hands, he continued, "Tomorrow doesn't come with guarantees, and the lives we live make tomorrow even less likely."

"What are you saying?"

"I'm saying, promise me that we are forever. No matter what happens…no matter what comes…this is it. This is us."

Grabbing his wrists, she held them tight. "Nothing and no one will ever come between us. This is us. Ash and Jules forever. I promise."

Ash kissed her then, with all the fervent and pent-up need he'd been feeling since she'd been taken. No, there were no guarantees, but knowing she'd be with him every step of the way made the journey much more bearable.

A throat cleared behind them. Slowing releasing her lips, Ash glanced over his shoulder.

Jazz was grinning at them. "I would tell you to get a room, but you might want to find a better place than this." She walked in a small circle, looking up at the enormous mansion. "Bet there's a camera in every bedroom in this place."

Jules smiled at Ash. "And the bathrooms, too."

Remembering the hot, steamy kiss they'd shared, he whispered against her lips, "But there are plenty of ways to avoid cameras. You just have to get creative."

Another throat was cleared, and Ash reluctantly released Jules. "Let's get out of here."

With Jules's hand in his, they walked out the door together.

Hours later, they were sitting in the back of the plane, holding hands. Except for a trip to the bathroom to shower and change clothes, Ash had not let her out of his sight. That was quite all right with her. This had been a disquieting reminder to them both that anything could happen at any time.

Other than hugs from Serena and Jazz and welcome-back pats on the back from Xavier and Sean, the team had made themselves scarce. Jules could hear them in the front of the plane, talking, but behind this curtain, she and Ash were in their own little world.

"Is there any way to trace the people who hacked us?"

Settling her closer to his side, Ash shrugged. "Serena's team is working on it, but if they're good enough to hack us, they're good enough to hide their tracks."

"And you're sure Turner had nothing to do with it?"

"She may have instigated it, but the hack came after her death. And whoever it was knew what to do with the intel."

"But how—"

Ash's phone chimed. He pulled it from his pocket, and they both noted it was Gideon. Putting the call on speaker, Ash asked, "What do you know?"

"Not much more than we did before. Schrader says someone with an androgynous voice called and told him Humphrey's real identity, as well as Elsa Olsen's real name. Nothing more. His people did some quick research for him. They didn't find that much."

"Which is why he wasn't prepared for the OZ team," Jules said.

"Yeah, he believed Humphrey and Elsa were doing this all on their own."

Jules shook her head in wonder. How on earth Omar Schrader had been dealing with some of the most dangerous people in the world for almost a decade and was still alive was a mystery. He might know weapons, but he was incredibly naïve about the people who purchased and used them.

"What about our location in Tahiti?" Ash said. "How'd he get that?"

"A bike messenger delivered a note to him a couple of days ago. I've got it right here. Just says, 'Asher Drake and Juliet Stone are at the Zanzibar Resort in Tahiti.'"

"That's it?"

"Yeah. We can try to get prints off it or the envelope, but I doubt we'll find anything other than Schrader's."

"What about the messenger?"

"I watched the surveillance footage of the delivery. Can't even tell if it's male or female. Whoever it was knew exactly where the cameras are."

"Yeah, they're not going to make it easy for us."

"Question is, who are they?"

"Hell if I know. What about Schrader? He behaving?"

"Remarkably so. He's a bit incensed about not being able to make more money, but when I described to him the accommodations given to a convicted terrorist, he changed his tune. He's quite fond of his house and his lifestyle."

"You tell him about the tracker?"

"Yes. Didn't seem to bother him, but my guess is he's a little overwhelmed. We'll let him get a good night's sleep, and over breakfast we'll reinforce our message."

"Sounds good. Keep me posted."

"Will do."

Ash pocketed his phone and then drew Jules back into his arms. He held her for several moments without saying a word. There was no need. She felt the same way. What could have been a disaster had turned out much better than they could have imagined.

"Who's behind all this, Ash?"

"I don't know. Every time I think we have a lead, it evaporates into thin air."

"Turner's death didn't end it."

"No, I think Turner was a pawn. There's someone else out there—someone with a whole lot more money and influence—calling the shots."

"But what's their endgame?"

"I don't know that either, but we won't stop until we find them."

Jules let that settle in her mind. This was what OZ did on a daily basis. Fighting against evil, corruption, and injustice. They wouldn't stop until they'd tracked down and exposed everyone involved.

"This arrangement with Omar. That's how you get some of your intel, isn't it?"

"If you mean using him as an asset, then yeah. Putting Omar behind bars would solve almost nothing. There are always going to be brokers connecting evil with evil. Keeping Omar in play will yield us a lot more intel than putting him behind bars ever would."

"How many assets does OZ have?"

"Hard to say. Maybe a hundred. They're not always reliable. And keeping them in play means they're still dealing with dangerous people. If we can, we protect them."

"Do they ever go rogue?"

"Oh yeah."

"Which is the reason for the tracker."

"Yeah."

"You never sent anyone to remove mine."

"Couldn't bring myself to do it."

"I'm glad." Turning in his arms, she cupped his face with her palm. "Seems weird, but that's a connection I don't mind anymore."

"Speaking of connections." He lowered his head and put his mouth to hers in a sweet promise. Pulling away, he looked down at her. "So, that forever we were talking about."

"Yes?"

"When you came to OZ, you only planned to stay until we brought Turner down. You have a life and a business back in Arizona. And OZ…" He blew out an explosive sigh. "It doesn't get any less dangerous."

"Hey, I hunt serial killers. I eat danger for breakfast."

"I'm serious, Jules. We're targets all over the world. We're—"

Jules put her finger on Ash's lips. "Are you trying to fire me, Mr. Drake?"

"Hell no. I'm trying in an ass-awkward way to ask you to stay on permanently with OZ…and with me."

"We belong to each other now, Ash. That's what forever means. And as for OZ, they're my people now."

"I love you, Jules."

She would never get tired of hearing him say those words. "And I love you, Ash. More than I ever thought possible."

"Marry me?"

Happiness bloomed throughout her body. "Just name the date, and I'll be there."

"Today?"

She glanced out the window at the sunrise. It was a new day. And a perfect day to marry the hero of her dreams.

"Yes."

Sealing her promise with a kiss, Jules gave herself up to the glorious beauty of being in the arms of the man she adored. Life, in all its messiness and ugliness, had led her to this incredible man and a love she'd always dreamed of but never thought possible.

No matter what happened in the future, no matter what evil came their way, they would face it together.

# THANK YOU

Thank you so much for reading **Merciless**. I sincerely hope you enjoyed Jules and Ash's love story. If you would be so kind as to leave a review to help other readers find this book, I would sincerely appreciate it.

Next up in the OZ series is Liam Stryker and Aubrey Starr's story. I'm only a few chapters into their book but I am loving them already! To learn more about their story and all my other books, come join my Reece's Readers Reading Group on Facebook *https://www.facebook.com/groups/reecesreaders/*

If you would like to be notified when I have a new release, be sure to sign up for my newsletter *https://christyreece.com/sign-up-newsletter.html*

To learn about my other books and what I'm currently writing, please visit my website *http://www.christyreece.com/*

Follow me on:

Facebook *https://www.facebook.com/AuthorChristyReece*
Twitter *https://twitter.com/ChristyReece*
Bookbub *https://www.bookbub.com/profile/christy-reece?*
*list=author_books*

**The Wildfire Series Writing as Ella Grace**

Midnight Secrets, A Wildefire Novel

Midnight Lies, A Wildefire Novel

Midnight Shadows, A Wildefire Novel

# ACKNOWLEDGMENTS

I am beyond blessed in many ways and one of the most significant is the number of wonderful people in my life. Writing can be a lonely, solitary endeavor but I could not do what I do without the support and love of the following people:

My husband, Jim, who loves and supports me in ways too numerous to mention. Thank you for the laughter, for bringing me goodies to keep me going, and for handling a million things that I take for granted. You are one in a billion!

My beautiful mom, who inspires me everyday.

My incredible and precious fur-babies who bring me smiles and more love than I ever thought possible. I would mention all their names but I would run out of room!

The amazing Joyce Lamb whose copyediting and fabulous advice are always on point.

Tricia Schmitt (Pickyme) for your gorgeous cover art.

The Reece's Readers Facebook groups, for all their support, encouragement, and wonderful sense of humor.

Anne, my first reader, who always goes above and beyond

in her advice and encouragement, and knows just what to say to keep me going.

My beta readers, Crystal, Hope, Julie, Alison, and Kris who always offer fabulous suggestions and encouragement.

Kara for reading the finished version and finding those things I missed even after reading it a thousand times.

Linda Clarkson of Black Opal Editing, who, as always, did an amazing job of finding those superfluous words and that one specific thing that made so much difference! So appreciate your eagle eye, Linda.

Special thanks to Hope for your help and assistance in a multitude of things. Thank you for your generous heart and for keeping me on track.

To my readers, thank you for your patience and encouragement as I learned my way around a new series and brand new characters. I hope you love them as much as I do!

# ABOUT THE AUTHOR

Christy Reece is the award winning, NYT Bestselling Author of dark romantic suspense. She lives in Alabama with her husband and a menagerie of pets.

Christy loves hearing from readers and can be contacted at Christy@ChristyReece.com.

**The Grey Justice Group**
*There's More Than One Path To Justice*

Justice isn't always swift or fair and only those who have felt the pain of denied justice can truly understand its bitter taste. But justice delayed doesn't have to be justice denied. Enter the Grey Justice Group, ordinary citizens swept up in extraordinary circumstances. Led by billionaire philanthropist Grey Justice, this small group of operatives gains justice for victims when other paths have failed.

NOTHING TO LOSE

**Choices Are Easy When You Have
Nothing Left To Lose**

Kennedy O'Connell had all the happiness she'd ever dreamed
—until someone stole it away. Now on the run for her life,
she has a choice to make—disappear forever or make those
responsible pay. Her choice is easy.

Two men want to help her, each with their own agenda.

Detective Nick Gallagher is accustomed to pursuing
killers within the law. Targeted for death, his life turned
inside out, Nick vows to bring down those responsible, no
matter the cost. But the beautiful and innocent Kennedy
O'Connell brings out every protective instinct. Putting aside
his own need for vengeance, he'll do whatever is necessary to
keep her safe and help her achieve her goals.

Billionaire philanthropist Grey Justice has a mission, too.
Dubbed the 'White Knight' of those in need of a champion,
few people are aware of his dark side. Having seen and experienced injustice—Grey knows its bitter taste. Gaining

justice for those who have been wronged is a small price to pay for a man's humanity.

With the help of a surprising accomplice, the three embark on a dangerous game of cat and mouse. The stage is set, the players are ready…the game is on. But someone is playing with another set of rules and survivors are not an option.

***Turn the page to read an excerpt of Nothing To Lose!***

NOTHING TO LOSE

A GREY JUSTICE NOVEL

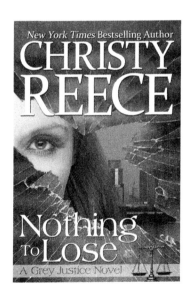

**Prologue**

**Houston, Texas**

The man's plane landed at William P. Hobby Airport. Like

any other businessman, he disembarked and headed with the seemingly endless throng of people toward ground transportation. Having no luggage other than his carry-on, he was standing in line for a taxi within minutes.

Innocuous looking, he blended into the mass of people as if he didn't exist. If a thousand people were later asked if they had seen a slender man of medium height with short, brown hair and pleasant features, most would say no. A few might say yes and yet be unable to describe him. Blending in was part of his trade, and he was very good at his chosen profession.

When an overaggressive traveler grabbed the taxi meant for him, he did nothing but step back and wait for the next one. Attracting attention would be unwise. The rude man would never know that he came in close contact with Death today.

Finally procuring a cab, the man gave the name of a hotel in the city. Nothing particularly expensive—just one of the many hotels on the outer edges of the big metropolitan area where one wouldn't be noticed.

After checking in, he followed a large family onto the elevator. All eyes were on the overexcited, squealing children. No one noticed the silent stranger in the corner.

Reaching his room on the third floor, he slid his key card into the slot and pushed open the door. A sniff of air brought a scowl to his bland features. He'd asked for a non-smoking room, and this one had definitely housed a smoker. A complaint or a room-change request would only bring unwanted attention and make him memorable. Shrugging philosophically, he set his bag on the luggage rack, withdrew his new, unused phone from his pocket, and punched in a number.

On the first ring, a male voice answered, "Yes?"

"I'm here," the man said. Not waiting for a reply, he ended the call.

Most people would unpack their clothing or check the television guide. Others might take a quick look over the room service menu. He did none of those. His total focus was on the job. Once that was finished, he would leave and go about his business. He wouldn't stay in the same hotel. Instead, he would head into the city and pay an exorbitant price for a one-night-only stay. Then he would return to his home and be someone else until another employment opportunity presented itself again.

Three minutes after making the call, a soft chime indicated he had a text message. Clicking on the message icon, he quickly took in the brief but significant information. Two targets. Both events were to look like random acts of violence—a specialty for him.

All relevant information gathered and memorized, he deleted the message, then efficiently and thoroughly demolished the phone. He would drop the decimated parts into a dumpster on the way to his first job.

After a quick check in the mirror to ensure his pleasant, nondescript appearance was still in place, he walked out the door with nothing more on his mind than to complete a successful business transaction—just like any other businessman.

### Chapter One

Kennedy O'Connell stepped back to admire her work and released a contented sigh. *Yes.* Even though she'd painted only a quarter of a wall with one coat, she was almost sure this color was the right one.

"Oh holy hell, you changed your mind again."

Grinning, she glanced over her shoulder at her husband. "Eighth time's the charm."

His arms wrapped around her and pulled her against his hard body. As he nuzzled her neck, she could feel his smile against her skin. Kennedy knew if she looked at his face, his eyes would be dancing with good humor. Thomas O'Connell was a patient, even-keeled man, but her indecisiveness about the color for the nursery had put him to the test.

Snuggling back into his arms, she asked, "So do you like this color better than the last one?"

Without raising his head, Thomas growled, "It's perfect."

She snorted softly. "That's what you said about the first seven."

"That's because they were perfect, too. Anything you pick is going to look great."

She appreciated his faith in her. Having grown up in various foster homes, her priorities had been getting enough food to fill her belly and staying out of trouble. Surviving her childhood hadn't involved learning about colors, textures, and fabrics.

When she and Thomas had married, almost everything she owned was secondhand and ragged. Since then, she'd been learning little by little, mostly by experimenting, what she liked. She had delighted in setting up their home, creating a beautiful environment she and Thomas could enjoy together. Now that their first child was on the way, she wanted everything to be just right, so she had taken experimentation to a whole new level.

She was on winter break from her first year of law school. In her spare time, she freelanced as a researcher for several law firms. She had considered taking on some jobs to earn a little extra money while on break, but Thomas had encouraged her to take her time off seriously by doing nothing at all. Never one to be idle, she couldn't stop herself from working on the nursery. This wasn't dry contracts, torts, or mind-numbing procedure. This was relaxing and fun.

Thomas's big hands covered her protruding belly and caressed. At just over twenty-two weeks, she was all baby. The weight she had gained—thirteen pounds so far—had gone straight to her stomach.

"How's Sweet Pea doing today?"

Smiling at the nickname Thomas had taken to calling their baby, Kennedy covered his hands with her own. "Sweet Pea is doing wonderful." She tilted her head to look up at him. "But you know, if it's a boy, you cannot call him Sweet Pea, right?"

"It's a girl," he assured her. "As sweet and beautiful as her mother."

"I hope you're right, if only because everything I've bought so far is pink."

"I'm right." He kissed the nape of her neck. "So. No queasiness?"

"Nope. I think she's decided to take the day off."

Warm breath caressed her ear as Thomas gently bit her lobe. "I'd say that calls for a celebration."

Heat licked up her spine. Morning sickness that lasted long past morning had put a damper on their lovemaking lately. When she wasn't in the bathroom throwing up, she was concentrating on staying still to keep from getting sick. But today, for whatever reason, the baby had decided to give her a break.

Turning in his arms, she whispered against his mouth. "I've missed you."

His mouth covered hers, and Kennedy gave herself up to the delicious and familiar taste of the man she adored. Two years of marriage had only increased her love for him.

He raised his head and dropped a quick kiss on her nose. "Think that'll hold you till tonight?"

Her smile teasing, she winked at him. "Yes, but don't blame me if I get started early."

His gruff laughter was cut off abruptly as he kissed her once more. Before she could pull him in for a deeper connection, he backed away. "Save some for me."

Already tingling in anticipation of the coming night, Kennedy watched him walk away, loving how his swagger denoted confidence without a hint of conceit.

Thomas stopped at the door and looked over his shoulder. "I'll call you before I head home to see what you need."

Blowing him a kiss in thanks, Kennedy turned back to her project, blissfully unaware that it would be the last time she would see her husband alive.

Detective Nick Gallagher slid into the front seat of his car, started the engine and flipped on his headlights. Damn, it was already dark. He pulled out of the parking lot and headed in the opposite direction of his apartment, pushing the vision of going home for a quick shower out of his mind. In fact, he'd be lucky to make his date on time. This was the first time today he'd had a few minutes to himself. This morning he'd been tied up in court, waiting to testify in a murder trial. The minute he'd walked out of the courtroom after his testimony, he'd been called in on a double homicide.

He took all of that in stride. He had played this dice when he'd chosen his career path. Sometimes, though, a little downtime to handle personal issues would have been nice.

With that thought in mind, he grabbed his cellphone and punched the speed dial for Thomas. His best friend was a detective in the Narcotics Division. Lately, the only way they'd communicated was through text messages and emails.

Yesterday, Nick had gotten an oddly obscure text from him that had put his cop instincts on high alert.

Thomas answered on the first ring. "You forget something?"

"How's that?" Nick asked.

Thomas chuckled. "Hey, Nick. Sorry. I was just talking to Kennedy. She's been having some wild cravings lately, and I figured she'd thought of something else she wanted."

"So you're headed home for the night?"

"After I make a stop at Bailey's grocery."

"Where's that?"

"Corner of Kendrick and Mulberry."

"That's on the other side of town. Why so far?"

"I'm on a mango run. I was in the area last week and picked up some fruit at the store. Kennedy went crazy over the mangoes and asked me to pick up some more. I think she's got some sort of special dessert in mind for tonight."

Nick didn't question his friend's need to please his wife. He'd seen Thomas's devotion to Kennedy firsthand…there was almost nothing he wouldn't do for her. And Kennedy was the same way about her husband. If anyone had the perfect marriage, it was the O'Connells.

"Sounds like you guys have plans for the evening."

"Yeah, something like that. Why? What's up?"

"I thought we might meet later and talk about that text you sent me yesterday. You know…about the Slaters."

The slight pause before Thomas answered told Nick that plans or not, his friend didn't want to discuss the subject. "It's nothing, really. I made a couple of calls, thinking I'd found something interesting, but nothing panned out. Forget about it."

Thomas O'Connell was the finest man Nick knew, but he couldn't lie for shit. Something was definitely going on. "What do you mean you made a couple of calls? To who?"

"No one…really. Just forget I mentioned anything, okay?"

"Look, I'll be the first to admit there's no way the Slaters are as squeaky clean as they pretend. But if you are right, they'll screw up big-time one day and get what's coming to them."

"Yeah, I know that. Like I said, it was just an idea that didn't pan out. I'm over it now. So who's the hottie of the night?"

The less-than-smooth effort to change the subject made Nick even more suspicious. Letting him off the hook for the time being, he said, "Louisa something or other."

"Where'd you meet this one?"

"Belden's party last week."

"Where're you taking her before you take her to bed?"

Nick snorted his disgust. His reputation of being a lady's man was mostly fictional. Yeah, he dated a lot of different women, because he enjoyed their company. Somehow, even Thomas was under the impression that it also meant he had a lot of sex.

"I don't sleep with all of them."

Thomas gave his own snort, this one of disbelief. "Yeah. Right."

Knowing whatever protests he made would only be construed as modest, Nick decided to go back to their original discussion. "Seriously, let's talk about the Slaters tomorrow. If you've got something on your mind, I want to hear about it. Want to meet for lunch at Barney's?"

"Um…yeah…sure, lunch sounds good. But I promise there's nothing to talk about. Gotta go. Catch you later."

Nick cursed softly at the abrupt end to the call. Thomas was definitely keeping something from him. Tomorrow he'd get in his face and make him talk. Screwing around with the Slaters wasn't a good career move. With their kind of influence, they could end a career with a phone call. On the other hand, if Thomas did have something significant on the family, then Nick wanted to know about it.

Mathias Slater and his clan were Texas royalty. Few people in America, much less Texas, hadn't heard of the Slaters. They were one of the oldest and wealthiest families in the country with descendants dating back to the first American settlers. Nothing seemed to tarnish their good image. Even the arrest and conviction of the youngest Slater, Jonah, on a major drug-smuggling charge had done nothing more than elicit sympathy. Shit bounced off of them like they had some kind of protective shield.

Nick knew almost nothing personally about the family—just what he'd seen on the news or read in the paper. One thing he did know was they had major connections. Hell, last week he'd seen a photo of Mathias Slater shaking hands with the president. The family had the kind of influence that most people could only dream of having.

A few months back, Thomas had handled the investigation of Jonah Slater and had given Nick the lowdown. Slater had been caught red-handed with a boatload of illegal drugs. In fact, he'd looked so stinking guilty that Thomas had said he would have suspected the guy had been framed if he hadn't been a Slater. According to Thomas, it'd taken almost no investigation or effort to put Jonah away. He was now serving a hefty sentence in Brownsville.

Mathias Slater had made the most of the publicity. He'd held a press conference, stating that he still loved his son and offered his full support. He'd even donated millions to a drug-rehab facility. Nick had caught the press conference on television and had seen more than a few people wipe away tears.

Thomas had described an incident the day Jonah Slater was sentenced. Said it had given him several sleepless nights. Jonah had been about to walk from the courtroom, his hands and ankles shackled, but he'd stopped in front of Thomas and said, "Hell of an investigation, O'Connell. Hope you didn't break a nail."

Nick agreed it was strange but had encouraged Thomas to let it go. Cryptic remarks from convicted criminals weren't exactly unusual. And prisons were filled with criminals who swore they were innocent. Few freely admitted their guilt.

As Nick pulled in front of Louisa's apartment complex, he glanced at the dashboard clock. Yeah, seven minutes late. Jerking the car door open, Nick strode up the sidewalk. Before he got to Louisa's front door, she had it open for him. Long-legged, honey blond hair, full pouty lips, and exotic eyes. She looked exactly like her magazine photo that had been splashed all over the country last month. Many men would have given their eyeteeth to talk with a cover model much less date one. So why did he want to turn around and walk the other way? Since he already knew the answer to that, he kept moving forward.

Giving her one of his stock smiles in greeting, Nick listened to her chatter with half an ear as he led her to the car. Had she been this talkative last week?

Thankfully, the restaurant wasn't far away. Within minutes of leaving her apartment, they were seated and had ordered their meal.

They were almost through with their appetizer when Nick had to stifle a giant yawn. For the past ten minutes, Louisa had droned on about her weekend in St. Moritz with some Hollywood celebrity. Taking a large bite of his ravioli so he wouldn't have to respond verbally, he chewed, nodded, and did his best to put on an interested expression, wishing like hell he'd never made this date.

"And then Maurice said the funniest thing. He—"

The abrupt ringing of his cellphone was a welcome

distraction. Holding his hand up to stop her chatter, Nick answered, "Gallagher."

"Nick, it's Lewis Grimes."

Before he could wonder why the captain of the Narcotics Division was calling, the man continued, "There's been a shooting."

The fine hairs on the back of his neck rose. The instant he heard the victim's name, he went to his feet. "I'll be right there."

He threw a wad of cash on the table. "I gotta go. That should pay for dinner and a cab home."

Before she could open her mouth to answer, Nick was already running toward the door, his date forgotten. His mind screamed a denial, but Grimes's stark words reverberated in his head, refusing to allow him to deny the truth. "Thomas O'Connell has been shot."

## Chapter Two

Kennedy stretched her back and winced at its tightness. This kind of work was nothing to a full day of research at her laptop. Still, she was exhausted. The first coat of paint looked wonderful. The second one she would apply tomorrow would look even better. She couldn't wait to see Thomas's grin when he saw that she had indeed changed her mind once more. Apparently, the ninth time was the charm, because the jewel-toned lilac was perfect. The people at Lloyd's Paint and Wallpaper would probably be just as happy as Thomas that she'd at last made her final choice.

She might be tired, but tonight was going to be perfect. She had taken a break late in the afternoon and prepared lasagna—one of Thomas's favorite dishes. The delicious fragrance now wafted through the air, and her stomach grumbled—a reminder that her early afternoon peanut butter and banana sandwich was long gone. What a blessing to have hunger pains in place of queasiness.

Thomas should be home soon. She would have to rush through her shower, but she wanted to be dressed and ready when he walked through the front door. Or undressed, in this case. On her way back from the paint store, she'd slipped into Victoria's Secret and found a negligee on sale that would probably make Thomas forget all about dinner.

She dashed from the nursery and ran to the master bedroom. Toeing off her sneakers, she was about to unzip her jeans when the sound of the doorbell chimes stopped her. Could she ignore it? If she'd been in the shower, she wouldn't have even heard it. She shrugged resignedly and headed downstairs. Curiosity was the bane of her existence…she had to know. Besides, if she was still in the shower when Thomas got home, he could join her and they could get started even earlier than planned.

The delightful thought cheering her, Kennedy opened the door with a big smile on her face. Thomas's best friend stood before her.

"Nick! Hey! Come on in." Even as she said the words, she inwardly sighed, seeing the romantic evening with her husband fizzling fast.

He didn't speak. The odd look in his eyes puzzled her until she realized what a mess she must look. Her chestnut hair, pulled up into a halfhearted ponytail, had more than a few streaks of lilac in it. She had a feeling that she had a few spots on her face, too.

"I know I must look a fright, but I just finished painting the nursery." She stepped back. "Come in and see it. Thomas isn't home yet. I asked him to pick up a couple of things at the store, but he should be here soon."

When he still said nothing and just kept looking at her, she frowned. "Nick? What's wrong?"

The woman before him was disheveled, messy and absolutely lovely. She was his best friend's wife…one of the sweetest people Nick had ever known. And he was about to destroy her world.

He opened his mouth to speak, but before he could say the words, she started shaking her head and said a very soft but emphatic, "No."

"Kennedy, I—"

She backed away, head still shaking. "You are not here to tell me anything bad, Nick. You got that? Thomas is on his way home. He's not on duty. He is fine."

Reaching out his hand for her, he wasn't surprised when she tried to close the door. Unfortunately, closing him out wasn't going to stop the truth.

He grabbed the edge of the door to keep it from slamming in his face, the words grinding from his mouth, "There was a robbery at the grocery store. Thomas tried to stop it. He was shot."

Her head continued to shake. "No. You made a mistake. Thomas will be home any minute." She looked wildly around the room, as if trying to hold back reality. But her face had paled to a sickly color, and her mouth trembled with emotion.

He took a step inside the house, and she backed away again. Tears swimming in her eyes, she whispered, "This is all wrong. This can't happen. It. Can't. Happen. Do you hear me? It can't."

He reached for her. Wanting to hold her, comfort her. When she jerked away, his hand dropped, and he whispered hoarsely, "I'm so sorry, Kennedy. So damn sorry."

Kennedy turned away from the sorrow on Nick's face. This couldn't be happening. It just couldn't. As a cop's wife, she knew this kind of news could come at any time. She lived with that knowledge daily. Having lost both her parents as a child, she knew more than most people about unexpected tragedies. But this? This wasn't something she could ever have expected. Thomas had been in a grocery store, off duty. Just like any other citizen.

Nick's gruff voice penetrated her blurred thoughts. "I've called Julie…she's on her way."

Julie was her best friend, also a cop's wife. She had been in Julie's place before. Last year, Sara White's husband, Rick, had been killed in the line of duty. Kennedy had been there when they'd told Sara. Had held Rick's widow in her arms and whispered to her that everything was going to be okay. Kennedy now realized she had lied. Everything wasn't going to be okay. Never would be again. How Sara must have wanted to wail and scream those very words.

No! She refused to accept it. Kennedy whirled, shouted, "He's not dead, dammit! I won't allow it. I will damn well not allow it. You hear me? It's a mistake."

His eyes glittering with tears, Nick pulled her into his arms and whispered, "It's going to be okay, Kennedy. I promise."

Hysterical laughter bubbled in her chest, and Kennedy jerked out of his arms. "No, it's not. That's the funny thing about those words. They're only said when it's not going to be okay." Tears blurred Nick's face as Kennedy felt them come. She froze, held her breath…willing them away. She couldn't cry. If she did, it would be admitting the truth.

She gazed blindly around at her house, her happy home. The home she and Thomas shared together. The one their baby would soon share with them. This couldn't be happening!

A female voice, filled with sympathy and sadness, said, "Kennedy?"

Julie stood at the door, tears streaming down her face.

Agony shot through Kennedy, almost bending her double. It was true. Oh God, it was true.

Thomas was gone.

Nick watched as Julie led Kennedy into the living room. As they got to the entrance, Julie twisted around and mouthed, "Hot, sweet tea."

With a nod, Nick headed to the kitchen, grateful to have a task. He'd never felt more helpless in his life. Nothing he could say or do would change the situation. Hot tea was about as good as anything.

He entered the kitchen and then stopped for a moment. How many times had he been in this house? Dozens. And they had all been happy times. Cookouts, dinners, the occasional brunch. Laughter had filled the rooms, and Kennedy had been the biggest cause of that. She had a dry, witty sense of humor and could deliver punch lines like a pro. She also had a smile that could light up the darkest of hearts, and not once had he heard her say an unkind word about anyone.

Every room in the house bore Kennedy's vibrant personality, but he'd always felt the kitchen showed the soul of the woman—sunny and inviting but with a calm serenity. He shoved his fingers through his hair. Hell, grief was turning him into some kind of lame-assed poet.

Nick opened a cabinet. Tea bags and sugar were to the left of the stove. Kennedy had once mentioned that her need for organization was rooted in the chaos of her childhood. Nick identified with her need to control her environment. Control gave power. And when your life goes to shit, control means everything.

He filled the teakettle, set it on the burner and sat down to wait for the whistle. As he waited, the memory of sitting beside his best friend as he bled out ran like a horror movie through his mind.

Nick's car had slid almost sideways into the parking lot, while the words "it's a mistake, it's a mistake" drummed like a mantra in his mind. The identification was wrong. It was someone who looked like Thomas.

He'd jumped out of the car and shoved open the store door, barely slowing to flash his badge. Uniformed and plainclothes cops had hovered around, their faces wearing the same bleak look of hopelessness.

"Back here, Gallagher," a voice called out.

Nick ran to the sound and then skidded to a stop. Thomas lay on his back, the front of his shirt covered in blood. His eyes were closed, and two EMTs were working on him.

"Dammit…no," Nick whispered.

Amazingly, Thomas must have heard him. His eyes flickered open, and he muttered a faint, "Nick…need to talk…Nick."

"We need to get him to a hospital," one of the EMTs stated.

The other EMT scooted out of the way. "Sit here. I'll get the transfer ready."

Nick knelt beside his best friend and could literally feel his own heart breaking. They'd known each other since college—cheerful, charming Thomas and angry, sarcastic Nick. Their friendship shouldn't have worked, but somehow it had. He gave Thomas all the credit. The man had tenaciously pursued him as a friend. For which Nick would be forever grateful.

Thomas's eyes glittered with a strange, intense light. Pain? Fear? Somehow, Nick got the idea there was another reason

"Need you…do me a favor," Thomas whispered.

"Anything. Name it."

"Take care of Kennedy for me. She's going to take it hard."

He swallowed and added, "And our little girl. Please…take care of her."

His eyes stinging, Nick said, "I promise, Thomas. I'll take care of both of them."

"You're a good man." A small smile lifted his mouth. "Despite what your ex-girlfriends say."

Nick forced a laugh. "Always joking."

His eyes opened wider, and Thomas said softly, "Tell Kennedy…" He drew in a rattling breath. "Tell her…best… thing…ever happened to me. Love her…" His eyes closed, and then he opened them even wider. Grabbing Nick's arm in a surprisingly strong grip, he rasped, "Don't let them hurt—"

The hand on Nick's arm went slack, and Thomas gave a final gasp.

"Thomas!" Nick shouted.

"Back away."

Nick jumped out of the way and watched as the two EMTs worked frantically. When one of them said, "It's no use," Nick yelled, "What do you mean it's no use? Do some-thing. He's a healthy man. He's got a wife…a kid on the way. Do something!"

"I'm sorry…he's gone."

Nick looked blankly over at Lewis Grimes. "What happened?"

Grief filled his eyes as he muttered, "Robbery. Thomas tried to stop it." He gestured to a black body bag. "At least he got the little bastard."

The whistle of the kettle drew Nick back to the present. Feeling like he'd aged a hundred years in the last hour, Nick prepared the tea and headed to the living room. Kennedy sat on the sofa, staring into space. Julie was talking softly to her, but he doubted any of the words penetrated.

He'd seen this reaction dozens of times. Had been there himself. First, there was the denial. The push back against a truth so horrific, your mind refused to acknowledge its existence. Then came the inevitable numbing shock. That was actually a welcoming place. Everything went on shutdown. You didn't think about the agony ripping at your heart. There was no knowledge of reality. You didn't think, period. You breathed in and out. You swallowed, occasionally nodded at the soft murmurings around you, even though you didn't comprehend the words. You just existed.

Nick had been eighteen years old when he had experienced that pain firsthand. His mother had been driving home from work, and some drugged-out bastard had decided to do a little target practice. Eight people had been shot. His mother had been one of three who'd died.

He had been home, cooking dinner, when the doorbell rang. Unaware that his life was about to be completely changed, he'd casually opened the door and faced two policemen. He still remembered their words, their solemn expressions...the sympathy in their eyes. He remembered the bellowing cries of their next-door neighbor, his mother's best friend. He even remembered the dog across the street that barked incessantly at all the cars and people who'd showed up a few minutes later. Those kinds of details—innocuous and unimportant—were ingrained in his memory.

Years later, even when the pain had dimmed, Nick knew Kennedy would remember these odd, unimportant moments, too. They lingered like small dark clouds. Not necessarily painful but just little reminders of life in all its messed-up glory.

He held the hot tea in front of Kennedy, wrapping both of her hands around the mug until she had a good grip. Assured she did, he dropped into a chair across from her and watched her carefully. Soon, the shock would wear off, and the truth would hit her once more. Only this time the pain would be harder to bear, because denial was no longer something to fall back on.

An ache developed in his chest as he watched her struggle to hold it together. He'd been a homicide detective for two years now, delivered news of a loved one's death to countless families. Though he'd always felt a measure of sympathy for them, he had always been able to hold himself apart. But there was no way in hell to separate himself from this tragedy. His best friend was gone.

Thomas had asked him to take care of Kennedy, and though it was something he would have done in the first place, the vow he'd made held extra weight. Nick would do whatever it took…give her whatever she needed, no matter what. From now on, Kennedy and her baby were his responsibilities. Whatever anyone said about him, no one could dispute that he took care of his own. And that's what Kennedy was now. *His.*

Printed in Great Britain
by Amazon